PAUL WENT UP TO HER, AND QUICKLY SEIZING HER HANDS
HELD THEM IN HIS FIRM GRIP.

—Paul Patoff.

THE COMPLETE WORKS OF
F. MARION CRAWFORD
In Thirty-two Volumes ✏ *Authorized Edition*

PAUL PATOFF

BY
F. MARION CRAWFORD

WITH FRONTISPIECE

P. F. COLLIER & SON
NEW YORK

THE COMPLETE WORKS OF F. MARION CRAWFORD

—8—

PAUL PATOFF.

MY dear lady — my dear friend — you have asked me
to tell you a story, and I am going to try, because there is
not anything I would not try if you asked it of me. I do
not yet know what it will be about, but it is impossible that I
should disappoint you; and if the proverb says, "Needs
must when the devil drives," I can mend the proverb into a
show of grace, and say, The most barren earth must needs
bear flowers when an angel sows the seed.

When you asked for the story I could only find a dry tale
of my own doings, which I detailed to you somewhat at
length, as we cantered down into the Valley of the Sweet
Waters. The south wind was warm this afternoon, though
it brought rain with it and wetted us a little as we rode; it
was soft and dreamy, and made everything look sleepy, and
misty, and a little uncertain in outline. Baghdad sniffed it
in his deep red nostrils, for it was the wind of his home;
but Haroun al Raschid shook the raindrops restlessly from
his gray mane, as though he hated to be damp, and was
thinking longingly of the hot sand and the desert sun. But
he had no right to complain, for water must needs come in
the oases, — and truly I know of no fairer and sweeter resting-place in life's journey than the Valley of the Sweet
Waters above the Golden Horn.

That same south wind — when I think, it is a point or two
easterly, and it seems to smell of Persia — well, that same
soft wind is blowing at my windows now in the dark night,
and is murmuring, sometimes almost complaining, then

dying away in a fitful, tearful sigh, sorry even to weeping for its restless fate, sorry perhaps for me and sighing for me. God knows, there is enough to sigh for in this working-day world, is there not? I have heard you sigh, too, very sadly, as though something hurt you, although you are so bright and young and fair. The wind sighs hopelessly, in great sobs of weariness and despair, for he is filled with the ghosts of the past; but your breath has a music in it that is more like the song of the sunrise that used to break out from the heart of the beautiful marble at dawn.

Poor wind! He is trying to speak to me through the pines, — perhaps he is bringing a message. It is long since any one brought me a message I cared to hear. I will open the door to the terrace and let him in, and see what he has to say.

Truly, he speaks great words: —

"I am the belt and the girdle of this world. I carry in my arms the souls of the dead and the sins of them; the souls of them that have not yet lived, with their deeds, are in my bosom. I am sorrowful with the sorrow of ages, and strong with the strength of ages yet unlived. What is thy sorrow to my sorrow, or thy strength to my strength? Listen.

"Knowest thou whence I come, or whither I go? Fool, thou knowest not even of thyself what thou shalt do to-morrow, and it may be that on the next day I shall have thy soul, to take it away, and hold it, and buffet it, and tear it as I will. Fool, thou knowest little! The gardens of Persia are sweet this night; this night the maidens of Hindustan have gone forth to greet the new moon, and I am full of their soft prayers and gentle thoughts, for I am come from them. But the north, whither I go, is cold and cruel, full of snow and darkness and gloom. Along the lands where I will pass I shall see men and women dying in the frost, and little children, too, poor and hungry, and shivering out the last breathings of a wretched life; and some of them I will take with me this night, to my journey's end among the ice-floes and the brown, driving mists of the uttermost north. Dost thou wonder that I am sad?

"That is thy life. Thou art come from the sweet-scented gardens of thy youth, thou must go to the ice desert of thine old age; and now thou art full of strength and boastfulness, and thinkest thou shalt perchance be the first mortal who shall cheat death. Go to! Thou shalt die like the rest, the more miserably that thou lovest life more than the others."

The wind is in an ill humor to-night; I should not have thought he could say such hard things. But he is a hopeless old cynic, even when he blows warm from the south; he has seen so much and done so much, and has furnished so many metaphors to threadbare poets, that he believes in nothing good, or young, or in any way fresh. He is bad company, and I have shut the window again. You asked me for a story, and you are beginning to wonder why I do not tell you one. Do you like long stories or short stories? Sad or gay? True or fanciful? What shall it be? My true stories are all sad, but the ones I imagine are often merry. Could I not think of one true, and gay as well? There was once a bad old man who said that when the truth ceased to be solemn it became dull. Between solemnity and dullness you would not find what you want, which, I take it, is a little laughter, a little sadness, and, when it is done, the comfortable assurance of your own senses that you have been amused, and not bored. The bad old gentleman was right. When our lives are not filled with great emotions they are crammed with insignificant details, and one may tell them ever so well, they will be insignificant to the end. But the fancy is a great store-house, filled with all the beautiful things that we do not find in our lives. My dear friend, if true love were an every-day phenomenon, experienced by everybody, it would cease to be in any way interesting; people would be so familiar with it that it

would bore them to extinction; they would have it for
breakfast, dinner, and supper as a matter of course, and
would be as fastidious of its niceties as an Anglo-Indian
about the quality of the pepper. It is because only one
man or woman in a hundred thousand is personally acquainted with the sufferings of true-love fever that the other
ninety-nine thousand nine hundred and ninety-nine take delight in observing the contortions and convulsions of the patient. It is a great satisfaction to them to compare the
slight touch of ague they once had when they were young
with the raging sickness of a breaking heart; to see a resemblance between the tiny scratch upon themselves, which
they delight in irritating, and the ghastly wound by which
the tortured soul has sped from its prison.

To tell the truth, they are not so very much to blame.
Even the momentary reflection of love is a good thing; at
least, it is better than to know nothing of it. One can
fancy that a violin upon which no one had ever played
would yet be glad to vibrate faintly in unison with the music
of a more favored neighbor; it would bring a sensation of
the possibility of music. The stronger harmony is caught
up and carried on forever in endless sound waves, but the
slight responsive murmur of the passive strings is lost and
forgotten.

And now you will tell me that I am making phrases.
That is my profession : I am a twister of words; I torture
language by trade. You know it, for you have known me
a long time, and, if you will pardon my vanity, or rudeness,
I observe that my mode of putting the dictionary on the
rack amuses you. The fact that you ask for a story shows
that well enough. I am a plain man, and there never was
any poetry in me, but I have seen it in other people, and I
understand why some persons like it. As for stories, I
have plenty of them. I, Paul Griggs, have seen a variety
of sights, and I have a good memory. There is the south-
east wind again. I was speaking of love, a moment ago, —

there is a story of the wind falling in love. There is a garden of roses far away to the east, where a maiden lies
asleep; the roses have no thorns in that garden, and they
grow softly about her and make a pillow for her fair head.
A blustering wind came once and nearly waked her, but she
was so beautiful that he fell deep in love; and he turned
into the softest breeze that ever fanned a woman's cheek in
summer, for fear lest he should trouble her sleep. There
was a poor woman in rags, in the streets of London, on
that March night, but she could not soften the heart of the
cruel blast for all her shivering and praying; for she was
very poor and wretched, and never was beautiful, even
when she was young.

That is a short tale, and it has no moral application, for
it is too common a truth. If people would only act directly
on things instead of expecting the morality of their cant
phrases to act for them, to feed the hungry, to clothe the
naked, to pay their bills, and to save their souls into the
bargain, what a vast deal of good would be done, and what
an incalculable amount of foolish talk would be spared!
But there is a diplomatic spirit abroad in our day, and it is
necessary to enter into polite relations with a drowning man
before it is possible to pull him out of the water.

But the story, you say, — where is it? Forgive me. I
am rusty and ponderous at the start, like an old dredger
that has stuck too long in the mud. Let me move a little
and swing out with the tide till I am in clearer waters, and
I will promise to bring up something pretty from the bottom
of the sea for you to look at. I would not have you see any
of the blackness that lies in the stagnant harbor.

I will tell you the story of Paul Patoff. I played a small
part in it myself last summer, and so, in a certain way, it is
a tale of my own experience. I say a tale, because it is emphatically a tale, and nothing else. I might almost call it
a yarn, though the word would look strangely on a printed
title-page. We are vain in our generation; we fancy we

have discovered something new under the sun, and we give the name "novel" to the things we write. I will not insult literature by honoring this story with any such high-sounding designation. A great many of the things I am going to tell you were told to me, so that I shall have some difficulty in putting the whole together in a connected shape, and I must begin by asking your indulgence if I transgress all sorts of rules, and if I do not succeed in getting the interesting points into the places assigned to them by the traditional laws of art. I tell what happened, and I do not pretend to tell any more.

I.

IF places could speak, they would describe people far better than people can describe places. No two men agree together in giving an account of a country, of natural scenery, or of a city; and though we may read the most accurate descriptions of a place, and vividly picture to ourselves what we have never seen, yet, when we are at last upon the spot, we realize that we have known nothing about it, and we loudly blame the author, whose word-painting is so palpably false. People will always think of places as being full of poetry if they are in love, as being beautiful if they are well, hideous if they are ill, wearisome if they are bored, and gay if they are making money.

Constantinople and the Bosphorus are no exceptions to this general rule. People who live there are sometimes well and sometimes ill, sometimes rich and sometimes poor, sometimes in love with themselves and sometimes in love with each other. A grave Persian carpet merchant sits smoking on the quay of Buyukdere. He sees them all go by, from the gay French secretary of embassy, puffing at a cigarette as he hurries from one visit to the next, to the neat and military German diplomat, landing from his steam launch on his return from the palace; from the devil-may-care English youth in white flannel to the graceful Turkish adjutant on his beautiful Arab horse; from the dark-eyed Armenian lady, walking slowly by the water's edge, to the terrifically arrayed little Greek dandy, with a spotted waistcoat and a thunder-and-lightning tie. He sees them all: the Levantine with the weak and cunning face, the swarthy Kurdish porter, the gorgeously arrayed Dalmatian embassy servant, the huge, fair Turkish waterman in his spotless white dress, and the countless veiled Turkish women from the small harems of the little town, shuffling along in silence, or squatted peacefully upon a jutting point of the pier, veiled in *yashmaks*, the more transparent as they have the more beauty to show or the less ugliness to conceal. The carpet merchant sees them all, and sits like Patience upon a monumental heap of stuffs, waiting for customers and smoking his water-pipe. His eyes are greedy and his fingers are long, but the peace of a superior mendacity is on his brow, and in his heart the lawful price of goods is multiplied exceedingly.

By the side of the quay, separated from the quiet water by the broad white road, stand the villas, the embassies, the houses, large and small, a varying front, following the curve of the Bosphorus for half a mile between the Turkish towns of Buyukdere and Mesar Burnu. Behind the villas rise the gardens, terraces upon terraces of roses, laurels, lemons, Japanese medlars, and trees and shrubs of all sorts, with a stone pine or a cypress here and there, dark green against the faint blue sky. Beyond the breadth of smooth sapphire water, scarcely rippling under the gentle northerly breeze, the long hills of the Asian mainland stretch to the left as far as the mouth of the Black Sea, and to the right until the quick bend of the narrow channel hides Asia from view behind the low promontories of the European shore. Now and then a big ferry-boat puffs into sight, churning the tranquil waters into foam with her huge paddles; a dozen sailing craft are in view, from Lord Mavourneen's smart yawl to the outlandishly rigged Turkish schooner, her masts raking forward like the antlers of a stag at bay, and spreading a motley collection of lateen-sails, stay-sails, square top-sails, and vast spinnakers rigged out with booms and sprits, which it would puzzle a northern sailor to name. Far to the right, towards Therapia, glimmer the brilliant uniforms and the long bright oars of an ambassador's twelve-oared caïque, re-turning from an official visit at the palace; and near the shore are loitering half a dozen *barcas*, — commodious row-boats, with awnings and cushioned seats, — on the lookout for a fare.

It is the month of June, and the afternoon air is warm and hazy upon the land, though a gentle northerly breeze is on the water, just enough to fill the sails of Lord Mavour-neen's little yacht, so that by making many short tacks he may beat up to the mouth of the Black Sea before sunset. But his excellency the British ambassador is in no hurry; he would go on tacking in his little yawl to all eternity of nautical time, with vast satisfaction, rather than be bored and worried and harrowed by the predestinating servants of Allah, at the palace of his majesty the commander of the faithful. Even Fate, the universal Kismet, procrasti-nates in Turkey, and Lord Mavourneen's special mission is to out-procrastinate the procrastinator. For the present the little yawl is an important factor in his operations, and as he stands in his rough blue clothes, looking up through his single eyeglass at the bellying canvas, a gentle smile upon his strongly marked face betrays considerable satisfaction. Lord Mavourneen is a very successful man, and his smile and his yacht have been elements of no small importance in his success. They characterize him historically, like the tear which always trembles under the left eyelid of Prince Bismarck, like the gray overcoat of Bonaparte, the black tights and gloomy looks of Hamlet the Dane, or Richelieu's kitten. Lord Mavourneen is a man of action, but he can wait. When he came to Constantinople the Turks thought they could keep him waiting, but they have discovered that they are more generally kept waiting themselves, while his excellency is up the Bosphorus, beating about in his little yawl near the mouth of the Black Sea. His actions are thought worthy of high praise, but on some occasions his inaction borders upon the sublime. Of the men who moved

along the Buyukdere quay, many paused and glanced out
over the water at the white-sailed yawl, with the single
streamer flying from the mast-head; and some smiled as
they recognized the ambassadorial yacht, and some looked
grave.

The sun sank lower towards the point where he disap-
pears from the sight of the inhabitants of Buyukdere; for
he is not seen to set from this part of the upper Bosphorus.
He sinks early behind the wooded hills above Therapia, and
when he is hidden the evening freshness begins, and the
crowd upon the quay swells to a multitude, as the people
from the embassies and villas sally forth to mount their
horses or to get into their caïques.

Two young men came out of the white gates of the Russian embassy, and, crossing the road, stood upon the edge
of the stone pier. They were brothers, but the resemblance
was slight between them. The one looked like an Englishman, tall, fair, and rather angular, with hard blue eyes, an
aquiline nose, a heavy yellow mustache concealing his
mouth, and a ruddy complexion. He was extremely well
dressed, and, though one might detect some awkwardness
in his movements, his manner had that composure which
comes from a great knowledge of the world, and from a
natural self-possession and independence of character.

His brother, though older by a year, might have passed
for being several years younger. He was in reality two
and thirty years of age, but his clear complexion was that
of a boy, his dark brown hair curled closely on his head,
and his soft brown eyes had a young and trustful look in
them, which contrasted strangely with his brother's hard and
dominating expression. He was shorter, too, and more
slender, but also more graceful; his hands and feet were
small and well shaped. Nevertheless, his manner was at
least as self-possessed as that of his tall brother, and there
was something in his look which suggested the dashing,
reckless spirit sometimes found in delicately constituted

men. Alexander Patoff was a soldier, and had obtained leave to visit his younger brother Paul in Constantinople, where the latter held the position of second secretary in the Russian embassy. At first sight one would have said that Paul should have been the cavalry officer, and Alexander the diplomatist: but fate had ordered it otherwise, for the elder son had inherited the bulk of his father's fortune, and was, consequently, able to bear the expenses of a career in a guard regiment; while Paul, the younger, just managed to live comfortably the life of a fashionable diplomacy, by dint of economy and an intelligent use of his small income.

They were Russians, but their mother was an English-woman. Their father had married a Miss Anne Dabstreak, with whom he had fallen in love when in London, shortly before the Crimean War. She was a beautiful woman, and had a moderate portion. Old Patoff's fortune, however, was sufficient, and they had lived happily for ten years, when he had died very suddenly, leaving a comfortable provision for his wife, and the chief part of his possessions to Alexander Paolovitch Patoff, his eldest boy. Paul, he thought, showed even as a child the character necessary to fight his own way; and as he had since advanced regularly in the diplomacy, it seemed probable that he would fulfill his father's predictions, and die an embassador.

At the time when this story opens Madame Patoff was traveling in Switzerland for her health. She was not strong, and dared not undertake a journey to Constantinople at present. On the other hand, the climate of northern Russia suited her even less well in summer than in winter, and, to her great regret, her son Alexander, whom she loved better than Paul, as he was also more like herself, had persisted in spending his leave in a visit to his brother.

Madame Patoff had been surprised at Alexander's determination. Her sons were not congenial to each other. They had been brought up differently to different careers, which might partially account for the lack of sympathy between them, but in reality the evil had a deeper root. Madame Patoff had either never realized that Alexander had been the favored son, and that Paul had suffered acutely from the preference shown to his elder brother, or she had loved the latter too passionately to care to hide her preference.   Alexander had been a beautiful child, full of grace, and gifted with that charm which in young children is not easily resisted.   Paul was ugly in his boyhood, cold and reserved, rarely showing sympathy, and too proud to ask for what was not given him freely.   Alexander was quick-witted, talented, and showy, if I may use so barbarous a word.   Paul was slow at first, ungainly as a young foal, strong without grace, shy of attempting anything new to him, and not liking to be noticed.   Both father and mother, as the boys grew up, loved the older lad, and spoiled him, while the younger was kept forever at his books, was treated coldly, and got little praise for the performance of his tasks.   Had Paul possessed less real energy of character, he must have hated his brother ; as it was, he silently disliked him, but inwardly resolved to outshine him in everything, laboring to that end from his boyhood, and especially after his father's death, with a dogged determination which promised success.   The result was that, although Paul never outgrew a certain ungainliness of appearance, due to his large and bony frame, he nevertheless acquired a perfection of manner, an ease and confidence in conversation, which, in the end, might well impress people who knew him more favorably than the bearing of Alexander, whose soft voice and graceful attitudes began to savor of affectation when he had attained to mature manhood.   As they stood together on the quay at Buyukdere, one could guess that, in the course of years, Alexander would be an irritable, peevish old dandy, while Paul would turn out a stern, successful old man.

They stood looking at the water, watching the caïques

shoot out from the shore upon the bosom of the broad stream.

"Have you made up your mind?" asked Paul, without looking at his brother.

"Oh, yes. I do not care where we go. I suppose it is worth seeing?"

"Well worth seeing. You have never seen anything like it."

"Is it as fine as Easter Eve in Moscow?" asked Alexander, incredulously.

"It is different," said Paul. "It corresponds to our Easter Eve in some ways. All through the Ramazán they fast all day — never smoke, nor drink a glass of water, and of course they eat nothing — until sunset, when the gun is fired. During the last week there are services in Santa Sophia every night, and that is what is most remarkable. They go on until the news comes that the new moon has been seen."

"That does not sound very interesting," remarked Alexander, languidly, lighting a cigarette with a bit of yellow fuse that dangled from his heavy Moscow case.

"It is interesting, nevertheless, and you must see it. You cannot be here at this time and not see what is most worth seeing."

"Is there nothing else this evening?" asked Alexander.

"No. We have to respect the prejudices of the country a little. After all, we really have a holiday during this month. Nothing can be done. The people at the palace do not get up until one o'clock or later, so as to make the time while they fast seem shorter."

"Very sensible of them. I wonder why they get up at all, until their ridiculous gun fires, and they can smoke."

"Whether you like it or not, you must go to Santa Sophia to-night, and see the service," said Paul, firmly. "You need not stay long, unless you like."

"If you take me there, I will stay rather than have the

trouble of coming away," answered the other. "Bah!" he exclaimed suddenly, "there is that caïque again!"

Paul followed the direction of his brother's glance, and saw a graceful caïque pulling slowly up-stream towards them. Four sturdy Turks in snow-white cotton tugged at the long oars, and in the deep body of the boat, upon low cushions, sat two ladies, side by side. Behind them, upon the stern, was perched a hideous and beardless African, gorgeously arrayed in a dark tunic heavily laced with gold, a richly chased and adorned scimiter at his side, and a red fez jauntily set on one side of his misshapen head. But Alexander's attention was arrested by the ladies, or rather by one of them, as the caïque passed within oar's length of the quay.

"She must be hideous," said Paul, contemptuously. "I never saw such a yashmak. It is as thick as a towel. You cannot see her face at all."

"Look at her hand," said Alexander. "I tell you she is not hideous."

The figures of the two ladies were completely hidden in the wide black silk garments they wore, the eternal ferigee which makes all women alike. Upon their heads they wore caps, such as in the jargon of fashion are called toques, and their faces were enveloped in yashmaks, white veils which cross the forehead above the eyes and are brought back just below them, so as to cover the rest of the face. But there was this difference; that whereas the veil worn by one of the ladies was of the thinnest gauze, showing every feature of her dark, coarse face through its transparent texture, the veil of the other was perfectly opaque, and disguised her like a mask. Paul Patoff justly remarked that this was very unusual. He had observed the same peculiarity at least twenty times; for in the course of three weeks, since Alexander arrived, the brothers had seen this same lady almost every day, till they had grown to expect her, and had exhausted all speculation in regard to her personality.

Paul maintained that she was ugly, because she would not show her face. Alexander swore that she was beautiful, because her hand was young and white and shapely, and because, as he said, her attitude was graceful and her head moved well when she turned it. Concerning her hand, at least, there was no doubt, for as the delicate fingers stole out from the black folds of the ferigee their whiteness shone by contrast upon the dark silk ; there was something youthful and nervous and sensitive in their shape and movement which fascinated the young Russian, and made him mad with curiosity to see the face of the veiled woman to whom they belonged. She turned her head a little, as the caïque passed, and her dark eyes met his with an expression which seemed one of intelligence ; but unfortunately all black eyes look very much alike when they are just visible between the upper and the lower folds of a thick yashmak, and Alexander uttered an exclamation of discontent.

Thereupon the hideous negro at the stern, who had noticed the stare of the two Russians, shook his light stick at Alexander, and hissed out something that sounded very like " Kiope 'oul kiopek," — dog and son of a dog ; the oarsmen grinned and pulled harder than ever, and the caïque shot past the pier. Paul shrugged his shoulders contemptuously, but did not translate the Turkish ejaculation to his brother. A boatman stood lounging near them, leaning on a stone post, and following the retreating caïque with his eyes.

" Ask that fellow who she is," said Alexander.

" He does not know," answered Paul. " Those fellows never know anything."

" Ask him," insisted his brother. " I am sure he knows." Paul was willing to be obliging, and went up to the man.

" Do you know who that Khanum is ? " he asked, in Turkish.

" Bilmem, — I don't know," replied the man, without moving a muscle of his face.

"Do you know who her father is ? "

"Allah bilir, — God knows.   Probably Abraham, who is the father of all the faithful."   Paul laughed.

"I told you he knew nothing about her," he said, turning to his brother.

"It did you no harm to ask," answered Alexander testily. "Let us take a caïque and follow her."

"You may, if you please," said Paul.   "I have no intention of getting myself into trouble."

"Nonsense!   Why should we get into trouble?   We have as good a right to row on the Bosphorus as they have."

"We have no right to go near them.   It is contrary to the customs of the country."

"I do not care for custom," retorted Alexander.

"If you walked down the Boulevard des Italiens in Paris on Easter Day and kissed every woman you met, merely saying, 'The Lord is risen,' by way of excuse, as we do in Russia, you would discover that customs are not the same everywhere."

"You are as slow as an ox-cart, Paul," said Alexander.

"The simile is graceful.   Thank you.   As I say, you may do anything you please, as you are a stranger here. But if you do anything flagrantly contrary to the manners of the country, you will not find my chief disposed to help you out of trouble.   We are disliked enough already, — hated expresses it better.   Come along.   Take a turn upon the quay before dinner, and then we will go to Stamboul and see the ceremony."

"I hate the quay," replied Alexander, who was now in a very bad humor.

"Then we will go the other way.   We can walk through Mesar Burnu and get to the Valley of Roses."

"That sounds better."

So the two turned northwards, and followed the quay up-stream till they came to the wooden steamboat landing, and then, turning to the left, they entered the small Turkish village of Mesar Burnu. While they walked upon the road Alexander could still follow the caïque, now far ahead, shooting along through the smooth water, and he slackened his pace more slowly when it was out of sight. The dirty little bazaar of the village did not interest him, and he was not inclined to talk as he picked his way over the muddy stones, chewing his discontent and regretting the varnish of his neat boots. Presently they emerged from the crowd of vegetable venders, fishmongers, and sweetmeat sellers into a broad green lane between two grave-yards, where the huge silent trees grew up straight and sad from the sea of white tombstones which stood at every angle, some already fallen, some looking as though they must fall at once, some still erect, according to the length of time which had elapsed since they were set up. For in Turkey the head-stones of graves are narrow at the base and broaden like leaves towards the top, and they are not set deep in the ground ; so that they are top-heavy, and with the sinking of the soil they invariably fall to one side or the other.

Paul turned again, where four roads meet at a drinking fountain, and the two brothers entered the narrow Valley of Roses. The roses are not, indeed, so numerous as one might expect, but the path is beautiful, green and quiet, and below it the tinkle of a little stream is heard, flowing down from the spring where the lane ends. There they sat down beneath a giant tree on a beaten terrace, where a Kaffegee has his little shop. The water pours from the spring in the hillside into a great basin bordered with green, the air is cool, and there is a delicious sense of rest after leaving the noise and dust of the quay. Both men smoked and drank their coffee in silence. Paul could not help wishing that his brother would take a little more interest in Turkey and a little less in the lady of the thick yashmak ; and especially he wished that Alexander might finish his visit without get-ting into trouble. He had successfully controlled him dur-

ing three weeks, and in another fortnight he must return to
Russia. Paul confessed to himself that his brother's visit
was not an unmitigated blessing, and found it hard to explain the object of it. Indeed, it was so simple that his diplomatic mind did not find it out; for Alexander had
merely said to himself that he had never seen Constantinople, and that, as his brother was there, in the embassy, he
could see it under favorable circumstances, at a very moderate cost. He was impetuous, spoiled by too much flattery,
and incapable of imagining that Paul could consider his
visit in any light but that of a compliment. Accordingly
he had come, and had enjoyed himself very much.

"Let us dine here," he said suddenly, as he finished his
coffee.

"There is nothing to eat," answered Paul. "Coffee,
cold water, and a few cakes. That is all, and that would
hardly satisfy you."

"What a nuisance!" exclaimed the elder brother.
"What a barbarous country this is! Nothing to eat but
coffee, cold water, and cakes!"

"It is rather hard on the Turks to abuse them for not
keeping restaurants in their woods," remarked Paul.

"I detest the Turks. I shall never forget the discomfort
I had to put up with in the war. They might have learned
something from us then; but they never learn anything.
Come along. Let us go and dine in your rooms."

"It is impossible to be more discontented than you are,"
said Paul, rather bitterly. "It is utterly impossible to
please you, — and yet you have most things which are necessary to happiness."

"I suppose you mean the money?" sneered his brother.
But Paul kept his temper.

"I mean everything," he answered. "You have money,
youth, good looks, and social success; and yet you can
hardly see anything without abusing it."

"You forget that I do not know the name of the lady in
the yashmak," objected Alexander.

Paul shrugged his shoulders, and said nothing. Both men rose, and began to go down the green lane, returning towards Mesar Burnu. By this time the sun had sunk low behind the western hills, and the cool of the evening had descended on the woods and the Valley of Roses. The green grass and the thick growth of shrubs took a darker color, and the first dampness of the dew was in the air. The two walked briskly down the path. Suddenly a turn in the narrow way brought them face to face with a party of three persons, strolling slowly towards them.

"Luck!" ejaculated Alexander. "Here they are again!"

He was right. There was no mistaking the lady with the thick, impenetrable veil, nor her companion, whose heavy dark face was distinctly visible through the thin Indian gauze. Behind them walked the hideous negro, swinging his light cane jauntily, but beginning to cast angry glances at the two Russians, whom he had already recognized. The way was very narrow, and the ladies saw that retreat was impossible. Paul bit his lip, fearing some foolish rashness on the part of his brother. As they all met, the ladies drew close to the hedge on one side of the path, their black attendant standing before them, as though to prevent the Giaours from even brushing against the wide silken ferigees of his charges. Paul pushed his brother in front of him, hoping that Alexander would have the sense to pass quietly by; but he trembled for the result.

Alexander moved slowly forward, turning his head as he passed, and looking long into the black eyes of the veiled lady.

"Pek güzel, — very pretty indeed," he said aloud, using the only words of Turkish he had learned in three weeks. But they were enough; the effect was instantaneous. Without a word and without hesitation, the tall negro struck a violent blow at Alexander with the light bamboo he carried. Paul, who was immediately behind his brother, saw the action and caught the man's hand in the air, but the end of the flexible cane flew down and knocked Alexander's hat from his head.

"Run!" cried Paul excitedly, as the negro struggled in his grip.

The two Turkish ladies laughed aloud. They were used to such adventures, but the spectacle of the negro beating a Frank gentleman was novel and refreshing. Alexander picked up his hat, but showed no disposition to move. The African struggled vainly in Paul's powerful arms.

"Go, I say!" cried the latter authoritatively. "There will be trouble if any one comes."

But Alexander had received a blow, and his blood was up. Moreover, he was a Russian, and utterly regardless of consequences, — or perhaps he only wanted to annoy his brother by a show of violence.

"I think I will shoot him," he said, quietly producing a small revolver from his pocket.

At the sight of the weapon, the two ladies, who, on seeing the fight prolonged, had retired a few paces up the path, began to scream loudly for help. The negro, who was proof against blows and would not have shown much fear at the sight of a knife, fell on his knees, crying aloud for mercy. Thereupon Paul released him and bid him go.

"For God's sake, Alexander, do not make a fool of yourself!" he said coldly, walking up to his brother. But he turned once more to the black attendant, and added quietly in Turkish, "You had better go. We both have pistols."

The negro did not wait, but sprang back and flew towards the two ladies, speaking excitedly, and imploring them to make haste. The two brothers made their way quickly down the path, Paul pushing Alexander before him.

"You have done it now. You will have to leave Constantinople to-morrow," he said, sternly. "You cannot play these tricks here."

"Bah!" returned Alexander, "it is of no consequence. They do not know who we are."

"They have not seen us coming out of our embassy half a dozen times without knowing where to look for us. There will be a complaint made within two hours, and there will be trouble. The law protects them. These fellows are authorized to strike anybody who speaks to the women they have in charge, or who even goes too near them. Be quick! We must get back to the quay before there is any alarm raised."

Alexander knew that his brother Paul was no coward, and, being thoroughly convinced of the danger, he quickened his walk. In twenty minutes they reached Mesar Burnu, and in five minutes more they were within the gates of the embassy. The huge Cossack who stood by the entrance saluted them gravely, and Paul drew a long breath of relief as he entered the pretty pavilion in the garden in which he had his quarters. Alexander threw himself upon a low divan, and laughed with true Russian indifference. Paul pretended not to notice him, but silently took up the local French paper, which came every evening, and began to read.

"You are excellent company, upon my word!" exclaimed Alexander, irritated at his brother's coldness. Paul laid down the paper, and stared at him with his hard blue eyes.

"Alexander, you are a fool," he said coolly.

"Look here," said the other, suddenly losing his temper, and rising to his feet, "I will not submit to this sort of language."

"Then do not expose yourself to it. Are you aware that you do me very serious injury by your escapades?"

"Escapades indeed!" cried Alexander indignantly. "As if there were any harm in telling a woman she is pretty!"

"You will probably have occasion to hear what the chief thinks of it before long," retorted his brother. "There will be a complaint. It will get to the palace, and the result will be that I shall be sent to another post, with a black mark in the service. Do you call that a joke? It is very

well for you, a rich officer in the guards, taking a turn in
the East by way of recreation. You will go back to Petersburg and tell the story and enjoy the laugh. I may be
sent to China or Japan for three or four years, in consequence."

"Bah!" ejaculated the soldier, sitting down on the
divan. "I do not believe it. You are an old woman.
You are always afraid of injuring your career."

"If it is to be injured at all, I prefer that it should be by
my own fault."

"What do you want me to do?" asked Alexander, rising once more. "I think I will go back to the Valley of
Roses, and see if I cannot find her again." Suiting the
action to the word, he moved towards the door. All the
willfulness of the angry Slav shone in his dark eyes, and he
was really capable of fulfilling his threat.

"If you try it," said Paul, touching an electric bell behind his chair, "I will have you arrested. We are in Russia inside these gates, and there are a couple of Cossacks
outside. I am quite willing to assume the responsibility."

Paul was certainly justified in taking active measures to
coerce his headstrong brother. The spoilt child of a brilliant society was not accustomed to being thwarted in his
caprices, and beneath his delicate pale skin the angry blood
boiled up to his face. He strode towards his brother as
though he would have struck him, but something in Paul's
eyes checked the intention. He held his heavy silver cigarette case in his hand; turning on his heel with an oath, he
dashed it angrily across the room. It struck a small mirror that stood upon a table in the corner, and broke it into
shivers with a loud crash. At that moment the door
opened, and Paul's servant appeared in answer to the bell.

"A glass of water," said Paul calmly. The man
glanced at Alexander's angry face and at the broken look-
ing-glass, and then retired.

"What do you mean by calling in your accursed servants

when I am angry?" cried the soldier. "You shall pay for this, Paul, — you shall pay for it!" His soft voice rose to loud and harsh tones, as he impatiently paced the room. "You shall pay for it!" he almost yelled, and then stood still, suddenly, while Paul rose from his chair. The door was opened again, but instead of the servant with the glass of water a tall and military figure stood in the entrance. It was the ambassador himself. He looked sternly from one brother to the other.

"Gentlemen," he said, "what is this quarrel? Lieutenant Patoff, I must beg you to remember that you are my guest as well as your brother's, and that the windows are open. Even the soldiers at the gates can hear your cries. Be good enough either to cease quarreling, or to retire to some place where you cannot be heard."

Without waiting for an answer, the old diplomat faced about and walked away.

"That is the beginning," said Paul, in a low voice. "You see what you are doing? You are ruining me, — and for what? Not even because you have a caprice for a woman, but merely because I have warned you not to make trouble."

Paul crossed the room and picked up the fallen cigarette case. Then he handed it to his brother, with a conciliatory look.

"There, — smoke a cigarette and be quiet, like a good fellow," he said.

The servant entered with the glass of water, and put it down upon the table. Glancing at the fragments of the mirror upon the floor, he looked inquiringly at his master. Paul made a gesture signifying that he might leave the room. The presence of the servant did not tend to pacify Alexander, whose face was still flushed with anger, as he roughly took the silver case and turned away with a furious glance. The servant had noticed, in the course of three weeks, that the brothers were not congenial to each other, but this was the first time he had witnessed a violent quarrel between them. When he was gone Alexander turned again and confronted Paul.

"You are insufferable," he said, in low tones.

"It is easy for you to escape my company," returned the other. "The Varna boat leaves here to-morrow afternoon at three."

"Set your mind at rest," said Alexander, regaining some control of his temper at the prospect of immediate departure. "I will leave to-morrow."

He went towards the door.

"Dinner is at seven," said Paul quietly. But his brother left the room without noticing the remark, and, retiring to his room, he revenged himself by writing a long letter to his mother, in which he explained at length the violence and, as he described it, the "impossibility" of his brother's character. He had all the pettiness of a bad child; he knew that he was his mother's favorite, and he naturally went to her for sympathy when he was angry with his brother, as he had done from his infancy. Having so far vented his wrath, he closed his letter without re-reading it, and delivered it to be posted before the clock struck seven.

He found Paul waiting for him in the sitting-room, and was received by him as though nothing had happened. Paul was indeed neither so forgiving nor so long-suffering as he appeared. He cordially disliked his brother, and was annoyed at his presence and outraged at his rashness. He felt bitterly enough that Alexander had quartered himself in the little pavilion for nearly a month without an invitation, and that, even financially, the visit caused him inconvenience; but he felt still more the danger to himself which lay in Alexander's folly, and he was not far wrong when he said that the ambassador's rebuke was the beginning of trouble. Accustomed to rely upon himself and his own wise conduct in the pursuance of his career, he resented the injury done him by such incidents as had taken place that afternoon. On the other hand, since Alexander had expressed his determination to leave Buyukdere the next day, he was determined that on his side the parting should be amicable. He could control his mood so far as to be civil during dinner, and to converse upon general topics. Alexander sat down to table in silence. His face was pale again, and his eyes had regained that simple, trustful look which was so much at variance with his character, and which, in the opinion of his admirers, constituted one of his chief attractions. It is unfortunate that, in general, the expression of the eyes should have less importance than that of the other features, for it always seems that by the eyes we should judge most justly. As a matter of fact, I think that the passions leave no trace in them, although they express the emotions of the moment clearly enough. The dark pupils may flash with anger, contract with determination, expand with love or fear; but so soon as the mind ceases to be under the momentary influence of any of these, the pupil returns to its normal state, the iris takes its natural color, and the eye, if seen through a hole in a screen, expresses nothing. If we were in the habit of studying men's mouths rather than their eyes, we should less often be deceived in the estimates we form of their character. Alexander Patoff's eyes were like a child's when he was peaceably inclined, like a wild-cat's when he was angry; but his nervous, scornful lips were concealed by the carefully trained dark brown mustache, and with them lay hidden the secret of his ill-controlled, ill-balanced nature.

When dinner was finished, the servant announced that the steam launch was at the pier, and that the embassy *kaváss* was waiting outside to conduct them to Santa Sophia. Alexander, who wanted diversion of some kind during the evening, said he would go, and the two brothers left the pavilion together.

The kaváss is a very important functionary in Constantinople, and, though his office is lucrative, it is no sinecure.

In former times the appearance of Franks in the streets of
Constantinople was very likely to cause disturbance.   Those
were the great days of Turkey, when the Osmanli was master of the East, and regarded himself as the master of the
world.   A Frank — that is to say, a person from the west
of Europe — was scarcely safe out of Pera without an es-
cort ; and even at the present day most people are advised
not to venture into Stamboul without the attendance of a
native, unless willing to wear a fez instead of a hat.   It became necessary to furnish the embassies with some outward
and visible means of protection, and the kaváss was accordingly instituted.   This man, who was formerly always a
Janizary, is at present a veteran soldier, and therefore a
Mussulman ; for Christians rarely enter the army in Constantinople, being permitted to buy themselves off.   He is
usually a man remarkable for his trustworthy character, of
fine presence, and generally courageous.   He wears a magnificent Turkish military dress, very richly adorned with
gold embroidery, girt with a splendid sash, in which are
thrust enough weapons to fill an armory, — knives, dirks,
pistols, and daggers, — while a huge scimiter hangs from
his sword-belt.   When he is on active service, you will detect somewhere among his trappings the brown leather case
of a serviceable army revolver.   The reason of this outfit is
a very simple one.   The kaváss is answerable with his head
for those he protects, — neither more nor less.   Whenever
the ambassador or the minister goes to the palace, or to
Stamboul, or on any expedition whatsoever, the kaváss follows him, frequently acting as interpreter, and certainly
never failing to impose respect upon the populace.   Moreover, when he is not needed by the head of the mission in
person, he is ready to accompany any member of the household when necessary. A lady may cross Stamboul in
safety with no other attendant, for he is answerable for her
with his life.   Whether or not, in existing circumstances,
he would be put to death, in case his charge were killed by

a mob, is not easy to say ; it is at least highly probable that
he would be executed within twenty-four hours.

It chanced, on the evening chosen by Paul and Alexander for their visit to Santa Sophia, that no other members
of the embassy accompanied them. Some had seen the ceremony before, some intended to go the next day, and some
were too lazy to go at all. They followed the kaváss in
silence across the road, and went on board the beautiful
steam launch which lay alongside the quay. The night was
exceedingly dark, for as the appearance of the new moon
terminates the month Ramazán, and as the ceremonies take
place only during the last week of the month, there can, of
course, be no moonlight. But a dark night is darker on the
black waters of the Bosphorus than anywhere else in the
world ; and the darkness is not relieved by the illumination
of the shores. On the contrary, the countless twinkling
points seem to make the shadow in midstream deeper, and
accidents are not unfrequent. In some places the current is
very rapid, and it is no easy matter to steer a steam launch
skillfully through it, without running over some belated fisherman or some shadowy caïque, slowly making way against
the stream in the dark.

The two brothers sat in the deep cane easy-chairs on the
small raised deck at the stern, the weather being too warm
to admit of remaining in the cushioned cabin. The sailors
cast off the moorings, and the strong little screw began to
beat the water. In two minutes the launch was far out in
the darkness. The kaváss gave the order to the man at the
wheel, an experienced old pilot : —

" To the Vinegar Sellers' Landing."

The engine was put at full speed, and the launch rushed
down stream towards Constantinople. Paul and Alexander
looked at the retreating shore and at the lights of the embassy, fast growing dim in the distance. Paul wished himself alone in his quiet pavilion, with a cigarette and one of

Gogol's novels. His brother, who was ashamed of his violent temper and disgusted with his brother's coldness,
wished that he might never come back. Indeed, he was inclined to say so, and to spend the night at a hotel in Pera;
but he was ashamed of that too, now that his anger had
subsided, and he made up his mind to be morally uncomfortable for at least twenty-four hours. For it is the nature
of violent people to be ashamed of themselves, and then to
work themselves into new fits of anger in order to escape
their shame, a process which may be exactly compared to
the drunkard's glass of brandy in the morning, and which
generally leads to very much the same result.

But Paul said nothing, and so long as he was silent it
was impossible to quarrel with him. Alexander, therefore,
stretched out his legs and puffed at his cigarette, wondering
whether he should ever see the lady in the yashmak again,
trying to imagine what her face could be like, but never
doubting that she was beautiful. He had been in love with
many faces. It was the first time he had ever fallen in
love with a veil. The sweet air of the Bosphorus blew in
his face, the distant lights twinkled and flashed past as the
steam launch ran swiftly on, and Alexander dozed in his
chair, dreaming that the scented breeze had blown aside
the folds of the yashmak, and that he was gazing on the
most beautiful face in the world. That is one of the characteristics of the true Russian. The Slav is easily roused
to frenzied excitement, and he as easily falls back to an in-
dolent and luxurious repose. There is something poetic in
his temperament, but the extremes are too violent for all
poetry. To be easily sad and easily gay may belong to the
temper of the poet, but to be bloodthirsty and luxurious by
turns savors of the barbarian.

Alexander was aroused by the lights of Stamboul and by
the noise of the large ferry-boats just making up to the
wooden piers of Galata bridge, or rushing away into the

darkness amidst tremendous splashing of paddles and blowing of steam whistles. A few minutes later the launch ran
alongside of the Vinegar Sellers' Landing on the Stamboul
shore, and the kaváss came aft to inform the brothers that
the carriage was waiting by the water-stairs.

II.

THERE is probably no nation in the world more attached to religion, both in form and principle, than the Osmanli; and it is probably for this reason that their public ceremonies bear a stamp of vigor and sincerity rarely equaled in Christian countries. No one can witness the rites practiced in the mosque of Agia Sophia without being profoundly impressed with the power of the Mohammedan faith. The famous church of Justinian is indeed in itself magnificent and awe-inspiring; the vast dome is more effective than that of Saint Peter's, in proportion as the masses which support it are smaller and less apparent; the double stories of the nave are less burdened with detail and ornament, and are therefore better calculated to convey an impression of size; the view from the galleries is less obstructed in all directions, and there is something startling in the enormous shields of green inscribed in gold with the names of God, Mohammed, and the earliest khalifs. Everything in the building produces a sensation of smallness in the beholder, almost amounting to stupor. But the Agia Sophia seen by day, in the company of a chattering Greek guide, is one thing; it is quite another when viewed at night from the solitude of the vast galleries, during the religious ceremonies of the last week in the month Ramazán.

Paul and Alexander Patoff were driven through dark streets to a narrow lane, where the carriage stopped before a flight of broad steps which suddenly descended into blackness. The kaváss was at the door, and seemed anxious that they should be quick in their movements. He held a small lantern in his hand, and, carrying it low down, showed

them the way. Entering a gloomy doorway, they were
aware of a number of Turks, clad mostly in white tunics,
with white turbans, and congregated near the heavy leathern curtain which separates this back entrance from the
portico. One of these men, a tall fellow with an ugly scowl,
came forward, holding a pair of keys in his hand, and after
a moment's parley with the kaváss unlocked a heavily
ironed door, lighting a taper at the lantern.

As they entered, both the brothers cast a glance at the
knot of scowling men, and Alexander felt in his pocket for
his pistol. He had forgotten it, and the discovery did not
tend to make him feel more safe. Then he smiled to himself, recognizing that it was but a passing feeling of distrust which he experienced, and remembering how many
thousands of Franks must have passed through that very
door to reach the winding staircase. As for Paul, he had
been there the previous year, and was accustomed to the
sour looks of Mussulmans when a Frank visitor enters one
of their mosques. He also went in, and the kaváss, who
was the last of the party, followed, pulling the door on its
hinges behind him. During several minutes they mounted
the rough stone steps in silence, by the dim light of the
lantern and the taper. Then emerging into the gallery
through a narrow arch, a strange sound reached them, and
Alexander stood still for a moment.

Far down in the vast church an Imam was intoning a
passage of the Koran in a voice which hardly seemed human; indeed, such a sound is probably not to be heard
anywhere else in the world. The pitch was higher than
what is attainable by the highest men's voices elsewhere,
and yet the voice possessed the ringing, manly quality of
the tenor, and its immense volume never dwindled to the
proportions of a soprano. The priest recited and modu-
lated in this extraordinary key, introducing all the orna-
ments peculiar to the ancient Arabic chant with a facility
which an operatic singer might have envied. Then there

was a moment's silence, broken again almost immediately by a succession of heavy sounds which can only be described as resembling rhythmical thunder, rising and falling three times at equal intervals; another short but intense silence, and again the voice burst out with the wild clang of a trumpet, echoing and reverberating through the galleries and among the hundred marble pillars of the vast temple.

The two brothers walked forward to the carved stone balustrade of the high gallery, and gazed down from the height upon the scene below. The multitude of worshipers surged like crested waves blown obliquely on a shingly shore. For the apse of the Christian church is not built so that, facing it, the true believer shall look towards Mecca, and the Mussulmans have made their *mihrab* — their shrine — a little to the right of what was once the altar, in the true direction of the sacred city. The long lines of matting spread on the floor all lie evenly at an angle with the axis of the nave, and when the mosque is full the whole congregation, amounting to thousands of men, are drawn up like regiments of soldiers in even ranks to face the mihrab, but not at right angles with the nave. The effect is startling and strangely inharmonious, like the studied distortions of some Japanese patterns, but yet fascinating from its very contrariety to what the eye expects.

There they stand, the ranks of the faithful, as they have stood yearly for centuries in the last week of Ramazán. As the trumpet notes of each recited verse die away among the arches, every man raises his hands above his head, then falls upon his knees, prostrates himself, and rises again, renewing the act of homage three times with the precision of a military evolution. At each prostration, performed exactly and simultaneously by that countless multitude, the air is filled with the tremendous roar of muffled rhythmical thunder, in which no voice is heard, but only the motion of ten thousand human bodies, swaying, bending, and kneeling in unison. Nor is the sound alone impressive. From the

vaulted roof, from the galleries, from the dome itself, are
hung hundreds of gigantic chandeliers, each having concen-
tric rings of lighted lamps, suspended a few feet above the
heads of the worshipers. Seen from the great height of the
gallery, these thousands of lights do not dazzle nor hide the
multitude below, which seems too great to be hidden, as the
heavens are not hid by the stars; but the soft illumination
fills every corner and angle of the immense building, and,
lest any detail of the architecture and splendid music should
escape the light, rows of little lamps are kindled along the
cornices of the galleries and roof, filling up the interstices
of darkness as a carver burnishes the inner petals of the
roses on a huge gilt frame of exquisite design, in which not
the smallest beauty of the workmanship can be allowed to
pass unnoticed.

This whole flood of glorious illumination descends then to
the floor of the nave, and envelops the ranks of white and
green clothed men, who rise and fall in long sloping lines,
like a field of corn under the slanting breeze. There is
something mystic and awe-inspiring in the sight, the sound,
the whole condition, of this strange worship. A man looks
down upon the serried army of believers, closely packed,
but not crowded nor irregular, shoulder to shoulder, knee
to knee, not one of them standing a hair's breadth in front
of his rank nor behind it, moving all as one body, animated
by one principle of harmonious motion, elevated by one un-
questioning faith in something divine, — a man looks down
upon this scene, and, whatever be his own belief, he cannot
but feel an unwonted thrill of admiration, a tremor of awe,
a quiver of dread, at the grand solemnity of this unanimous
worship of the unseen. And then, as the movement ceases,
and the files of white turbans remain motionless, the unearthly voice of the Imam rings out like a battle signal
from the lofty balcony of the *mastaba*,[1] awaking in the fer-

---

[1] The tribune, or marble platform, from which the prayers are
read; not to be confounded with the *minber*, or pulpit, from which the
Khatib preaches on Fridays, with a drawn sword in his hand.

vent spirits of the believers the warlike memories of mighty
conquest. For the Osmanli is a warrior, and his nation is a
warrior tribe; his belief is too simple for civilization, his
courage too blind and devoted for the military operations of
our times, his heart too easily roused by the bloodthirsty
instincts of the fanatic, and too ready to bear the misfortunes of life with the grave indifference of the fatalist.
He lacks the balance of the faculties which is imposed upon
civilized man by a conscious distinction of the possible from
the impossible; he lacks the capacity for being contented
with that state of life in which he is placed. Instead of the
quiet courage and self-knowledge of a serviceable strength, he
possesses the reckless and all-destroying zeal of the frenzied
inconoclast; in place of patience under misfortune, in the
hope of better times, he cultivates the insensibility begotten
of a belief in hopeless predestination, — instead of strength
he has fury, instead of patience apathy. He is a strange
being, beyond our understanding, as he is too often beyond
our sympathy. It is only when we see him roused to the
highest expression of his religious fervor that we involuntarily feel that thrill of astonishment and awe which in our
hearts we know to be genuine admiration.

Alexander Patoff stood by his brother's side, watching
the ceremony with intense interest. He hated the Turks
and despised their faith, but what he now saw appealed to
the Orientalism of his nature. Himself capable of the most
distant extremes of feeling, sensitive, passionate, and accustomed to delight in strong impressions, he could not fail to
be moved by the profound solemnity of the scene and by
the indescribable wildness of the Imam's chant. Paul, too,
was silent, and, though far less able to feel such emotions
than his elder brother, the sight of such unanimous and
heart-felt devotion called up strange trains of thought in his
mind, and forced him to speculate upon the qualities and
the character which still survived in these hereditary enemies of his nation. It was not possible, he said to himself,

that such men could ever be really conquered. They might
be driven from the capital of the East by overwhelming
force, but they would soon rally in greater numbers on the
Asian shore. They might be crushed for a moment, but
they could never be kept under, nor really dominated.
Their religion might be oppressed and condemned by the
oppressor, but it was of the sort to gain new strength at
every fresh persecution. To slay such men was to sow
dragon's teeth and to reap a harvest of still more furious
fanatics, who, in their turn being destroyed, would multiply
as the heads of the Hydra beneath the blows of Heracles.
The even rise and fall of those long lines of stalwart Mussulmans seemed like the irrepressible tide of an ocean, which
if restrained, would soon break every barrier raised to ob-
struct it. Paul sickened at the thought that these men
were bowing themselves upon the pavement from which
their forefathers had washed the dust of Christian feet in
the blood of twenty thousand Christians, and the sullen
longing for vengeance rankled in his heart. At that moment he wished he were a soldier, like his brother ; he
wished he could feel a soldier's pride in the strong fellow-
ship of the ranks, and a soldier's hope of retaliation. He
almost shuddered when he reflected that he and his brother
stood alone, two hated Russians, with that mighty, rhythmi-
cally surging mass of enemies below. The bravest man
might feel his nerves a little shaken in such a place, at such
an hour. Paul leaned his chin upon his hand, and gazed
intently down into the body of the church. The armed
kaváss stood a few paces from him on his left, and Alexander was leaning against a column on his right.

The kaváss was a good Mussulman, and regarded the
ceremony not only with interest, but with a devotion akin
to that of those who took part in it. He also looked fixedly
down, turning his eyes to the mihrab, and listening attentively to the chanting of the Imam, of whose Arabic recita-
tion, however, he could not understand any more than Paul

himself. For a long time no one of the three spoke, nor indeed noticed his companions.

"Shall we go to the other side of the gallery?" asked
Paul, presently, in a low voice, but without looking round.
Alexander did not answer, but the kaváss moved, and uttered a low exclamation of surprise. Paul turned his head
to repeat his question, and saw that Alexander was no
longer in the place where he had been standing. He was
nowhere to be seen.

"He is gone round the gallery alone," said Paul to the
kaváss, and leading the way he went to the end of the balcony, and turning in the shadow looked down the long gallery which runs parallel with the nave. Alexander was not
in sight, and Paul, supposing him to be hidden behind one
of the heavy pillars which divided the balustrade into equal
portions, walked rapidly to the end. But his brother was
not there.

"Bah!" Paul exclaimed to the kaváss, "he is on the
other side." He looked attentively at the opposite balconies, across the brilliantly lighted church, but saw no one.
He and the soldier retraced their steps, and explored every
corner of the galleries, without success. The kaváss was
pale to the lips.

"He is gone down alone," he muttered, hastening to the
head of the winding stair in the northwest corner of the dim
gallery. He had left his lantern by the door, but it was
not there. Alexander must have taken it with him. The
Turk with the keys and the taper had long since gone down,
in expectation of some other Frank visitors, but as yet none
had appeared. Paul breathed hard, for he knew that a stranger could not with safety descend alone, on such a night, to
the vestibule of the mosque, filled as it was with turbaned
Mussulmans who had not found room in the interior, and who
were pursuing their devotions before the great open doors.
On the other hand, if Alexander had not entered the vestibule, he must have gone out into the street, where he would

not be much safer, for his hat proclaimed him a Frank to every party of strolling Turks he chanced to meet.

Paul lit a wax taper from his case, and, holding others in readiness, began to follow the rugged descent, the kaváss close at his elbow. It seemed interminable. At every deep embrasure Paul paused, searching the recess by the flickering glare of the match, and then, finding nothing, both men went on. At last they reached the bottom, and the heavy door creaked as the kaváss pressed it back.

" You must stay here," he said, in his broken jargon. " Or, better still, you should go outside with me and get into the carriage. I will come back and search."

" No," said Paul. " I will go with you. I am not afraid of them."

" You cannot," answered the kaváss firmly. " I cannot protect you inside the vestibule."

" I tell you I will go ! " exclaimed Paul impatiently. " I do not expect you to protect me. I will protect myself." But the kaváss would not yield so easily. He was a powerful man, and stood calmly in the doorway. Paul could not pass him without using violence.

" Effendim," said the man, speaking Turkish, which he knew that Paul understood, " if I let you go in there, and anything happens to you, my life is forfeited."

Paul hesitated. The man was in earnest, and they were losing time which might be precious. It was clear that Alexander might already be in trouble, and that the kaváss was the only person capable of imposing respect upon the crowd.

" Go," said Paul. " I will wait by the carriage."

The kaváss opened the door, and both men went out into the dim entry. Paul turned to the right and the soldier to the left, towards the heavy curtain which closed the entrance of the vestibule. The knot of Turks who had stood there when the Russians had arrived had disappeared, and the place was silent and deserted, while from behind the curtain

faint echoes of the priest's high voice were audible, and at
intervals the distant thundering roll from the church told
that the worshipers were prostrating themselves in the intervals of the chanting.   Paul retired up the dark way, but
paused at the deserted gate, unwilling to go so far as the
carriage, and thus lengthen the time before the kaváss could
rejoin him with his brother.   He trembled lest Alexander
should have given way to some foolhardy impulse to enter
the mosque in defiance of the ceremony which was then proceeding, but it did not strike him that anything very serious
could have occurred, nor that the kaváss would really have
any great difficulty in finding him.   Alexander would probably escape with some rough treatment, which might not be
altogether unprofitable, provided he sustained no serious injury.   It was indeed a rash and foolish thing to go alone
and unarmed among a crowd of fanatic Mohammedans at
their devotions; but, after all, civilization had progressed in
Turkey, and the intruder was no longer liable to be torn in
pieces by the mob.   He would most likely be forcibly ejected
from the vestibule, and left to repent of his folly in peace.

All these reflections passed through Paul's mind, as he
stood waiting in the shadow of the gate at the back of the
mosque; but the time began to seem unreasonably long, and
his doubts presently took the shape of positive fears.   Still
the echoes came to his ears through the heavy curtain, while
from without the distant hum of the city, given up to gayety
after the day's long fast, mingled discordantly with the
sounds from within.   He was aware that his heart was beating faster than usual, and that he was beginning to suffer
the excitement of fear.   He tried to reason with himself,
saying that it was foolish to make so much of so little; but
in the arguments of reason against terror, the latter generally gets the advantage and keeps it.   Paul had a strong desire to follow the kaváss into the vestibule, and to see for
himself whether his brother were there or not.   He rarely
carried weapons, as Alexander did, but he trusted in his

own strength to save him. He drew his watch from his pocket, resolving to wait five minutes longer, and then, if the kaváss did not return, to lift the curtain, come what might. He struck a match, and looked at the dial. It was a quarter past ten o'clock. Then, to occupy his mind, he began to try and count the three hundred seconds, fancying that he could see a pendulum swinging before his eyes in the dark. At twenty minutes past ten he would go in.

But he did not reach the end of his counting. The curtain suddenly moved a little, allowing a ray of bright light to fall out into the darkness, and in the momentary flash Paul saw the gorgeous uniform and accoutrements of the embassy kaváss. He was alone, and Paul's heart sank. He remembered very vividly the dark and scowling faces and the fiery eyes of the turbaned men who had stood before the door an hour earlier, and he began to fear some dreadful catastrophe. The kaváss came quickly forward, and Paul stepped out of the shadow and confronted him.

" Well ? "

" He has not been there," answered the soldier, in agitated tones. " I went all through the crowd, and searched everywhere. I asked many persons. They laughed at the idea of a Frank gentleman in a hat appearing amongst them. He must have gone out into the street."

"We searched the gallery thoroughly, did we not ? " asked Paul. " Are you sure he could not have been hidden somewhere ? "

" Perfectly, Effendim. He is not there."

" Then we must look for him in the streets," said Paul, growing very pale. He turned to ascend the steps from the gate to the road.

" It is not my fault, Effendim," answered the soldier. " Did you not see him leave the gallery ? "

" It is nobody's fault but his own," returned Patoff. " I was looking down at the people. He must have slipped away like a cat."

They reached the carriage, and Paul got inside. It was a landau, and the kaváss and the coachman opened the front, so that Patoff might get a better view of the streets. The kaváss mounted the box, and explained to the coachman that they must search Stamboul as far as possible for the lost Effendi. But the coachman turned sharply round on his seat and spoke to Paul.

"The gentleman did not come out," he said emphatically. "I have been watching for you ever since you went in. He is inside the Agia Sophia — somewhere."

Paul was disconcerted. He had not thought of making inquiries of the coachman, supposing that Alexander might easily have slipped past in the darkness. But the man seemed very positive.

"Wait in the carriage, Effendim," said the kaváss, once more descending from his seat. "If he is inside I will find him. I will search the galleries again. He cannot have gone through the vestibule."

Before Paul could answer him the man had plunged once more down the black steps, and the Russian was condemned a second time to a long suspense, during which he was frequently tempted to leave the carriage and explore the church for himself. He felt the cold perspiration on his brow, and his hand trembled as he took out his watch again and again. It was nearly a quarter of an hour before the kaváss returned. The man was now very pale, and seemed as much distressed as Paul himself. He silently shook his head, and, mounting to the box seat, ordered the coachman to drive on.

The city was ablaze with lights. Every mosque was illuminated, and the minarets, decked out with thousands of little lamps, looked like fiery needles piercing the black bosom of the sky. The carriage drove from place to place, passing where a crowd was gathered together, hastening down dark and deserted streets, to emerge again upon some brilliantly lighted square, thronged with men in fez and turban and

with women veiled in the eternal yashmak. More than
once Paul started in his seat, fancying that he could discover
on the borders of the crowd the two ladies, with their attendant, who had been the cause of the scuffle in the Valley of
Roses that afternoon. Again, he thought he could distinguish his brother's features among the moving faces, but
always the sight of the dark red fez told him that he was
wrong. He was driven round Agia Sophia, beneath the
splendid festoons of lamps, some hung so as to form huge
Arabic letters, some merely bound together in great ropes of
light; back towards the water and through the Atmaidam,
the ancient Hippodrome, down to the Serai point, then up to
the Seraskierat, where the glorious tower shot upwards like
the pillar of flame that went before the Israelites of old ; on
to the mosque of Suleiman, over whose tomb the great dome
burned like a fiery mountain, round once more to the Atmaidam, past the tall trees amidst which blazed the six minarets of Sultan Achmet; then, trying a new route, down by
the bazaar gates to Sultan Validé and the head of Galata
bridge, and at last back again to the Seraskierat, and, leaving the Dove Mosque of Bajazet on the right, once more to
the Vinegar Sellers' Landing, in the vain hope that Alexander might have found his way down to the quay where the
steam launch was moored.

In vain did the terrified kaváss bid the coachman turn
and turn again ; in vain did Paul, in agonized excitement,
try to pierce the darkness with his eyes, and to distinguish
the well-known face in the throngs that crowded the brightly
lighted squares. At the end of two hours he began to realize the hopelessness of the search. Suddenly it struck him
that Alexander might have found the bridge, and, recognizing it, might have crossed to Pera rather than run the risk
of losing himself in Stamboul again.

"Tell the launch to be at Beschik Tasch to-morrow morning at ten o'clock," said Paul. "Take me to Galata bridge.
I will cross on foot to Pera. Then go back and wait be-

hind Agia Sophia, in case he comes that way again to look
for the carriage. If I find him in Pera, I will send a mes-
senger to tell you. If he does not come, meet me at Missiri's early to-morrow morning."

"Pek eyi — very good," answered the kaváss, who understood the wisdom of the plan. Again the carriage
turned, and in five minutes Paul was crossing Galata bridge,
alone, on his way to Pera.

He was terribly agitated. Stories of the disappearance
of foreigners in the labyrinths of Stamboul rose to his mind,
and though he had never known of such a case in his own
experience, he did not believe the thing impossible. His
brother was the rashest and most foolhardy of men, capable
of risking his life for a mere caprice, and perhaps the more
inclined to do so on that night because he had had a violent
quarrel with Paul that very afternoon, about his own foolish conduct. Of all nights in the year, the last four or five
of Ramazán are the most dangerous to unprotected foreigners, and as he walked the spectacle of the scowling Turks
thrust itself once more before Paul's mental vision. If Alexander had descended the steps, and had ventured, as well
he might, to push past those fellows into the vestibule of the
mosque, it must have gone hard with him. The fanatic
worshipers of Allah were not in a mood that night to bear
with the capricious humors of a haughty Frank ; and though
Alexander was active, strong, and brave, his strength would
avail him little against such odds. He would be overpow-
ered, stunned, and thrown out before he could utter a cry,
and he might think himself lucky if he escaped with one or
two broken bones. But then, again, if he had suffered such
treatment, some one must have heard of it, and Paul remembered the blank face and frightened look of the kaváss when
he returned the second time from his search. They had
gone carefully round the great building, and must have seen
such an object as the body of a man lying in the street.
Perhaps Alexander had broken away without injury, and

fled out into the streets of Stamboul. If so, he was in no common danger, for, utterly ignorant of the topography of the great city, he might as easily have gone towards the Seven Towers or to Aiwán Serai as to Galata bridge or Topkapussi, the Canon Gate at Serai point. There was still one hope left. He might have reached Pera, and be at that very moment refreshing himself with coffee and cigarettes at Missiri's hotel.

Paul hastened his walk, and, reaching Galata, began at once to ascend the steep street which further on is called the Grande Rue, but which of all " great " streets least deserves the name. He then walked slowly, scrutinizing every face he saw. But indeed there were few people about, for Christian Pera does not fast in Ramazán, and consequently does not spend the night in parading the streets. Nevertheless, Paul began a systematic search, leaving no small café or eating-house unvisited, rousing the sleepy porters of the inns with his inquiries, and finally entering the hotel. It was now past midnight, but he would not give up the quest. He caused all the guides to be collected from their obscure habitations by messengers from the hotel, and representing to them the urgency of the case, and giving them money in advance with the promise of more to come, he dispatched them in all directions. Alexander had been at the hotel very often during the last month, while visiting the sights of the city, and most of these fellows knew him by sight. At all events, it would be easy for them to recognize a well-dressed Frank gentleman in trouble.

Patoff saw the last of them leave the hotel, and stood staring out upon the Grande Rue de Pera, wondering what should be done next. The town residence of the embassy was closed for the summer, and there were only two or three sleepy servants in the place, who could be of no use. He thought of getting a horse and riding rapidly back to Buyukdere, in order to warn the ambassador of his bro-

ther's disappearance; but on reflection it seemed that he
would do better to stay where he was. The short June
night would soon be past, and by daylight he could at once
prosecute his search in Stamboul with safety and with far
greater probability of finding the lost man. He knew that
the kaváss would remain with the carriage all night behind
Santa Sophia, and then at dawn he should still find them
there. Meanwhile, he took a *hamál*, — a luggage porter
from the hotel, — and, armed with a lantern and a stick,
began to beat the different quarters of Pera, judging that
in the three or four hours before daylight he could pass
through most of the streets.

Hour after hour he trudged along, pale with fatigue and
anxiety, his big features hardening with despairing determination as he walked. He searched every street and al-
ley; he interviewed the Bekjees, who stamp along the
streets, pounding the pavement with their iron-shod clubs;
he tramped out to the Taksim, and down again to Galata
tower, plunging into the dark alleys about the Oriental
Bank, skirting lower Pera to the Austrian embassy, and
climbing up the narrow path between tall houses, till he
was once more in the Grande Rue; crossing to the filthy
quarters of Kassim Paschá and emerging at the German
Lutheran church, crossing, recrossing, stumbling over gut-
ters and up dirty back lanes, silent and determined still,
addressing only the sturdy Kurd by his side to ask if there
were any streets still unexplored, and entering every new
by-path with new hope. At last he found himself once
more at Galata bridge, and the light of the lantern began
to pale before the grayness of the coming morning. He
paid the Kurdish porter a generous fee, and giving his tiny
coin to the tall keeper of the bridge, whose white garments
looked whiter in the dawn, he walked on until he was half
way over the Golden Horn.

Stepping aside on to the wooden pier where the great
ferry-boats were moored, he leaned upon the rail and looked

out over the water, momentarily exhausted and unable to
go further. The tender light tinged the southeastern sky.
and the far mist of the horizon seemed already hot with the
rising day. On the lapping water of the Horn the light
fell like petals of roses tossed in a mantle of some soft dark
fabric interwoven with a silvery sheen. Far across the
mouth of the Bosphorus the minarets of Scutari came
faintly into view, and on the Stamboul side the few lingering lamps which had outlasted the darkness, upon the lofty
minarets, paled and lost their yellow color, and then ceased
to shine, outdone in their turn by the rosy morning light.
A wonderful stillness had fallen on the great city, as one
by one the tired parties of friends had gone to rest, to
shorten the day of fasting by prolonging their sleep till late
in the hot afternoon. The clank of some capstan on one
of the ferry-boats struck loud and clear on the still air, as
the reluctant sailors and firemen prepared for their first
run to the Black Sea, or across to Kadi Köi on the Sea of
Marmara. Paul turned and looked towards the mighty
dome of Santa Sophia, and his haggard face was almost as
pale as the white walls. He lingered still, and suddenly
the sun sprang up behind the Serai, and gilded the delicate
spires, and caught the gold of the crescents on the mosques,
and shone full upon the broad water. Paul followed the
light as it touched one glorious building after another, and
his hand trembled convulsively on the railing. Somewhere
in that great awakening city — his brother was somewhere,
alive or dead, amongst those white walls and glittering crescents and towering minarets — somewhere, and he must be
found. Paul bent his head, and turning away hurried across
the bridge, and plunged once more into Stamboul, alone as
he had come.

The streets were deserted, and the early morning air was
full of the smell of thousands of extinguished oil lamps,
that peculiar and pervading odor which suggests past rev-
elry, sleepless hours, and the vanity of turning night into

day. It oppressed Paul's overwrought senses, as he passed the melancholy remains of the illumination before the post-office and the Sultan Validé mosque, and he hurried on towards the more secluded streets leading to Santa Sophia, in which the night's gayety had left no perceptible signs. At last he came to the narrow lane behind the huge pile, feeling that he had at last reached the end of his five hours' tramp.

There stood the carriage, all dusty with the night's driving, looking dilapidated and forlorn; the tired horses drooped their heads in the flaccid and empty canvas nose-bags. The extinguished lamps were black with the smoke from the last flare of their sputtering wicks. The coachman lay inside, snoring, — a mere heap of cloth and brass buttons surmounted by a shapeless fez. On the stone steps leading down to the church sat the kaváss; his head had fallen on the low parapet behind him, and his half-shaved scalp was bare. His face was deadly pale, and his mouth was wide open as he slept, breathing heavily; his left hand rested on the hilt of his scimiter; his right was extended, palm upwards, on the stone step on which he sat, the very picture of exhaustion.

At any other time Paul would have laughed at the scene. But he was very far from mirth now, as he bent down and laid his hand upon the sleeping kaváss's shoulder.

III.

At ten o'clock on that morning, Paul and the kaváss went on board the steam launch at Beschik Tasch, the landing most convenient for persons coming from the upper part of Pera. They had done everything possible, and it was manifestly Paul's duty to inform his chief of the occurrences of the night. The authorities had been put in possession of the details of Alexander's disappearance, and the scanty machinery of the Stamboul police had been set in motion; notice had been given at every hotel and circulated to every place of resort, and it was impossible that if Alexander showed himself in Pera he should escape observation, even if he desired to do so. But Stamboul was not Pera, and as Paul gave the order to steam to Buyukdere he resolutely turned his back on the eastern shore of the Golden Horn, unable to bear the sight of the buildings so intimately associated with his night's search. He was convinced that his brother was in Stamboul, and he knew that the search in Pera was a mere formality. He knew, also, that to find any one in Stamboul was only possible provided the person were free, or at least able to give some sign of his presence; and he began to believe that Alexander had fallen a victim to some rash prank. He had, perhaps, repeated his folly of the previous afternoon, — had wandered into the streets, had foolishly ventured to look too closely at a pair of black eyes, and had been spirited away by the prompt vengeance of the lady's attendants.

But Paul's speculations concerning the fate of his brother were just now interrupted by the consideration of the difficulties which lay before him. Cold and resolute by nature,

he found himself in a position in which any man's calmness
would have been shaken. He knew that he must tell his
tale to his chief, and he knew that he was to blame for not
having watched Alexander more closely. It was improbable that any one who had not been present could understand
how, in the intense interest caused by the ceremony, Paul
could have overlooked his brother's departure from the
gallery. But not only had Paul failed to notice his going;
the kaváss had not observed the lost man's movements any
more than Paul himself. It was inconceivable to any one
except Paul that Alexander should have been capable of
creeping past him and the soldier, on tip-toe, purposely eluding observation; nevertheless, such an action would not be
unnatural to his character. He had perhaps conceived a
sudden desire to go down into the church and view the ceremony more closely. He must have known that both his
companions would forcibly prevent him from such a course,
and it was like him to escape them, laughing to himself at
their carelessness. The passion for adventure was in his
blood, and his training had not tended to cool it; fate had
thrown an attractive possibility into his way, and he had
seized the opportunity of doing something unusual, and an-
noying his more prudent brother at the same time.

But though Paul understood this clearly enough, he felt
that it would be anything but easy to make it clear to his
chief; and yet, if he did not succeed in doing so, it would
be hard for him to account for his carelessness, and he
might spend a very unpleasant season of waiting until the
missing man was found. In such a case as this, Paul was
too good a diplomatist not to tell the truth very exactly.
Indeed, he was always a truthful man, according to his
lights; but had it been necessary to shield his brother's reputation in any way, he would have so arranged his story as
not to tell any more of the truth than was necessary. What
had occurred was probably more to his own discredit than
to Alexander's, and Paul reflected that, on the other hand,

there was no need to inform the ambassador of the quarrel on the previous afternoon, since the chief had overheard it, and had himself interposed to produce quiet, if not peace. He resolved, therefore, to tell every particular, from the moment of his arrival with Alexander at the Vinegar Sellers' Landing to the time of his leaving Pera, that morning, on his way back to Buyukdere.

There was some relief in having thus decided upon the course he should follow; but the momentary satisfaction did not in the least lighten the burden that weighed upon his heart. His anxiety was intense, and he could not escape it, nor find any argument whereby to alleviate it. He did not love his brother, or at least had never loved him before; but we often find in life that a sudden fear for the safety of an individual, for whom we believe we care nothing, brings out a latent affection which we had not expected to feel. The bond of blood is a very strong one, and asserts itself in extreme moments with an unsuspected tenacity which works wonders, and which astonishes ourselves. The silken cord is slender, but the hands must be strong that can break it. In spite of all the misery his brother had caused him in boyhood, in spite of the coolness which had existed between them in later years, in spite of the humiliation he had so often suffered in seeing Alexander preferred before him, yet at this moment, when, for a time, the only man who bore his name had suddenly disappeared from the scene of life, Paul discovered deep down in his heart a strange sympathy for the lost man. He blamed himself bitterly for his carelessness, and, going back in his memory, he recalled with sorrow the hard words which had passed between them. He would have given much to be able to revoke the past and to weave more affection into his remembrance of his brother; and at the idea that he might perhaps never see him again, he turned pale, and twisted his fingers uneasily in his agitation.

Meanwhile, the launch steamed bravely against the cur-

rent, deftly avoiding the swift eddies under the skillful
hand of the pilot, slackening her pace to let a big ferry-boat
cross before her from Europe to Asia, facing the fierce
stream at Bala Hissar, — the devil's stream, as the Turks
call it, — and finally ploughing through the rushing waters
of Yeni Köj round the point where the Therapia pier juts
out into the placid bay of Buyukdere. Paul could see far
down the pier the white gates of the Russian embassy, and
when, some ten minutes later, the launch ran alongside the
landing, he gathered his courage with all his might, and
stepped boldly ashore, and entered the grounds, the kaváss
following him with bent head and dejected looks.

His excellency the Russian ambassador was seated in his
private study, alternately sipping a cup of tea and puffing
at a cigarette. The green blinds were closed, and the air of
the luxurious little apartment was cool and refreshing.
The diplomatist had very little to do, as no business could
be transacted until after the Bairam feast, which begins
with the new moon succeeding the month Ramazán ; he sat
late over his tea, smoking and turning over a few letters,
while he enjoyed the gentle breeze which found its way into
his room with the softened light. He was a gray-headed
man, but not old. His keen gray eyes seemed exceedingly
alive to every sight presented to them, and the lines on his
face were the expression of thought and power rather than
of age. He was tall, thin, and soldier-like, extremely courteous in manner and speech, but grave and not inclined to
mirth ; he belonged to that class of active men in whom the
constant exercise of vitality and intelligence appears to prolong life instead of exhausting its force, who possess a constitution in which the body is governed by the mind, and
who, being generally little capable of enjoying the pleasure
of the moment, find it easy to devote their energies to the
attainment of an object in the future. Count Ananoff was
the ideal diplomatist : cautious, far-sighted, impenetrable,
and exact, outwardly ceremonious and dignified, not too

skeptical of other men's qualities nor too confident of his
own. His convictions might be summed up, according to
the old Russian joke, in the one word Nabuchadnezar, —
Na Bogh ad ne Czar, — "There is no God but the Czar."

As Paul entered the ambassador's study, he was glad
that he had always been on good terms with his chief. Indeed, there was much sympathy between them, and it might
well have been predicted at that time that Paul would some
day become just such a man as he under whom he now
served. Convinced as he was that in his present career
quite as much of success depended upon the manner of carrying out a scheme as on the scheme itself, Paul had long
come to the conclusion that no manner could possibly be so
effective as that of Count Ananoff, and that in order to cultivate it the utmost attention must be bestowed upon the
study of his chief's motives. Himself grave and cautious,
he possessed the two main elements noticeable in the character of his model, and to acquire the rest could only be a
matter of time. The ambassador noticed the ease with
which Paul comprehended his point of view, and fancied
that he saw in his secretary a desire to imitate himself,
which of course was flattering. The result was that a sincere good feeling existed between the two, made up of a
genuine admiration on the one side, and of considerable
self-satisfaction on the other. Patoff felt that the moment
had come when he must test the extent of the regard his
chief felt for him, and, considering the difficulty of his position and the personal anxiety he felt for his brother, it is
not surprising that he was nervous and ill at ease.

"I have a painful story to tell, excellency," he said,
standing before the broad writing-desk at which the count
was sitting. The latter looked up from his tea.

"Be seated," he said gravely, but fixing a keen look on
Paul's haggard face.

"I will tell you everything, with all the details," said
Patoff, sitting down ; and he forthwith began his story. The

narrative was clear and connected, and embraced the history of the night from the time when Paul had left Buyukdere with his brother to the time of his return. Nothing
was omitted which he could remember, but when he had
done he was conscious that he had only told the tale of his
long search for the missing man. He had thrown no light
upon the cause of the disappearance. The ambassador
looked very grave, and his thoughtful brows knit themselves
together, while he never took his eyes from Paul's face.

"It is very serious," he said at last. "Will you kindly
explain to me, if you can do so without indiscretion, the
causes of the violent quarrel which took place between you
yesterday afternoon ? "

Paul had foreseen the question, and proceeded to detail
the occurrences in the Valley of Roses, explaining the part
he had played, and how he had remonstrated with Alexander. The latter, he said, had lost his temper, after they
had got home.

"I would not tell that story to any one else," said Paul,
in conclusion. "It shows the disposition of my brother,
and does him no credit. It was a foolish escapade, but I
should be sorry to have it known. I expected that a complaint would have been lodged already."

"None has been made. Is the kaváss who went with
you come back ? "

"Yes."

"Do you think," said the count, looking quietly at Paul,
"that he can tell us anything you have forgotten ? "

There was a peculiar emphasis upon the last words which
did not escape the secretary, though in that first moment he
did not understand what was meant.

"No," he answered, quite simply, returning his chief's
look with perfect calmness. "I do not believe he can tell
anything more. I will call him."

"By all means. There is the bell," said the ambassador.
Paul rang, and sent the servant to call his kaváss, who had

been waiting, and appeared immediately, looking very ill and exhausted with the fatigue of the night. He trembled visibly, as he stood before the table and made his military salute, bringing his right hand quickly to his mouth, then to his forehead, and letting it drop again to his side. Count Ananoff cross-examined him with short, sharp questions. The man was very pale, and stammered his replies, but the extraordinary accuracy with which he recounted the details already given by Patoff did not escape the diplomatist.

"Have you anything more to tell?" asked the ambassador, at last.

"It was not my fault, Effendim," said the kaváss, in great agitation. "Paul Effendi and I were looking at the people, and when we turned Alexander Effendi was gone, and we could not find him. I had warned him beforehand not to separate himself from us" —

"Do you think he can be found?" inquired Ananoff, cutting short the man's repetitions.

"Surely, the Effendi can be found," returned the kaváss. "But it may take time."

"Why should it take time? Unless he is injured or imprisoned somewhere, he ought to find his way to Pera today."

"Effendim, he may have strayed into the dark streets. If the *bekji* found him without a lantern, he would be arrested, according to the law."

"He had our lantern," said Paul. "We could not find it."

"That is true," answered the kaváss, in dejected tones. "There is the Persian ambassador, Effendim," he said, with a sudden revival of hope.

"What can he do?" asked the count.

"He is lord over all the donkey-drivers in Stamboul, Effendim. The Sultan allows him to exact tribute of them, which is the most part of his fortune.[1] Perhaps if he gave

[1] Fact.

orders that they should all be beaten unless they found Alexander Effendi, they would find him. They go everywhere
and see everybody."

"That is an idea," said the ambassador, hardly able to
repress a grim smile. "I will send word to his excellency
at once. I have no doubt but that he will do it."

"But it was not my fault" — began the kaváss again.

"I am not sure of that," answered the diplomatist. "If
you find him, you will be excused."

"I think the man is not to be blamed," remarked Paul,
who had not forgotten the anxiety the kaváss had shown
in trying to find Alexander. "It is my belief that my
brother's disappearance did not occur in any ordinary way."

"I think so, too," replied the count. "You may go," he
said to the soldier, who at once left the room. A short
silence followed his departure.

"Monsieur Patoff," resumed the elder man presently,
"you are in a very dangerous and distressing position."

"Distressing," said Paul. "Not dangerous, so far as I
can see."

"Let us be frank," answered the other. "Alexander
Patoff is your elder brother. You feel that he had too
large a share of your father's fortune. You have never
liked him. He came here without an invitation, and made
himself very disagreeable to you. You had a violent quarrel yesterday afternoon, and you were justly provoked, —
quite justly, I have no doubt. You go to Stamboul at night
with only one man to attend you. You come back without
your rich, overbearing, intolerable brother. What will the
world say to all that?"

In spite of his pallor, the blood rushed violently to Paul's
face, and he sprang from his chair in the wildest excitement.

"You have no right — you do not mean to say it —
Great God! How can you think of such a" —

"I do not think it," said the ambassador, seizing him by

the arm and trying to calm him. "I do not think any-thing of the kind. Command yourself, and be a man. Sit down, — there, be reasonable. I only mean to put you in your right position."

"You will drive me mad," answered Paul in low tones, sinking into the chair again.

"Now listen to me," continued the count, "and under-stand that you are listening to your best friend. The world will not fail to say that you have spirited away your brother, — got rid of him, in short, for your own ends. There is no one but a Turkish soldier to prove the contrary. No, do not excite yourself again. I am telling you the truth. I know perfectly well that Alexander has lost him-self by his own folly, but I must foresee what other people will say, in case he is not found " —

"But he must be found!" interrupted Paul. "I say he shall be found!"

"Yes, so do I. But there is just a possibility that he may not be found. Meanwhile, the alarm is given. The story will be in every one's mouth to-night, and to-morrow you will be assailed with all manner of questions. My dear Patoff, if Alexander does not turn up in a few days, you had better go away, until the whole matter has blown over. You can safely leave your reputation in my hands, as well as the care of finding your brother, if he can be found at all, and you will be spared much that is painful and em-barrassing. I will arrange that you may be transferred for a year to some distant post, and when the mystery is cleared up you can come back and brave your accusers."

"But," said Paul, who had grown pale again, "it seems to me impossible that I could be accused of murdering my brother on such slender grounds, even if the worst were to happen and he were never found. It is an awful imputa-tion to put upon a man. I do not see how any one would dare to suggest such a thing."

"In the first place," answered the ambassador, arguing

the point as he would have discussed the framing of a dispatch, "the Turks are very cunning, and they hate us. They will begin by saying that you had an interest in disposing of Alexander. They will search out the whole story, and will assert the fact because they will be safe in saying that there is no evidence to the contrary. They will take care that the suggestion shall reach our ears, and that it shall spread throughout our little society. What can you answer to the question, 'Where is your brother?' If people do not ask it, they will let you know that it is in their hearts."

"I do not know," said Paul, stunned by the possible truth of his chief's argument.

"Exactly. You do not know, nor I either. But if you stay here, you will have to fight for your own reputation. If you are absent, I can put down such scandal by my authority, and it will soon be forgotten. I do not believe that this disappearance can remain a secret forever. At present, and for some time to come, it is only a disappearance, and it will be expected that your brother may yet come back. But when months are past, — should such a catastrophe occur, — people will find another word, and the murder of Alexander Patoff will be the common topic of conversation."

"It is awful to think of," murmured Paul. "But why do you suppose that he will not come back? He may have got into some scrape, and he may appear this evening. There is hope yet and for days to come."

"I am sorry to say I do not believe it," answered the count. "There have been several disappearances of insignificant individuals since I have been here. No pains were spared to find them, but no one ever obtained the smallest trace of their fate. They were probably murdered for the small sums of money they carried. Of course there is possibility, but I think there is very little hope."

"But I cannot bear to think that poor Alexander should

have come to such an end," cried Paul. "I could not go away feeling that I had left anything untried in searching for him. I never loved him, God forgive me! But he was my brother, and my mother's favorite son. He was with me, and by my carelessness he lost himself. Who is to tell her that? No, I cannot go until I know what has become of him."

"My friend," said old Ananoff gently, "you have all my sympathy, and you shall have all my help. I will myself write to your mother, if Alexander does not return in a week. But if in a month he is not heard of, there will be no hope at all. Then you must go away, and I will shut the mouths of the gossips. Now go and rest, for you are exhausted. Be quite sure that between the measures you have taken yourself and those which I shall take, everything possible will be done."

Paul rose unsteadily to his feet, and took the count's hand. Then, without a word, he went to his pavilion, and gave himself up to his own agonizing thoughts.

The ambassador lost no time, for he felt how serious the case was. In spite of the heat, he proceeded to Stamboul at once, visited Santa Sophia, and explored every foot of the gallery whence Alexander had disappeared, but without discovering any trace. He asked questions of the warden of the church, the scowling Turk who had admitted the brothers on the previous night; but the man only answered that Allah was great, and that he knew nothing of the circumstances, having left the two gentlemen in charge of their kaváss. Then the count went to the house of the Persian ambassador, and obtained his promise to aid in the search by means of his army of donkey-drivers. He went in person to the Ottoman Bank, to the chief of police, to every office through which he could hope for any information. Returning to Buyukdere, he sent notes to all his colleagues, informing them of what had occurred, and requesting their assistance in searching for the lost man. At last he felt that he had done everything in his power, and he desisted from his labors. But, as he had said, he had small expectation of ever hearing again from Lieutenant Alexander Patoff, and he meditated upon the letter he had promised to write to the missing man's mother. He was shocked at the accident, and he felt a real sympathy for Paul, besides the responsibility for the safety of Russian subjects in Turkey, which in some measure rested with him.

As for Paul, he paced his room for an hour after he had left his chief, and then at last he fell upon the divan, faint with bodily fatigue and exhausted by mental anxiety. He slept a troubled sleep for some hours, and did not leave his apartments again that day.

The view of the situation presented to him by Count Ananoff had stunned him almost beyond the power of thought, and when he tried to think his reflections only confirmed his fears. He saw himself branded as a murderer, though the deed could not be proved, and he knew how such an accusation, once put upon a man, will cling to him in spite of the lack of evidence. He realized with awful force the meaning of the question, "Where is your brother?" and he understood how easily such a question would suggest itself to the minds of those who knew his position. That question which was put to the first murderer, and which will be put to the last, has been asked many times of innocent men, and the mere fact that they could find no ready answer has sufficed to send them to their death. Why should it not be the same with him? Until he could show them his brother, they would have a right to ask, and they would ask, rejoicing in the pain inflicted. Paul cursed the day when Alexander had come to visit him, and he had received him with a show of satisfaction. Had he been more honest in showing his dislike, the poor fellow would perhaps have gone angrily away, but he would not have been lost in the night in the labyrinths of Stamboul. And then again Paul repented bitterly of the hard words he had spoken, and, working himself into a fever of unreasonable remorse, walked the floor of his room as a wild beast tramps in its cage.

The night was interminable, though there were only six hours of darkness; but when the morning rose the light was more intolerable still, and Paul felt as though he must go mad from inaction. He dressed hastily, and went out into the cool dawn to wait for the first boat to Pera. Even the early shadows on the water reminded him of yesterday, when he had crossed Galata bridge on foot, still feeling some hope. He closed his eyes as he leaned upon the rail of the landing, wishing that the sun would rise and dispel at least some portion of his sorrow.

He reached Pera, and spent the whole day in fruitless inquiries. In the evening he returned, and the next morning he went back again; sleeping little, hardly eating at all, speaking to no one he knew, and growing hourly more thin and haggard, till the Cossacks at the gate hardly recognized him. But day after day he searched, and all the countless messengers, officials, guides, porters, and people of every class searched, too, attracted by the large reward which the ambassador offered for any information concerning Alexander Patoff. But not the slightest clue could be obtained. Alexander Patoff had disappeared hopelessly and completely, and had left no more trace than if he had been thrown into the Bosphorus, with a couple of round shot at his neck. The days lengthened into weeks, and the weeks became a month, and still Paul hoped against all possibility of hope, and wearied the officials of every class with his perpetual inquiries.

Count Ananoff had long since communicated the news of Alexander's disappearance to the authorities in St. Petersburg, thinking it barely possible that he might have gone home secretly, out of anger against his brother. But the only answer was an instruction to leave nothing untried in attempting to find the lost man, provided that no harm

should be done to the progress of certain diplomatic negotiations then proceeding. As the count had foreseen, the
Turkish authorities, while exhibiting considerable alacrity
in the prosecution of the search, vaguely hinted that Paul
Patoff himself was the only person able to give a satisfactory explanation of the case ; and in due time these hints
found their way into the gossip of the Bosphorus tea-parties.
Paul was not unpopular, but in spite of his studied ease in
conversation there was a reserve in his manner which many
persons foolishly resented ; and they were not slow to find
out that his brother's disappearance was very odd, — so
strange, they said, that it seemed impossible that Paul
should know nothing of it. The ambassador thought it was
time to speak to him on the subject. Moreover, in his present state of excitement Paul was utterly useless in the embassy, and the work which had accumulated during the
month of Ramazán was now unusually heavy. Count Ananoff had arranged this matter, without speaking of it to
any one, a fortnight after Alexander's disappearance, and
now a secretary who had been in Athens had arrived, osten-
sibly on a visit to the ambassador. But Ananoff had Paul's
appointment to Teheran in his pocket, with the permission
to take a month's leave for procuring his outfit for Persia.

The explanation was inevitable. It was impossible that
things should go on any longer as they had proceeded during the last fortnight ; and now that there was really no
hope whatever, and people were beginning to talk as they
had not talked before, the best thing to be done was to send
Paul away. Count Ananoff came to his rooms one morning, and found him staring at the wall, his untasted breakfast on the table beside him, his face very thin and drawn,
looking altogether like a man in a severe illness. The ambassador explained the reason of his visit, reminded him of
what had been said at their first interview, and entreated
him to spend his month's leave in regaining some of his
former calmness.

"Go to the Crimea, or to Tiflis," he said. "You will not be far from your way. I will write to Madame Patoff."

"You are kind, — too kind," answered Paul. "Thank you, but I will go to my mother myself. I will be back in time," he added bitterly. "She will not care to keep me, now that poor Alexander is gone. Yes, I know; you need not tell me. There is no hope left. We shall not even find his body now. But I must tell my mother. I have already written, for I thought it better. I told her the story, just as it all happened. She has never answered my letter. I fancy she must have had news from some one else, or perhaps she is ill."

"Do not go," said his chief, looking sorrowfully at Paul's white face and wasted, nervous hands. "You are not able to bear the strain of such a meeting. I will write to her, and explain.'

"No," answered Paul firmly. "I must go myself. There is no help for it. May I leave to-day? I think there is a boat to Varna. As for my strength, I am as strong as ever, though I am a little thinner than I was."

The old diplomatist shook his head gravely, but he knew that it was of no use to try and prevent Paul from undertaking the journey. After all, if he could bear it, it was the most manly course. He had done his best, had labored in the search as no one else could have labored, and if he were strong enough he was entitled to tell his own tale.

The two men parted affectionately that day, and when Paul was fairly on board the Varna boat Count Ananoff owned to himself that he had lost one of the best secretaries he had ever known.

IV.

THREE days later Paul descended from the train which runs twice a day from Pforzheim to Constance, at a station in the heart of the Swabian Black Forest. The name painted in black Gothic letters over the neat, cottage-like building before which the train stopped was *Teinach*. Paul had never heard of the place until his mother had telegraphed that she was there, and he looked about him with curiosity, while a dark youth, in leather breeches, rough stockings, and a blouse, possessed himself of the traveler's slender luggage, and began to lead the way to the hotel.

It was late in the afternoon, and the sinking sun had almost touched the top of the hill. On all sides but one the pines and firs presented a black, absorbing surface to the light, while at the upper end of the valley the ancient and ruined castle of Zavelstein caught the sun's rays, and stood clearly out against the dark background. It is impossible to imagine anything more monotonous in color than this boundless forest of greenish-black trees, and it is perhaps for this reason that the ruins of the many old fortresses, which once commanded every eminence from Weissenstein to the Boden-See, are seen to such singular advantage. The sober gray or brown masonry, which anywhere else would offer but a neutral tint in the landscape, here constitutes high lights as compared with the impenetrable shadows of the woods; and even the sky above, generally seen through the thick masses of evergreen, seems to be of a more sombre blue. In the deep gorges the black water of the Nagold foams and tumbles among the hollow rocks, or glides smoothly over the long and shallow races by which the

jointed timber rafts are shot down to the Neckar, and
thence to the Rhine and the ocean, many hundreds of miles
away. For the chief wealth of Swabia and of the kingdom
of Würtemberg lies in the splendid timber of the forest,
which is carefully preserved, and in which no tree is felled
without the order of the royal foresters. Indeed, Nature
herself does most of the felling, for in winter fierce wind-
storms gather and spread themselves in the winding valleys,
tearing down acres of trees upon the hill-sides in broad,
straight bands, and leaving them there, uprooted and fallen
over each other in every direction, like a box of wooden
matches carelessly emptied upon a dark green table. Then
come the wood-cutters in the spring, and lop off the branches,
and roll the great logs down to the torrent below, and float
them away in long flexible rafts, which spin down the
smooth water-ways at a giddy speed, or float silently along
the broad, still reaches of the widening river, or dash over
the dangerous rapids, skillfully guided by the wild rafts-
men, bare-legged and armed with long poles, whose practiced feet support them as safely on the slippery, rolling
timber as ours would carry us on the smoothest pavement.

At Teinach the valley is wider than in other places, and
a huge establishment, built over the wonderful iron springs,
rears above the tops of the trees its walls of mingled stone,
wood and stucco, gayly painted and ornamented with balconies and pavilions, in startling and unpleasant contrast
with the sober darkness of the surroundings. The broad
post-road runs past the hotels and bath-houses, and a great
garden, or rather an esplanade with a few scattered beds of
flowers, has been cleared and smoothed for the benefit of
the visitors, who take their gentle exercise in the wide
walks, or sip their weak German coffee, to the accompani-
ment of a small band, at the wooden tables set up under the
few remaining trees. The place is little known, either to
tourists or invalids, beyond the limits of the kingdom of
Würtemberg, but its waters are full of healing properties,

and the seclusion of the little village amidst the wild scenery of the Black Forest is refreshing to soul and body.

Paul followed his guide along the winding path which leads from the railway station to the hotel, smelling with delight the aromatic odor of the pines, and enjoying the coolness of the evening air. The fatigues of the last month and of the rapid journey from Varna had told upon his strength, as the fearful anxiety he had endured had wearied his brain. He felt, as he walked, how delicious it would be to forget all the past, to shoulder a broad axe, and to plunge forever into the silent forest; to lead the life of one of those rude woodmen, without a thought at night save of the trees to be felled to-morrow; to rise in the morning with no care save to accomplish the daily task before night; to sleep in summer on the carpet of sweet pine needles, and to watch the stars peep through the lofty branches of the ancient trees; in winter to lie by the warm fire of some mountain hut, with no disturbing dreams or nervous wakings, master of himself, his axe, and his freedom.

But the thought of such peace only made the present moment more painful, and Paul bent his head as though to shut out all pleasant thoughts, till presently he reached the wide porch of the hotel, and, summoning his courage, asked for Madame Patoff.

"Number seventeen," said the Swiss clerk, laconically, to the waiter who stood at hand, by way of intimating that he should conduct the gentleman to the number he had mentioned. As Paul turned to follow the functionary in the white tie and the shabby dress-coat, he was stopped by a thick-set, broad-shouldered man, with gold-rimmed spectacles and a bushy beard, who addressed him in English:—

"I beg your pardon, I heard you ask for Madame Patoff. Have I the honor of addressing her son?"

"Yes," said Paul, bowing stiffly, for the man was evidently a gentleman. "May I ask to whom"—

"I am Dr. Cutter," replied the other, interrupting him. "Madame Patoff is ill, and I am taking care of her."

The average doctor would have said, "I am attending her," and Paul, whose English mother had brought him up to speak English as fluently and correctly as Russian, noticed the shade in the expression. But he was startled by the news of his mother's illness, and did not stop to think of such a trifle.

"What is the matter with her?" he asked briefly, turning from the desk of the hotel office, and walking across the vestibule by Dr. Cutter's side.

"I don't know," replied the doctor, quietly.

"You are a strange physician, sir," said Paul sternly. "You tell me that you are attending my mother, and yet you do not know what is the matter with her."

The doctor was not in the least offended by Paul's sharp answer. He smiled a little, but instantly became grave again, as he answered, —

"I am not a practicing physician. I am a specialist, and I devote my life to the study of mental complaints. Your mother is ill in mind, not in body."

"Mad!" exclaimed Paul, turning very pale. His life seemed to be nothing but a series of misfortunes.

"Certainly not hopelessly insane," replied Dr. Cutter, in a musing tone. "She has suffered a terrible shock, as you may imagine."

"Yes," said Paul, "of course. That is the reason why I have come all the way from Constantinople to see her. I could not go to my new post without telling her the whole story myself."

"Her manner is very strange," returned the other. "That is the reason why I waited for you here. I could not have allowed you to see her without being warned. She has a strange delusion, and you ought to know it."

"What is it?" asked Paul, in a thick voice.

"It is a very delicate matter. Come out into the garden, and I will tell you what I know."

The two men went out together, and walked slowly along

the open path towards the woods. In the distance a few invalids moved painfully about the garden, or rested on the benches beneath the trees. Far off a party of children were playing and laughing merrily at their games.

"It is a delicate matter," repeated Dr. Cutter. " In the first place, I must explain my own position here. I am an Englishman, devoted to scientific pursuits. Originally a physician, subsequently professor in one of our universities, I have given up both practice and professorship in order to be at liberty to follow my studies. I am often abroad, and I generally spend the summer in Switzerland or somewhere in South Germany. I was at Rugby with Madame Patoff's brother-in-law, John Carvel, whom I dare say you know, and I met Madame Patoff two years ago at Wiesbaden. I met her there again, last year, and this summer, as I was coming to the South, I found her in the same place, — little more than a month ago. In both the former years your brother Alexander came to visit her, on leave from St. Petersburg. I knew him, therefore, and was aware of her deep affection for him. This time I found her very much depressed in spirits because he had resolved to join you in Constantinople. Excuse me if I pain you by referring to him. It is unavoidable. One morning she told me that she had made up her mind to go to Turkey, traveling by easy stages through Switzerland to Italy, and thence by steamer to the East. She dreaded the long railway journey through Austria, and preferred the sea. She was in bad health, and seemed very melancholy, and I proposed to accompany her as far as the Italian frontier. We went to Lucerne, and thence to Como, where I intended to leave her. She chose to wait there a few days, in order to have her letters sent on to her before going to the East. Among those which came was a long letter from you, in which you told in detail the story of your brother's disappearance. Your mother was alone in her sitting-room when she received it, but the effect of the news was such that her maid found her lying insensible in her chair some time afterwards, and thought it best to call me. I easily revived her from the fit of fainting, and when she came to herself she thrust your letter into my hand, and insisted that I should read it. She was very hysterical, and I judged that I should comply with her request. The scene which followed was very painful."

"Well?" asked Paul, who was visibly agitated. "What then?" he inquired rather sharply, seeing that Dr. Cutter was silent.

"To be short about it," said the professor, "it has been evident to me from that moment that her mind is deranged. No argument can affect the distorted view she takes."

"But what is the view? What does she think?" inquired Paul, trembling with excitement.

"She thinks that you were the cause of your brother's death," answered Cutter shortly.

"That I murdered him?" cried Paul, feeling that his worst fears were realized.

"Poor lady!" exclaimed the professor, fixing his gray eyes on Paul's face. "It is of no use to go over the story. That is what she thinks."

Paul turned from his companion, and leaned against a tree for support. He was utterly overcome, and unmanned for the moment. Cutter stood beside him, fearing lest he might fall, for he could see that he was wasted with anxiety and weak with fatigue. But he possessed great strength of will and that command of himself which is acquired by living much among strangers. After a few seconds he stood erect, and, making a great effort, continued to walk upon the road, steadying himself with his stick.

"Go on, please," he said. "How did you come here?"

"You will understand that I could not leave Madame Patoff at such a time," continued the professor, inwardly admiring the strength of his new acquaintance. "She insisted upon returning northwards, saying that she would go to her relations in England. Fearing lest her mind should become more deranged, I suggested traveling slowly by an unfrequented route. I intended to take her to England by short stages, endeavoring to avoid all places where she might, at this season, have met any of her numerous acquaintances. I chose to cross the Splügen Pass to the Lake of Constance. Thence we came here by the Nagold railway. I propose to take her to the Rhine, where we will take the Rhine boat to Rotterdam. Nobody travels by the Rhine nowadays. You got my telegram at Vienna? Yes. Yours went to Wiesbaden, was telegraphed to Como, and thence here. I had just time to send an answer directed to you at Vienna, as a passenger by the Oriental Express, giving you the name of this place. I signed it with your mother's name."

"She does not know I have left Constantinople, then?"

"No. I feared that the news would have a bad effect. She receives her letters, of course, but telegrams often do harm to people in her state, — so I naturally opened yours."

"Is she perfectly sane in all other respects?" asked Paul, speaking with an effort.

"Perfectly."

"Then she is not insane at all," said Paul, in a tone of conviction.

"I do not understand you," answered the professor, staring at him in some surprise.

"If you knew how she loved my poor brother, and how little she loves me, you would understand better. Without being insane, she might well believe that I had let him lose himself in Stamboul, or even that I had killed him. You read my letter, — you can remember how strange a story it was. There is nothing but the evidence of a Turkish soldier to show that I did not contribute to Alexander's disappearance."

"It was certainly a very queer story," said the professor gravely. "Nevertheless, I am of opinion that Madame Patoff is under the influence of a delusion. I cannot think that if she were in her right mind she would insist as she does, and with such violence, that you are guilty of making away with your brother."

" I must see her," said Paul firmly. " I have come from Constantinople to see her, and I cannot go back disappointed."

" I think it would be a great mistake for you to seek an interview," answered the professor, no less decidedly. " It might bring on a fit of anger."

" Which might be fatal ? " inquired Paul.

" No, but which might affect her brain."

" I do not think so. Pardon my contradicting you, professor, but I have a very strong impression that my mother is not in the least insane, and that I may succeed in bringing her to look at this dreadful business in its true light."

" I fear not," answered Dr. Cutter sadly.

" But you do not know," insisted Paul. " Unless you are perfectly sure that my mother is really mad, you can have no right to prevent my seeing her. I may possibly persuade her. I am the only one left," he added bitterly, " and I must be a son to her in fact as well as in relation. I cannot, for my own sake, let her go to our English relatives, with this story to tell, without at least contradicting it."

" It is of no use to contradict it to her."

" Of no use ! " exclaimed Paul, impatiently. " Do you think that if the slightest suspicion, however unfounded, had rested on me, my chief would have allowed me to leave Constantinople without clearing it up ? I should think that anybody in his senses would see that ! "

" Yes, — anybody in his or her senses," answered the professor coldly.

Paul stopped in his walk, and faced the strong man with the gold spectacles and the intelligent features who had thus obstinately thrust himself in his path.

"Sir," he said, "I know you very slightly, and I do not want to insult you. But if you continue to oppose me, I shall begin to think that you have some other object in view besides a concern for my mother's health." His drawn and haggard features wore an expression of desperate determination as he spoke, and his cold blue eyes began to brighten dangerously.

"I have nothing more to say," replied the scientist, meeting his look with perfect steadiness. "I admit the justice of your argument. I can only implore you to take my advice, and to reflect on what you are doing. I have no moral right to oppose you."

"No," said Paul, "and you must not prevent this meeting. I wish to see her only once. Then I will go. I need not tell you that I am deeply indebted to you for the assistance you have rendered to my mother in this affair. If she does not believe my story, she will certainly not tolerate my presence, and I venture to hope that you will see her safely to England. If possible, I should like to meet her to-night."

"You shall," replied the professor. "But if any harm comes of it, remember that I protested against the meeting. That is all I ask."

"I will remember," answered Paul quietly. Both men turned in their walk, and went back towards the hotel.

"You must give me time to warn her of your presence," said Cutter, as they reached the steps.

Paul nodded, and they both went in. Cutter disappeared up-stairs, and Patoff was shown to his room by a servant.

"I shall probably leave to-morrow morning," he remarked, as the man deposited his effects in the corner, and looked round, waiting for orders. Paul threw himself on the bed, closing his eyes, and trying to collect his courage and his senses for this meeting, which had turned out so much more difficult than he had expected. Nevertheless, he was glad that Cutter had met him, and had warned him of the state of his mother's mind. He did not in the least believe her insane, — he almost wished that he could. Lying there on his bed, he remembered his youth, and the time when he had longed for some little portion of the affection lavished on his elder brother. He remembered how often he had in vain looked to his mother for a smile of approbation, and how he had ever been disappointed. He had grown up feeling that, by some fault not his own, he was disliked and despised, a victim to one of those unreasoning antipathies which parents sometimes feel for one of their children. He remembered how he had choked down his anger, swallowed his tears, and affected indifference to censure, until his child's heart had grown case-hardened and steely; asking nothing, doing his tasks for his own satisfaction, and finally taking a sad pleasure in that silence which was so frequently imposed upon him. Then he had grown up, and the sullen determination to outdo his brother in everything had got possession of his strong nature. He remembered how, coming home from school, he had presented his mother with the report which spoke of his final examinations as brilliant compared with Alexander's; how his mother had said a cold word of praise; and how he himself had turned silently away, able already, in his young self-dependence, to rejoice secretly over his victory, without demanding the least approbation from those who should have loved him best. He remembered, when his brother was an ensign in the guards, spoiled and reckless, making debts and getting into all kinds of trouble, how he himself had labored at the dry work assigned to him in the foreign office, without amusements, without pleasure, and without pocket money, toiling day and night to win by force that position which Alexander had got for nothing; never relaxing in his exertions, and scrupulous in the performance of his duties. Even in the present moment of anxiety he thought with satisfaction of his well-earned advancement, and of the promotion which could not now be far distant. He remembered himself a big, bony youth of twenty, and he reflected that he had made himself what he now was, the accomplished man of the world, the rising diplomatist among those of his years, steadily moving on to success. But he saw that he was the same to-day as he had been then; if he had not gained affection in his life, he had gained strength and hardness and indifference to opposition.

Then this blow had come upon him. This brother, whom he had striven to surpass in everything, had been suddenly and mysteriously taken from his very side; and not that only, but the mother who had borne them both had put the crowning touch to her life-long injustice, and had accused him of being his brother's murderer, — accused him to a stranger, or to one who was little nearer than a stranger, — refusing to hear him in his own defense.

He wished that she might be indeed mad. He hoped that she was beside herself with grief, even wholly insane, rather than that he should be forced to believe that she could be so unjust. What construction the world would put upon the catastrophe he knew from Count Ananoff; but surely he might expect his mother to be more merciful. A mother should hope against hope for her child's innocence, even when every one else has forsaken him; how was it possible that this mother of his could so harden her heart as to be first to suspect him of such a crime, and to be of all people the one to refuse to hear his defense! He hoped she was mad, as he lay there on his bed, in the little room of the hotel, in the gathering gloom.

At last some one knocked at the door, and Professor Cutter entered, admitting a stream of light from the corridor outside. Paul sprang to his feet, pale and haggard.

" You are in the dark," said the professor quietly, as he shut the door behind him. Then he struck a match, and lit the two candles which stood on each side of the mirror on the bare dressing-table.

" Can I go now?" asked Paul. The scientist eyed him deliberately.

"Pardon me," he said. "You have not thought of your appearance. You have traveled for three or four days, and look rather disheveled."

Paul understood. The professor did not want him to be seen as he was. He was wild and excited, and his clothes were in disorder. Silently he unlocked his dressing-case and bag, and proceeded to dress himself. Cutter sat quietly watching him, as though still studying his character; for he was a student of men, and prided himself on his ability to detect people's peculiarities from their unconscious movements. Paul dressed rapidly, with the neatness of a man accustomed to wait upon himself. In twenty minutes his toilet was completed, during which time neither of the two spoke a word. At last Paul turned to the professor. "Did you have difficulty in arranging it?" he asked coldly.

"Yes. But you may see her, if you go at once," answered the other.

"I am ready," said Paul. "Let us go." They left the room, and went down the corridor together. The quiet and solitude of his room had strengthened Paul's nerves, and he walked more erect and with a firmer step than before. Presently the professor stopped before one of the doors.

"Go in," he said. "This is a little passage room. Knock at the door opposite. She is there, and will receive you."

Paul followed the professor's instructions, and knocked at the door within. A voice which he hardly recognized as his mother's bid him enter, and he was in the presence of Madame Patoff.

A bright lamp, unshaded and filling the little sitting-room with a broad yellow light, stood upon the table. The details of the apartment were insignificant, and seemed to throw the figure of the seated woman into strong relief. She had been beautiful, and was beautiful still, though now in her fifty-second year. Her features were high and noble, and her rich dark hair was only lightly streaked with gray. Her eyes were brown, but of that brown which easily looks black when not exposed directly to the light. Her face was now very pale, but there was a slight flush upon her cheeks, which for a moment brought back a reflection of her former brilliant beauty. She was dressed entirely in black, and her thin white hands lay folded on the dark material of her gown; she wore no ring save the plain band of gold upon the third finger of her left hand.

Paul entered, and closed the door behind him without taking his eyes from his mother. She rose from her seat as he came forward, as though to draw back. He came nearer, and bending low would have taken her hand, but she stepped backwards and withdrew it, while the flush darkened on her cheek.

"Mother, will you not give me your hand?" he asked, in a low and broken voice.

"No," she answered sternly. "Why have you come here?"

"To tell you my brother's story," said Paul, drawing himself up and facing her. When he entered the room he had felt sorrow and pity for her, in spite of Cutter's account, and he would willingly have kneeled and kissed her hand. But her rough refusal brought vividly to his mind the situation.

"You have told me already, by your letter," she replied. "Have you found him, that you come here? Do you think I want to see you — you?" she repeated, with rising emphasis.

"I might think it natural that you should," said Paul, very coldly. "Be calm. I am going to-morrow. Had I supposed that you would meet me as you have, I should have spared myself the trouble of coming here."

"Indeed you might!" she exclaimed scornfully. "Have you come here to tell me how you did it?" Her voice trembled hysterically.

"Did what?" asked Paul, in the same cold tone. "Do

you mean to accuse me to my face of my brother's death, as your doctor says you do behind my back? And if you dare to do so, do you think I will permit it without defending myself?"

His mother looked at him for one moment; then, clasping her hands to her forehead, she staggered across the room, and hid her face in the cushions of the sofa, moaning and crying aloud.

"Alexis, Alexis!" she sobbed. "Ah — my beloved son — if only I could have seen your dear face once more — to close your eyes — and kiss you — those sweet eyes — oh, my boy, my boy! Where are you — my own child?"

She was beside herself with grief, and ceased to notice Paul's presence for some minutes, moaning, and tossing herself upon the sofa, and wringing her hands as the tears streamed down. Paul could not look unmoved on such a sight. He came near and touched her shoulder.

"You must not give up all hope, mother," he said softly. "He may yet come back." He did not know what else to say, to comfort her.

"Come back?" she cried hysterically, suddenly sitting up and facing him. "Come back, when you are standing there with his blood on your hands! You murderer! You monster! Go — for God's sake, go! Don't touch me! Don't look at me!"

Paul was horrified at her violence, and could not believe that she was in her senses. But he had heard the words she had spoken, and the wound had entered into his soul. His look was colder than ever as he answered.

"You are evidently insane," he said

"Go — go, I tell you! Let me never see you again!" cried the frantic woman, rising to her feet, and staring at him with wide and blood-shot eyes.

Paul went up to her, and quickly seizing her hands held them in his firm grip, without pressure, but so that she could not withdraw them.

"Mother," he said, in low and distinct tones, "I believe you are mad. If you are not, God forgive you, and grant that you may forget what you have said. I am as innocent of Alexander's death — if indeed he is dead — as you are yourself."

She seemed awed by his manner, and spoke more quietly.

"Where is he, then? Paul, where is your brother?"

"I cannot tell where he is. He left me and never returned, as the man who was with me can testify. I came here to tell you the story with my own lips. If you do not care to hear it, I will go, and you shall have your wish, for you need never see me again." He released her hands, and turned from her as though to leave the room.

Madame Patoff's mood changed. Though Alexander was more like her, she possessed, too, some of the inexorable coldness which Paul had inherited so abundantly. She now drew herself up, and retired to the other side of the room. Paul's hand was on the door. Then she turned once more, and he saw that her face was as pale as death.

"Go," she said, for the last time. "And above all, do not come back. Unless you can bring Alexis with you, and show him to me alive, I will always believe that you killed him, like the heartless, cruel monster you have been from a child."

"Is that your last word, mother?" asked Paul, controlling his voice by a great effort.

"My very last word, to you," she answered, pointing to the door.

Paul went out, and left her alone. In the corridor he found Professor Cutter, calmly walking up and down. The scientist stopped, and looked at Paul's pale face.

"Was I right?" he asked.

"Too right."

"I thought so," said the professor. "Do you mean to leave to-morrow?"

"Yes," answered Paul quietly. "I must eat something. I am exhausted."

He staggered against Dr. Cutter's strong arm, and caught himself by it. The professor held him firmly on his feet, and looked at him curiously.

"You are worn out," he said. "Come with me."

He led him through the corridor to the restaurant of the hotel, and poured out a glass of wine from a bottle which stood on a table set ready for dinner. Paul drank it slowly, stopping twice to look at his companion, who watched him with the eye of a physician.

"Have you ever had any trouble with your heart?" asked the latter.

"No," said Paul. "I have never been ill."

"Then you must have been half starved on your journey," replied the professor, philosophically. "Let us dine here."

They sat down, and ordered dinner. Paul was conscious that his manner must seem strange to his new acquaintance, and indeed what he felt was strange to himself. He was conscious that since he had left his mother his ideas had undergone a change. He was calmer than he had been before, and he could not account for it on the ground of his having begun to eat something. He was indeed exhausted, for he had hardly thought of taking any nourishment during his long journey, and the dinner revived him. But the odd consciousness that he was not exactly the same man he had been before had come upon him as he closed the door of his mother's room. Up to the time he had entered her presence he had been in a state of the wildest anxiety and excitement. The moment the interview was over his mind worked normally and easily, and he felt himself completely master of his own actions.

Indeed, a change had taken place. He had gone to his mother feeling that he was accountable to her for his brother's disappearance, and prepared to tell his story with every detail he could recall, yet knowing that he was wholly innocent of the catastrophe, and that he had done everything in his power to find the lost man. But in that moment he was unconscious of two things : first, of the extreme hardness of his own nature ; and secondly, that he had not in reality the slightest real love either for his mother or for Alexander. The moral sufferings of his childhood had killed the natural affections in him, and there had remained nothing in their stead but a strong sense of duty to his nearest relations. It was this sense which had prompted him to receive Alexander kindly, and to take the utmost care of him during his visit; and it was the same feeling which had impelled him to come to his mother, in order to give the best account he could of the terrible catastrophe. But the frightful accusation she had put upon him, and her stubborn determination to abide by it, had destroyed even that lingering sense of duty which he had so long obeyed. He knew now that he experienced no more pain at Alexander's loss than he would naturally have felt at the death of an ordinary acquaintance, and that his mother had absolved him by her crowning injustice from the last tie which bound him to his family. In the first month at Buyukdere, after Alexander had disappeared, he had been overcome by the horror of the situation, and by the knowledge that he must tell his mother of the loss of her favorite son. He had mistaken these two incentives to the search for a feeling of love for the missing man. A quarter of an hour with his mother had shown him how little love there had ever been between them, and her frantic behavior, which he felt was not insanity, had disgusted him, and had shown him that he was henceforth free from all responsibility towards her.

The love of a child for his mother may be instinctive in the first instance, but as the child grows to manhood he becomes subject to reason ; and that which reason first rejects is injustice, because injustice is the most destructive form of lie imaginable. Paul had borne much, had cherished to the last his feeling of duty and his outward rendering of respect, but his mother had gone too far. He felt that she was not mad, and that in accusing him she was only treating him as she had always done since he was a boy; giving way to her unaccountable dislike, and suffering her antipathy to get the better of all sense of truth.

As Paul sat at table with Professor Cutter, he felt that the yoke had suddenly been taken from his neck, and that he was henceforth free to follow his own career and his own interests, without further thought for her who had cast him off. He was not a boy, to grow sulky at an unkind word, or to resent a fancied insult. He was a grown man, more than thirty years of age, and he fully realized his position, without exaggeration and without any superfluous exhibition of feeling. All at once he felt like a man who has done his day's work, and has a right to think no more about it.

"I am glad to see that you have a good appetite," observed the professor.

"I am conscious of not having eaten for a long time," answered Paul. "I suppose I was too much excited to be hungry before."

"You are not excited any longer?" inquired Dr. Cutter, with a smile.

"No. I believe I am perfectly calm. I have accomplished the journey, I have seen my mother, I have heard her last word, and I shall go to Persia to-morrow."

"Your programme is a simple one," answered his companion. "However, I am sure you can be of no use here. Your mother is quite safe under my care."

"It is my belief that she would be quite safe alone," said Paul, "though your presence is a help to her. You are a friend of her family, you knew my poor brother, you are intimate with my uncle by marriage, Mr. John Carvel. I am sure that, since you are good enough to accompany my mother, she cannot fail to appreciate your kindness and to enjoy your society. But I do not think she really stands in need of assistance."

"That is a matter of opinion," replied the professor, sipping his wine.

"Yes; but shall I be frank with you, Dr. Cutter? I fancy that, as a scientist and a student of diseases of the mind, you are over-ready to suspect insanity where my mother's conduct can be explained by ordinary causes."

"My dear sir," said the professor, "if I am a scientist, I am not one for nothing. I know how very little science knows, and in due time I shall be quite ready to own myself mistaken, if your mother turns out to be perfectly sane."

"You are very honest," returned Patoff. "All I want to express is that, although I am grateful to you for taking her home, I think she is quite able to take care of herself. I should be very sorry to think that you felt yourself bound not to leave her. She is fifty-two years old, I believe, but she is very strong, though she used to fancy herself in bad health, for some reason or other; she has a maid, a courier, and plenty of money. You yourself admit that she has no delusion except about this sad business. I think that under the circumstances she could safely travel alone."

"Possibly. But the case is an interesting one. I am a free man, and your mother's age and my position procure me the advantage of studying the state of her mind by traveling with her without causing any scandal. I am not disposed to abandon my patient."

"I can assure you," said Paul, "that if I thought she would tolerate my presence I should go with her myself, and I repeat that I am sincerely obliged to you. Only, I do not believe she is mad. I hope you will write to me, however, and tell me how she is."

"Of course. And I hope you will tell me whether you have changed your mind about her. I confess that you seem to me to be the calmest person I ever met."

"I?" exclaimed Paul. "Yes, I am calm now, but I have not had a moment's rest during the last month."

"I can understand that. You know the worst now, and

you have nothing more to anticipate. I have no right to inquire into your personal feelings, but I should say that you cared very little for your mother, and less for your brother, and that hitherto you had been animated by a sort of fictitious sense of responsibility. That has ceased, and you feel like a man released from prison."

The professor fixed his keen gray eyes on Paul's face as he spoke. His speech was rather incisive, considering how little he had seen of Paul. Perhaps he intended that it should be, for he watched the effect of his words with interest.

"You are not a bad judge of human nature," answered Patoff, coolly. But he did not vouchsafe any further answer.

"It is my business," said the professor. "If, as a friend of Madame Patoff's family, I take the liberty of being plain, and of telling you what I think, you may believe that I have not wholly misjudged your mother, since I have hit the mark in judging you."

"I am not sure that you have hit the mark," replied Paul. "Perhaps you have. Time will show. Meanwhile, I am going to Teheran to reflect upon it. It is impossible to choose a more secluded spot," he added, with a smile.

"Why do you not return to Constantinople?" asked the inquisitive professor.

"Because it has pleased the Minister for Foreign Affairs to send me to Persia. I am a government servant, and must go whither I am sent. I dare say I shall not be there very long. The climate is not very pleasant, and the society is limited. But it will be an agreeable change for me."

"I suppose that efforts will still be made to find your brother?"

"Yes. The search will never be given up while there is the least hope."

"I wonder what the effect would be upon Madame Patoff, if Alexander were found after six months?"

"I have not the least idea," answered Paul. "I suppose we should all return to our former relations with each other. Perhaps the shock might drive her mad in earnest, — I cannot tell. You are a psychologist; it is a case for you."

"A puzzle without an answer. I am afraid it can never be tried."

"No, I am afraid not," said Paul quietly.

The two men finished their dinner, and went out. Paul meant to leave early the next morning, and was anxious to go to bed. He felt that at last he could sleep, and he took his leave of Professor Cutter.

"Good-by," he said, with more feeling than he had shown since he had left his mother's room. "I am glad we have met. Believe me, I am really grateful to you for your kindness, and I hope you will let me know that you have reached England safely. If my mother refers to me, please tell her that after what she said to me I thought it best to leave here at once. Good-by, and thank you again."

"Good-by," said the professor, shaking Paul's hand warmly. "The world is a little place, and I dare say we shall meet again somewhere."

"I hope so," answered Paul.

And so these two parted, to go to the opposite ends of the earth, not satisfied with each other, and yet each feeling that he should like to meet his new acquaintance again. But Persia and England, in the present imperfect state of civilization, are tolerably far apart.

V.

EARLY on the next morning Paul was on his way to Munich, Vienna, and the East again, and on the afternoon of the same day Professor Cutter and Madame Patoff, with two servants, got into a spacious carriage, in which they had determined to drive as far as Weissenstein, the last village of the Black Forest before reaching Pforzheim. Pursuing his plan of traveling by unfrequented routes, the professor had proposed to spend the night in the beautiful old place which he had formerly visited, intending to proceed the next day by rail to Carlsruhe, and thence down the Rhine.

He had not seen Madame Patoff in the evening after her interview with Paul, and when he met her in the morning it struck him that her manner was greatly changed. She was very silent, and when she spoke at all talked of indifferent subjects. She never referred in any way to the meeting with her son, and the professor observed that for the first time she allowed the day to pass without once mentioning the disappearance of Alexander. He attributed this silence to the deep emotion she had felt on seeing Paul, and to her natural desire to avoid any reference to the pain she had suffered. As usual she allowed him to make all the necessary arrangements for the journey, and she even spoke with some pleasure of the long drive through the forest. She was evidently fatigued and nervous, and her face was much paler than usual, but she was quiet and did not seem ill. All through the long afternoon they drove over the beautiful winding road, enjoying the views, discussing the scenery, and breathing in the healthy odor of the pines.

The professor was an agreeable companion, for he had traveled much in Southern Germany, and amused Madame Patoff with all manner of curious information concerning the people, the legends connected with the different parts of the Black Forest, the fairy tales of the Rhine, and the history of the barons before Rudolf of Hapsburg destroyed them in his raid upon the freebooters. This he sprinkled with anecdotes, small talk about books, and comments on European society; speaking with ease and remarkable knowledge of his subjects, and so pleasantly that Madame Patoff never perceived that he wished to amuse her, and was trying to distract her thoughts from the one subject which too easily beset them. Indeed, the professor in the society of a woman of the world was a very different man from the earnest, plain-speaking person who had dined with Paul on the previous night. Even his gold-rimmed spectacles were worn with a less professional air. His well-cut traveling costume of plain tweed did not suggest the traditional scientist, and his bronzed and manly face was that of a sportsman or an Alpine Club man rather than of a student. Madame Patoff leaned back in the carriage, and fairly enjoyed the hours; saying to herself that Cutter had never been so agreeable before, and that indeed in her long life she had met few men who possessed so much charm in conversation. She was an old lady, and could judge of men, for she had spent nearly forty years in the midst of the most brilliant society in Europe, and was not to be deceived by the ring of false metal.

At last they reached the place in the road where they had to descend from the carriage and mount the ascent to Weissenstein. Madame Patoff was well pleased with the place, and said so as she slowly climbed the narrow path, leaning on the professor's arm. The inn — the old Gasthaus zum Goldenen Anker — stands upon the very edge of the precipice above the tumbling Nagold, and is indeed partly built down the face of the cliff. Rooms have been hollowed, so that their windows look down on the river from a sheer height of two hundred feet, the surface of the natural wall, broken only here and there by a projecting ledge, or by the crooked stem of a strong wild cherry tree which somehow finds enough soil and moisture there to support its hardy growth. The inn is very primitive, but comfortable in its simple way, and the scenery is surpassingly beautiful. Far below, on the other side of the torrent, the small village nestles among the dark pines, the single spire of the diminutive church standing high above the surrounding cottages. Above, the hill is crowned by the ruins of the ancient castle of Weissenstein, — the castle of Bellrem, the crusader, who fell from the lofty ramparts on a moonlight night in the twelfth century, terrified by the ghost of a woman he had loved and wronged. At least, the legend says so, and as the ruined ramparts are still there it is probably all quite true. On the back of the hill, where the narrow path descends from the inn to the road, the still, deep waters of the great mill pool lie stagnant in the hot air, and the long-legged water spiders shoot over the surface, inviting the old carp to snap at them, well knowing that they will not, but skimming away like mad when a mountain trout, who has strayed in from the river through the sluices, comes suddenly to the surface with a short, sharp splash. But there are flies for the trout, and he prefers them, so that the water spiders lead, on the whole, a quiet and unmolested life.

The travelers entered the inn, and were soon established for the night. Madame Patoff was still enchanted with the view, and insisted on sitting out upon the low balcony until late at night, though the air was very cool and the dampness rose from the river. There was something in the wild place which soothed her. She almost wished she could stay there forever, and hide her sorrow from the world in such a nest as this, overhanging the wild water, perched high in air, and surrounded on all sides by the soft black forest. For the Black Forest is indeed black, as only such impenetrable masses of evergreen can be.

In the early morning the tall old lady in black was again at her place on the balcony when Professor Cutter appeared. She sat by the low parapet, and gazed down as in a trance at the tumbling water, and at the solitary fisherman who stood bare-legged on a jutting rock, casting his rough tackle on the eddying stream. She was calmer than she had seemed for a long time, and the professor began seriously to doubt the wisdom of taking her to England, although he had already written to her brother-in-law, naming the date when they expected to arrive.

"Shall we go on this morning?" he asked, in a tone which left the answer wholly at Madame Patoff's decision.

"Where?" she asked, dreamily.

"Another stage on our way home," answered the professor.

"Yes," she said, with sudden determination. "If we stay here any longer, I shall be so much in love with the place that I shall never be able to leave it. Let us go at once. I feel as though something might happen to prevent us."

"Very well. I will make all the arrangements." Professor Cutter forthwith went to consult the landlord, leaving Madame Patoff upon the balcony. She sat there without moving, absorbed in the beauty of the scene, and happy to forget her troubles even for a moment in the sight of something altogether new. Her thoughts were indeed confused. It was but the day before yesterday that she had seen her son Paul after years of separation, and that alone was sufficient to disturb her. She had never liked him, — she could not tell why, except it were because she loved Alexander better, — and she could not help looking on Paul as on the man who had robbed her of what she loved best in the world. But the recollection of the interview was cloudy and uncertain. She had given way to a violent rst of anger, and was not quite sure of what had happened. She tried to thrust it all away from her weary brain, and she looked down again at the fisherman, far below. He had moved a little, and just then she could see him only through the branches of a projecting cherry-tree. He seemed to be baiting his hook for another cast in the river.

"Madame Patoff, are you quite ready?" asked the professor's voice from the window.

"Yes," she said, rising to her feet. "I am coming."

"One moment, — I am just paying the bill," answered Cutter from within; and Madame Patoff could hear the landlord counting out the small change upon a plate, the ringing silver marks and the dull little clatter of the nickel ten-pfennig pieces.

She was standing now, and she looked over the torrent at the dark forest beyond, endeavoring to fix the beautiful scene in her mind, and trying to forget her trouble. But it would not be forgotten, and as she stood up the whole scene with Paul came vividly to her mind. She remembered all her loathing for him, all the horror and all the furious anger she had felt at the sight of him. In the keen memory of that bitter meeting, rendered tenfold more vivid by the overwrought state of her brain, the blood rushed violently to her face, her head swam, and she put out her hand to steady herself, thinking there was a railing before her. But the parapet was low, scarcely reaching to her knees. She tottered, lost her balance, and with a wild shriek fell headlong into the abyss.

Cutter dropped his change and rushed frantically to the window, well-nigh falling over the low parapet himself. His face was ghastly, as he leaned far forward and looked down. Then he uttered an exclamation of terror, and seemed about to attempt to climb over the balcony. Not ten feet below him the wretched woman hung suspended in the thick branches of the wild cherry tree, caught by her clothes. Cutter breathed hard, for he had never seen so horrible a sight. At any moment the material of her dress might give way, the branches might break under the heavy

strain. He looked wildly round for help. Between the
balcony and the trees there were ten feet of smooth rock,
which would not have given a foothold to a lizard.

"Catch hold, there ! " cried a loud voice from above, and
Cutter saw a new rope dangling before him into the abyss.
He looked up as he seized the means of help, and saw at
the upper window the square dark face of a strong man, who
was clad in a flannel shirt and had a silver-mounted pipe in
his mouth.

"Go ahead, — it 's fast," said the man, letting out more
rope. " Or if you 're afraid, I 'll come down the rope myself."

But Cutter was not afraid. It was the work of a moment
to make a wide bowline knot in the pliant Manilla cord.
With an agility which in so heavily built a frame surprised
the dark man above, the doctor let himself down as far as
the tree ; then seizing the insensible lady firmly by the arm,
and bracing himself on the roots of the cherry close to the
rock, so that he could stand for a moment without support
from above, he deftly slipped the rope twice round her
waist with what are called technically two half hitches, close
to his own loop, in which he intended to sit, clasping her
body with his arms.

"Can you haul us up ? " he shouted.

Slowly the rope was raised, with its heavy burden. The
strong tourist had got help from the terrified landlord, who
had followed Cutter to the balcony, but who was a stalwart
Swabian, and not easily disconcerted. He had rushed up-
stairs, and was hauling away with all his might. In less
than a minute and a half Cutter was on a level with the balcony, and in a few seconds more he had disengaged himself and the rescued lady from the coils of the rope. It is
not surprising that his first thought should have been for
her, and not for the quiet man with the pipe, who had been
the means of her escape. He bore Madame Patoff to her
room, and with the assistance of her maid set about reviving

her as fast as possible, though the perspiration streamed from his forehead, and he was trembling with fright in every limb and joint.

The tourist wound up his rope, and took his pipe from his mouth, which he had forgotten to do in the hurry of the moment. Then he slipped on an old jacket, and descended the stairs, to inquire whether he could be of any use, and whether the lady were alive or dead. He was a strongly built man, with an ugly but not unkindly face, small gray eyes, and black hair just beginning to grizzle at the temples. He was an extremely quiet fellow, and the people of the inn remarked that he gave very little trouble, though he had been at Weissenstein nearly a week. He had told the landlord that he was going to Switzerland, but that he liked roundabout ways, and was loitering along the road, as the season was not yet far enough advanced for a certain ascent which he meditated. He had nothing with him but a knapsack, a coil of rope, and a weather-beaten ice-axe, besides one small book, which he read whenever he read at all. He spoke German fluently, but said he was an American. Thereupon the landlady, who had a cousin who had a nephew who had gone to Brazil, asked the tourist if he did not know August Bürgin, and was very much disappointed to find that he did not.

The excitement outside of Madame Patoff's room was intense. But the Herr Doctor, as the landlord called Cutter, had admitted no one but the maid, and as yet had not given any news of the patient. The little group stood in the passage a long time before Cutter came out.

"She is not badly hurt," he said, and was about to re-enter the apartment, when his eye fell on the tall tourist, who, on hearing the news, had turned quickly away. Cutter went hastily after him, and, grasping his hand, thanked him warmly for his timely help.

"Don't mention it," said the stranger. "You did the thing beautifully when once you had got hold of the rope.

Excuse me — I have an engagement — good-by — glad to hear the lady is not hurt." Wherewith the tourist quickly shook the professor's hand once more, and was gone before the latter could ask his name.

"Queer fellow," muttered Cutter, as he returned to Madame Patoff's side.

She was not injured, as he had at once announced, but it was impossible to say what effect the awful shock might produce upon her overwrought brain. She opened her eyes, indeed, but she did not seem to recognize any one; and when the professor asked her how she felt, in order to see if she could speak intelligibly, she laughed harshly, and turned her head away. She was badly bruised, but he could discover no mark of any blow upon the head which could have caused a suspension of intelligence. There was therefore nothing to be done but to take care of her, and if she recovered her normal health she must be removed to her home at once. All day he sat beside her bed, with the patience of a man accustomed to tend the sick, and to regard them as studies for his own improvement. Towards evening she slept, and Cutter went out, hoping to find the tourist again. But the landlord said he was gone, and as the little inn kept no book wherein strangers were asked to register their names, and as the landlord could only say that the gentleman had declared his name to be Paul, Cutter was obliged to suffer the pangs of unsatisfied curiosity.

"I am sick of the name of Paul!" exclaimed the professor, half angrily. "Is the fellow a Russian, too, I wonder? Paul, Paul, — everybody seems to be called Paul!" Therewith he turned away, and began to walk up and down before the house, lighting a cigar, and smoking savagely in his annoyance with things in general.

He was thinking that if it had been so easy for Madame Patoff to throw herself over the balcony, just when he was not looking, it was after all not so very improbable that Alexander might have slipped away from his brother in the

dark. The coincidence of the two cases was remarkable.
As for Madame Patoff, he did not doubt for a moment that
she had intended to commit suicide by throwing herself
down the precipice. According to his theory, all her calmness of yesterday and this morning, succeeding the great
excitement of her meeting with Paul, proved that she had
been quietly meditating death. She had escaped. But
had her mind escaped the suicide she had attempted on her
body ? In its effects, her anger against Paul and her fixed
idea concerning him were as nothing when compared with
the terrible shock she had experienced that morning. It
was absolutely impossible to predict what would occur:
whether she would recover her faculties, or remain apathetic
for the rest of her life. She was a nervous, sensitive, and
overstrung woman at all times, and would suffer far more
under a sudden and violent strain than a duller nature
could. The view she took in regard to Alexander's disappearance proved that her faculties were not evenly balanced.
Of course the story was a very queer one, and Russians are
queer people, as the professor said to himself. It was not
going beyond the bounds of possibility to suppose that Paul
might have murdered his brother, but Cutter would have
expected that Madame Patoff would be the last person to
suspect it, and especially to say it aloud. The way she had
raved against Paul on more than one occasion sufficiently
showed that she seized at false conclusions, like a person of
unsound mind. Alexander had resembled her, too, and
had always acted like an irritable, beautiful, spoiled child.
There was a distinct streak of "queerness," as Cutter expressed it, in the family. Probably Paul had inherited it
in a different way. His conduct at Teinach, after leaving
his mother, had been strange. He had shown no sorrow,
scarcely any annoyance, indeed, and during their dinner
had seemed thoroughly at his ease. Scientifically speaking,
the professor regretted the accident of the morning. Madame Patoff had been a very interesting study so long as

she was under the influence of a dominating idea. Her
case might now degenerate into one of common apathy,
such as Cutter had seen hundreds of times. There would
be nothing to be done but to try the usual methods, with the
usual unsatisfactory results, abandoning her at last to the
care of her relations and nurses as a hopeless idiot.

But Professor Cutter was not destined to such a disappointment. His patient recovered in a way which was new
to him, and he realized that in losing his former case he
had found one even more interesting. She was apathetic,
indeed, in a certain degree, and did not appear to understand everything that was said to her, but this was the only
sign of any degeneracy. She never again addressed by
name either the professor or her maid, and never spoke except to express her wants, which she did in few words, and
very concisely and correctly. Nothing would induce her,
in conversation, to make any answer save a simple yes or
no, and Cutter was struck by the fact that her color ceased
to change when he spoke of Alexander. This, he thought,
showed that she no longer associated any painful idea with
the name of her lost son. But there were none of the signs
of a softening brain, — no foolish ravings, nor any expressed
desire to do anything not perfectly rational. She accomplished the journey with evident comfort, and was evidently
delighted at the beautiful sights she saw on the way, though
she said nothing, but only smiled and looked pleased. Her
habitual expression was one of calm melancholy. Her features wore a sad but placid expression, and she appeared to
thrive in health, and to be better than when the professor
had first known her. She was more scrupulous than ever
about her appearance, and there was an almost unnatural
perfection in her dress and in her calm and graceful manner. Cutter was puzzled. With these symptoms he would
have expected some apparent delusion on one point. But
he could detect nothing of the kind, and he exhausted his
theories in trying to find out what particular form of in-

sanity afflicted her. He could see nothing and define nothing, save her absolute refusal to talk. She asked for what she wanted, or got it for herself, and she answered readily yes and no to direct questions. Gradually, as they traveled by short stages, drawing near to their destination, Cutter altogether lost the habit of talking to her, and almost ceased to notice her one peculiarity. She would sit for hours in the same position, apparently never wearied of her silence, her placid expression never changing save into a gentle smile when she saw anything that pleased her.

They reached England at last, and Madame Patoff was installed in her brother-in-law's house in the country. Cutter came frequently from town to see her, and always studied her case with new interest; but after a whole year he could detect no change whatever in her condition, and began to despair of ever classifying her malady in the scientific catalogue of his mind.

. . . .

It was at this point, my dear friend, that I became an actor in the story of Paul Patoff and his mother, and I will now for a time tell my tale in my own person, — in the prosaic person of Paul Griggs, with whom you are so well acquainted that you are good enough to call him your friend. To give you at once an idea of my own connection with this history, I will confess that it was I who dropped the rope out of the window at Weissenstein, as you may have already guessed from the description I have given of myself.

VI.

MANKIND may be divided and classified in many ways, according to the tests applied, and the reason why any new classification of people is always striking is not far to seek. For, since all the mental and moral qualities of which we have ever heard belong to men and women, it is obviously easy to say that we can divide our fellow-creatures into two classes, one class possessing the vice or virtue in point, and the other not possessing it. The only division which is hard to make is that which should separate the human race into classes of good and bad, — to speak biblically, the division of the sheep from the goats ; but as no one has ever been able to draw the line, some people have said, in their haste, that all men are bad, while others have arrived at the no less hasty and equally false conclusion that all men are good. The Preacher was nearer the truth when he said, " All is vanity," than was David when he said in his heart, " All men are liars ; " for if the bad man is foolish enough to boast of his error, the good man is generally inclined to vaunt his virtue after the most mature reflection, and the secret of success, whether in good or in evil, is not to allow the right hand to know the doings of the left. There are men who give lavishly with the one hand, while they steal even more freely with the other, and are covered with glory, until their biography is written by an intelligent enemy.

The faculty of persuading the world at large to consider that you are in the right is called your " prestige," a word closely connected with the term " prestidigitation," — if not in derivation, most certainly in meaning. Wnen you have found out your neighbor's sin, your prestige is increased; when your neighbor has found out yours, your prestige is gone. There is little credit to be got from charity; for if you conceal your good deeds it is certain that nobody will suspect you of doing them, and if you do them before the world every one will say that you are vainglorious and purse-proud, and altogether a dangerous hypocrite. On the other hand, there is undeniably much social interest attached to a man who is supposed to be bad, but who has never been caught in his wickedness; and if a thorough-going sinner is discovered, after having concealed his doings for many years, people at least give him all the credit he can expect, saying, "Surely he was a very clever fellow to deceive us for so long!" There are plenty of ways which serve to conceal evil doings, from the vulgar lies which make up the code of schoolboy honor, to the national bad faith which systematically violates all treaties when they cease to be lucrative; from the promising youth who borrows money from his tailor, and has it charged to his father with compound interest as "account rendered for clothes furnished," down to the driveling dishonesty of some old statesman who clings to office because his ornate eloquence still survives his scanty wit. Verily, if the boy be father to the man, it is not pleasant to imagine what manner of men they will be to whom the modern boy stands in the relation of paternity. The big boys who kill little ones with their fists, and spend a pleasant hour in watching a couple of cats, slung over a clothes-line by the tails, fight each other to death, are likely to be less remarkable for their singular lack of intelligence than for their extraordinary excess of brutality. It is true that a nation's greatest activity for good is developed in the time of its transition from coarseness to refinement. It may also be true that its period of greatest harmfulness is when, from a fictitious refinement, it is dragged down again by the natural brutality of its nature; when the ideal has ceased to correspond with the real; when the poet has lost his hold upon the hearts of the people; when poetry itself is no longer the strong fire bursting through the thick, foul crust of the earth, but is only the faint and shadowy smoke of the fire, wreathed for a moment into ethereal shapes of fleeting grace that have neither heat enough to burn the earth from which they come, nor strength to withstand the rough winds of heaven by which they shall soon be scattered. For as the evolution of the ideal from the real is life, so the final separation of the soul from the body is death.

Almost all men have the qualities which can give moderate success. Very few have those gifts which lead to greatness, and those who have them invariably become great. There is no unrecognized genius; for genius means the production of what is not only beautiful, but enduring, and the works of man are all sooner or later judged by his fellows, and judged fairly. But it is unprofitable to discuss these matters; for those who are very great seldom know that they are, and those who are not cannot be persuaded that they might not attain to greatness if circumstances were slightly changed in their favor. Perhaps also there is very little use in making any preamble to what I have to tell. I remember to have been at a great meeting of American bankers at Niagara some years ago, where, as usual at American meetings, many speeches were made. There was an old gentleman there from the West who appeared to have something to say, but although his voice rose to impassioned tones and his gestures were highly effective as he delivered a variety of ornate phrases, he did not come to the point. An irreverent hearer rose and inquired what was the object of his distinguished friend's discourse, which did not appear to bear at all upon the matters in hand. The old gentleman stopped instantly in his flow of words, and said very quietly and naturally, "I feel a little shy, and I want to speak some before getting to the point, so as to get used to you." There was a good-natured laugh, in which the speaker joined. But he presently began again, and before long he was talking very well and very much to the point. It may be doubted, however, whether any well-conditioned chronicler needs a preliminary breather before so short a race as this is likely to be. In these wild days there is small time for man to work or for woman to weep, and those who would tell a tale must tell it quickly, lest the traveler be out of hearing before the song is ended, and the minstrel be left harping at the empty air and wasting his eloquence upon the stones.

Last year I was staying in an English country house on the borders of Hertfordshire and Essex. It is not what is called a "romantic neighborhood," but there are plenty of pretty places and some fine old trees where the green lanes of Essex begin to undulate into the wooded valleys of Herts. The name of the place where I was stopping is Carvel Place, and the people who generally live in it are John Carvel, Esq., formerly member for the borough; Mary Carvel, his wife, who was a Miss Dabstreak; Hermione Carvel, their daughter; and, when he is at home on leave, Macaulay Carvel, their son, a young man who has been in the diplomatic service several years, and who once had the good fortune to be selected as private secretary to Lord Mavourneen, when that noble diplomatist was sent on a special mission to India. Mrs. Carvel has a younger sister, a spinster, thirty-eight years of age, who rejoices in the name of Chrysophrasia. Her parents had christened their eldest daughter Anne, their second Mary, and had regretted the simple appellations bitterly, so that when a third little girl came into the world, seven years afterwards, their latent love for euphony was poured out upon her in a double measure at the baptismal font. Anne, eldest sister of Mrs. Carvel and Miss Chrysophrasia Dabstreak, married a Russian in the year 1850, and was never mentioned after the Crimean War, until her son, Paul Patoff, being a diplomatist, made the acquaintance of his first cousin in the person of Macaulay Carvel, who happened to be third secretary in Berlin, when Paul passed through that capital, on his return from a distant post in the East.

It is taken for granted that the Carvels have lived at Carvel Place since the memory of man. I know very little of their family history; my acquaintance with John Carvel is of comparatively recent date, and Miss Chrysophrasia eyes me with evident suspicion, as being an American and probably an adventurer. I cannot say that Carvel and I are precisely old friends, but we enjoy each other's society, and have been of considerable service to each other in the last ten years. There is a certain kind of mutual respect, not untempered by substantial mutual obligation, which very nearly approaches to friendship when the parties concerned have common tastes and are not unsympathetic. John Carvel is a man fifty years of age : he is short, well built, and active, delighting in the chase; slender rather than stout, but not thin ; red in the face from constant exposure, scrupulous in the shaving of his smooth chin and in the scrubbing processes, dressed with untarnishing neatness ; having large hands with large nails, smooth and tolerably thick gray hair, strongly marked eyebrows, and small, bright eyes of a gray-blue color. In his personal appearance he is a type of a fine race ; in character and tastes he is a specimen of the best class of men to be met with in our day. He is a country gentleman, educated in the traditions of Rugby and Oxford at a time when those institutions had not succumbed to the subtle evils of our times, whereby the weak are corrupted into effeminate fools and the strong into abominable bullies. John Carvel's Latin has survived his school-days, and his manliness has outlived the university. He belongs to that class of Englishmen who proverbially speak the truth.

When he began life, an orphan at twenty-two years of age, he found himself comparatively poor, but in spite of the prejudices of those days he was not ashamed to better his fortunes by manufacture. and he is now a rich man. He married Mary Dabstreak for love, and has never regretted it. He has lived most of his life at Carvel Place, has hunted perpetually, and has of late years developed a taste for books which is likely to stand him in good stead in his old age. There is a fine library in the house, and much has been added to it in the last ten years. Miss Chrysophrasia occasionally strays into the repository of learning, but she has little sympathy with the contents of the shelves.

Miss Chrysophrasia Dabstreak is a lady concerning whom there is much speculation, to very little purpose, in the world as represented by the select society in which she droops, — not moves. She is an amateur.

Her eye rejoices only in the tints of the crushed strawberry and the faded olive; her ear loves the limited poetry of doubtful sound produced by abortive attempts to revive the unbarred melodies of the troubadours; and her soul thrills responsively in the checkered light falling through a stained-glass window, as a sensitive-plant waves its sticky leaves when a fly is in the neighborhood.

But life has attractions for Chrysophrasia. She enjoys it after her own fashion. It is a little disconnected. The relation between cause and effect is a little obscure. She is fragmentary. She is a series of unfinished sketches in various manners. She has her being in the past tense, and her future, if she could have it after her taste, would be the past made present. She has many aspirations, and few of them are realized, but all of them are sketched in faint hues upon the mist of her mediæval atmosphere. She is, in the language of a lyric from her own pen,

" The shadow of fair and of joyous impossible, infinite, faintness
That is cast on the mist of the sea by the light of the ages to come."

Her handwriting is Gothic. Her heart is of the type created by Mr. Swinburne in the minds of those who do not understand him, — in their minds, for in the flesh the type is not found. Moreover, she resents modernness of every kind, including the steam-engine, the electric telegraph, the continent of North America, and myself. Her political creed shadows forth the government of the future as a pleasant combination of communism and knight-baronry, wherein all oppressed persons shall have republics, and all nice people shall wear armor, and live in castles, and strew the floors of their rooms with rushes and their garments with the anatomic monstrosities of heraldic blazon.

As for religion, her mind is disturbed in its choice between a palatable form of Buddhism and a particularly luscious adaptation of Greek mythology ; but in either case as much Christianity would be indispensable as would give the whole a flavor of crusading. I hope I am not hard upon Miss Chrysophrasia, but the fact is she is not — what shall I say ? — not sympathetic to me. John Carvel does not often speak of her, but he has more than once attempted to argue with her, and on these occasions his sister-in-law invariably winds up her defense by remarking very wearily that " argument is the negation of poetry, and, indeed, of all that is fair and joyous."

Personally Miss Dabstreak is a faded blonde, with a very large nose, a wide mouth garnished with imperfect teeth, a very thin figure of considerable height, a poor complexion ill set off by scanty, straggling fair hair ; garments of unusual greenish hues, fitted in an unusual and irregular manner, hang in fantastic folds about the angles of her frame, and her attitudes are strange and improbable. I repeat that I do not mean to be hard upon Chrysophrasia, but her looks are not much to my taste. She is too strongly contrasted with her niece, Miss Carvel. There is, besides, something in Chrysophrasia's cold green eyes which gives me an unpleasant sensation. She was at Carvel Place when I arrived, and she is generally there, although she has a little house in Brompton, where she preserves the objects she most loves, consisting chiefly of earthen vessels, abominable in color and useless to civilized man ; nevertheless, so great is her influence with her sister's family that even John speaks of majolica with a certain reverence, as a man lowers his voice when he mentions some dear relation not long dead. As for Mrs. Carvel, she is silent when Chrysophrasia holds forth concerning pots and plates, though I have seen her raise her gentle face and cast up her eyes with a faint, hopeless smile when her sister was more than usually eloquent about her Spanow-Morescow things, as she calls them, her Marstrow-Geawgiow and her Robby-ah. It seems to me that objects of that description are a trifle too perishable. Perhaps John Carvel wishes Miss Dabstreak were perishable, too; but she is not.

I would not weary you with too many portraits, my dear lady, and I will describe the beautiful Hermione another day. As for her mother, Mary Carvel, she is an angel upon earth, and if her trials have not been many until lately, her good deeds are without number as the sands of the sea; for it is a poor country that lies on the borders of Essex, and there have been bad times in these years. The harvests have failed, and many other misfortunes have happened, not the least of which is that the old race of farmers is dying out, and that the young ones cannot live as their fathers did, but sell their goods and chattels and emigrate, one after another, to the far, rich West. Some of them prosper, and some of them die on the road; but they leave the land behind them a waste, and there are eleven millions of acres now lying fallow in England which were ploughed and sowed and reaped ten years ago. People are poor, and Mrs. Carvel takes care of them. Her soft brown eyes have a way of finding out trouble, and when it is found her great heart cannot help easing it. She loves her husband and her daughter, understanding them in different degrees. She loves her son also, but she does not pretend to understand him; he is the outcome of a new state of things; but he has no vices, and is thought exceedingly clever. As for her sister, she is very good to her, but she does not profess to understand her, either.

I had been in Persia and Turkey some time, and had not been many days in London, when John Carvel wrote to ask me if I would spend the winter with him. I was tired and wanted to be quiet, so I accepted his offer. Carvel Place is peaceful, and I like the woods about it, and the old towers, and the great library in the house itself, and the general sense of satisfaction at being among congenial people who are friendly. I knew I should have to encounter Miss Chrysophrasia, but I reflected that there was room for both of us, and that if it were not easy to agree with her it was not easy to quarrel with her, either. I packed my traps, and went down to the country one afternoon in November.

John Carvel had grown a trifle older; I thought he was a little less cheerful than he had been in former days, but I was welcomed as warmly as ever. The great fire burned brightly in the old hall, lighting up the dark wainscoting and the heavy furniture with a glow that turned the old oak from brown to red. The dim portraits looked down as of old from the panels, and Fang, the white deerhound, shook his shaggy coat and stretched his vast jaws as I came in. It was cold outside, and the rain was falling fast, as the early darkness gathered gloomily over the landscape, so that I was glad to stand by the blazing logs after the disagreeable drive. John Carvel was alone in the hall. He stretched out his broad hand and grasped mine, and it did my heart good to see the smile of honest gladness on his clean, manly face.

"I hardly thought you would come," he said, looking into my eyes. "I was never so glad to see you in my life. You have been wandering again, — half over the world. How are you? You look tougher than ever, and here am I growing palpably old. How in the world do you manage it?"

"A hard heart, a melancholy temperament, and a large appetite," I answered, with a laugh. "Besides, you have four or five years the better of me."

"The worse, you mean. I'm as gray as a badger."

"Nonsense. It is your climate that makes people gray. How is Mrs. Carvel, and Hermione, — she must have grown up since I saw her, — and Miss Dabstreak?"

"She is after her pots and pans as usual," said John. "Mary and Hermy are all right, thank you. We will have tea with them presently."

He turned and poked the fire with a huge pair of old-fashioned tongs. I thought his cheerful manner subsided a little as he took me to my room. He lingered a moment, till the man who brought in my boxes had unstrapped them, and trimmed the candles, and was gone.

"Is there anything you would like?" he asked. "A little whiskey? a glass of sherry?"

"No, thanks, — nothing. I will come down to tea in a few minutes. It is in the same old room, I suppose?"

"Oh, yes, same as ever. By the bye, Griggs," he added suddenly, as he laid his hand on the handle of the door, "how long is it since you were here?"

"Three years and a month," I answered, after a moment's thought. "It does not seem so long. I suppose that is because we have met abroad since then."

"No, it does not seem long," said John Carvel, thoughtfully. Then he opened the door, and went out without another word.

Nothing especially worthy of mention happened on that evening, nor on the next day, nor for many days. I hunted a little, and shot a great deal more, and spent many hours in the library. The weather improved in the first week of December; it was rather warmer, and the scent lay very well. I gave myself up to the pleasant country life, and enjoyed the society of my host, without much thought of the present or care for the future. Hermione had grown, since I had seen her, from a grave and rather silent girl of seventeen to a somewhat less reserved young woman of twenty, always beautiful, but apparently not much changed. Her mother had taken her out in London during the previous season, and there was occasionally some talk about London and society, in which the young girl did not appear to take very much interest. With this exception the people and things at Carvel Place were the same as I had always known them. I was treated as one of the household, and was allowed to go my own ways without question or interference. Of course, I had to answer many questions about my wanderings and my doings in the last years, but I am used to that and do not mind it.

All this sounds as though I were going to give you some quiet chronicle of English country life, as if I were about to begin a report of household doings: how Mrs. Carvel and Hermione went to church on Sunday; how the Rev. Trumpington Soulsby used to stroll back with them across the park on fine days, and how he and Miss Dabstreak raved over the joyousness of a certain majolica plate; how the curate gently reproved, yet half indulged, Chrysophrasia's erratic religionism; how Mrs. Carvel distributed blankets to the old men and red cloaks to the old women; how the deerhound followed Hermione like Mary's little lamb, and how the worthy keeper, James Grubb, did not quite catch the wicked William Saltmarsh in the act of setting a beautiful new brass wire snare at a particular spot in the quickset hedge between the park and the twelve-acre field, but was confident he would catch him the next time he tried it; how Moses Skingle, the sexton, fell out with Mr. Speller, the superannuated village schoolmaster, because the juvenile Spellers would not refrain from the preparation of luscious mud pies upon the newly made grave of the late Peter Sullins, farmer, whose promising heir had not yet recovered sufficiently from the dissipation attending the funeral to erect a monument to his uncle; and so on and so forth, cackling through a volume or two of village chronicle, "and so home to bed."

I do not care a straw for the ducks in the horse-pond,

nor for the naughty boy who throws stones at them, robs bird's-nests, and sets snares for hares under the wire fence of Carvel Park. I blush to say I have done most things of that kind myself, in one part of the world or in another, and they no longer have any sort of interest for me. No, my dear friend, the world is not yet turned into a farm-yard ; there are other things to tell of besides the mud pies of the Speller children and the marks of little Billy Salt-marsh's hob-nailed shoes in the grass where he set the snare. The Turks say that a fool has three points in com-mon with an ass, — he eats, he drinks, and he brays at other asses. I must fain eat and drink ; let me at least re-frain from braying.

It is not every one who cares for the beauty of nature as reflected in a horse-pond, or for the conversations of a class of people who have not more than seven or eight hundred words in their language, and with whom every word does not by any means correspond with an idea ; we cannot all be farmer's lads, nor, if we were, could each of us find a Wordsworth to describe feelings we should certainly not possess.

I had been nearly a month at Carvel Place, and Christ-mas was approaching. We sat one afternoon in the draw-ing-room, drinking tea. John Carvel was turning over the leaves of a rare book he had just received, before transfer-ring it to its place in the library. His heavy brows were contracted, and his large, clean hands touched the pages lovingly. Mrs. Carvel was installed in her favorite upright chair near an enormous student-lamp that had a pink shade, and her fingers were busy with some sort of needle-work. She, too, was silent, and her gentle face was bent over her hand. I can remember exactly how she always looks when she is working, and how her soft brown hair, that is just turning a little gray at the temples, waves above her fore-head. Chrysophrasia Dabstreak lay languidly extended upon a couch, her thin hands clasped together in a studied attitude. She was bemoaning the evils of civilization, and no one was listening to her, for Hermione and I were engaged in putting a new silver collar round the neck of Fang; the great hound sat up patiently between us, yawning prodigiously from time to time, for the operation was tedious, and the patent lock of the collar would not fasten.

"I was just going to say it was time the letters came," said Mrs. Carvel, as the door opened and a servant entered with the post-bag. The master of the house unlocked the leathern case, and distributed the contents. We each received our share, and without ceremony opened our letters. There was a short silence while we were all reading.

"Macaulay has got his leave," said Mrs. Carvel, joyfully. "Is not that delightful! And he is going to bring — wait a minute — I cannot make out the name — let me get nearer to the light, dear — John, look here, is it not Paul Patoff? Look, dear!"

John looked. "It is certainly Paul Patoff," he said quietly. "I told Macaulay to bring him."

"Gracious!" ejaculated Hermione.

"How extremely interesting!" said Miss Chrysophrasia. "I adore Russians! They have such a joyous savor of the wild, free steppes!"

"You have exactly described the Russian of the steppes, Miss Dabstreak," I remarked. "His savor is so wild that it is perceptible at a great distance. But Patoff is not at all a bad fellow. I met him in Teheran last year. He had a trick of beating his servants which excited the wildest admiration among the Persians. The Shah decorated him before he left."

"Do you know him?" asked John Carvel quickly, as he caught my last words.

"Yes. I was just telling Miss Dabstreak that I met Paul Patoff last year. He was at the Russian legation in Teheran." John showed no surprise, and relapsed into silence.

"He and Macaulay are both in Paris," said Mrs. Carvel, "and I suppose Macaulay has made up his mind that we must know his cousin."

"Is not Professor Cutter coming, too, mamma?" asked Hermione. "I heard papa say so the other day."

"Oh, dear, yes!" exclaimed Chrysophrasia, wearily. "Professor Cutter is coming, with his nasty science, and his lenses, and his mathematics. Of course he will wear those vivid green spectacles morning, noon, and night, — such a dreadfully offensive color."

"Yes," said John, gazing down at his neat shoes, as he stood rubbing his broad hands slowly together before the fire, "Cutter is coming, too. What a queer party we shall be at Christmas."

And when Christmas came, we were a very queer party indeed.

At the prospect of seeing united, under an English roof, an English family, consisting of a great manufacturer, — at the same time a thorough-going country gentleman of old descent, — his wife, his beautiful daughter, and his æsthetic sister-in-law, having with them as guests the son of the master of the house, being a young English diplomatist; an English professor, who had given up his professorship to devote himself to the study of diseases of the mind; a Russian secretary of the embassy, who had seen the world, and was thirty years old; and, lastly, your humble slave of the pen, being an American, — at the prospect of such a heterogeneous assembly of men and women, you will suppose, my dear lady, that I am about to embark upon the cerulean waters of a potentially platonic republic, humbly steering my craft by the charts of a recent voyager, who, after making a noble but ineffectual attempt to discover the Isles of the Blessed, appears to have stumbled into the drawing-rooms of the Damned.

I am not going to do anything of the kind. My story is written for the sole purpose of amusing you, and as a form of diversion for your leisure moments I would select neither the Wordsworthian pastoral, nor the platonic doctrine of Ideas. Mary Carvel would give her vote for the Dalesman, and Chrysophrasia for Plato, but I have not consulted them; and if I do not consult you, it is because I think I understand your tastes. You will, moreover, readily understand that in telling this tale I sometimes speak of things I did not actually see, because I know the people concerned very well, and some of them told me at the time, and have told me since, what they felt and thought about the things they did and saw done. For myself, I am the man you have long known, Paul Griggs, the American; a man of many acquaintances and of few friends, who has seen the world, and is forty-three years of age, ugly and tough, not so poor as I have been, not so good as I might be, melancholic by temperament, and a little sour by force of circumstances.

VII.

IT chanced, one evening, that I was walking alone through the park. I had been on foot to the village to send a telegram, which I had not cared to trust to a servant. The weather had suddenly cleared, and there had been a sharp frost in the morning; towards midday it had thawed a little, but by the time it was dark everything was frozen hard again. The moon was nearly full, and shone brightly upon the frozen grass, casting queer shadows through the bare branches of the trees; it was very cold, and I walked fast; the brittle, frozen mud of the road broke beneath my feet with a creaking, crunching sound, and startled the deep stillness. As I neared the house the moon was before me, and the mass of buildings cast a dark shadow.

Carvel Place is like many old country houses in England; it is a typical dwelling of its kind, irregular, yet imposing, and though it has no plan, for it has been added to and enlarged, and in part rebuilt, it is yet harmonious and of good proportion. I had often reflected that it was too large for the use of the present family, and I knew that there must be a great number of rooms in the house which were never opened; but no one had ever proposed to show them to me, and I was not sufficiently curious to ask permission to visit the disused apartments. I had observed, however, that a wing of the building ran into an inclosure, surrounded by a wall seven or eight feet high, against which were ranged upon the one side a series of hot-houses, while another formed the back of a covered tennis court. The third wall of the inclosure was covered with a lattice, upon which fruit trees had been trained without any great success, and I had noticed that the lattice now completely covered an old oak door which led into the inclosure. I had never seen the door open, but I remembered very well that it was uncovered the last time I had been at Carvel Place.

When I reached the house I was no longer cold, and the night was so clear and sparkling that I idly strolled round the great place, wandering across the frozen lawn and through the winding paths of the flower garden beyond, till I came to the wall I have described, and stood still, half wondering why the door had been covered over with fruit trees, as though no one would ever wish to enter the house from that side. The space could hardly be so valuable for gardening purposes, I thought, for the slender peach-trees that were bound upon the lattice on each side of the door had not thriven. There was something melancholy about the unsuccessful attempt to cultivate the delicate southern fruit in the unkindly air of England, and the branches and stems, all wrapped in straw against the frost, looked unhappy and unnatural in the cold moonlight. I stood looking at them, with my hands in my pockets, thinking somewhat regretfully of my southern birthplace. I smiled at myself and turned away, but as I went the very faintest echo of a laugh seemed to come from the other side of the wall. It sounded disagreeably in the stillness, and I slowly finished my walk around the house and came back to the front door, still wondering who it was that had laughed at me from behind the wall in the moonlight. There was certainly no original reason in the nature of things why it should not chance that some one should laugh on the other side of the wall just as I happened to be standing before the closed gate. The inclosure was probably in connection with the servants' apartments; or it might be the exclusive privilege of Chrysophrasia to walk there, composing anapæstic verse to the infinite faintness of the moon, — or anything. A quarter of an hour later I was in the drawing-room drinking a cup of tea. I came in when the others had finished reading their evening letters, and there were none for me. The tea was cold. I wished I had walked half an hour longer, and had not come into the drawing-room at all.

"Let me make you a fresh cup, Mr. Griggs," said Hermione ; " do, — it will be ready in a moment ! "

I politely declined, and the conversation of the rest soon began where it had left off. It appeared that Professor Cutter was expected that night, and the son of the house, with Patoff, on the following day. It was Thursday, and Christmas was that day week. John Carvel seemed unusually depressed ; his words were few and very grave, and he did not smile, but answered in the shortest manner possible the questions addressed to him. He thought Cutter might arrive at any moment. Hermione hazarded a remark to the effect that the professor was rather dull.

"No, my dear," answered John, "he is not at all dull."

"But, papa, I thought he was so immensely learned "—

"He is very learned," said her father, shortly, and buried himself in his newspaper, so that hardly anything was visible of him but his feet, encased in exceedingly neat shoes ; those nether extremities moved impatiently from time to time. Chrysophrasia was not present, a circumstance which made it seem likely that she might have been the person who had laughed behind the wall. Mary Carvel, like her husband, was unusually silent, and I was sitting not far from Hermione. She looked at me after her father's curt answer to her innocent remark, and smiled faintly.

The drawing-room where we sat exhibited a curious instance of the effect produced upon inanimate things when subjected to the contact of persons who differ widely from each other in taste. You smile, dear lady, at the complicated form of expression. I mean merely that if two people who like very different things live in the same room, each of them will try to give the place the look he or she likes. At Carvel Place there were four to be consulted, instead of two; for John had his own opinions as to taste, and they were certainly sounder than those of his wife and sister-in-law, and at least as clearly defined.

John Carvel liked fine pictures, and he had placed three or four in the drawing-room, — a couple of good Hogarths, a beautiful woman's head by Andrea del Sarto, and a military scene by Meissonnier, — about as heterogeneous a quartette of really valuable works as could be got for money; and John had given a great deal of money for them. Besides the pictures, there stood in the drawing-room an enormous leathern easy-chair, of the old-fashioned type with semicircular wings projecting forward from the high back on each side, made to protect the rheumatic old head of some ancestor who suffered from the toothache before the invention of dentists. Near this stood a low, square, revolving bookcase, which always contained the volumes which John was reading at the time, to be changed from day to day as circumstances required.

Mary Carvel was, and is, an exceedingly religious woman, and her tastes are to some extent the expression of her religious feelings. She has a number of excellent engravings of celebrated pictures, such as Holbein's Madonna, Raphael's Transfiguration, and the Dresden Madonna di San Sisto; she owns the entire collection of chromo-lithographs published by the Arundel Society, and many other reproductions of a similar nature. Many of these she had hung in the drawing-room at Carvel Place. Here and there, also, were little shelves of oak in the common Anglomaniac style of woodwork, ornamented with trefoils, crosses, circles, and triangles, and containing a curious collection of sacred literature, beginning with the ancient volume entitled Wilberforce's View, including the poetry published in a series of Lyras, — Lyra Anglicana, Lyra Germanica, and so on, — culminating at last in the works of Dr. Pusey; the whole perhaps exhibiting in a succinct form the stages through which Mary Carvel had passed, or was still passing, in her religious convictions. And here let me say at once that I am very far from intending to jest at those same convictions of Mary Carvel's, and if you smile it is because the picture is true, not because it is ridiculous. She may read what she pleases, but the world would be a better place if there were more women like her.

There were many other possessions of hers in the drawing-room : for instance, upon the mantel-piece were placed three magnificent Wedgwood urns, after Flaxman's designs, inherited from her father, and now of great value; upon the tables there were several vases of old Vienna, but of a green color, vivid enough to elicit Chrysophrasia's most eloquent disapprobation; there were several embroideries of a sufficiently harmless nature, the work of Mary Carvel's patient fingers, but conceived in a style no longer popular; and on the whole, there was a great number of objects in the drawing-room which belonged to her and by which she set great store, but which bore decidedly the character of English household decoration and furniture at the beginning of the present century, and are consequently abhorrent to the true æsthete.

Chrysophrasia Dabstreak, however, had sworn to cast the shadow of beauty over what she called the substance of the hideous, and to this end and intention, by dint of honeyed eloquence and stinging satire, she had persuaded John and Mary to allow her to insert stained glass in one of the windows, which formerly opened upon and afforded a view of a certain particularly brilliant flower bed. Beneath the many-colored light from this Gothic window — for she insisted upon the pointed arch — Miss Dabstreak had made her own especial corner of the drawing-room. There one might see strange pots and plates, and withered rushes, and fantastic greenish draperies of Eastern weft, which, however, would not fetch five piastres a yard in the bazaar of Stamboul, curious water-colors said to represent " impressions," though one would be shy of meeting, beyond the bounds of an insane asylum, the individual whose impressions could take so questionable a shape; lastly, the centre of the collection, a " polka mazurka harmony in yellow," by Sardanapalus Stiggins, the great impressionist painter of the day. Chrysophrasia paid five hundred pounds for this little gem.

But it was not enough for Miss Dabstreak to have collected so many worthless objects of price in her own little corner of the room. She had encumbered the tables with useless articles of pottery ; she had fastened a green plate between the better of the two Hogarths and an Arundel chromo-lithograph, and connected it with both the pictures by a drooping scarf of faint pink silk ; she had adorned the engraving of Raphael's Transfiguration with a bit of Broussa embroidery, because it looked so very Oriental; and she had bedizened Mary Carvel's water-color view of Carisbrooke Castle with peacock's feathers, because they looked so very English. There was no spot in the room where Chryso. phrasia's hand had not fallen, and often it had fallen heavily. She had respected John Carvel's easy-chair and revolving book-case, but she had respected nothing else.

There was a fourth person, however, who had set her especial impress on the appearance of the room where all met in common. I mean Hermione Carvel. Educated and brought up among the conflicting tastes and views of her parents and her aunt, she had imbibed some of the characteristics of each, although in widely different degrees. At that time, perhaps, the various traits which were united in her had not yet blended harmoniously so as to form a satisfactory whole. The resultant of so many more or less conflicting forces was prone to extremes of enthusiasm or of indifference. Her heart was capable of feeling the warmest sympathy, but was liable also to conceive unwarrantable antipathies ; her mind was of admirable quality, fairly well gifted and sensibly trained ; though not marvelously quick to understand, yet tenacious and slow to forget. The con-

stant attempt to reconcile the irreconcilable opinions of her
mother and aunt had given Hermione a certain versatility
of thought, and a certain capacity to see both sides of the
question when not under the momentary influence of her
enthusiasm.   She is, and was even then, a fine type of the
English girl who has grown up under the most favorable
circumstances; that is to say, with an excellent education
and a decided preference for the country.   It is not necessary to allow her any of the privileges and immunities usually granted to exceptional people; in any ordinary position
of life she would bear the test of any ordinary difficulty very
well.   She inherits common sense from her father, an honest
country gentleman of the kind now unfortunately growing
every day more rare ; a man not so countrified as to break
his connection with the intelligent world, nor so foolishly
ambitious as to abandon a happy life in the country in
order to pursue the mirage of petty political importance: a
man who holds humbug in supreme contempt, and having
purged it from his being has still something to fall back
upon.   From her mother Hermione inherits an extreme
conscientiousness in the things of every-day life ; but whereas
in Mary Carvel this scrupulous pursuance of what is right
is on the verge of degenerating into morbid religionism, in
Hermione it is tempered by occasional bursts of enthusiasm,
and relieved by a wholesome and natural capacity for liking
some people and disliking others.

   In the drawing-room I have been describing, Hermione
touched everything, and did her best to cast over the various objects some grace, some air of harmony, which should
make the contrasted tastes of the rest of her family less
glaring and unpleasant to the eye.   Her task was not easy,
and it was no fault of hers if the room was out of joint.
Her love of flowers showed itself everywhere, and she knew
how to take advantage of each inch of room on shelf, or
table, or window-seat, filling all available spaces with a pro-
fusion of roses, geraniums, and blossoms of every kind that

chanced to be in season. . Flowers in a room will do what
nothing else can accomplish. The eye turns gladly to the
living plant, when wearied and strained with the incongrui-
ties of inanimate things. A pot of pinks makes the lowliest
and most dismal cottage chamber look gay by comparison;
a single rose in a glass of water lights up the most dusty
den of the most dusty student. A bit of climbing ivy con-
verts a hideous ruin into a bower, as the Alp roses and the
Iva make a garden for one short month of the roughest
rocks in the Grisons. Only that which lives and of which
the life is beautiful can reconcile us to those surroundings
which would otherwise offend our sense of harmony, or op-
press us with a dullness even more deadly than mere ugliness can ever be.

Hermione loves all flowers, and at Carvel Place she was
the sweetest blossom of them all. Her fresh vitality is of
the contagious kind, and even plants seem to revive and
get new life from the touch of her small fingers, as though
feeling the necessity of growing like her. Her beauty may
not last. It is not of the imperious kind, nor even quite
classic, but it has a wonderful fineness and delicacy. Her
soft brown hair coils closely on her small, well-shaped head;
her gentle, serious blue eyes look tenderly on all that lives
and has being within the circle of her sight; her small
mouth smiles graciously and readily, though sometimes a
little sadly; and her pleasant voice has a frank ring in it
that is good to hear. Her slight fingers, neither too long
nor too short, are often busy, but her labors are generally
labors of love, and she is never weary of them. Of middle
height, she has the grace of a taller woman, and the ease
in motion which comes only from natural, healthy, elastic
strength, not weakened by enforced idleness, not overdevel-
oped by abominable and unwomanly gymnastic exercises.
Everything she does is graceful.

It is very strange and interesting to see in her the combination of such different elements. Even her aunt Chryso-

phrasia's queer nature is represented, though it needs some ingenuity to trace the resemblance between the two. There are indeed tones of the voice, phrases and expressions, which seem to belong to particular families, and by which one may sometimes discover the relationship. But the modification of leading characteristics in the individual is not so easily detected. Miss Dabstreak is eccentric, but the wild ideas which continue to flourish in the æsthetic cells of Chrysophrasia's brain are softened and made more gentle and delicate in Hermione, so that even if they were inconsequent they would not seem offensive; though one might not admire them, one could not despise them. The young girl loves all that is beautiful : not as Chrysophrasia loves it, by sheer force of habitual affectation, without discernment and without real enjoyment, but from the bottom of her heart, from the well-springs of her own beautiful soul; knowing and understanding the great divisions between the graceful and the clumsy, between the true and the false, the lovely and the unlovely. The extraordinary passion for the eccentric is tempered to an honest and natural craving after the beautiful; the admixture of the gentleness the girl has inherited from her saintly mother and of the genuine common sense which characterizes her father has produced a rational desire and ability to do good to every one. Mary Carvel is sometimes exaggerated in her ideas of charity, and John on rare occasions — very rarely — used to be a little too much inclined to the practice of economy; "near" was the term applied by the village people. It was at first with him but the reminiscence of poorer years, when economy was necessary, and forethought was an indispensable element in his life ; but the tendency has remained and sometimes shows itself. All that can be traced of this quality in the daughter is a certain power of keen discernment, which saves her from being cheated by the sham paupers who abound in the neighborhood of Carvel Place, and from being led into spoiling the school-children with too many feasts of tea, jam, and cake.

It is not easy to be brief in describing Hermione Carvel, because in her fair self she combines a great many qualities belonging to contradictory persons, which one would suppose impossible to unite in one harmonious whole; and yet Hermione is one of the most harmonious persons I ever knew. Nothing about her ever offended my sense of fitness. I often used to wonder how she managed to be loved equally by the different members of the household, but there is no doubt of the fact that all the members of her family not only love her, but excuse readily enough those of their own bad qualities which they fancy they recognize in her; for, indeed, nothing ever seems bad in Hermione, and I doubt greatly whether there is not some touch of white magic in her nature that protects her and shields her, so that bad things turn to good when they come near her. If she likes the curious notions of her aunt, she certainly changes them so that they become delicate fancies, and agree together with the gentle charity she has from her mother and the sterling honesty she gets from her father. John sometimes shrugs his shoulders at what he calls his wife's extraordinary faith in human nature, and both he and Mary are sometimes driven to the verge of distraction by Chrysophrasia's perpetual moaning over civilization; but no one is ever out of temper with Hermione, nor is Hermione ever impatient with any one of the three. She is the peacemaker, the one whose sympathy never fails, whose gentleness is never ruffled, and whose fair judgment is never at fault.

When John Carvel answered Hermione's question about Professor Cutter by a simple affirmation to the effect that he was a very learned man, the young girl did not press her father with any more inquiries, but turned to me.

"Do you not think learned people are very often dull, Mr. Griggs?" she asked.

"Oppressively," I answered.

"What makes them so?"

"It is the very low and common view which they take of life," put in Miss Dabstreak, who entered the room while we were speaking, and sank upon the couch with a little sigh. "They have no aspirations after the beautiful, — and what else can satisfy the human mind? The Greeks were never dull."

"What do you call dull?" asked Mrs. Carvel very mildly.

"Oh — anything; parliamentary reports, for instance, and agricultural shows, and the Rural Dean, — anything of that sort," answered Miss Chrysophrasia languidly.

"In other words, civilization as compared with barbarism," I suggested. "It is true that there cannot be much boredom among barbarous tribes who are always scalping their enemies or being scalped themselves; those things help to pass the time."

"Yes, scalping must be most interesting," murmured Chrysophrasia, with an air of conviction.

Hermione laughed.

"I really believe you would like to see it done, aunt Chrysophrasia," said she.

"Hermy, Hermy, what dreadful ideas you have!" exclaimed Mrs. Carvel, in gentle horror. But she immediately returned to her embroidery, and relapsed into silence.

"It is Mr. Griggs, mamma," said Hermione, still laughing. "He agrees with me that learned people are all oppressively dull, and that the only tolerably exciting society is found among scalping Indians."

"Did you not once scalp somebody yourself, Griggs?" asked John, suddenly lowering his newspaper.

"Not quite," I answered; "but I once shaved a poodle with a pocket-knife. Perhaps you were thinking of that?"

While I spoke there was a sound of wheels without, and John rose to his feet. He seemed impatient.

"That must be Cutter at last!" he exclaimed, moving towards the door that led into the hall. "I thought he was never coming."

I rose also, and followed him. It was Cutter. The learned professor arrived wrapped in a huge ulster overcoat, his hands in the deep pockets thereof, and the end of an extinguished cigar between his teeth. He furtively disposed of the remains of the weed before shaking hands with our host. After the first greetings John led him away to his room, and I remained standing in the hall. The professor's luggage was rather voluminous, and various boxes, bags, and portmanteaus bore the labels of many journeys. The men brought them in from the dog-cart; the strong cob pawed the gravel a little, and the moonlight flashed back from the silver harness, from the smooth varnished dashboard, the polished chains, and the plated lamps. I stood staring out of the door, hardly seeing anything. Indeed, I was lost in a fruitless effort of memory. The groom gathered up the reins and drove away, and presently I was aware that Stubbs, the butler, was offering me a hat, as a hint, I supposed, that he wanted to shut the front door. I mechanically covered my head and strolled away.

I was trying to remember where I had seen Professor Cutter. I could not have known him well, for I never forget a man I have met three or four times; and yet his face was perfectly familiar to me, and came vividly before me as I paced the garden walks. Instinctively I walked round the house again, and paused before the door that had attracted my attention an hour earlier. I listened, but heard nothing, and still I tried to recall my former meeting with Cutter. Strange, I thought, that I should seem to know him so well, and that I should nevertheless be unable to connect him in my mind with any date, or country, or circumstance. In vain I went over many scenes of my life, endeavoring to limit this remembrance to a particular period. I argued that our meeting, if we really had met, could not have taken place many years ago, for I recognized exactly the curling gray hairs in the professor's beard, the wrinkles in his forehead, and a slight mark upon one cheek,

just below the eye. I recollected the same spectacles; the
same bushy, cropped gray hair; the same massive, square
head set upon a short but powerful body; the same huge
hands, spotlessly clean, the big nails kept closely pared and
polished, but so large that they might have belonged to an
extinct species of gigantic man. The whole of him and his
belongings, to the very clothes he wore, seemed familiar to
me and witnesses to his identity; but though I did my best
for half an hour, I could not bring back one circumstance
connected with him. I grew impatient and returned to
the house, for it was time to dress for dinner, and I felt
cold as I strolled about in the frosty moonlight.

We met again before dinner, for a few minutes, in the
drawing-room. I went near to the professor, and examined
his appearance very carefully. His evening dress set off
the robust proportions of his frame, and the recollection I
had of him struck me more forcibly than ever. I am not
superstitious, but I began to fancy that we must have met
in some former state, in some other sphere. He stood before the fire, rubbing his hands and answering all manner
of questions that were put to him. He appeared to be an
old friend of the family, to judge by the conversation, and
yet I was positively certain that I had never seen him at
Carvel Place. He knew all the family, however, and
seemed familiar with their tastes and pursuits: he inquired
about John's manufacturing interests, and about Mrs. Carvel's poor people; he asked Hermione several questions
about the recent exhibitions of flowers, and discussed with
Chrysophrasia a sale of majolica which had just taken place
in London. After this round of remarks I suspected that
the professor would address himself to me, for his gray eyes
rested on me from time to time with a look of recognition.
But he held his peace, and we presently went to dinner.

Professor Cutter talked much and talked well, in a con-
tinuous, consistent manner that was satisfactory for a time,
but a little wearisome in the long run. His ideas were

often brilliant, and his expression of them was always orig-inal, but he had an extraordinary faculty of dominating the conversation. Even John Carvel, who knew a great deal in his way, found it hard to make any headway against the professor's eloquence, though I could sometimes see that he was far from being convinced. The professor had been everywhere and had seen most things; he talked with abso-lute conviction of what he had seen, and avoided talking of what he had not seen, doubtless inferring that it was not worth seeing. Nevertheless, he was not a disagreeable per-son, as such men often are; on the contrary, there was a charm of manner about him that was felt by every one pres-ent. I longed for the meal to be over, however, for I in-tended to seize the first opportunity which presented itself of asking him whether he remembered where we had met before.

I was destined to remain in suspense for some time. We had no sooner risen from dinner than John Carvel came up to me and spoke in a low voice.

"Will you excuse me if I leave you alone, Griggs?" he said. "I have very important business with Professor Cut-ter, which will not keep until to-morrow. We will join you in the drawing-room in about an hour."

It was nothing to me if the two men had business to-gether; I was sufficiently intimate in the house to be treated without ceremony, and I did not care for anybody's com-pany until I could find what I was searching for in the for-gotten corners of my brain.

"Do not mind me," I answered, and I retired into the smoking-room, and began to turn over the evening papers. How long I read I do not know, nor whether the news of the day was more or less interesting and credible than usual; I do not believe that an hour elapsed, either, for an hour is a long time when a man is not interested in what he is doing, and is trying to recall something to his mind. I cannot even tell why I so longed to recollect the professor's face; I only remember that the effort was intense, but wholly fruitless. I lay back in the deep leathern easy-chair, and all sorts of visions flitted before my half-closed eyes, — visions of good and visions of evil, visions of yesterday and visions of long ago. Somehow I fell to thinking about the lattice-covered door in the wall, and I caught myself wondering who had been behind it when I passed; and then I laughed, for I had made up my mind that it must have been Miss Chrysophrasia, who had entered the drawing-room five minutes after I did. I sat staring at the fire. I was conscious that some one had entered the room, and presently the scratching of a match upon something rough roused me from my reverie. I looked round, and saw Professor Cutter standing by the table.

It sometimes happens that a very slight thing will recall a very long chain of circumstances; a look, the intonation of a word, the attitude of a moment, will call up other looks and words and attitudes in quick succession, until the chain is complete. So it happened to me, when I saw the learned professor standing by the table, with a cigar in his mouth, and his great gray eyes fixed upon me from behind his enormous spectacles. I recognized the man, and the little I knew of him came back to me.

The professor is one of the most learned specialists in neurology and the study of the brain now living; he is, moreover, a famous anthropologist. He began his career as a surgeon, and would have been celebrated as an operator had he not one day inherited a private fortune, which permitted him to abandon his surgical practice in favor of a special branch for which he knew himself more particularly fitted. So soon as I recalled the circumstances of our first meeting I realized that I had been in his company only a few moments, and had not known his name.

He came and sat himself down in an easy-chair by my side, and puffed in silence at a big cigar.

"We have met before," I said. "I could not make you

out at first.   You were at Weissenstein last year.   You remember that affair ? "

Professor Cutter looked at me curiously for several seconds before he answered.

" You are the man who let down the rope," he said at last.   " I remember you now very well."

There was a short pause.

" Did you ever hear any more of that lady ? " asked he, presently.

" No, I did not even know her name, any more than I knew yours," I replied.   " I took you for a physician, and the lady for your patient."

We heard steps on the polished floor outside the smoking-room.

" If I were you, I would not say anything to Carvel about that matter," said the professor quickly.

The door opened, and John entered the room.   He was a little pale and looked nervous.

" Ah," he ejaculated, " I thought you would fraternize over the tobacco."

" We are doing our best," said I.

" It is written that the free should be brothers and equal," said the professor, with a laugh.

" I never knew two brothers who were equal," said Carvel, in reflective tones.   " I do not know why the ideal freedom and equality, attaching to the ideal brothers, should not be as good as any other visionary aim for tangible earthly government ; but it certainly does not seem so easy of realization, nor so sound in the working, as our good English principle that exceptions prove the rule, and that the more exceptions there are the better the rule will be."

" Is that speech an attack upon American freedom ? " asked the professor, laughing a little.   " I believe Mr. Griggs is an American."

" No, indeed.   Why should I attack American freedom ? " said John.

"American freedom is not so easily attacked," I remarked. "It eludes definition and rejects political para-
dox. No one ever connects our republic with the fashionable liberty-fraternity-and-equality doctrines of European
emancipation; still less with the communistic idea that,
although men have very different capacities for originating
things, all men have an equal right to destroy them."

"Griggs is mounted upon his hobby," remarked John
Carvel, stretching his feet out towards the fire. The professor turned the light of his spectacles upon me, and puffed
a cloud of smoke.

"Are you a political enthusiast and a rider of hobby-
horses, Mr. Griggs?" he asked.

"I do not know; you must ask our host."

"Pardon me. I think you know very well," said the
professor. "I should say you belonged to a class of persons who know very well what they think."

"How do you judge?"

"That is, of all questions a man can ask, the most difficult to answer. How do you judge of anything?"

"By applying the test of past experience to present fact,"
I replied.

"Then past experience is that by which I judge. How
can you expect me to tell you the whole of my past experience, in order that you may understand how my judgment
is formed? It would take years."

"You are a pair of very singular men," remarked John
Carvel. "You seem to take to argument as fish to the
water. You ought to be successful in a school of walking
philosophers."

John seemed more depressed than I had ever seen him,
and only made an observation from time to time, as though
to make a show of hospitality. The professor interested
me, but I could see that we were boring Carvel. The conversation languished, and before long the latter proposed
that we should go into the drawing-room for half an hour
before bed-time.

We found the ladies seated around the fire. Their voices fell suddenly as we entered the room, and all of them looked towards John and the professor, as though expecting something. It struck me that they had been talking of some matter which was not intended for our ears.

"We have been making plans for Christmas," said Mrs. Carvel, as though to break the awkward silence that followed our entrance.

VIII.

EARLY on the following morning John Carvel came to my room. He looked less anxious than on the previous night, but he was evidently not altogether his former self.

"Would you care to drive to the station and meet those boys?" he asked, cheerfully.

The weather was bright and frosty, and I was glad enough of an excuse for being alone for half an hour with my friend. I assented, therefore, to his proposition, and presently we were rattling along the hard road through the park. The hoar-frost was on the trees and on the blue-green frozen grass beneath them, and on the reeds and sedges beside the pond, which was overspread with a sheet of black ice. The breath flew from the horses' nostrils in white clouds to right and left, and the low morning sun flashed back from the harness, and made the little icicles and laces of frost upon the trees shine like diamonds.

"Carvel," I said presently, as we spun past the lodge, through the great iron gates, "I am not inquisitive, but it is easy to see that there is something going on in your house which is not agreeable to you. Will you tell me frankly whether you would like me to go away?"

"Not for worlds," my companion ejaculated, and he turned a shade paler as he spoke. "I would rather tell you all about it — only " — He paused.

"Don't," said I. "I don't want to know. I merely thought you might prefer to be left free of outsiders at present."

"We hardly look upon you as an outsider, Griggs," said John, quietly. "You have been here so much and we have been so intimate that you are almost like one of the family. Besides, you know this young nephew of my wife's, Paul Patoff; and your knowing him will make matters a little easier. I am not at all sure I shall like him."

"I think you will. At all events, I can give you some idea of him."

"I wish you would," answered John.

"He is a thorough Russian in his ideas and an Englishman in appearance, — perhaps you might say he is more like a Scotchman. He is fair, with blue eyes, a brown mustache, and a prominent nose. He is angular in his movements and rather tall. He has a remarkable talent for languages, and is regarded as a very promising diplomatist. His temper is violent and changeable, but he has excellent manners and is full of tact. I should call him an extremely clever fellow in a general way, and he has done wisely in the selection of his career."

"That is not a bad description. Is there anything against him?"

"I cannot say; I only knew him in Persia, — a chance acquaintance. People said he was very eccentric."

"Eccentric?" asked John. "How?"

"Moody, I suppose, because he would sometimes shut himself up for days, and see nobody unless the minister sent for him. He used to beat his native servants when he was in a bad humor, and was said to be a reckless sort of fellow."

"I hope he will not indulge his eccentricities here. Heaven knows, he has reason enough for being odd, poor fellow. We must make the best of him," continued John hurriedly, as though regretting his last remark, "and you must help us to amuse him and keep him out of mischief. Those Russians are the very devil, sometimes, as I have no doubt you know, and just at present our relations with them are not of the best; but, after all, he is my nephew and one of the family, so that we must do what we can for him, and avoid trouble. Macaulay likes him, and I dare say he likes Macaulay. They will get on together very well."

"Yes — perhaps so — though I do not see what the two can have in common," I answered. "Macaulay can hardly have much sympathy for Patoff's peculiarities, however much he may like the man himself."

"Macaulay is very young, although he has seen something of the world. He has not outgrown the age which mistakes eccentricity for genius and bad temper for boldness. We shall see, — we shall see very soon. They will both hate Cutter, with his professorial wisdom and his immense experience of things they have never seen. How do you like him yourself?"

"Without being congenial to me, he represents what I would like to be myself."

"Would you change with him, if you could?" asked John.

"No, indeed. I, in my person, would like to be what he is in his, — that is all. People often talk of changing. No man alive would really exchange his personality for that of another man, if he had the chance. He only wishes to adorn what he most admires in himself with those things which, in his neighbor, excite the admiration of others. He meditates no change which does not give his vanity a better appearance to himself, and his reputation a dash of more brilliant color in the popular eye."

"Perhaps you are right," said John. "At all events, the professor has qualities that any man might envy."

We reached the station just as the train ran in, and Macaulay Carvel and Patoff waved their hats from the carriage window. In a moment we were all shaking hands upon the platform.

"Papa, this is cousin Paul," said Macaulay, and he turned to greet me next. He is a good-looking fellow, with rather delicate features and a quiet, conscientious sort of expression, exquisite in his dress and scrupulous in his manners, with more of his mother's gentleness than of his father's bold frankness in his brown eyes. His small hand grasped mine readily enough, but seemed nerveless and lacking in vitality, a contrast to Paul Patoff's grip. The Russian was as angular as ever, and his wiry fingers seemed to discharge an electric shock as they touched mine. I realized that he was a very tall man, and that he was far from ugly. His prominent nose and high cheek-bones gave a singular eagle-like look to his face, and his cold, bright eyes added to the impression. He lacked grace of form, but he had plenty of force, and though his movements were sometimes sudden and ungainly he was not without a certain air of nobility. His brown mustache did not altogether hide the half-scornful expression of his mouth.

"How is everybody?" asked Macaulay Carvel of his father. "We shall have a most jolly Christmas, all together."

"Well, Mr. Griggs," said Patoff to me, "I did not expect, when we parted in Persia, that we should meet again in my uncle's house, did you? You will hardly believe that this is my first visit to England, and to my relations here."

"You will certainly not be taken for a foreigner here," I said, laughing.

"Oh, of course not. You see my mother is English, so that I speak the language. The difficulty for me will lie in learning the customs. The English have so many peculiar habits. Is Professor Cutter at the house?"

"Yes. You know him?"

"Very well. He has been my mother's physician for some time."

"Indeed — I was not aware that he practiced as a physician." I was surprised by the news, and a suspicion crossed my mind that the lady at Weissenstein might have been Patoff's mother. Instantly the meaning of the professor's warning flashed upon me, — I was not to mention that

affair in the Black Forest to Carvel. Of course not.
Carvel was the brother-in-law of the lady in question.
However, I kept my own counsel as we drove rapidly home-
wards. The sun had risen higher in the cloudless sky, and
the frozen ground was beginning to thaw, so that now and
then the mud splashed high from under the horses' hoofs.
The vehicle in which we drove was a mail phaeton, and
Macaulay sat in front by his father's side, while Patoff and
I sat behind. We chatted pleasantly along the road, and in
half an hour were deposited at Carvel Place, where the ladies came out to meet us, and the new cousin was introduced to every one. He seemed to make himself at home
very easily, and I think the first impression he produced
was favorable. Mrs. Carvel held his hand for several seconds, and looked up into his cold blue eyes as though searching for some resemblance to his mother, and he met her
gentle look frankly enough. Chrysophrasia eyed him and
eyed him again, trying to discover in him the attributes she
had bestowed upon him in her imagination; he was certainly a bold-looking fellow, and she was not altogether disappointed. She allowed her hand to linger in his, and her
sentimental eyes turned upwards towards him with a look
that was intended to express profound sympathy. As for
Paul, he looked at his aunt Chrysophrasia with a certain
surprise, and he looked upon Hermione with a great admiration as she came forward and put out her hand. John
Carvel stood near by, and I thought his expression changed
as he saw the glance his nephew bestowed upon his daughter. I slipped away to the library, and left the family party
to themselves. Professor Cutter had not yet appeared, and
I hoped to find him. Sure enough, he was among the
books. Three or four large volumes lay open upon a table
near the window, and the sturdy professor was turning over
the leaves, holding a pencil in his mouth and a sheet of
paper in one hand, the image of a student in the pursuit of
knowledge. I went straight up to him.

"Professor Cutter," I said, "you asked me last night whether I had ever heard anything more of the lady with whom I met you at Weissenstein. I have heard of her this morning."

The scientist took the pencil from his mouth, and thrust his hands into his pockets, gazing upon me through the large round lenses of his spectacles. He glanced towards the door before he spoke.

"Well, what have you heard?" he asked.

"Only that she was Paul Patoff's mother," I answered.

"Nothing else?"

"Nothing."

"And how did you come by the information, if you please?" he inquired.

"Very simply. Paul Patoff volunteered to tell me that you had been his mother's physician for some time. I remembered that you warned me not to speak of the Weissenstein affair to our friend Carvel; that was natural enough, since the lady was his sister-in-law. She did not look at all like Paul, it is true, but you are not in the habit of playing physician, and it is a thousand to one that you have attended no one else in the last year who is in any way connected with John Carvel."

The learned doctor smiled.

"You have made a very good guess, Mr. Griggs," he said. "Paul Patoff is a silly fellow enough, or he would not have spoken so plainly. Why do you tell me that you have found me out?"

"Because I imagine that you are still interested in the lady, and that you had better be informed of everything connected with the case."

"The case — yes — it is a very singular case, and I am intensely interested in it. Besides, it has very nearly cost me my reputation, as well as my life. I assure you I have rarely had to do with such a case, nor have I ever experienced such a sensation as when I went over the cliff at Weissenstein after Madame Patoff."

"Probably not," I remarked. "I never saw a braver thing more successfully accomplished."

"There is small courage in acting under necessity," said the professor, walking slowly across the room towards the fire. "If I had not rescued my patient, I should have been much more injured than if I had broken my neck in the attempt. I was responsible for her. What would have become of the 'great neurologist,' the celebrated 'mad-doctor,' as they call me, if one of the few patients to whom I ever devoted my whole personal attention had committed suicide under my very eyes? You can understand that there was something more than her life and mine at stake."

"I never knew exactly how it happened," I replied. "I was looking out of my window, when I saw a woman fall over the balcony below me. Her clothes caught in the crooked branches of a wild cherry tree that grew some ten feet below; and as she struggled, I saw you leaning over the parapet, as if you meant to scramble down the face of the cliff after her. I had a hundred feet of manilla rope which I was taking with me to Switzerland for a special expedition, and I let it down to you. The people of the inn came to my assistance, and we managed to haul you up together, thanks to your knowing how to tie the rope around you both. Then I saw you down-stairs for a few minutes and you told me the lady was not hurt. I left almost immediately. I never knew what led to the accident."

Professor Cutter passed his heavy hand slowly over his thick gray hair, and looked pensively into the fire.

"It was simple enough," he said at last. "I was paying our bill to the landlord, and in doing so I turned my back upon Madame Patoff for a moment. She was standing on a low balcony outside the window, and she must have thrown herself over. Luckily she was dressed in a gown of strong Scotch stuff, which did not tear when it caught in the tree. It was the most extraordinary escape I ever saw."

" I should think so, indeed. But why did she want to kill herself ? Was she insane ? "

" Are people always insane who try to kill themselves ? " asked the professor, eying me keenly through his glasses.

" Very generally they are. I suppose that she was."

" That is precisely the question," said the scientist. " Insanity is an expression that covers a multitude of sins of all kinds, but explains none of them, nor is itself explained. If I could tell you what insanity is, I could tell you whether Madame Patoff was insane or not. I can say that a man possesses a dog, because I can classify the dogs I have seen all over the world. But supposing I had never met any specimen of the canine race but a King Charles spaniel, and on seeing a Scotch deerhound in the possession of a friend was told that the man had a ' dog : ' I should be justified in doubting whether the deerhound was a dog at all in the sense in which the tiny spaniel — the only dog I had ever seen — represented the canine race in my mind and experience. The biblical ' devil,' which ' possessed ' men, took as many shapes and characteristics as the *genus* ' dog ' does : there was the devil that dwelt in tombs, the devil that tore its victim, the devil that entered into swine, the devil that spoke false prophecies, and many more. It is the same with insanity. No two mad people are alike. If I find a person with any madness I know, I can say he is mad ; but if I find a person acting in a very unusual way under the influence of strong and protracted emotion, I am not justified in concluding that he is crazy. I have not seen everything in the world yet. I have not seen every kind of dog, nor every kind of devil, nor every kind of madness."

" You choose strange illustrations," I said, " but you speak clearly."

" Strange cases and strange examples. Insanity is the strangest phase of human nature, because it is the least common state of humanity. If a majority of men were mad, they would have a right to consider themselves sane, and sane men crazy. Your original question was whether, when she attempted suicide, Madame Patoff were sane or not. I do not know. I have known many persons to attempt to take their lives when, according to all their other actions, they were perfectly sane. The question of their sanity could be decided by placing a large number of sensible people in similar circumstances, in order to see whether the majority of them would kill themselves or not. That sort of experiment is not likely to be tried. I found Madame Patoff placed in very extraordinary circumstances, but I did not know her before she was so placed. The case interests me exceedingly. I am still trying to understand it."

"You speak as though you were still treating it," I remarked.

"A physician, in his imagination, will continue to study a case for years after it has passed out of his treatment," answered my companion. "I must go and see Paul, however, since he was good enough to mention me to you." Whereupon Professor Cutter buttoned up his coat and went away, leaving me to my reflections by the library fire.

If Carvel had intended to have a family party in his house at Christmas, including his nephew whom he had never seen, and whose mother had been mad, and the great scientist who had attended her, it seemed strange that he should have asked me as directly as he had done to spend the whole winter under his roof. I had never been asked for so long a visit before, and had never been treated with such confidence and received so intimately as I now was. I could not help wondering whether I was to be told the reason of what was going on, whether, indeed, anything was going on at all, and whether the air of depression and mystery which I thought I observed were not the result of my own imagination, rather than of any actual foundation in fact. The professor might be making a visit for his pleasure, but I knew how valuable his time must be, and I wondered how he could afford to spend it in mere amusement.

I remembered John Carvel's hesitation as we drove to the
station that morning, and his evident annoyance when I
proposed to leave. He knew me well enough to say, " All
right, if you don't mind, run up to town for a day or two,"
but he had not said it. He had manifested the strongest
desire that I should stay, and I had determined to comply
with his request. At the same time I was left entirely in
the dark as to what was going on in the family, and whispered words, conversations that ceased abruptly on my approach, and many other little signs told me beyond all doubt
that something was occurring of which I had no knowledge.
Without being inquisitive, it is hard to live in such surroundings without having one's curiosity roused, and the
circumstance of my former meeting with the professor, now
so suddenly illuminated by the discovery that the lady
whose life he had saved was the sister-in-law of our host,
led me to believe, almost intuitively, that the mystery, if
mystery there were, was connected in some way with Madame Patoff. As I thought of her, the memory of the little
inn, the Gasthof zum Goldenen Anker, in Weissenstein, came
vividly back to me. The splash of the plunging Nagold
was in my ears, the smell of the boundless pine forest was
in my nostrils; once more I seemed to be looking down
from the upper window of the hostelry upon the deep ra-
vine, a sheer precipice from the back of the house, broken
only by some few struggling trees that appeared scarcely
able to find roothold on the straight fall of rock, — one tree
projecting just below the foundations of the inn, ten feet
lower than the lowest window, a knotted wild cherry, storm-
beaten and crooked, — and then, suddenly, something of uncertain shape, huddled together and falling from the balcony
down the precipice, — a woman's figure, caught in the
gnarled boughs of the cherry-tree, hanging and swinging
over the abyss, while shriek on shriek echoed down to the
swollen torrent and up to the turrets of the old inn in an
agonized reverberation of horror.

It was a fearful memory, and the thought of being brought into the company of the woman whose life I had seen so . risked and so saved was strange and fascinating. Often and often I had wondered about her fate, speculating upon the question whether her fall was due to accident or to the intention of suicide, and I had tried to realize the terrible waking when she found herself saved from the destruction she sought by the man I had seen, — perhaps by the very man from whom she was endeavoring to escape. I was thrown off my balance by being so suddenly brought face to face with this woman's son, the tall, blue-eyed, awkward fine gentleman, Paul Patoff. I sat by the library fire and thought it all over, and I said to myself at last, " Paul Griggs, thou art an ass for thy pains, and an inquisitive idiot for thy curiosity." I, who am rarely out of conceit with myself, was disgusted at my lack of dignity at actually desiring to find out things that were in no way my business, nor ever concerned me. So I took a book and fell to reading. Far off in the house I could hear voices now and then, the voices of the family making the acquaintance of their new-found relation. The great fire blazed upon the broad hearth within, and the wintry sun shone brightly without, and there came gradually upon me the delight of comfort that reigns within a luxurious library when the frost is biting without, and there is no scent upon the frozen fields, — the comfort that lies in the contrasts we make for ourselves against nature ; most of all, the peace that a wanderer on the face of the earth, as I am, can feel when he rests his weary limbs in some quiet home, half wishing he might at last be allowed to lay down the staff and scrip, and taste freely of the world's good things, yet knowing that before many days the devil of unrest will drive him forth again upon his road. So I sat in John Carvel's library, and read his books, and enjoyed his cushioned easy-chair with the swinging desk ; and I envied John Carvel his home, and his quiet life, and his defenses against intrusion, saying that

I also might be made happy by the trifling addition of twenty thousand pounds a year to my income.

But I was not long permitted to enjoy the undisturbed possession of this temple of sweet dreams, reveling in my imagination at the idea of what I should do if I possessed such a place. The door of the library opened suddenly with the noise of many feet upon the polished floor.

"And this is the library," said the voice of Hermione, who led the way, followed by her mother and aunt and Paul; John Carvel brought up the rear, quietly looking on while his daughter showed the new cousin the wonders of Carvel Place.

"This is the library," she repeated, "and this is Mr. Griggs," she added, with a little laugh, as she discovered me in the deep easy-chair. "This is the celebrated Mr. Griggs. His name is Paul, like yours, but otherwise he is not in the least like you, I fancy. Everybody knows him, and he knows everybody."

"We have met before," said Patoff, "not only this morning, but in the East. Mr. Griggs certainly seemed to know everybody there, from the Shah to the Greek consul. What a splendid room! It must have taken you years of thought to construct such a literary retreat, uncle John," he added, turning to the master of the house as he spoke.

Indeed, Paul Patoff appeared much struck with everything he saw at Carvel Place. I left my chair and joined the party, who wandered through the rooms and into the great conservatory, and finally gravitated to the drawing-room. Patoff examined everything with an air of extreme interest, and seemed to understand intuitively the tastes of each member of the household. He praised John's pictures and Mrs. Carvel's engravings; he admired Chrysophrasia's stained-glass window, and her pots, and plates, and bits of drapery, he glanced reverently at Mrs. Carvel's religious books, and stopped now and then to smell the flowers Hermione loved. He noted the view upon the park from the

south windows, and thought the disposal of the shrubbery
near the house was a masterpiece of landscape gardening.
As he proceeded, surrounded by his relations, remarking
upon everything he saw, and giving upon all things opinions
which marvelously flattered the individual tastes of each
one of the family, it became evident that he was making a
very favorable impression upon them.

"It is delightful to show you things," said Hermione.
"You are so appreciative."

"It needs little skill to appreciate, where everything is so
beautiful," he answered. "Indeed," he continued, addressing himself to all present, "your home is the most charming I ever saw : I had no idea that the English understood
luxury so well. You know that with us Continental people
you have the reputation of being extravagant, even magnificent, in your ideas, but of being also ascetics in some measure, — loving to make yourselves strangely uncomfortable,
fond of getting very hot, and of taking very cold baths, and
of living on raw meat and cold potatoes and all manner of
strange things. I do not see here any evidences of great
asceticism."

"How wonderfully he speaks English!" exclaimed
Mrs. Carvel, aside, to her husband.

"I should say," continued Paul, without noticing the
flattering interruption, "that you are the most luxurious
people in the world, that you have more taste than any
people I have ever known, and that if I had had the least
idea how charming my relations were, I should have come
from our Russian wilds ten years ago to visit you and tell
you how superior I think you are to ourselves."

Paul laughed pleasantly as he made this speech, and
there was a little murmur of applause.

"We were very different, ten years ago," said John Carvel. "In the first place, there was no Hermione then, to
do the honors and show you the sights. She was quite a
little thing, ten years ago."

"That would have made no difference in the place, though," said Hermione, simply.

"On the contrary, said Paul. "I am inclined to think, on reflection, that I would have postponed my visit, after all, for the sake of ˙ aving my cousin for a guide."

"Ah, how gracefully these wild northern men can turn a phrase!" whispered Chrysophrasia in my ear, — "so strong and yet so tender!" She could not take her eyes from her nephew, and he appeared to understand that he had already made a conquest of the æsthetic old maid, for he took her admiration for granted, and addressed himself to Mrs. Carvel; not losing sight of Chrysophrasia, however, but looking pleasantly at her as he talked, though his words were meant for her sister.

"It is the whole atmosphere of this life that is delightful, and every little thing seems so harmonious," he said. "You have here the solidity of traditional English country life, combined with the comforts of the most advanced civilization ; and, to make it all perfection, you have at every turn the lingering romance of the glorious mediæval life," with a glance at Miss Dabstreak, "that middle age which in beauty was the prime of age, from which began and spread all your most glorious ideas, your government, your warfare, your science. Did you never have an alchemist in your family, Uncle John? Surely he found for you the golden secret, and it is his touch which has beautified these old walls!"

"I don't know," said John Carvel.

"Indeed there was!" cried Chrysophrasia, in delight. "I have found out all about him. He was not exactly an alchemist; he was an astrologer, and tnere are the ruins of his tower in the park. There are some old books up-stairs, upon the Black Art, with his name in them, Johannes Carvellius, written in the most enchanting angular hand-writing."

"I believe there was somebody of that name," remarked John.

"They are full of delicious incantations for raising the devil, — such exquisite ceremonies, with all the dress described that you must wear, and the phases of the moon, and hazel wands cut at midnight. Imagine how delightful ! "

" The tower in the park is a beautiful place," said Hermione. " I have it all filled with flowers in summer, and the gardener's boy once saw a ghost there on All Hallow E'en."

" You must take me there," said Paul, smiling good-humoredly at the reference to the alchemist. " I have a passion for ruins, and I had no idea that you had any ; nothing seems ruined here, and yet everything appears old. What a delightful place ! " Paul sat far back in his comfortable chair, and inserted a single eyeglass in the angle between his heavy brow and his aquiline nose ; his bony fingers were spotless, long, and white, and as he sat there he had the appearance of a personage receiving the respectful homage of a body of devoted attendants, the indescribable air of easy superiority and condescending good-nature which a Roman patrician might have assumed when visiting the country villa of one of his clients. Everybody seemed delighted to be noticed by him and flattered by his words.

I am by nature cross-grained and crabbed, I presume. I admitted that Paul Patoff, though not graceful in his movements, was a fine-looking fellow, with an undeniable distinction of manner ; he had a pleasant voice, an extraordinary command of English, though he was but half an Englishman, and a tact which he certainly owed to his foreign blood ; he was irreproachable in appearance, in the simplicity of his dress, in the smoothness of his fair hair and well-trimmed mustache ; he appeared thoroughly at home among his new-found relations, and anxious to please them all alike ; he was modest and unassuming, for he did not speak of himself, and he gave no opinion saving such as should be pleasing to his audience. He had all this, and yet in the cold stare of his stony eyes, in the ungainly twist of his broad white hand, where the bones and sinews crossed and recrossed like a network of marble, in the decisive tone with which he uttered the most flattering remarks, there was something which betrayed a tyrannical and unyielding character, — something which struck me at first sight, and which suggested a nature by no means so gentle and amiable as he was willing it should appear.

Nevertheless, I was the only one to notice these signs, to judge by the enthusiasm which Patoff produced at Carvel Place in those first hours of his stay. It is true that the professor was not present, although he had left me on the pretense of going to see Paul, and Macaulay Carvel was resting from his journey in his own rooms, in a remote part of the house; but I judged that the latter had already fallen under the spell of Patoff's manner, and that it would not be easy to find out what the man of science really thought about the Anglo-Russian. They probably knew each other of old, and whatever opinions they held of each other were fully formed.

Paul sat in his easy-chair in the midst of the family, and smiled and surveyed everything through his single eyeglass, and if anything did not please him he did not say so. John had something to do, and went away, then Mrs. Carvel wanted to see her son alone, and she left us too; so that Chrysophrasia and Hermione and I remained to amuse Patoff. Hermione immediately began to do so after her own fashion. I think that of all of us she was the one least inclined to give him absolute supremacy at first, but he interested her, for she had seen little of the world, and nothing of such men as her cousin Paul, who was thirty years of age, and had been to most of the courts of the world in the course of twelve years in the diplomatic service. She was not inclined to admit that knowledge of the world was superiority of itself, nor that an easy manner and an irreproachable appearance constituted the ideal of a man; but she was barely twenty, and had seen little of those things. She recognized their importance, and desired to understand them ; she felt that wonderful suspicion of possibilities which a young girl loves to dwell on in connection with every exceptional man she meets ; she unconsciously said to herself that such a man as Patoff might possibly be her ideal, because there was nothing apparent to her at first sight which was in direct contradiction with the typical picture she had conceived of the typical man she hoped to meet.

Every young girl has an ideal, I presume. If it be possible to reason about so unreasonable a thing as love, I should say that love at first sight is probably due to the sudden supposed realization in every respect of an ideal long cherished and carefully developed in the imagination. But in most cases a young girl sees one man after another, hopes in each one to find those qualities which she has elected to admire, and finally submits to be satisfied with far less than she had at first supposed could satisfy her. As for young men, they are mostly fools, and they talk of love with a vast deal of swagger and bravery, laughing it to scorn, as a landsman talks of seasickness, telling you it is nothing but an impression and a mere lack of courage, till one day the land-bred boaster puts to sea in a Channel steamer, and experiences a new sensation, and becomes a very sick man indeed before he is out of sight of Dover cliffs.

But with Hermione there was certainly no realization of her ideal, but probably only the faint, unformulated hope that in her cousin Paul she might find some of those qualities which her own many-sided nature longed to find in man.

"You must tell us all about Russia, cousin Paul," she said, when her father and mother were gone. "Aunt Chrysophrasia believes that you are the most extraordinary set of barbarians up there, and she adores barbarians, you know."

"Of course we are rather barbarous."

"Hermione ! How can you say I ever said such a

thing!" interposed Miss Dabstreak, with a deprecating glance at Paul. "I only said the Russians were such a young and manly race, so interesting, so unlike the inhabitants of this dreary den of printing-presses and steam-engines, so" —

"Thanks, aunt Chrysophrasia," said Paul, "for the delightful ideal you have formed of us. We are certainly less civilized than you, and perhaps, as you are so good as to believe, we are the more interesting. I suppose the unbroken colt of the desert is more interesting than an American trotting horse, but for downright practical use " —

"There is such a tremendous talk of usefulness!" ejaculated Chrysophrasia, a faint, sad smile flickering over her sallow features.

"Usefulness is so remarkably useful," I remarked.

"Oh, Mr. Griggs," exclaimed Hermione, "what an immensely witty speech!"

"There is nothing so witty as truth, Miss Carvel, though you laugh at it," I answered, "for where there is no truth, there is no wit. I maintain that usefulness is really useful. Miss Dabstreak, I believe, maintains the contrary."

"Indeed, I care more for beauty than for usefulness," replied the æsthetic lady, with a fine smile.

"Beauty is indeed truly useful," said Paul, with a very faint imitation of Chrysophrasia's accent, "and it should be sought in everything. But that need not prevent us from seeing true beauty in all that is truly useful."

I had a faint suspicion that if Patoff had mimicked Miss Dabstreak in the first half of his speech, he had imitated me in the second portion of the sentiment. I do not like to be made game of, because I am aware that I am naturally pedantic. It is an old trick of the schools to rouse a pedant to desperate and distracted self-contradiction by quietly imitating everything he says.

"You are very clever at taking both sides of a question at once," said Hermione, with a smile.

"Almost all questions have two sides," answered Paul, "but very often both sides are true. A man may perfectly appreciate and approve of the opinions of two persons who take diametrically opposite views of the same point, provided there be no question of right and wrong involved."

"Perhaps," retorted Hermione; "but then the man who takes both sides has no opinion of his own. I do not like that."

"In general, cousin Hermione," said Paul, with a polite smile, "you may be sure that any man will make your opinion his. In this case, I submit that both beauty and usefulness are good, and that they need not at all interfere with each other. As for the compliment my aunt Chrysophrasia has paid to us Russians, I do not think we can be said to have gone very far in either direction as yet." After which diplomatic speech Paul dropped his eyeglass, and looked pleasantly round upon all three of us, as much as to say that it was impossible to draw him into the position of disagreeing with any one present by any device whatsoever.

IX.

PROFESSOR CUTTER and I walked to the village that afternoon. He is a great pedestrian, and is never satisfied unless he can walk four or five miles a day. His robust and somewhat heavy frame was planned rather for bodily labor than for the housing of so active a mind, and he often complains that the exercise of his body has robbed him of years of intellectual labor. He grumbles at the necessity of wasting time in that way, but he never omits his daily walk.

"I should like to possess your temperament, Mr. Griggs," he remarked, as we walked briskly through the park. "You might renounce exercise and open air for the rest of your life, and never be the worse for it."

"I hardly know," I answered. "I have never tried any regular method of life, and I have never been ill. I do not believe in regular methods."

"That is the ideal constitution. By the by, I had hoped to induce Patoff to come with us, but he said he would stay with the ladies."

"You will never induce him to do anything he does not want to do," I replied. "However, I dare say you know that as well as I do."

"What makes you say that?"

"I can see it, — it is plain enough. Carvel wanted him to go and shoot something after lunch, you wanted him to come for a walk, Macaulay wanted him to bury himself upstairs and talk out the Egyptian question, I wanted to get him into the smoking-room to ask him questions about some friends of mine in the East, Miss Dabstreak had plans to waylay him with her pottery. Not a bit of it! He smiled at us all, and serenely sat by Mrs. Carvel, talking to her and Miss Hermione. He has a will of his own."

"Indeed he has," assented the professor. "He is a moderately clever fellow, with a smooth tongue and a despotic character, a much better combination than a weak will and the mind of a genius. You are right, he is not to be turned by trifles."

"I see that he must be a good diplomatist in these days."

"Diplomacy has got past the stage of being intellectual," said the professor. "There was a time when a fine intellect was thought important in an ambassador; nowadays it is enough if his excellency can hold his tongue and show his teeth. The question is, whether the low estimate of intellect in our day is due to the exigency of modern affairs, or to the exiguity of modern intelligence."

"Men are stronger in our time," I answered, "and consequently have less need to be clever. The transition from the joint government of the world by a herd of wily foxes to the domination of the universe by the mammoth ox is marked by the increase of clumsy strength and the disappearance of graceful deception."

"That is true; but the graceful deception continues to be the more interesting, if not the more agreeable. As for me, I would rather be gracefully deceived, as you call it, than pounded to jelly by the hoofs of the mammoth, — unless I could be the mammoth myself."

"To return to Patoff," said I, "what are they going to do with him?"

"The question is much more likely to be what he will do with them, I should say," answered the scientist, looking straight before him, and increasing the speed of his walk. "I am not at all sure what he might do, if no one prevented him. He is capable of considerable originality if left to himself, and they follow him up there at the Place as the boys and girls followed the Pied Piper."

"Is he at all like his mother?" I asked.

" In point of originality ? " inquired the professor, with a curious smile. " She was certainly a most original woman. I hardly know whether he is like her. Boys are said to resemble their mother in appearance and their father in character. He is certainly not of the same type of constitution as his mother, he has not even the same shape of head, and I am glad of it. But his father was a Slav, and what is madness in an Englishwoman is sanity in a Russian. Her most extraordinary aberrations might not seem at all extraordinary when set off by the natural violence he inherits from his father."

" That is a novel idea to me," I remarked. " You mean that what is madness in one man is not necessarily insanity in another; besides, you refused to allow this morning that Madame Patoff was crazy."

" I did not refuse to allow it ; I only said I did not know it to be the case. But as for what I just said, take two types of mankind, a Chinese and an Englishman, for instance. If you met a fair-haired, blue-eyed, sanguine Englishman, whose head and features were shaped precisely like those of a Chinaman, you could predicate of him that he must be a very extraordinary creature, capable, perhaps, of becoming a driveling idiot. The same of a Chinese, if you met one with a brain shaped like that of an Englishman, and similar features, but with straight black hair, a yellow skin, and red eyes. He would have the brain of the Anglo-Saxon with the temperament of the Mongol, and would probably become a raving maniac. It is not the temperament only, nor the intellect only, which produces the idiot or the madman ; it is the lack of balance between the two. Arrant cowards frequently have very warlike imaginations, and in their dreams conceive themselves doing extremely violent things. Suppose that with such an imagination you unite the temperament of an Arab fanatic, or the coarse, brutal courage of an English prize-fighter, you can put no bounds to the possible actions of the monster you create. The salvation of the human race lies in the fact that very strong and brave people commonly have a peaceable disposition, or else commit murder and get hanged for it. It is far better that they should be hanged, because nobody knows where violence ends and insanity begins, and it is just as well to be on the safe side. Whenever a given form of intellect happens to be joined to a totally inappropriate temperament, we say it is a case of idiocy or insanity. Of course there are many other cases which arise from the mind or the body being injured by extraneous causes ; but they are not genuine cases of insanity, because the evil has not been transmitted from the parents, nor will it be to the children."

The professor marched forward as he gave his lecture on unsoundness of brain, and I strode by his side, silent and listening. What he said seemed very natural, and yet I had never heard it before. Was Madame Patoff such a monster as he described ? It was more likely that her son might be, seeing that he in some points answered precisely to the description of a man with the intellect of one race and the temperament of another ; and yet any one would scoff at the idea that Paul Patoff could go mad. He was so correct, so staid, so absolutely master of what he said, and probably of what he felt, that one could not imagine him a prey to insanity.

" What you say is very interesting," I remarked, at last, " but how does it apply to Madame Patoff ? "

" It does not apply to her," returned Professor Cutter. " She belongs to the class of people in whom the mind has been injured by extraneous circumstances."

" I suppose it is possible. I suppose a perfectly sound mind may be completely destroyed by an accident, even by the moral shock from a sorrow or disappointment."

" Yes," said the professor. " It is even possible to produce artificial insanity, — perfectly genuine while it lasts ; but it is not possible for any one to pretend to be insane."

"Really? I should have thought it quite possible," said I.

"No. It is impossible. I was once called to give my opinion in such a case ; he man betrayed himself in half an hour, and yet he was ı very clever fellow. He was a servant ; murdered his master to rob him ; was caught, but succeeded in restoring the valuables to their places, and pretended to be crazy. It was very well managed and he played the fool splendidly, but I caught him."

"How?" I asked.

"Simply by bullying. I treated him roughly, and never stopped talking to him, — just the worst treatment for a person really insane. In less than an hour I had wearied him out, his feigned madness became so fatiguing to him that there was finally only a spasmodic attempt, and when I had done with him the sane man was perfectly apparent. He grew too much frightened and too tired to act a part. He was hanged, to the satisfaction of all concerned, and he made a complete confession."

"But how about the artificial insanity you spoke of? How can it be produced "

"By any poison, from coffee to alcohol, from tobacco to belladonna. A man who is drunk is insane."

"I wonder whether, if a madman got drunk, he would be sane?" I said.

"Sometimes. A man who has delirium tremens can be brought to his right mind for a time by alcohol, unless he is too far gone. The habitual drunkard is not in his right mind until he has had a certain amount of liquor. All habitual poisons act in that way, even tea. How often do you hear a woman or a student say, 'I do not feel like myself to-day, — I have not had my tea'! When a man does not feel like himself, he means that he feels like some one else, and he is mildly crazy. Generally speaking, any sudden change in our habits of eating and drinking will produce a temporary unsoundness of the mind. Every one knows that thirst sometimes brings on a dangerous madness, and hunger produces hallucinations and visions which take a very real character."

" I know, — I have seen that. In the East it is thought that insanity can be caused by mesmerism, or something like it."

" It is not impossible," answered the scientist. "We do not deny that some very extraordinary circumstances can be induced by sympathy and antipathy."

" I suppose you do not believe in actual mesmerism, do you ? "

" I neither affirm nor deny, — I wait ; and until I have been convinced I do not consider my opinion worth giving."

" That is the only rational position for a man of science. I fancy that nothing but experience satisfies you, — why should it ? "

" The trouble is that experiments, according to the old maxim, are generally made, and should be made, upon worthless bodies, and that they are necessarily very far from being conclusive in regard to the human body. There is no doubt that dogs are subject to grief, joy, hope, and disappointment ; but it is not possible to conclude from the conduct of a dog who is deprived of a particularly interesting bone he is gnawing, for instance, how a man will act who is robbed of his possessions. Similarity of misfortune does not imply analogy in the consequences."

"Certainly not. Otherwise everybody would act in the same way, if put in the same case."

The professor's conversation was interesting if only on account of the extreme simplicity with which he spoke of such a complicated subject. I was impressed with the belief that he belonged to a class of scientists whose interest in what they hope to learn surpasses their enthusiasm for what they have already learned, — a class of scientists unfortunately very rare in our day. For we talk more nonsense

about science than would fill many volumes, because we devote so much time to the pursuit of knowledge; nevertheless, the amount of knowledge actually acquired, beyond all
possibility of contradiction, is ludicrously small as compared
with the energy expended in the pursuit of it and the noise
made over its attainment.   Science lays many eggs, but few
are hatched.   Science .oasts much, but accomplishes little;
is vainglorious, puffed up, and uncharitable; desires to be
considered as the root of all civilization and the seed of all
good, whereas it is the heart that civilizes, never the head.

I walked by the professor's side in deep thought, and he,
too, became silent, so that we talked little more until we
were coming home and had almost reached the house.

"Why has Patoff never been in England before?" I
asked, suddenly.

"I believe he has," answered Cutter.

"He says he has not."

"Never mind.   I believe he was in London during nearly
eighteen months, about four or five years ago, as secretary in
the Russian embassy.   He never went near his relations."

"Why should he ay now that he never was in the country?"

"Because they would not like it, if they knew he had
been so near them without ever visiting them."

"Was his mother with him?   Did she never write to her
people?"

"No," said Cutter, with a short laugh, "she never wrote
to them."

"How very odd!" I exclaimed, as we entered the hall-
door.

"It was odd," answered my companion, and went up-
stairs.   There was something very unsatisfactory about him,
I thought; and then I cursed my own curiosity.   What
business was it all of mine?   If Paul Patoff chose to tell a
diplomatic falsehood, it certainly did not concern me.   It
was possible that his mother might have quarreled with her

family, — indeed, in former years I had sometimes thought
as much from their never mentioning her; and in that case
it would be natural that her son might not have cared to
visit his relations when he was in England before. He need
not have made such a show of never having visited the country, but people often do that sort of thing. And now it was
probable that since Madame Patoff had been insane there
might have been a reconciliation and a smoothing over of the
family difficulties. I had no idea where Madame Patoff
might be. I could not ask any one such a delicate question, for I supposed she was confined in an asylum, and no
one volunteered the information. . Probably Cutter's visit
to Carvel Place was connected with her sad state; perhaps
Patoff's coming might be the result of it, also. It was impossible to say. But of this I was certain: that John Carvel
and his wife had both grown older and sadder in the past
two years, and that there was an air of concealment about
the house which made me very uncomfortable. I have been
connected with more than one odd story in my time, and I
confess that I no longer care for excitement as I once did.
If people are going to get into trouble, I would rather not
be there to see it, and I have a strong dislike to being suddenly called upon to play an unexpected part in sensational
events. Above all, I hate mystery; I hate the mournful air
of superior sorrow that hangs about people who have a disagreeable secret, and the constant depression of long-pro-
tracted anxiety in those about me. It spoiled my pleasure
in the quiet country life to see John's face grow every day
more grave and Mary Carvel's eyes turn sadder. Pain of
any sort is unpleasant to witness, but there is nothing so
depressing as to watch the progress of melancholy in one's
friends; to feel that from some cause which they will not
confide they are losing peace and health and happiness.
Even if one knew the cause one might not be able to do anything to remove it, for it is no bodily ill, that can be doc-
tored and studied and experimented upon, a subject for dis-

sertation and barbarous, semi-classic nomenclature ; quacks
do not pretend to cure it with patent medicines, and great
physicians do not write nebulous articles about it in the re-
views.   There is little room for speculation in the matter of
grief, for most people know well enough what it is, and need
no Latin words with Greek terminations to express it.   It
is the breaking of the sea of life over the harbor bar where
science ends and humanity begins.

Poor John !   It needed something strong indeed to sad-
den his cheerfulness and leaden his energy.   That evening
I talked with Hermione in the drawing-room.   She looked
more lovely than ever dressed all in white, with a single
row of pearls around er roat. Her delicate features were
pale and luminous, and her brown eyes brighter than usual,
—a mere girl, scarcely yet gone into the world, but such
a woman !   It was no wonder that Paul glanced from time
to time in admiration at is cousin.

We were seated in Chrysophrasia's corner, Hermione and
I.   There was nothing odd in that ; the young girl likes me
and enjoys talking to me, and I am no longer young.   You
know, dear friend, that I am forty-six years old this summer, and it is a long time since any one thought of flirting
with me.   I am not dangerous, — nature has taken care
of that, — and I am thought very safe company for the
young.

"Tell me one of your stories, Mr. Griggs. I am so
tired this evening," said Hermione.

"I do not know what to tell you," I answered. "I was
hoping that you would tell me one of yours, all about the
fairies and the elves in the park, as you used to when you
were a little girl."

"I do not believe in fairies any more," said Hermione,
with a little sigh. "I believed in them once, — it was so
nice. I want stories of real life now, — sad ones, that end
happily."

"A great many happy stories end sadly," I replied, "but

few sad ones end happily. Why do you want a sad story? You ought to be gay."

"Ought I? I am not, I am sure. I cannot take everything with a laugh, as some people can; and I cannot be always resigned and religious, as mamma is."

"The pleasantest people are the ones who are always good, but not always alike," I remarked. "It is variety that makes life charming, and goodness that makes it worth living."

Hermione laughed a little.

"That sounds very good, — a little goody, as we used to say when we were small. I wonder whether it is true. I suppose I have not enough variety, or not enough goodness, just at present."

"Why?" I asked. "I should think you had both."

"I do not see the great variety," she answered.

"Have you not found a new relation to-day? An interesting cousin who has seen the whole world ought to go far towards making a variety in life."

"What should you think of a man, Mr. Griggs, whose brother has not been dead eighteen months, and whose mother is dangerously ill, perhaps dying, and who shows no more feeling than a stone?"

The question came sharply and distinctly; Hermione's short lip curled in scorn, and the words were spoken through her closed teeth. Of course she was speaking of Paul Patoff. She turned to me for an answer, and there was an angry light in her eyes.

"Is your cousin's mother very ill?" I asked.

"She is not really dying, but she can never get well. Oh, Mr. Griggs," she cried, clasping her hands together on her knees, and leaning back in her seat, "I wish I could tell you all about it! I am sure you might do some good, but they would be very angry if I told you. I wonder whether he is really so hard-hearted as he looks!"

"Oh, no," I answered. "Men who have lived so much in the world learn to conceal their feelings."

"It is not thought good manners to have any feeling, is it ? "

"Most people try to hide what they feel. What is good of showing every one that you are hurt, when nobody can do anything to help you ? It is undignified to make an exhibition of sorrow for the benefit of one's neighbors."

"Perhaps. But I almost think aunt Chrysophrasia is right : the world was a nicer place, and life was more interesting, when everybody showed what they felt, and fought for what they wanted, and ran away with people they loved, and killed people they hated."

"I think you would get very tired of it," I said, laughing. "It is uncomfortable to live in constant danger of one's life. You used not to talk so, Miss Carvel ; what has happened to you ? "

"Oh, I do not know ; everything is happening that ought not. I should think you might see that we are all very anxious. But I do not half understand it myself. Will you not tell me a story, and help me to forget all about it ? Here comes papa with Professor Cutter, looking graver than ever ; they have been to see — I mean they have been talking about it again."

"Once upon a time there was a " — I stopped. John Carvel came straight across the room to where we were sitting.

"Griggs," he said, in a low voice, "will you come with me for a moment ? " I sprang to my feet. John laid his hand upon my arm ; he was very pale. "Don't look as though anything were the matter," he added.

Accordingly I sauntered across the room, and made a show of stopping a moment before the fire to warm my hands and listen to the general conversation that was going on there. Presently I walked away, and John followed me. As I passed, I looked at the professor, who seemed already absorbed in listening to one of Chrysophrasia's speeches.

He did not return my glance, and I left the room with my friend. A moment later we were in his study. A student's lamp with a green shade burned steadily upon the table, and there was a bright fire on the hearth. A huge writing-table filled the centre of the room, covered with papers and pamphlets. John did not sit down, but stood leaning back against a heavy bookcase, with one hand behind him.

"Griggs," he said, and his voice trembled with excitement, "I am going to ask you a favor, and in order to ask it I am obliged to take you into my confidence."

"I am ready," said I. "You can trust me."

"Since you were here last, very painful things have occurred. In consequence of the death of her eldest son, and of certain circumstances attending it which I need not, cannot, detail, my wife's sister, Madame Patoff, became insane about eighteen months ago. Professor Cutter chanced to be with her at the time, and informed me at once. Her husband, as you know, died twenty years ago, and Paul was away, so that Cutter was so good as to take care of her. He said her only chance of recovery lay in being removed to her native country and carefully nursed. Thank God, I am rich. I received her here, and she has been here ever since. Do not look surprised. For the sake f all I have taken every precaution to keep her absolutely removed from us, though we visit her from time to time. Cutter told me that dreadful story of her trying to kill herself in Suabia. He has just informed me that it was you who saved both her life and his with your rope, — not knowing either of them. I need not tell you my gratitude."

John paused, and grasped my hand; his own was cold and moist.

"It was nothing," I said. "I did not even incur any danger; it was Cutter who risked his life."

"No matter," continued Carvel. "It was you who saved them both. From that time she has recognized no one. Cutter brought her here, and the north wing of the house

was fitted up for her. He has come from time to time to
see her, and she has proper attendants. You never see
them nor her, for she has a walled garden, — the one
against which the hot-houses and the tennis-court are built.
Of course the servants know, — everybody in the house
knows all about it; but this is a huge old place, and there
is plenty of room. It is not thought safe to take her out,
and there appears to be something so peculiar about her
insanity that Cutter discourages the idea of the ordinary
treatment of placing the patient in the company of other
insane, giving them all manner of amusement, and so on.
He seems to think that if she is left alone, and is well cared
for, seeing only, from time to time, the faces of persons she
has known before, she may recover."

"I trust so, indeed," I said earnestly.

"We all pray that she may, poor thing!" rejoined Carvel, very sadly.

"Now listen. Her son, Paul Patoff, arrived this morning, and insisted upon seeing her this afternoon. Cutter
said it could do no harm, as she probably would not recognize him. To our astonishment and delight she knew him
at once for her son, though she treated him with a coldness
almost amounting to horror. She stepped back from him,
and folded her arms, only saying, over and over again,
'Paul, why did you come here, — why did you come?'
We could get nothing more from her than that, and at the
end of ten minutes we left her. She seemed very much exhausted, excited, too, and the nurse who was with her advised us to go."

"It is a great step, however, that she should have recognized any one, especially her own son," I remarked.

"So Cutter holds. She never takes the least notice of
him. But he has suggested to me that while she is still in
this humor it would be worth while trying whether she has
any recollection of you. He says that anything which re-
calls so violent a shock as the one she experienced when

you saved her life may possibly recall a connected train of thought, even though it be a very painful reminiscence; and anything which helps memory helps recovery. He considers hers the most extraordinary case he has ever seen, and he must have seen a great many; he says that there is almost always some delusion, some fixed idea, in insanity. Madame Patoff seems to have none, but she has absolutely no recognition for any one, nor any memory for events beyond a few minutes. She can hardly be induced to speak at all, but will sit quite still for hours with any book that is given her, turning over the pages mechanically. She has a curious fancy for big books, and will always select the thickest from a number of volumes; but whether or not she retains any impression of what she reads, or whether, in fact, she really reads at all, it is quite impossible to say. She will sometimes answer 'yes' or 'no' to a question, but she will give opposite answers to the same question in five minutes. She will stare stolidly at any one who talks to her consecutively; or will simply turn away, and close her eyes as though she were going to sleep. In other respects she is in normal health. She eats little, but regularly, and sleeps soundly; goes out into her garden at certain hours, and seems to enjoy fine weather, and to be annoyed when it rains. She is not easily startled by a sudden noise, or the abrupt appearance of those of us who go to see her. Cutter does not know what to make of it. She was once a very beautiful woman, and is still as handsome as a woman can be at fifty. Cutter says that if she had softening of the brain she would behave very differently, and that if she had become feeble-minded the decay of her faculties would show in her face; but there is nothing of that observable in her. She has as much dignity and beauty as ever, and, excepting when she stares blankly at those who talk to her, her face is intelligent, though very sad."

"Poor lady!" I said. "How old did you say she is?"

" She must be fifty-two, in her fifty-third year.   Her hair is gray, but it is not white."

" Had she any children besides Paul and his brother ? "

" No.   I know very little of her family life.   It was a love match ; but old Patoff was rich.   I never heard that they quarreled.   Alexander entered the army, and remained in a guard regiment in St. Petersburg, while Paul went into the diplomacy.   Madame Patoff must have spent much of her time with Alexander until he died, and Cutter says he was always the favorite son.   I dare say that Paul has a bad temper, and he may have been extravagant.   At all events, she loved Alexander devotedly, and it was his death that first affected her mind."

John had grown more calm during this long conversation. To tell the truth, I did not precisely understand why he should have looked so pale and seemed so anxious, seeing that the news of Madame Patoff was decidedly of an encouraging nature.   I myself was too much astonished at learning that the insane lady was actually an inmate of the house, and I was too much interested at the prospect of seeing her so soon, to think much of John and his anxiety ; but on looking back I remember that his mournful manner produced a certain impression upon me at the moment.

The story was strange enough.   I began to comprehend what Hermione had meant when she spoke of Paul's cold nature.   An hour before dinner the man had seen his mother for the first time in eighteen months, — it might be more, for all I knew, — for the first time since she had been out of her mind.   I had learned from John that she had recognized him, indeed, but had coldly repulsed him when he came before her.   If Paul Patoff had been a warm-hearted man, he could not have been at that very moment making conversation for his cousins in the drawing-room, laughing and chatting, his eyeglass in his eye, his bony fingers toying with the flower Chrysophrasia had given him. It struck me that neither Mrs. Carvel nor her sister could have known of the interview, or they would have manifested some feeling, or at least would not have behaved just as they always did. I asked John if they knew.

"No," he answered. "He told my daughter because he broke off his conversation with her to go and see his mother, but Hermy never tells anything except to me."

"When would you like me to go?" I asked.

"Now, if you will. I will call Cutter. He thinks that, as she last saw you with him, your coming together now will be more likely to recall some memory of the accident. Besides, it is better to go this evening, before she has slept, as the return of memory this afternoon may have been very transitory, and anything which might stimulate it again should be tried before the mood changes. Will you go now?"

"Certainly," I replied, and John Carvel left the room to call the professor.

While I was waiting alone in the study, I happened to take up a pamphlet that lay upon the table. It was something about the relations of England with Russia. An idea crossed my mind.

"I wonder," I said to myself, "whether they have ever tried speaking to her in Russian. Cutter does not know a word of the language; I suppose nobody else here does, either, except Paul, and she seems to have spoken to him in English."

The door opened, and John entered with the professor. I laid down the pamphlet, and prepared to accompany them.

"I suppose Carvel has told you all that I could not tell you, Mr. Griggs," said the learned man, eying me through his glasses with an air of inquiry, and slowly rubbing his enormous hands together.

"Yes," I said. "I understand that we are about to make an experiment in order to ascertain if this unfortunate lady will recognize me."

"Precisely. It is not impossible that she may know you, though, if she saw you at all, it was only for a moment. You have a very striking face and figure, and you have not changed in the least. Besides, the moment was that in which she experienced an awful shock. Such things are sometimes photographed on the mind."

"Has she never recognized you in any way?" I asked.

"Never since that day at Weissenstein. There is just a faint possibility that when she sees us together she may recall that catastrophe. I think Carvel had better stay behind."

"Very well," said John, "I will leave you at the door."

Carvel led the way to the great hall, and then turned through a passage I had never entered. The narrow corridor was brightly lighted by a number of lamps; at the end of it we came to a massive door. John took a little key from a niche in the wall, and inserted it in the small metal plate of the patent lock.

"Cutter will lead you now," he said, as he pushed the heavy mahogany back upon its hinges. Beyond it the passage continued, still brilliantly illuminated, to a dark curtain which closed the other end. It was very warm. Carvel closed the door behind us, and the professor and I proceeded alone.

X.

THE professor pushed aside the heavy curtain, and we entered a small room, simply furnished with a couple of tables, a bookcase, one or two easy-chairs, and a divan. The walls were dark, and the color of the curtains and carpet was a dark green, but two large lamps illuminated every corner of the apartment. At one of the tables a middle-aged woman sat reading; as we entered she looked up at us, and I saw that she was one of the nurses in charge of Madame Patoff. She wore a simple gown of dark material, and upon her head a dainty cap of French appearance was pinned, with a certain show of taste. The nurse had a kindly face and quiet eyes, accustomed, one would think, to look calmly upon sights which would astonish ordinary people. Her features were strongly marked, but gentle in expression and somewhat pale, and as she sat facing us, her large white hands were folded together on the foot of the open page, with an air of resolution that seemed appropriate to her character. She rose deliberately to her feet, as we came forward, and I saw that she was short, though when seated I should have guessed her to be tall.

"Mrs. North," said the professor, "this is my friend Mr. Griggs, who formerly knew Madame Patoff. I have hopes that she may recognize him. Can we see her now?"

"If you will wait one moment," answered Mrs. North, "I will see whether you may go in." Her voice was like herself, calm and gentle, but with a ring of strength and determination in it that was very attractive. She moved to the door opposite to the one by which we had entered, and opened it cautiously; after looking in, she turned and beck-

oned to us to advance.   We went in, and she softly closed
the door behind us.

I shall never forget the impression made upon me when I
saw Madame Patoff.   She was tall, and, though she was
much over fifty years of age, her figure was erect and commanding, slight, but of good proportion ; whether by nature,
or owing to her mental disease, it seemed as though she had
escaped the effects of time, and had she concealed her hair
with a veil she might easily have passed for a woman still
young.   Mary Carvel had been beautiful, and was beautiful
still in a matronly, old-fashioned way ; Hermione was beautiful after another and a smaller manner, slender and delicate and lovely ; but Madame Patoff belonged to a very
different category.   She was on a grander scale, and in her
dark eyes there was room for deeper feeling than in the
gentle looks of her sister and niece.   One could understand
how in her youth she had braved the opposition of father
and mother and sisters, and had married the brilliant Russian, and had followed him to the ends of the earth during
ten years, through peace and through war, till he died.   One
could understand how some great trouble and despair, which
would send a duller, gentler soul to prayers and sad medita-
tions, might have driven this grand, passionate creature to
the very defiance of all despair and trouble, into the abyss
of a self-sought death.   I shuddered when I remembered
that I had seen this very woman suspended in mid-air, her
life depending on the slender strength of a wild cherry tree
upon the cliff side.   I had seen her, and yet had not seen
her ; for the sudden impression of that terrible moment
bore little or no relation to the calmer view of the present
time.

Madame Patoff stood before us, dressed in a close-fitting
gown of black velvet, closed at the throat with a clasp of
pearls ; her thick hair, just turning gray, was coiled in
masses low behind her head, drawn back in long broad
waves on each side, in the manner of the Greeks.   Her

features, slightly aquiline and strongly defined, wore an expression of haughty indifference, not at all like the stolid
stare which John Carvel had described to me, and though
her dark eyes gazed upon us without apparent recognition,
their look was not without intelligence. She had been
walking up and down in the long drawing-room where we
found her, and she had paused in her walk as we entered,
standing beneath a chandelier which carried five lamps;
there were others upon the wall, high up on brackets and
beyond her reach. There was no fireplace, but the air was
very warm, heated, I suppose, by some concealed apparatus.
The furniture consisted of deep chairs, lounges and divans
of every description; three or four bookcases were filled
with books, and there were many volumes piled in a disor-
derly fashion upon the different tables, and some lay upon
the floor beside a cushioned lounge, which looked as though
it were the favorite resting-place of the inmate of the apartment. At first sight it seemed to me that few precautions
were observed; the nurse was seated in an outer apartment,
and Madame Patoff was quite alone and free. But the
room where she was left was so constructed that she could
do herself no harm. There was no fire; the lamps were
all out of reach; the windows were locked, and she could
only go out by passing through the antechamber where the
nurse was watching. There was a singular lack of all those
little objects which encumbered the drawing-room of Carvel
Place; there was not a bit of porcelain or glass, nor a pa-
per-knife, nor any kind of metal object. There were a few
pictures upon the walls, and the walls themselves were hung
with a light gray material, that looked like silk and brilliantly reflected the strong light, making an extraordinary
background for Madame Patoff's figure, clad as she was in
black velvet and white lace.

We stood before her, Cutter and I, for several seconds,
watching for some change of expression in her face. He
had hoped that my sudden appearance would arouse a mem-

ory in her disordered mind. I understood his anxiety, but
it appeared to me very unlikely that when she failed to recognize him she should remember me. For some moments
she gazed upon me, and then a slight flush rose to her
pale cheeks, her fixed stare wavered, and her eyes fell. I
could hear Cutter's long-drawn breath of excitement. She
clasped her hands together and turned away, resuming her
walk. It was strange, — perhaps she really remembered.

"He saved your life in Weissenstein," said Cutter, in
loud, clear tones. "You ought to thank him for it, — you
never did."

The unhappy woman paused in her walk, stood still, then
came swiftly towards us, and again paused. Her face had
changed completely in its expression. Her teeth were
closely set together, and her lip curled in scorn, while a dark
flush overspread her pale face, and her hands twisted each
other convulsively.

"Do you remember Weissenstein?" asked the professor,
in the same incisive voice, and through his round glasses he
fixed his commanding glance upon her. But as he looked
her eyes grew dull, and the blush subsided from her cheek.
With a low, short laugh she turned away.

I started. I had forgotten the laugh behind the latticed
wall, and if I had found time to reflect I should have known,
from what John Carvel had told me, that it could have
come from no one but the mad lady, who had been walking
in the garden with her nurse, on that bright evening. It
was the same low, rippling sound, silvery and clear, and it
came so suddenly that I was startled. I thought that the
professor sighed as he heard it. It was, perhaps, a strong
evidence of insanity. In all my life of wandering and various experience I have chanced to be thrown into the society
of but one insane person besides Madame Patoff. That
was a curious case : a hardy old sea-captain, who chanced
to make a fortune upon the New York stock exchange, and
went stark mad a few weeks later. His madness seemed to

come from elation at his success, and it was very curious to watch its progress, and very sad. He was a strong man, and in all his active life had never touched liquor nor tobacco. Nothing but wealth could have driven him out of his mind; but within two months of his acquiring a fortune he was confined in an asylum, and within the year he died of softening of the brain. I only mention this to show you that I had had no experience of insanity worth speaking of before I met Madame Patoff. I knew next to nothing of the signs of the disease.

Madame Patoff turned away, and crossed the room; then she sank down upon the lounge which I have described as surrounded with books, and, taking a volume in her hand, she began to read, with the utmost unconcern.

"Come," said the professor, "we may as well go."

"Wait a minute," I suggested. "Stay where you are." Cutter looked at me, and shrugged his shoulders.

"You can't do any harm," he replied, indifferently. "I think she has a faint remembrance of you."

You know I can speak the Russian language fairly well, for I have lived some time in the country. It had struck me, while I was waiting in the study, that it would be worth while to try the effect of a remark in a tongue with which Madame Patoff had been familiar for over thirty years. I went quietly up to the couch where she was lying, and spoke to her.

"I am sorry I saved your life, since you wished to die," I said, in a low voice, in Russian. "Forgive me."

Madame Patoff started violently, and her white hands closed upon her book with such force that the strong binding bent and cracked. Cutter could not have seen this, for I was between him and her. She looked up at me, and fixed her dark eyes on mine. There was a great sadness in them, and at the same time a certain terror, but she did not speak. However, as I had made an impression, I addressed her again in the same language.

" Do you remember seeing Paul to-day ? " I asked.

" Paul ? " she repeated, in a soft, sad voice, that seemed to stir the heart into sympathy. " Paul is dead."

I thought it might have been her husband's name as well as her son's.

" I mean your son. He was with you to-day ; you were unkind to him."

" Was I ? " she asked. " I have no son." Still her eyes gazed into mine as though searching for something, and as I looked I thought the tears rose in them and trembled, but they did not overflow. I was profoundly surprised. They had told me that she had no memory for any one, and yet she seemed to have told me that her husband was dead, — if indeed his name had been Paul, — and although she said she had no son, her tears rose at the mention of him. Probably for the very reason that I had not then had any experience of insane persons, the impression formed itself in my mind that this poor lady was not mad, after all. It seemed madness on my own part to doubt the evidence before me, — the evidence of attendants trained to the duty of watching lunatics, the assurances of a man who had grown famous by studying diseases of the brain as Professor Cutter had, the unanimous opinion of Madame Patoff's family. How could they all be mistaken ? Besides, she might have been really mad, and she might be now recovering ; this might be one of her first lucid moments. I hardly knew how to continue, but I was so much interested by her first answers that I felt I must say something.

" Why do you say you have no son ! He is here in the house ; you have seen him to-day. Your son is Paul Patoff. He loves you, and has come to see you."

Again the low, silvery laugh came rippling from her lips. She let the book fall from her hands upon her lap, and leaned far back upon the couch.

" Why do you torment me so ? " she asked. " I tell you I have no son." Agaih she laughed, — less sweetly than before. " Why do you torment me ? "

"I do not want to torment you. I will leave you. Shall I come again?"

"Again?" she repeated, vacantly, as though not understanding. But as I stood beside her I moved a little, and I thought her eyes rested on the figure of the professor, standing at the other end of the room, and her face expressed dislike of him, while her answer to me was a meaningless repetition of my own word.

"Yes," I said. "Shall I come again? Do you like to talk Russian?" This time she said nothing, but her eyes remained fixed upon the professor. "I am going," I added. "Good-by."

She looked up suddenly. I bowed to her, out of habit, I suppose. Do people generally bow to insane persons? To my surprise, she put out her hand and took mine, and shook it, in the most natural way imaginable; but she did not answer me. Just as I was turning from her she spoke again.

"Who are you?" she asked in English.

"My name is Griggs," I replied, and lingered to see if she would say more. But she laughed again, — very little this time, — and she took up the book she had dropped and began to read.

Cutter smiled, too, as we left the room. I glanced back at the graceful figure of the gray-haired woman, extended upon her couch. She did not look up, and a moment later Cutter and I stood again in the antechamber. The professor slowly rubbed his hands together, — his gigantic hands, modeled by nature for dealing with big things. Mrs. North rose from her reading.

"I have an idea that our patient has recognized this gentleman," said the scientist. "This has been a remarkably eventful day. She is probably very tired, and if you could induce her to go to bed it would be a very good thing, Mrs. North. Good-evening."

"Good-evening," I said. Mrs. North made a slight inclination with her head, in answer to our salutation. I

pushed aside the heavy curtain, and we went out. Cutter
had a pass-key to the heavy door in the passage, and opened
it and closed it noiselessly behind us. I felt as though I
had been in a dream, as we emerged into the dimly lighted
great hall, where a huge fire burned in the old-fashioned
fireplace, and Fang, the white deerhound, lay asleep upon
the thick rug.

"And now, Mr. Griggs," said the professor, stopping
short and thrusting his hands into his pockets, "will you
tell me what she said to you, and whether she gave any
signs of intelligence?" He faced me very sharply, as
though to disconcert me by the suddenness of his question.
It was a habit he had.

"She said very little," I replied. "She said that 'Paul'
was dead. Was that her husband's name as well as her
son's?"

"Yes. What else?"

"She told me she had no son; and when I reminded her
that she had seen him that very afternoon, she laughed and
answered, 'I tell you I have no son, — why do you torment me?' She said all that in Russian. As I was going
away you heard her ask me who I was, in English. My
name appeared to amuse her."

"Yes," assented Cutter, with a smile. "Was that all?"

"That was all she said," I answered, with perfect truth.
Somehow I did not care to tell the professor of the look I
thought I had seen in her face when her eyes rested on
him. In the first place, as he was doing his best to cure
her, it seemed useless to tell him that I thought she disliked
him. It might have been only my imagination. Besides,
that nameless, undefined suspicion had crossed my brain
that Madame Patoff was not really mad; and though her
apparently meaningless words might have been interpreted
to mean something in connection with her expression of
face in speaking, it was all too vague to be worth detailing.
I had determined that I would see her again and see her

alone, before long. I might then make some discovery, or satisfy myself that she was really insane.

" Well," observed the professor, " it looks as though she remembered her husband's death, at all events ; and if she remembers that, she has the memory of her own identity, which is something in such cases. I think she faintly recognized you. That flush that came into her face was there when she saw her son this afternoon, so far as I can gather from Carvel's description. I wish they had waited for me. This remark about her son is very curious, too. It is more like a monomania than anything we have had yet. It is like a fixed idea in character ; she certainly is not sane enough to have meant it ironically, — to have meant that Paul Patoff is not a son to her while thinking only of the other one who is dead. Did she speak Russian fluently ? She has not spoken it for more than eighteen months, — perhaps longer."

" She speaks it perfectly," I replied.

" What strange tricks this brain of ours will play us ! " exclaimed the professor. " Here is a woman who has forgotten every circumstance of her former life, has forgotten her friends and relations, and is puzzling us all with her extraordinary lack of memory, and who, nevertheless, remembers fluently the forms and expressions of one of the most complicated languages in the world. At the same time we do not think that she remembers what she reads. I wish we could find out. She acts like a person who has had an injury to some part of the head which has not affected the rest. But then, she never received any injury, to my knowledge."

" Not even when she fell at Weissenstein ? "

" Not the least. I made a careful examination."

" I do not see that we are likely to arrive at a conclusion by any amount of guessing," I remarked. " Nothing but time and experiments will show what is the matter with her."

"I have not the time, and I cannot invent the experiments," replied the professor, impatiently. "I have a great mind to advise Carvel to put her into an asylum, and have done with all this sort of thing."

"He will never consent to do that," I answered. "He evidently believes that she is recovering. I could see it in his face this evening. What do the nurses think of it?"

"Mrs. North never says anything very encouraging, excepting that she has taken care of many insane women before, and remembers no case like this. She is a famous nurse, too. Those people, from their constant daily experience, sometimes understand things that we specialists do not. But on the other hand, she is so taciturn and cautious that she can hardly be induced to speak at all. The other woman is younger and more enthusiastic, but she has not half so much sense."

I was silent. I was thinking that, according to all accounts, I had been more successful than any one hitherto, and that a possible clue to Madame Patoff's condition might be obtained by encouraging her to speak in her adopted language. Perhaps something of the sort crossed the professor's mind.

"Should you like to see her again?" he inquired. "It will be interesting to know whether this return of memory is wholly transitory. She recognized her son to-day, and I think she had some recognition of you. You might both see her again to-morrow, and discover if the same symptoms present themselves."

"I should be glad to go again," I replied. "But if I can be of any service, it seems to me that I ought to be informed of the circumstances which led to her insanity. I might have a better chance of rousing her attention."

"Carvel will never consent to that," said the professor, shortly, and he looked away from me as I spoke.

I was about to ask whether Cutter himself was acquainted with the whole story, when Fang, the dog, who had taken no notice whatever of our presence in the hall, suddenly sprang to his feet and trotted across the floor, wagging his tail. He had recognized the tread of his mistress, and a moment later Hermione entered and came towards us. Hermione did not like the professor very much, and the professor knew it; for he was a man of quick and intuitive perceptions, who had a marvelous understanding of the sympathies and antipathies of those with whom he was thrown. He sniffed the air rather discontentedly as the young girl approached, and he looked at his watch.

"Fang has good ears, Miss Carvel," said he. "He knew your step before you came in."

"Yes," answered Hermione, seating herself in one of the deep chairs by the fireside, and caressing the dog's head as he laid his long muzzle upon her knee. "Poor Fang, you know your friends, don't you? Mr. Griggs, this new collar is always unfastening itself. I believe you have bewitched it! See, here it is falling off again."

I bent down to examine the lock. The professor was not interested in the dog nor his collar, and, muttering something about speaking to Carvel before he went to bed, he left us.

"I could not stay in there," said Hermione. "Aunt Chrysophrasia is talking to cousin Paul in her usual way, and Macaulay has got into a corner with mamma, so that I was left alone. Where have you been all this time?"

"I have heard what you could not tell me," I answered. "I have been to see Madame Patoff with the professor."

"Not really? Oh, I am so glad! Now I can always talk to you about it. Did papa tell you? Why did he want you to go?"

I briefly explained the circumstances of my seeing Madame Patoff in the Black Forest, and the hope that was entertained of her recognizing me.

"Do you ever go in to see her, Miss Carvel?" I asked.

"Sometimes. They do not like me to go," said she;

" they think it is too depressing for me. I cannot tell why. Poor dear aunt! she used to be glad to see me. Is not it dreadfully sad? Can you imagine a man who has just seen his mother in such a condition, behaving as Paul Patoff behaves this evening? He talks as if nothing had happened."

" No, I cannot imagine it. I suppose he does not want to make everybody feel badly about it."

" Mr. Griggs, is she really mad?" asked Hermione, in a low voice, leaning forward and clasping her hands.

" Why," I began, very much surprised, " does anybody doubt that she is insane?"

" I do," said the young girl, decidedly. " I do not believe she is any more insane than you and I are."

" That is a very bold thing to say," I objected, " when a man of Professor Cutter's reputation in those things says that she is crazy, and gives up so much time to visiting her."

" All the same," said Hermione, " I do not believe it. I am sure people sometimes try to kill themselves without being insane, and that is all it rests on."

" But she has never recognized any one since that," I urged.

" Perhaps she is ashamed," suggested my companion, simply.

I was struck by the reply. It was such a simple idea that it seemed almost foolish. But it was a woman's thought about another woman, and it had its value. I laughed a little, but I answered seriously enough.

" Why should she be ashamed?"

" It seems to me," said the young girl, " that if I had done something very foolish and wicked, like trying to kill myself, and if people took it for granted that I was crazy, I would let them believe it, because I should be too much ashamed of myself to allow that I had consciously done anything so bad. Perhaps that is very silly; do you think so?"

" I do not think it is silly," I replied. " It is a very original idea."

"Well, I will tell you something. Soon after she was first brought here I used to go and see her more often than I do now. She interested me so much. I was often alone with her. She never answered any questions, but she would sometimes let me read aloud to her. I do not know whether she understood anything I read, but it soothed her, and occasionally she would go to sleep while I was reading. One day I was sitting quite quietly beside her, and she looked at me very sadly, as though she were thinking of somebody she had loved, — I cannot tell why; and without thinking I looked at her, and said, " Dear aunt Annie, tell me, you are not really mad, are you?" Then she turned very pale and began to cry, so that I was frightened, and called the nurse, and went away. I never told anybody, because it seemed so foolish of me, and I thought I had been unkind, and had hurt her feelings. But after that she did not seem to want to see me when I came, and so I have thought a great deal about it. Do you see? Perhaps there is not much connection."

"I think you ought to have told some one; your father, for instance," I said. "It is very interesting."

"I have told you, though it is so long since it happened," she answered; and then she added, quickly, "Shall you tell Professor Cutter?"

"No," I replied, after a moment's hesitation. "I do not think I shall. Should you like me to tell him?"

"Oh, no," she exclaimed quickly, "I should much rather you would not."

"Why?" I inquired. "I agree with you, but I should like to know your reason."

"I think Professor Cutter knows more already than he will tell you or me" — She checked herself, and then continued in a lower voice: "It is prejudice, of course, but I do not like him. I positively cannot bear the sight of him."

"I fancy he knows that you do not like him," I remarked.

"Tell me, Miss Carvel, do you know anything of the rea-

son why Madame Patoff became insane? If you do know,
you must not tell me what it was, because your father does
not wish me to hear it. But I should like to be sure whether
you know all about it or not; whether you and I judge her
from the same point of view, or whether you are better in-
structed than I am."

"I know nothing about it," said Hermione, quietly.

She sat gazing into the great fire, one small hand support-
ing her chin, and the other resting upon the sharp white
head of Fang, who never moved from her knee. There
was a pause, during which we were both wondering what
strange circumstance could have brought the unhappy
woman to her present condition, whether it were that of
real or of assumed insanity.

"I do not know," she repeated, at last. "I wish I did;
but I suppose it was something too dreadful to be told.
There are such dreadful things in the world, you know."

"Yes, I know there are," I answered, gravely; and in
truth I was persuaded that the prime cause must have been
extraordinary indeed, since even John Carvel had said that
he could not tell me.

"There are such dreadful things," Hermione said again.
"Just think how horrible it would be if"— She stopped
short, and blushed crimson in the ruddy firelight.

"What?" I asked. But she did not answer, and I saw
that the idea had pained her, whatever it might be. Presently she turned the phrase so as to make it appear natural
enough.

"What a horrible thing it would be if we found that poor
aunt Annie only let us believe she was mad, because she
had done something she was sorry for, and would not own
it!"

"Dreadful indeed," I replied. Hermione rose from her
deep chair.

"Good-night, Mr. Griggs," she said. "I hope we may
all understand everything some day."

" Good-night, Miss Carvel."

" How careful you are of the formalities ! " she said, laughing. " How two years change everything ! It used to be ' Good-night, Hermy,' so short a time ago ! "

" Good-night, Hermy," I said, laughing too, as she took my hand. " If you are old enough to be called Miss Carvel, I am old enough to call you Hermy still."

" Oh, I did not mean that," she said, and went away.

I sat a few minutes by the fire after she had gone, and then, fearing lest I should be disturbed by the professor or John Carvel, I too left the hall, and went to my own room, to think over the events of the day. I had learned so much that I was confused, and needed rest and leisure to reflect. That morning I had waked with a sensation of unsatisfied curiosity. All I had wanted to discover had been told me before bedtime, and more also ; and now I was unpleasantly aware that this very curiosity was redoubled, and that, having been promoted from knowing nothing to knowing something, I felt I had only begun to guess how much there was to be known.

Oh, this interest in other people's business ! How grand and beautiful and simple a thing it is to mind one's own affairs, and leave other people to mind what concerns them ! And yet I defy the most indifferent man alive to let himself be put in my position, and not to feel curiosity ; to be taken into a half confidence of the most intense interest, and not to desire exceedingly to be trusted with the remainder ; to be asked to consider and give an opinion upon certain effects, and to be deliberately informed that he may never know the causes which led to the results he sees.

On mature reflection, what had struck me as most remarkable in connection with the whole matter was Hermione's simple, almost childlike guess, — that Madame Patoff was ashamed of something, and was willing to be considered insane, rather than let it be thought she was in possession of her faculties at the time when she did the deed, whatever it might be. That this was a conceivable hypothesis there was no manner of doubt, only I could hardly imagine what action, apart from the poor woman's attempt at suicide, could have been so serious as to persuade her to act insanity for the rest of her life. Surely John Carvel, with his great, kind heart, would not be unforgiving. But John Carvel might not have been concerned in the matter at all. He spoke of knowing the details and being unable to tell them to me, but he never said they concerned any one but Madame Patoff.

Strange that Hermione should not know, either. Whatever the details were, they were not fit for her young ears. It was strange, too, that she should have conceived an antipathy for the professor. He was a man who was generally popular, or who at least had the faculty of making himself acceptable when he chose ; but it was perfectly evident that the scientist and the young girl disliked each other. There was more in it than appeared upon the surface. Innocent young girls do not suddenly contract violent prejudices against elderly and inoffensive men who do not weary them or annoy them in some way ; still less do men of large intellect and experience take unreasoning and foolish dislikes to young and beautiful maidens. We know little of the hidden sympathies and antipathies of the human heart, but we know enough to say with certainty that in broad cases the average human being will not, without cause, act wholly in contradiction to the dictates of reason and the probabilities of human nature.

I lay awake long that night, and for many nights afterwards, trying to explain to myself these problems, and planning ways and means for discovering whether or not the beautiful old lady downstairs was in her right mind, or was playing a shameful and wicked trick upon the man who sheltered her. But though other events followed each other

with rapidity, it was long before I got at the truth and settled the question. Whether or not I was right in wishing
to pursue the secret to its ultimate source and explanation,
I leave you to judge. I will only say that, although I was
at first impelled by what seems now a wretched and worthless curiosity, I found, as time went on, that there was such
a multiplicity of interests at stake, that the complications
were so singular and unexpected and the passions aroused so
masterful and desperate, that, being in the fight, I had no
choice but to fight it to the end. So I did my very best in
helping those to whom I owed allegiance by all the laws of
hospitality and gratitude, and in concentrating my whole
strength and intelligence and activity in the discovery of
an evil which I suspected from the first to be very great,
but of which I was far from realizing the magnitude and
extent.

You will forgive my thus speaking of myself, and this
apology for my doings at this stage of my story; but I am
aware that my motives hitherto may have appeared contemptible, and I am anxious to have you understand that
when I found myself suddenly placed in what I regard as
one of the most extraordinary situations of my life, I honestly put my hand out, and strove to become an agent for
good in that strange series of events into which my poor
curiosity had originally brought me. And having thus explained and expressed myself in concluding what I may
regard as the first part of my story, I promise that I will
not trouble you again, dear lady, with any unnecessary as-
severations of my good faith, nor with any useless defense
of my actions; conceiving that although I am responsible to
you for the telling of this tale, I am answerable to many
for the part I played in the circumstances here related;
and that, on the other hand, though no one can find much
fault with me for my doings, none but you will have occasion to criticise my mode of telling them.

Henceforth, therefore, and to the end, I will speak of events which happened from an historical point of view, frequently detailing conversations in which I took no part and scenes of which I had not at the time any knowledge, and only introducing myself in the first person when the nature of the story requires it.

XI.

ONE might perhaps define the difference between Professor Cutter and Paul Patoff by saying that the Russian endeavored to make a favorable impression upon people about him, and then to lead them on by means of the impression he had created, whereas the scientist enjoyed feeling that he had a hidden power over his surroundings, while he allowed people to think that he was only blunt and outspoken. Essentially, there was between the two men the difference that exists between a diplomatist and a conspirator. Patoff loved to appear brilliant, to talk well, to be liked by everybody, and to accomplish everything by persuasion ; he seemed to enjoy the world and his position in it, and it was part of his plan of life to acknowledge his little vanities, and to make others feel that they need only take a sufficient pride in themselves to become as shining lights in the social world as Paul Patoff. At a small cost to himself, he favored the general opinion in regard to his eccentricity, because the reputation of it gave him a certain amount of freedom he would not otherwise have enjoyed. He undertook many obligations, in his constant readiness to be agreeable to all men, and perhaps, if he had not reserved to himself the liberty of some occasional repose, he would have found the burden of his responsibilities intolerable. It was his maxim that one should never appear to refuse anything to any one, and it is no easy matter to do that, especially when it is necessary never to neglect an opportunity of gaining an advantage for one's self. For the whole aim of Patoff's policy at that time was selfish. He believed that he possessed the secret of power in his own indomitable will, and he cultivated the science of persuasion, until he acquired an infinite art in adapting the means to the end. Every kind of knowledge served him, and though his mind was perhaps not really profound, it was far from being superficial, and the surface of it which he presented when he chose was vast. It was impossible to speak of any question of history, science, ethics, or æsthetics of which Patoff was ignorant, and his information on most points was more than sufficient to help him in artfully indorsing the opinions of those about him. He was full of tact. It was impossible to make him disagree with any one, and yet he was so skillful in his conversation that he was generally thought to have a very sound judgment. His system was substantially one of harmless flattery, and he never departed from it. He reckoned on the unfathomable vanity of man, and he rarely was out in his reckoning; he counted upon woman's admiration of dominating characters, and was not disappointed, for women respected him, and were proportionately delighted when he asked their opinion.

In this, as in all other things, the professor was the precise opposite of the diplomatist. Cutter affected an air of sublime simplicity, and cultivated a straightforward bluntness of expression which was not without weight. He prided himself on saying at once that he either had an opinion upon a subject, or had none; and if he chanced to have formed any judgment he was hot in its support. His intellect was really profound within the limits he had chosen for his activity, and his experience of mankind was varied and singular. He was a man who cared little for detail, except when details tended to elucidate the whole, for his first impressions were accurate and large. With his strong and sanguine nature he exhibited a rough frankness appropriate to his character. He was strong-handed, strong-minded, and strong-tongued; a man who loved to rule others, and who made no secret of it; impatient of contradiction when he stated his views, but sure never to assume a position in argument or in affairs which he did not believe himself able to maintain against all comers.

But with this appearance of hearty honesty the scientist possessed the remarkable quality of discretion, not often found in sanguine temperaments. He loved to understand the secrets of men's lives, and to feel that if need be he could govern people by main force and wholly against their will. He could conceal anything, any knowledge he possessed, any strong passion he felt, with amazing skill. At the very time when he seemed to be most frankly speaking his mind, when he made his honest strength appear as open as the day, as though scorning all concealment and courting inquiry into his motives, he was capable of completely hiding his real intentions, of professing ignorance in matters in which he was profoundly versed, of appearing to be as cold as stone when his heart was as hot as fire. He was a man of violent passions in love and hate, unforgetting and unforgiving, who never relented in the pursuit of an object, nor weighed the cruelty of the means in comparison with the importance of the end. He had by nature a temperament fitted for conspiracy and planned to disarm suspicion. He was incomparably superior to Paul Patoff in powers of mind and in the art of concealment, he was equal to him in the unchanging determination of his will, but he was by far inferior to him in those external gifts which charm the world and command social success.

These two remarkable men had met before they found themselves together under John Carvel's roof, but they did not appear to have been intimate. It was, indeed, very difficult to imagine what their relations could have been, for they occasionally seemed to understand each other perfectly upon matters not understood by the rest of us, whereas they sometimes betrayed a surprising ignorance in regard to each other's affairs.

From the time when the professor arrived it was apparent that Hermione did not like him, and that Cutter was aware of the fact. It had not needed the young girl's own assurance to inform me of the antipathy she felt for the man of science. He had seen her before, but Hermione had suddenly grown into a young lady since his last visit, and the consequence was that she was thrown far more often into the society of the man she disliked than had been the case when she was still in the school-room. John Carvel never liked governesses, and as soon as practicable the last one had been discharged, so that Hermione was left to the society of her mother and aunt and of such visitors as chanced to be staying in the house. She was fond of her brother, but had seen little of him, and stood rather in awe of his superior genius; for Macaulay was a young man who possessed in a very high degree what we call the advantages of modern education. She loved him and looked up to him, but did not understand him in the least, because people who have a great deal of heart do not easily comprehend the nature of people who have little; and Macaulay Carvel's manner of talking about men, and even nations, as though they were mere wooden pawns, or sets of pawns, puzzled his sister's simpler views of humanity. Her mother did not always interest her, either; she was devotedly attached to her, but Mrs. Carvel, as she grew older, became more and more absolved in the strange sort of inner religious life which she had created for herself as a kind of stronghold in the midst of her surroundings, and when alone with her daughter was apt to talk too much upon serious subjects. To a young and beautiful girl, who felt herself entering the vestibule of the world in the glow of a wondrous dawn, the somewhat mournful contemplation of the spiritual future could not possibly have the charm such meditation possessed for a woman in middle age, who had passed through the halls of the palace of life without seeing many of its beauties, and who already, in the dim distance, caught sight of the shadowy gate whereby we must all descend from this world's sumptuous dwelling, to tread the silent labyrinths of the unknown future.

Such society as Mrs. Carvel's was not good for Hermione. It is not good for any girl. It is before all things important that youth should be young, lest it should not know how to be old when age comes upon it. Nor is there anything that should be further removed from youth than the contemplation of death, which to old age is but a haven of rest to be desired, whereas to those who are still young it is an abyss to be abhorred. It is well to say, *Memento, homo, quia pulvis es,"* but not to say it too often, lest the dust of individual human existence make cobwebs in the existence of humanity.

As for her aunt Chrysophrasia, Hermione liked to talk to her, because Miss Dabstreak was amusing, with her everlasting paradoxes upon everything; and because, not being by nature of an evil heart, and desiring to be eccentric beyond her fellows, she was not altogether averse to the mild martyrdom of being thought ridiculous by those who held contrary opinions. Nevertheless, her aunt's company did not satisfy all Hermione's want of society, and the advent of strangers, even of myself, was hailed by her with delight. The fact of her conceiving a particular antipathy for the professor was therefore all the more remarkable, because she rarely shunned the society of any one with whom she had an opportunity of exchanging ideas. But Cutter did not like to be disliked, and he sought an occasion of making her change her mind in regard to him. A few days after my visit to Madame Patoff, the professor found his chance. Macaulay Carvel, Paul Patoff, and I left the house early to ride to a distant meet, for Patoff had expressed his desire to follow the hounds, and, as usual, everybody was anxious to oblige him.

After breakfast the professor watched until he saw Hermione enter the conservatory, where she usually spent a part of the morning alone among the flowers; sometimes making an elaborate inspection of the plants she loved best, sometimes sitting for an hour or two with a book in some remote corner, among the giant tropical leaves and the bright-colored blossoms. She loved not only the flowers, but the warmth of the place, in the bitter winter weather.

Cutter entered with a supremely unconscious air, as though he believed there was no one in the conservatory. There was nothing professorial about his appearance, except his great spectacles, through which he gazed benignly at the luxuriant growth of plants, as he advanced, his hands in the pockets of his plaid shooting-coat. He was dressed as any other man might be in the country; he had selected an unostentatious plaid for the material of his clothes, and he wore a colored tie, which just showed beneath the wave of his thick beard. He trod slowly but firmly, putting his feet down as though prepared to prove his right to the ground he trod on.

"Oh! Are you here, Miss Carvel?" he exclaimed, as he caught sight of Hermione installed in a cane chair behind some plants. She was not much pleased at being disturbed, but she looked up with a slight smile, willing to be civil.

"Since you ask me, I am," she replied.

"Whereas if I had not asked you, you would have affected not to be here, you mean? How odd it is that just when one sees a person one should always ask them if one sees them or not! In this case, I suppose the pleasure of seeing you was so great that I doubted the evidence of my senses. Is that the way to turn a speech?"

"It is a way of turning one, certainly," answered Hermione. "There may be other ways. I have not much experience of people who turn speeches."

"I have had great experience of them," said the professor, "and I confess to you that I consider the practice of turning everything into compliment as a disagreeable and tiresome humbug."

"I was just thinking the same thing," said Hermione.

"Then we shall agree."

"Provided you practice what you preach, we shall."

"Did you ever know me to preach what I did not practice?" asked Cutter, with a smile of honest amusement.

"I have not known much of you, either in preaching or in practicing, as yet. We shall see."

"Shall I begin now?"

"If you like," answered the young girl.

"Which shall it be, preaching or practicing?"

"I should say that, as you have me entirely at your mercy, the opportunity is favorable for preaching."

"I would not make such an unfair use of my advantage," said the professor. "I detest preaching. In practice I never preach" —

"You are making too much conversation out of those two words," interrupted Hermione. "If I let you go on, you will be making puns upon them."

"You do not like puns?"

"I think nothing is more contemptible."

"Merely because that way of being funny is grown old-fashioned," said Cutter. "Fifty or sixty years ago, a hundred years ago, when a man wanted to be very bitingly sarcastic, he would compose a criticism upon his enemy which was only a long string of abominable puns; each pun was printed in italics. That was thought to be very funny."

"You would not imitate that sort of fun, would you?" asked Hermione.

"No. You would think it no joke if I did," answered Cutter, gravely.

"I am not going to laugh," said Hermione. But she laughed, nevertheless.

"Pray do not laugh if you do not want to," said Cutter. "I am used to being thought dull. Your gravity would not wound me though I were chief clown to the whole universe, and yours were the only grave face in the world. By the by, you are laughing, I see. I am much obliged for the appreciation. Shall I go on being funny?"

"Not if you can help it," said Hermione.

"Do you insinuate that I am naturally an object for laughter?" asked Cutter, smiling. "Do you mean that 'I am not only witty in myself, but the cause that wit is in other men'? If so, I may yet make you spend a pleasant hour in despite of yourself, without any great effort on my own part. I will sit here, and you shall laugh at me. The morning will pass very agreeably."

"I should think you might find something better to do," returned Hermione. "But they say that small things amuse great minds."

"If I had a great mind, do you think I should look upon it as a small thing to be laughed at by you, Miss Carvel?" inquired Cutter, quietly.

"You offer yourself so readily to be my laughing-stock that I am forced to consider what you offer a small thing," returned his companion.

"You are exceedingly sarcastic. In that case, I have not a great mind, as you supposed."

"You are fishing for a compliment, I presume."

"Perhaps. I wish you would pay me compliments — in earnest. I am vain. I like to be appreciated. You do not like me, — I should like to be liked by you."

"You are talking nonsense, Professor Cutter," said the young girl, raising her eyebrows a little. "If I did not like you, it would be uncivil of you to say you had found it out, unless I treated you rudely."

"It may be nonsense, Miss Carvel. I speak according to my lights."

"Then I should say that for a luminary of science your light is very limited," returned Hermione.

"In future I will hide my light under a bushel, since it displeases you."

"Something smaller than a bushel would serve the purpose. But it does not please me that you should be in the dark ; I would rather you had more light."

"You have only to look at me," said the scientist, with a laugh.

"I thought you professed not to make silly compliments. My mother tells me that the true light should come from within," added Hermione, with a little scorn.

"Religious enthusiasts, who make those phrases, spend their lives in studying themselves," retorted Cutter. "They think they see light where they most wish to find it. I spend my time in studying other people."

"I should think you would find it vastly more interesting."

"I do; especially when you are one of the people I am permitted to study."

"If you think I will permit it long, you are mistaken," said Hermione, who was beginning to lose her temper, without precisely knowing why. She took up her book and a piece of embroidery she had brought with her, as though she would go.

"You cannot help my making a study of you," returned the professor, calmly. "If you leave me now, I regard it as an interesting feature in your case."

"I will afford you that much interest, at all events," answered Hermione, rising to her feet. She was annoyed, and the blood rose to her delicate cheeks, while her downcast lashes hid the anger in her eyes. But she did not know the man, if she thought he would let himself be treated so lightly. She knew neither him nor his weapons.

"Miss Carvel, permit me to ask your forgiveness," he said. "I am so fond of hearing myself talk that my tongue runs away with me."

"Why do you tease me so?" asked Hermione, suddenly raising her eyes and facing Cutter. But before he could answer her she laid down her work and her book, and walked slowly away from him. She reached the opposite side of the broad conservatory, and turned back.

Cutter's whole manner had changed the moment he saw that she was seriously annoyed. He knew well enough that he had said nothing for which the girl could be legiti-

mately angry, but he understood her antipathy to him too
well not to know that it could easily be excited at any moment to an open expression of dislike. On the present
occasion, however, he had resolved to fathom, if possible,
the secret cause of the feeling the beautiful Hermione entertained against him.

"Miss Carvel," he said, very gently, as she advanced
again towards him, " I like to talk to you, of all people, but
you do not like me, — forgive my saying it, for I am in
earnest, — and I lose my temper because I cannot find out
why."

Hermione stood still for a moment, and looked straight
into the professor's eyes ; she saw that they met hers with
such an honest expression of regret that her heart was
touched. She stooped and picked a flower, and held it in
her hand some seconds before she answered.

"It was I who was wrong," she said, presently. " Let
us be friends. It is not that I do not like you, — really I
believe it is not that. It is that, somehow, you do manage
to — to tease me, I suppose." She blushed. " I am sure
you do not mean it. It is very foolish of me, I know."

" If you could only tell me exactly where my fault lies,"
said Cutter, earnestly, " I am sure I would never commit it
again. You do not seriously believe that I ever intend to
annoy you ? "

"N—no," hesitated Hermione. " No, you do not intend
to annoy me, and yet I think it amuses you sometimes to
see that I am angry about nothing."

" It does not amuse me," said Cutter. " My tongue gets
the better of me, and then I am very sorry afterwards. Let
us be friends, as you say. We have more serious things to
think of than quarreling in our conversation. Say you forgive me, as freely as I say that it has been my fault."

There was something so natural and humble in the way
the man spoke that Hermione had no choice but to put out
her hand and agree to the truce. Professor Cutter was as

old as her father, though he looked ten years younger, or more ; he had a world-wide reputation in more than one branch of science ; he was altogether what is called a celebrated man ; and he stood before her asking to "make friends," as simply as a schoolboy. Hermione had no choice.

"Of course," she answered, and then added with a smile, " only you must really not tease me any more."

" I won't," said Cutter, emphatically.

They sat down again, side by side, and were silent for some moments. It seemed to Hermione as though she had made an important compact, and she did not feel altogether certain of the result. She could have laughed at the idea that her making up her differences with the professor was of any real importance in her life, but nevertheless she felt that it was so, and she was inclined to think over what she had done. Her hands lay folded upon her lap, and she idly gazed at them, and thought how small and white they looked upon the dark blue serge. Cutter spoke first.

" I suppose," he began, " that when we are not concerned with our own immediate affairs, we are all of us thinking of the same thing. Indeed, though we live very much as though nothing were the matter, we are constantly aware that one subject occupies us all alike."

To tell the truth, Hermione was not at that moment thinking of poor Madame Patoff. She raised her eyes with an inquiring glance.

" I am very much preoccupied," continued the professor. " I have not the least idea whether we have done wisely in allowing Paul to see his mother."

" If she knew him, I imagine it was a good thing," answered Hermione. " How long is it since they met ? "

" Eighteen months, or more. They met last in very painful circumstances, I believe. You see the impression was strong enough to outlive her insanity. She was not glad to see him."

" Why will they not tell me what drove her mad ? "
asked Hermione.

" It is not a very nice story," answered the professor.
" It is probably on account of Paul." There was a short
pause.

" Do you mean that she went mad on account of something Paul did ? " asked Hermione presently.

" I am not sure I can tell you that. I wish you could
know the whole story, but your father would never consent
to it, I am sure."

" If it is not nice, I do not wish to hear it," said Hermione, quietly. " I only wanted to know about Paul. You
gave me the impression that it was in some way his fault."

" In some way it was," replied Cutter. " Poor lady, —
I am not sure we should have let her see him."

" Does she suffer much, do you think ? "

" No. If she suffered much, she would fall ill and probably die. I do not think she has any consciousness of her
situation. I have known people like that who were mad
only three or four days in the week. She never has a lucid
moment. I am beginning to think it is hopeless, and we
might as well advise your father to have her taken to a private asylum. The experiment would be interesting."

" Why ? " asked Hermione. " She gives nobody any
trouble here. It would be unkind. She is not violent, nor
anything of that sort. We should all feel dreadfully if anything happened to her in the asylum. Besides, I thought it
was a great thing that she should have known Paul yesterday."

" Not so great as one might fancy. I think that if there
were much chance of her recovery, the recognition of her
son ought to have brought back a long train of memories,
amounting almost to a lucid interval."

" I understood that you had spoken more hopefully last
night," said Hermione, doubtfully. " You seem discour-
aged to-day."

"With most people it is necessary to appear hopeful at any price," answered Cutter. "I feel that with you I am perfectly safe in saying precisely what I think. You will not misinterpret what I say, nor repeat it to every other member of the household."

"No, indeed. I am glad you tell me the truth, but I had hoped it was not as bad as you say."

"Your aunt is very mad indeed, Miss Carvel," said the professor.

I may observe, in passing, that what the professor said to me differed very materially from what he said to Hermione, a circumstance we did not discover until a later date. For Hermione, having given her promise not to repeat what Cutter told her about her aunt, kept it faithfully, and did not even assume an air of superiority when speaking about the case to others. She believed exactly what the professor said, namely, that he trusted her, and no one else, with his true views of the matter; and that, to all others, he assumed an air of hopefulness very far removed from his actual state of mind.

Singularly, — or naturally, as you look at it, — the result of the conversation between Hermione and the professor was the complete disappearance, for some time, of all their differences. Cutter ceased to annoy her with his sharp answers to all she said, and she showed a growing interest in him and in his conversation. They were frequently seen talking together, apparently taking pleasure in each other's society, a fact which I alone noticed as interesting, for Patoff had not been long enough at Carvel Place to discover that there had ever been any antipathy between the two. On looking back, I ascribe the change to the influence Cutter obtained over Hermione by suddenly affecting a great earnestness and a sincere regret for the annoyance he had given in the past, and by admitting her, as he gave her to understand that he did, to his confidence in the matter of Madame Patoff's insanity. Be that as it may, the result

was obtained very easily by the professor; and when Hermione left him, before lunch, it is probable that in the solitude of the conservatory the man of science rubbed his
gigantic hands together, and beamed upon the orchids with
unusual benignity.

But while this new alliance was being formed in the conservatory, another conversation was taking place in a distant part of the house, not less interesting, perhaps, but not
destined to reach so peaceable a conclusion. The scene of
this other meeting was Miss Chrysophrasia Dabstreak's especial boudoir, an apartment so singular in its furniture and
adornment that I will leave out all description of it, and
ask you merely to imagine, at will, the most æsthetic retreat
of the most æsthetic old maid in existence.

After breakfast, that morning, Chrysophrasia had sent
word to Mrs. Carvel that she should be glad to see her, if
she could come up to her boudoir. Chrysophrasia never
came down to breakfast. She regarded that meal as a barbarism, forgetting that the mediæval persons she admired
began their days by taking to themselves a goodly supply of
food. She never appeared before lunch, but spent her
mornings in the solitude of her own apartment, probably in
the composition of verses which have remained hitherto un-
published. Mrs. Carvel at once acceded to the request conveyed in her sister's message, and went to answer the sum-
mons. She was not greatly pleased at the idea of spending
the morning with her sister, for she devoted the early hours
to religious reading whenever she was able; but she was the
most obliging woman in the world, and so she quietly put
aside her own wishes, and mounted the stairs to Miss Dabstreak's boudoir. She found the latter clad in loose garments of strange cut and hue, and a green silk handkerchief
was tied about her forehead, presumably out of respect for
certain concealed curl papers rather than for any direct
purpose of adornment. Chrysophrasia looked very faded in
the morning. As Mrs. Carvel entered the room, her sister

pointed languidly to a chair, and then paused a moment, as though to recover from the exertion.

"Mary," said she at last, and even from the first tone of her voice Mrs. Carvel felt that a severe lecture was imminent, — "Mary, this thing is a hollow sham. It cannot be allowed to go on any longer."

Mrs. Carvel's face assumed a sweet and sad expression, and folding her hands upon her knees, she leaned slightly forward from the chair upon which she sat, and prepared to soothe her sister's views upon hollow shams in general.

"My dear," said she, "you must endeavor to be charitable."

"I do not see the use of being charitable," returned Chrysophrasia, with more energy than she was wont to display. "Dear me, Mary, what in the world has charity to do with the matter? Can you look at me and say that it has anything to do with it?"

No. Mary could not look at her and say so, for a very good reason. She had not the most distant idea what Chrysophrasia was talking about. On general principles, she had made a remark about being charitable, and was now held to account for it. She smiled timidly, as though to deprecate her sister's vengeance.

"Mary," said Chrysophrasia, in a tone of sorrowful rebuke, "I am afraid you are not listening to me."

"Indeed I am," said Mrs. Carvel, patiently.

"Well, then, Mary, I say it is a hollow sham, and that it cannot go on any longer."

"Yes, my dear," assented her sister. "I have no doubt you are right; but what were you referring to as a hollow sham?"

"You are hopeless, Mary, — you have no intuitions. Of course I mean Paul."

Even this was not perfectly clear, and Mrs. Carvel looked inquiringly at her sister.

"Is it possible you do not understand?" asked Chrysophrasia. "Do you propose to allow my niece — my niece, Mary, and your daughter," she repeated with awful emphasis — "to fall in love with her own cousin?"

"I am sure the dear child would never think of such a thing," answered Mary Carvel, very gently, and as though not wishing to contradict her sister. "He has not been here twenty-four hours."

"The dear child is thinking of it at this very moment," said Chrysophrasia. "And what is more, Paul has come here with the deliberate intention of marrying her. I have seen it from the first moment he entered the house. I can see it in his eyes."

"Well, my dear, you may be right. But I have not noticed anything of the sort, and I think you go too far. You will jump at conclusions, Chrysophrasia."

"If I went at them at all, Mary, I would glide, — I certainly would not jump," replied the æsthetic lady, with a languid smile. Mrs. Carvel looked wearily out of the window. "Besides," continued Chrysophrasia, "the thing is quite impossible. Paul is not at all a match. Hermy will be very rich, some day. John will not leave everything to Macaulay: I have heard him say so."

"Why do you discuss the matter, Chrysophrasia?" objected Mrs. Carvel, with a little shade of very mild impatience. "There is no question of Hermy marrying Paul."

"Then Paul ought to go away at once."

"We cannot send him away. Besides, I think he is a very good fellow. You forget that poor Annie is in the house, and he has a right to see her, at least for a week."

"It seems to me that Annie might go and live with him."

"He has no home, poor fellow, — he is in the diplomatic service. He is made to fly from Constantinople to Persia, and from Persia to St. Petersburg; how could he take poor Annie with him?"

"If poor Annie chose," said Chrysophrasia, sniffing the

air with a disagreeable expression, "poor Annie could go. If she has sense enough to dress herself gorgeously and to read dry books all day, she has sense enough to travel."

"Oh, Chrysophrasia! How dreadfully unkind you are! You know how — ill she is."

Mrs. Carvel did not like to pronounce the word "insane." She always spoke of Madame Patoff's "illness."

"I do not believe it," returned Miss Dabstreak. "She is no more crazy than I am. I believe Professor Cutter knows it, too. Only he has been used to saying that she is mad for so long that he will not believe his senses, for fear of contradicting himself."

"In any case I would rather trust to him than to my own judgment."

"I would not. I am utterly sick of this perpetual disturbance about Annie's state of mind. It destroys the charm of a peaceful existence. If I had the strength, I would go to her and tell her that I know she is perfectly sane, and that she must leave the house. John is so silly about her. He turns the place into an asylum, just because she chooses to hold her tongue."

Mrs. Carvel rose with great dignity.

"I will leave you, Chrysophrasia," she said. "I cannot bear to hear you talk in this way. You really ought to be more charitable."

"You are angry, Mary," replied her sister. "Good-by. I cannot bear the strain of arguing with you. When you are calmer you will remember what I have said."

Poor Mrs. Carvel certainly exhibited none of the ordinary symptoms of anger, as she quietly left the room, with an expression of pain upon her gentle face. When Chrysophrasia was very unreasonable her only course was to go away ; for she was wholly unable to give a rough answer, or to defend herself against her sister's attacks. Mary went in search of her husband, and was glad to find him in the library, among his books.

"John dear, may I come in?" asked Mrs. Carvel, opening the door of her husband's library, and standing on the threshold.

"By all means," exclaimed John, looking up. "Anything wrong?" he inquired, observing the expression of his wife's face.

"John," said Mrs. Carvel, coming near to him and laying her hand gently on his shoulder, "tell me — do you think there is likely to be anything between Paul and Hermy?"

"Gracious goodness! what put that into your head?" asked Carvel.

"I have been with Chrysophrasia" — began Mary.

"Chrysophrasia! Oh! Is that it?" cried John in discontented tones. "I wish Chrysophrasia would mind her own business, and not talk nonsense!"

"It is nonsense, is it not?"

"Of course, — absolute rubbish! I would not hear of it, to begin with!" he exclaimed, as though that were sufficient evidence that the thing was impossible.

"No, indeed," echoed Mrs. Carvel, but in more doubtful tones. "Of course, Paul is a very good fellow. But yet"— She hesitated. "After all, they are cousins," she added suddenly, "and that is a great objection."

"I hope you will not think seriously of any such marriage, Mary," said John Carvel, with great decision. "They are cousins, and there are twenty other reasons why they should not marry."

"Are there? I dare say you are right, and of course there is no probability of either of them thinking of such a thing. But after all, Paul is a very marriageable fellow, John."

"I would not consent to his marrying my daughter, though," returned Carvel. "I have no doubt it is all right about his brother, who disappeared on a dark night in Constantinople. But I would not let Hermy marry anybody who had such a story connected with his name."

"Surely, John, you are not so unkind as to give any weight to that spiteful accusation. It was very dreadful, but there never was the slightest ground for believing that Paul had a hand in it. Even Professor Cutter, who does not like him, always said so. That was one of the principal proofs of poor Annie's madness."

"I know, my dear. But to the end of time people will go on asking where Paul's brother is, and will look suspicious when he is mentioned. Cutter, whom you quote, says the same thing, though he believes Paul perfectly innocent, as I do myself. Do you suppose I would have a man in the house whom I suspected of having murdered his brother?"

"What a dreadful idea!" exclaimed Mrs. Carvel. "But if you liked him very much, and wanted him to marry Hermy, would you let that silly bit of gossip stand in the way of the match?"

"I don't know what I should do. Perhaps not. But Hermy shall marry whom she pleases, provided she marries a gentleman. She has no more idea of marrying Paul than Chrysophrasia has, or than Paul has of marrying her. Besides, she is far too young to think of such things."

"Really, John, Hermy is nineteen. She is nearly twenty."

"My dear," retorted Carvel, "you will make me think you want them to marry."

"Nonsense, John!"

"Well, nonsense, if you like. But Chrysophrasia has been putting this ridiculous notion into your head. I believe she is in love with Paul herself."

"Oh, John!" exclaimed Mrs. Carvel, smiling at the idea.

But John rose from his chair, and indulged in a hearty laugh at the thought of Chrysophrasia's affection for Patoff. Then he stirred the fire vigorously, till the coals broke into a bright blaze.

"Annie is better," he said presently, without looking

round. "You know she recognized Paul; and Griggs thought she knew him, too, when he went in with Cutter, the other night."

"Would you like me to go and see her to-day?" asked Mrs. Carvel. Her husband had already told her the news and seemed to be repeating it now out of sheer satisfaction.

"Perhaps she may know you," he answered. "Have you seen Mrs. North this morning?"

"Yes. She says Annie has not slept very well since that day."

"The meeting excited her. Better wait a day or two longer, before doing anything else. At any rate, we ought to ask Cutter before making another experiment."

"Why did you not go to the meet to-day?" asked Mrs. Carvel suddenly.

"I wanted to have a morning at my books," answered John. His wife took the answer as a hint to go away, and presently left the room, feeling that her mind had been unnecessarily troubled by her sister. But in her honest self-examination, when she had returned to her own room and to the perusal of Jeremy Taylor's sermons, she acknowledged to herself that she had a liking for Paul Patoff, and that she could not understand why both her sister and her husband should at the very beginning scout the idea of his marrying Hermione. Of course there was not the slightest reason for supposing that Hermione liked him at all, but there was nothing to show that she would not like him hereafter.

Late in the afternoon we three came back from our long day with the hounds, hungry and thirsty and tired. When I came down from my room to get some tea, I found that Patoff had been quicker than I; he was already comfortably installed by the fireside, with Fang at his feet, while Hermione sat beside him. Mrs. Carvel was at the tea-table, at some little distance, with her work in her hands, but neither John nor Chrysophrasia was in the room. As I sat down and began to drink my tea, I watched Paul's face, and it seemed to me that he had changed since I had seen him in Teheran, six months ago. I had not liked him much. I am not given to seeking acquaintance, and had certainly not sought his, but in the Persian capital one necessarily knew every one in the little European colony, and I had met him frequently. I had then been struck by the stony coldness which appeared to underlie his courteous manner, and I had thought it was part of the strange temper he was said to possess. Treating his colleagues and all whom he met with the utmost affability, never sullenly silent and often even brilliant in conversation, he nevertheless had struck me as a man who hated and despised his fellow-creatures. There had been then a sort of scornful, defiant look on his large features, which inevitably repelled a stranger until he began to talk. But he understood eminently the science of making himself agreeable, and, when he chose, few could so well lead conversation without imposing themselves upon their hearers. I well remembered the disdainful coldness of his face when he was listening to some one else, and I recollected how oddly it contrasted with his courteous forbearing speech. He would look at a man who made a remark with a cynical stare, and then in the very next moment would agree with him, and produce excellent arguments for doing so. One felt that the man's own nature was at war with itself, and that, while forcing himself to be sociable, he despised society. It was a thing so evident that I used to avoid looking at him, because his expression was so unpleasant.

But as I saw him seated by Hermione's side, playing with the great hound at his feet, and talking quietly with his companion, I was forcibly struck by the change. His face could not be said to have softened ; but instead of the cold, defiant sneer which had formerly been peculiar to him, his look was now very grave, and from time to time a pleasant light passed quickly over his features. Watching him now,

I could not fancy him either violent or eccentric in temper, as he was said to be. It was as though the real nature of the man had got the better of some malady.

"This is like home," I heard him say. "How happy you must be!"

"Yes, I am very happy," answered Hermione. "I have only one unhappiness in my life."

"What is that?"

"Poor aunt Annie," said the girl. "I am so dreadfully sorry for her." The words were spoken in a low tone, and Mrs. Carvel said something to me just then, so that I could not hear Patoff's answer. But while talking with my hostess I noticed his earnest manner, and that he seemed to be telling some story which interested Hermione intensely. His voice dropped to lower key, and I heard no more, though he talked for a long time, as I thought. Then Macaulay Carvel and Professor Cutter entered the room. I saw Cutter look at the pair by the fire, and, after exchanging a few words with Mrs. Carvel, he immediately joined them. Paul's face assumed suddenly the expression of stony indifference, once so familiar to me, and I did not hear his voice again. It struck me that his more gentle look might have been wholly due to the pleasure he took in Hermione's society; but I dismissed the idea as improbable.

Macaulay sat down by his mother, and began telling the incidents of the day's hunting in his smooth, unmodulated voice. He was altogether smooth and unmodulated in appearance, in conversation, and in manner, and he reminded me more of a model schoolboy, rather vain of his acquirements and of the favor he enjoyed in the eyes of his masters, than of a grown Englishman. It would be impossible to imagine a greater contrast than that which existed between the two cousins, and, little as I was inclined to like Patoff at first, I was bound to acknowledge that he was more manly, more dignified, and altogether more attractive than Macaulay Carvel. It was strange that the sturdy, active,

intelligent John should have such a son, although, on looking at the mother, one recognized the sweet smile and gentle features, the dutiful submission and quiet feminine for-
bearance, which in her face so well expressed her character.

But in spite of the vast difference between them in temperament, appearance, and education, Macaulay was destined to play a small part in Patoff's life. He had from
the first taken a fancy to his big Russian cousin, and admired him with all his heart. Paul seemed to be his ideal,
probably because he differed so much from himself; and
though Macaulay felt it was impossible to imitate him, he
was content to give him his earnest admiration. It was to
be foreseen that if Paul fell in love with Hermione he would
find a powerful ally in her brother, who was prepared to say
everything good about him, and to extol his virtues to the
skies. Indeed, it was likely that during their short acquaintance Macaulay had only seen the best points in his cousin's
character; for the principal sins imputed to Patoff were his
violence of temper and his selfishness, and it appeared to
me that he had done much to overcome both since I had
last seen him. It is probable that in the last analysis, if
this reputation could have been traced to its source, it would
have been found to have arisen from the gossip concerning
his quarrel with his brother in Constantinople, and from his
having once or twice boxed the ears of some lazy Persian
servant in Teheran. None of the Carvel family knew much
of Paul's antecedents. His mother never spoke, and before
she was brought home in her present state, by Professor
Cutter, there had been hardly any communication between
her and her sisters since her marriage. Time had effaced
the remembrance of what they had called her folly when
she married Patoff, but the breach had never been healed.
Mrs. Carvel had made one or two efforts at reconciliation,
but they had been coldly received; she was a timid woman,
and soon gave up the attempt. It was not till poor Madame Patoff was brought home hopelessly insane, and Ma-

caulay had conceived an unbounded admiration for his
cousin, that the old affection was revived, and transferred
in some degree to this son of the lost sister.

As I sat with Mrs. Carvel listening to Macaulay's nerveless, conscientious description of the day's doings, I thought
over all these things, and wondered what would happen next.

The days passed much as usual at Carvel Place after the
first excitement of Paul's arrival had worn off; but I regretted that I saw less of Hermione than formerly, though
I found Cutter's society very interesting. Remembering
my promise to see Madame Patoff again, I visited her once
more, but, to my great disappointment, she seemed to have
forgotten me ; and though I again spoke to her in Russian,
she gave no answer to my questions, and after a quarter of
an hour I retired, much shaken in my theory that she was
not really as mad as was supposed. It was reserved for
some one else to break the spell, if it could be broken at
all, and I felt the hopelessness of making any further attempt. Though I was not aware of it at the time, I afterwards learned that Paul visited her again within a week of
his arrival. She behaved very much as on the first occasion,
it appears, except that her manner was more violent than
before, so that Cutter deemed it imprudent to repeat the
experiment.

One morning, three weeks after the events last recorded,
I was walking with Hermione in the garden. She was as
fond of me as ever, though we now saw little of each
other. But this morning she had seen me alone among the
empty flower-beds, smoking a solitary cigar after breakfast,
and, having nothing better to do, she wrapped herself in
a fur cloak and came out to join me. For a few minutes
we talked of the day, and of the prospect of an early spring,
though we were still in January. People always talk of
spring before the winter is half over. I said I wondered
whether Paul would stay to the end of the hunting season.

"I hope so," said Hermione.

"By the by," I remarked, "you seem to have overcome your antipathy for your cousin. You are very good friends."

"Yes, he is interesting," she answered. "I wonder"—She paused, and looked at me rather wistfully. "Have you known him long?" she asked, suddenly.

"Not very long."

"Do you know anything of his past life?"

"Nothing," I answered. "Nobody does, I fancy, unless it be Professor Cutter."

"He has been very unhappy, I should think," she said, presently.

"Has he? Has he told you so?" I resented the idea of Paul's confiding his woes, if he had any, to the lovely girl I had known from a child. It is too common a way of making love.

"No — that is — yes. He told me about his childhood; how his brother was the favorite, and he was always second best, and it made him very unhappy."

"Indeed!" I ejaculated, indifferently enough. I knew nothing about his brother except that he was dead, or had disappeared and was thought to be dead. The story had never reached my ears, and I did not know anything about the circumstances.

"How did his brother die?" I asked.

"Oh, he is dead," answered Hermione gravely. "He died in the East eighteen months ago. Aunt Annie worshiped him; it was his death that affected her mind. At least, I believe so. Professor Cutter says it is something else, — something connected with cousin Paul; but papa seems to think it was Alexander's death."

"What does the professor say?" I inquired.

"He will not tell me. He is a very odd person. He says it is something about Paul, and that it is not nice, and that papa would not like me to know it. And then papa tells me that it was only Alexander's death."

"That is very strange," I said. "If I were you, I would believe your father rather than the professor."

"Of course; how could I help believing papa?" Hermione turned her beautiful blue eyes full upon my face, as though wondering at the simplicity of my remark. Of course she believed her father.

"You would not think Paul capable of doing anything not nice, would you?" I asked.

Hermione blushed, and looked away towards the distant woods.

"I think he is very nice," she said.

I am Hermione's old friend, but I saw that I had no right to press her with questions. No friendship gives a man the right to ask the confidence of a young girl, and, moreover, it was evident from her few words and from the blush which accompanied them that this was a delicate subject. If any one were to speak to her, it must be her father. As far as I knew, there was no reason why she should not love her cousin P..ul, if she admired him half as much as her brother was inclined o do.

"There is only one thing about him which I cannot understand," she continued, after a short pause. "He seems not to care in the least for his mother; and yet," she added thoughtfully, "I cannot believe that he is heartless. I suppose it is because she did not treat him well when he was a child. I cannot think of any other reason."

"No," I echoed mechanically, "I cannot think of any other reason."

And indeed I could not. I had known nothing of his unhappy childhood before Hermione had told me of it, and though that did not afford a sufficient explanation of his evident indifference in regard to his mother, it was better than nothing. The whole situation seemed to me to be wrapped in impenetrable mystery, and I was beginning to despair of ever understanding what was going on about me. John Carvel treated me most affectionately, and delighted in entrapping me into the library to talk about books; but he scarcely ever referred to Madame Patoff. Cutter would walk or ride with me for hours, talking over the extraordinary cases of insanity he had met with in his experience; but he never would give me the least information in regard to the events which had preceded the accident at Weissenstein. I was entirely in the dark.

A catastrophe was soon to occur, however, which led to my acquaintance with all the details of Alexander's disappearance in Stamboul. I will tell what happened as well as I can from what was afterwards told me by the persons most concerned.

A week after my conversation with Hermione, the train was fired which led to a very remarkable concatenation of circumstances. You have foreseen that Paul would fall in love with his beautiful young cousin. Chrysophrasia foresaw it from the first moment of his appearance at Carvel Place, with that keen scent for romance which sometimes characterizes romantic old maids. If I were telling you a love story, I could make a great deal out of Paul's courtship. But this is the history of the extraordinary things which befell Paul Patoff, and for the present it is sufficient to say that he was in love with Hermione, and that he had never before cared seriously for any woman. He was cold by nature, and his wandering life as a diplomatist, together with his fixed determination to excel in his career, had not been favorable to the development of love in his heart. The repose of Carvel Place, the novelty of the life, and the comparative freedom from all responsibility, had relaxed the hard shell of his sensibilities, and the beauty and grace of Hermione had easily fascinated him. She, on her part, had distinguished with a woman's natural instinct the curious duality of his character. The grave, powerful, dominating man attracted her very forcibly; the cold, impenetrable, apparently heartless soul, on the other hand, repelled her, and almost inspired her with horror when it showed itself.

One afternoon in the end of January, Paul and Hermione were walking in the park. The weather was raw and gusty, and the ground hard frozen. They had been merely strolling up and down before the house, as they often did, but, being in earnest conversation, had forgotten at last to turn back, and had gone on along the avenue, till they were far from the old mansion and quite out of sight. They had been talking of Paul's approaching departure, and they were both in low spirits at the prospect.

"I am like those patches of snow," said Paul. "The clouds drop me in a beautiful place, and I feel very comfortable; and then I have to melt away again, and the clouds pick me up and carry me a thousand miles off, and drop me somewhere else. I wish they would leave me alone for a while."

"Yes," said Hermione. "I wish you could stay with us longer."

"It is of no use to wish," answered Paul bitterly. "I am always wishing for things I cannot possibly have. I would give anything to stay here. I have grown so fond of you all, and you have all been so kind to me — it is very hard to go, Hermione!"

He looked almost tenderly at the beautiful girl beside him, as he spoke. But she looked down, so that he could hardly see her face at all.

"I have never before felt as though I were at home," he continued. "I never had much of a home, at the best. Latterly I have had none at all. I had almost forgotten the idea when I came to England. It is hard to think how soon I must forget it again, and all the dear people I have known here."

"You must not quite forget us," said Hermione. Her voice trembled a little.

"I will never forget you — Hermione — for I love you with all my heart."

He took her little gloved hand in his, and held it tightly.

They stood still in the midst of the lonely park. Hermione blushed like an Alp-rose in the snow, and turned her head away from him. But her lip quivered slightly, and she left her hand in his.

"I love you, my darling," he repeated, drawing her to him, till her head rested for a moment on his shoulder. " I cannot live without you, — I cannot leave you."

What could she do? When he spoke in that tone his voice was so very gentle; she loved him, and she was under the fascination of his love. She said nothing, but she looked up into his face, and her blue eyes saw themselves in his. Then she bent her head and hid her face against his coat, and her small hand tightened convulsively upon his fingers.

"Do you really love me?" he asked as he bent down and kissed her white forehead.

"You know I do," she answered in a low voice.

That was all they said, I suppose. But it was quite enough. When a man and a woman have told each other their love, there is little more to say. They probably say it again, and repeat it in different keys and with different modulations. I can imagine that a man in love might find many pretty expressions, but the gist of the thing is the same. Model conversation as follows, in fugue form, for two voices : —

He. I love you. Do you love me? (Theme.)

She. Very much. I love you more than you love me. (Answer.)

He. No. I love you most. (Sub-theme.)

She. Not more. That is impossible. (Sub-answer.)

He and She. Then we love each other very much. (*A due voci.*)

She. Yes. But I am not sure that you *can* love me as much as I do you. (*Stretto.*) Etc., etc., etc.

By using these simple themes you may easily write a series of conversations in at least twenty-four keys, on the principle of Bach's Wohltemperirtes Klavier, but your

fugues must be composed for two voices only, unless you
are very clever. A third voice increases the difficulty, a
fourth causes a high degree of complication, five voices are
distracting, and six impossible.

It is certain that when Paul and Hermione returned from
their walk they had arranged matters to their own satisfaction, or had at least settled the preliminaries. I think
every one noticed the change in their manner. Hermione
was radiant, and talked better than I had ever heard her
talk before. Paul was quiet, even taciturn, but his silence
was evidently not due to bad temper. His expression was
serene and happy, and the cold look seemed to have left his
face forever. His peace of mind, however, was destined to
be shortlived.

Chrysophrasia and Professor Cutter watched the couple
with extreme interest when they appeared at tea, and each
arrived at the same conclusion. They had probably expected for a long time what had now occurred, and, as they
were eagerly looking for some evidence that their convictions were well founded, they did not overlook the sudden
change of manner which succeeded the walk in the park.
They did not communicate their suspicions to each other,
however. Chrysophrasia had protested again and again to
Mary Carvel and to John that things were going too far.
But Paul was a favorite with the Carvels, and they refused
to see anything in his conduct which could be interpreted to
mean love for Hermione. Chrysophrasia resolved at once
to throw a bomb into the camp, and to enjoy the effect of
the explosion.

Cutter's position was more delicate. He was very fond
of John, and was, moreover, his guest. It was not his business to criticise what occurred in the house. He was profoundly interested in Madame Patoff, but he did not like
Paul. Indeed, in his inmost heart he had never settled the
question of Alexander's disappearance from the world, and
in his opinion Paul Patoff was a man accused of murder,

who had not sufficiently established his innocence. In his desire to be wholly unprejudiced in judging mankind and their mental aberrations, he did not allow that the social position of the individual was in itself a guaranty against committing any crime whatever. On the contrary, he had found reason to believe, from his own experience, that people belonging to the higher classes have generally a much keener appreciation of the construction which will be put upon their smallest actions, and are therefore far more ingenious in concealing their evil deeds than the common ruffian could possibly be. John Carvel would have said that it was impossible that a gentleman should murder his brother. Professor Cutter said it was not only possible, but, under certain circumstances, very probable. It must also be remembered that he had got most of his information concerning Paul from Madame Patoff and from Alexander, who both detested him, in the two summers when he had met the mother and son at Wiesbaden. His idea of Paul's character had therefore received a bias from the first, and was to a great extent unjust. Conceiving it possible that Patoff might be responsible for his brother's death, he therefore regarded the prospect of Paul's marriage with Hermione with the strongest aversion, though he could not make up his mind to speak to John Carvel on the subject. He had told the whole story to him eighteen months earlier, when he had brought home Madame Patoff; and he had told it without ornament, leaving John to judge for himself. But at that time there had been no prospect whatever of Paul's coming to Carvel Place. Cutter might easily have turned his story in such a way as to make Paul look guilty, or at least so as to cast a slight upon his character. But he had given the plain facts as they occurred. John had said the thing was absurd, and a great injustice to the young man; and he had, moreover, told his wife and sister, as well as Cutter, that Hermione was never to know anything of the story. It was not right, he said, that the young girl should ever know that any member of the family had even been suspected of such a crime. She should grow up in ignorance of it, and it was not untruthful to say that Madame Patoff's insanity had been caused by Alexander's death.

But now Cutter regretted that he had not put the matter in a stronger light from the first, giving John to understand that Paul had never really cleared himself of the imputation. The professor did not know what to do, and would very likely have done nothing at all, had Miss Dabstreak not fired the mine. He had, indeed, endeavored to stop the progress of the attachment, but, in attempting always to intervene as a third person in their conversations, he had roused Paul's obstinacy instead of interrupting his love-making. And Paul was a very obstinate man.

As we sat at dinner that evening, the conversation turned upon general topics. Chrysophrasia sat opposite to Paul, as usual, and her green eyes watched him with interest for some time. As luck would have it, our talk approached the subject of crime in general, and John Carvel asked me some question about the average number of murders in India, taking ten years together, as compared with the number committed in Europe. While I was hesitating and trying to recollect some figures I had once known, Chrysophrasia rushed into the conversation in her usual wild way.

"I think murders are so extremely interesting," said she to Patoff. "I always wonder what it must be like to commit one, don't you?"

"No," said Paul, quietly. "I confess that I do not generally devote much thought to the matter. Murder is not a particularly pleasant subject for contemplation."

"Oh, do you think so?" answered Chrysophrasia. "Of course not pleasant, no, but so very interesting. I read such a delightfully thrilling account this morning of a man who killed his own brother, — quite like Cain."

Paul made no answer, and continued to eat his dinner in silence. Though at that time I knew nothing of his story, I remember noticing how Professor Cutter slowly turned his face towards Patoff, and the peculiar expression of his gray eyes as I saw them through the gold-rimmed spectacles. Then he looked at John Carvel, who grew very red in the pause which followed. Mrs. Carvel looked down at her plate, and her features showed that her sister's remark had given her some pain ; for she was quite incapable of concealing her slightest emotions, like many extremely truthful and sensitive people. But Chrysophrasia had launched herself, and was not to be silenced by an awkward pause. Not understanding the situation in the least, I nevertheless tried to relieve the unpleasantness by answering her.

"I think it is a great mistake that the newspapers should publish the horrible details of every crime committed," I said. "It is bad for the public morals, and worse for the public taste."

"Really, we must be allowed some emotion," answered Chrysophrasia. "It is so very thrilling to read about such cases. Now I can quite well imagine what it must be like to kill somebody, and then to hear every one saying to me, 'Where is thy brother?' Poor Cain! He must have had the most deliciously complicated feelings!"

She fixed her green eyes on Paul so intently as she spoke that I looked at him, too, and was surprised to see that he was very pale. He said nothing, however, but he looked up and returned her gaze. His cold blue eyes glittered disagreeably. At that moment, John Carvel, who was redder than ever, addressed me in loud tones. I thought his voice had an artificial ring in it as he spoke.

"Well, Griggs," he cried, "without going into the question of Cain and Abel, can you tell me anything about the figures?"

I said something. I gave some approximate account, and, speaking loudly, I ran on readily with a long string of statistics, most of them, I grieve to say, manufactured on the spur of the moment. But I knew that Carvel was not lis-

tening, and did not care what I said. Hermione was watching Paul with evident concern; Mrs. Carvel and Macaulay
at once affected the greatest interest in what I was saying,
while Professor Cutter looked at Chrysophrasia, as though
trying to attract her attention.

"What a wonderful memory you have, Mr. Griggs!"
said Macaulay Carvel, in sincere admiration.

"Oh, not at all," I answered, with perfect truth. "Statistics of that kind are very easily got."

By this time the awkwardness had disappeared, and by
dint of talking very loud and saying a great many things
which meant very little, John and I succeeded in making
the remainder of the dinner pass off very well. But every
one seemed to be afraid of Chrysophrasia, and when, once
or twice, she was on the point of making a remark, there
was a general attempt made to prevent her from leading the
conversation. As soon as dinner was over we scattered in
all directions, like a flock of sheep. Chrysophrasia retired
to her room. John Carvel went to the library, whither his
wife followed him in a few minutes. Macaulay, Patoff, and
I went to the smoking-room, contrary to all precedent;
but as Macaulay led the way, we followed with delight.
The result of this general separation was that Hermione
and Professor Cutter were left alone in the drawing-room.

"I want to ask you a question," said the young girl, as
they stood before the great fireplace.

"Yes," answered the scientist, anticipating trouble. "I
am at your service."

"Why did Paul turn so pale when aunt Chrysophrasia
talked about Cain at dinner, and why did everybody feel so
uncomfortable?"

"It is not surprising. But I cannot tell you the story."

"You must," said Hermione, growing pale, and laying
her hand upon his arm. "I must know. I insist that you
shall tell me."

"If I tell you, will you promise not to blame me hereafter?" asked Cutter.

"Certainly, — of course. Please go on."

"Do not be shocked. There is no truth in the story, I fancy. When Alexander Patoff was lost on a dark night in Constantinople, the world said that Paul had made away with him. That is all."

Hermione did not scream nor faint, as Cutter had expected. The blood rushed to her face, and then sank again as suddenly. She steadied herself with one hand on the chimney-piece before she answered.

"What a horrible, infamous lie!" she exclaimed in low tones.

"You insisted upon knowing it, Miss Carvel," said the professor quietly. "You must not blame me for telling you. After all, it was as well that you should know it."

"Yes — it was as well." She turned away, and with bent head left the room. So it came about that both Chrysophrasia and Cutter on the same evening struck a blow at the new-found happiness of the cousins, raising between them, as it were, the spectre of the lost man.

After what had occurred in the afternoon, Paul had intended to seek a formal interview with John Carvel. He had no intention of keeping his engagement a secret, and indeed he already felt that, according to his European notions, he had done wrong in declaring his love to Hermione before asking her father's consent. It had been an accident, and he regretted it. But after the scene at the dinner-table, he felt that he must see Hermione again before going to her father. Chrysophrasia's remarks had been so evidently directed against him that he had betrayed himself, and he knew that Hermione had noticed his expression, as well as the momentary stupefaction which had chilled the whole party. He had no idea whether Hermione had ever heard his story or not. She had of course never referred to it, and he thought it was now his duty to speak to her, to ascertain the extent of her information, and, if necessary, to tell her all the circumstances; honestly avowing that, although he had never been accused openly of his brother's death except by his mother, he knew that many persons had suspected him of having been voluntarily concerned in it. He would state the case plainly, and she might then decide upon her own course. But the question, " Where is your brother ? " had been asked again, and he was deeply wounded, — far more deeply than he would acknowledge to himself. As we three sat together in the smoking-room, keeping up a dry, strained conversation, the old expression returned to his face, and I watched him with a kind of regret as I saw the cold, defiant look harden again, where lately there had been nothing but gentleness.

Hermione left the drawing-room, and glided through the hall towards the passage which led to Madame Patoff's rooms. She had formed a desperate resolution, — one of those which must be carried out quickly, or not at all. Mrs. North, the nurse, opened the door at the end of the corridor, and admitted the young girl.

"Can I see my aunt ? " asked Hermione, trying to control her voice.

" Has anything happened, Miss Carvel ? " inquired Mrs. North, scrutinizing her features and noticing her paleness.

" No — yes, dear Mrs. North, something has happened. I want to see aunt Annie," answered Hermione. " Do let me go in ! "

The nurse did not suppose that anything Hermione could say would rouse Madame Patoff from her habitual apathy. After a moment's hesitation, she nodded, and opened the door into the sitting-room. Hermione passed her in silence, and entered, closing the door behind her. Her aunt sat as usual in a deep chair near the fire, beneath the brilliant light, the rich folds of her sweeping gown gathered around her, her face pale and calm, holding a book upon her knee. She did not look up as the young girl came in, but an uneasy expression passed over her features. Hermione had never believed that Madame Patoff was mad, in spite of

Professor Cutter's assurances to the contrary. On this occasion she resolved to speak as though her aunt were perfectly sane.

"Dear aunt Annie," she began, sitting down beside the deep chair, and laying her hand on Madame Patoff's apathetic fingers, — "dear aunt Annie, I have something to tell you, and I am sure you will listen to me."

"Yes," answered the lady, in her mechanical voice.

"Aunt Annie, Paul is still here. I love him, and we are going to be married."

"No," said Madame Patoff, in the same tone as before. Hermione's heart sank, for her aunt did not seem to understand in the least. But before she could speak again, a curious change seemed to come over the invalid's face. The features were drawn into an expression of pain, such as Hermione had never seen there before, the lip trembled hysterically, the blood rushed to her face, and Madame Patoff suddenly broke into a fit of violent weeping. The tears streamed down her cheeks, bursting between her fingers as she covered her eyes. She sobbed as though her heart would break, rocking herself backwards and forwards in her chair. Hermione was frightened, and rose to call Mrs. North; but to her extreme surprise her aunt put out her hand, all wet with tears, and held her back.

"No, no," she moaned; "let me cry."

For several minutes nothing was heard in the room but her passionate sobs. It seemed as though they would never stop, and again Hermione would have called the nurse, but again Madame Patoff prevented her.

"Aunt Annie, — dear aunt Annie!" said the young girl, trying to soothe her, and laying her hand upon the thick gray hair. "What is the matter? Can I do nothing? I cannot bear to see you cry like this!"

Gradually the hysteric emotion spent itself, and Madame Patoff grew more calm. Then she spoke, and, to Hermione's amazement, she spoke connectedly.

"Hermione, you must not betray my secret, — you will not betray me? Swear that you will not, my child!" She was evidently suffering some great emotion.

"Aunt Annie," said Hermione in the greatest excitement, "you are not mad! I always said you were not!"

Madame Patoff shook her head sorrowfully.

"No, child, I am not mad, — I never was. I am only unhappy. I let them think so, because I am so miserable, and I can live alone, and perhaps die very soon. But you have found me out."

Again it seemed as though she would burst into tears. Hermione hastened to reassure her, not knowing what she said, in the anxiety of the moment.

"You are safe with me, aunt Annie. I will not tell. But why, why have you deceived them all so long, a year and a half, — why?"

"I am the most wretched woman alive," moaned Madame Patoff. Then, looking suddenly into Hermione's eyes, she spoke in low, distinct tones. "You cannot marry Paul, Hermione. You must never think of it again. You must promise me never to think of it."

"I will not promise that," answered the young girl, summoning all her courage. "It is not true that he killed his brother. You never believed it, — nobody ever believed it!"

"It is true — true — truer than anything else can be!" exclaimed Madame Patoff, lowering her voice to a strong, clear whisper.

"No," said Hermione. "You are wrong, aunt Annie; it is an abominable lie."

"I tell you I know it is true," retorted her aunt, still whispering, but emphasizing every word with the greatest decision. "If you do not believe it, go to him and say, 'Paul, where is your brother?' and you will see how he will look."

"I will. I will ask him, and I will tell you what he says."

" He murdered him, Hermione," continued Madame Patoff, not heeding the interruption. " He murdered him in Constantinople, — he and a Turkish soldier whom he hired. And now he has come here to marry you. He thinks I am mad — he is the worst man that ever lived. You must never see him again. There is blood on his hands — blood, do you hear ? Rather than that you should love him, I will tell them all that I am a sane woman. I will confess that I have imposed upon them in order to be alone, to die in peace, or, while I live to mourn for my poor murdered boy, '—the boy I loved. Oh how I loved him ! "

This time her tears could not be controlled, and at the thought of Alexander she sobbed again, as she had sobbed before. Hermione was too much astonished and altogether thrown off her mental balance to know what to do. Her amazement at discovering that her aunt had for more than a year imposed upon Professor Cutter and upon the whole household was almost obliterated in the horror inspired by Madame Patoff's words. There was a conviction in her way of speaking which terrified Hermione, and for a moment she was completely unnerved.

Meanwhile, Madame Patoff's tears ceased again. In the strange deception she had practiced upon all around her for so long, she had acquired an extraordinary command of her features and voice. It was only Hermione's discovery which had thrown her off her guard, and once feeling that the girl knew her secret, she had perhaps enjoyed the luxury of tears and of expressed emotion. But this stage being past, she regained her self-control. She had meditated so long on the death of her eldest son that the mention of his name had ceased to affect her, and though she had been betrayed into recognizing Paul, she had cleverly resumed her play of apathetic indifference so soon as he had left her. Had Hermione known of the early stages which had led to her present state, she would have asked herself how Madame Patoff could have suddenly begun to act her part so well as to deceive even Professor Cutter from the first. But Hermione knew nothing of all those details. She only realized that her aunt was a perfectly sane woman, and that she had fully confirmed the fearful accusation against Paul.

"Go now, my child," said Madame Patoff. "Remember your promise. Remember that I am a wretched old woman, come here to be left alone, to die. Remember what I have told you, and beware of being deceived. You love a murderer — a murderer — remember that."

Hermione stood a moment and gazed at her aunt's face, grown calm and almost beautiful again. Her tears had left no trace, her thick gray hair was as smooth as ever, her great dark eyes were deep and full of light. Then, without another word, the young girl turned away and left the room, closing the door behind her, and nodding a good-night to Mrs. North, who sat by her lamp in the outer room, gray and watchful as ever.

If her aunt was sane, was she human? The question suggested itself to Hermione's brain as she walked along the passage; but she had not time to frame an answer. As she went out into the hall she saw Paul standing by the huge carved fireplace, his back turned towards her, his tall figure thrown into high relief by the leaping flames. She went up to him, and as he heard her step he started and faced her. He had finished his cigar with us, and was about to go quietly to his room in search of solitude, when he had paused by the hall fire. His face was very sad as he looked up.

"Paul," said the young girl, taking both his hands and looking into   eyes, "I believe in you, — you could not do anything ᴦ ᴦong. People would never suspect you if you answered them, if you would only take the trouble to defend yourself."

"Defend myself?" repeated Paul. "Against what, Hermione?"

"When people say, 'Where is your brother?' — or

mean to say it, as aunt Chrysophrasia did this evening, —
you ought to answer; you ought not to turn pale and be
silent."

"You too!" groaned the unhappy man, looking into her
eyes. "You too, my darling! Ah, no! It is too much."
He dropped her hands, and turned again, leaning on the
chimney-piece.

"How can you think I believe it? Oh, Paul! how unkind!" exclaimed Hermione, clasping her hands upon his
shoulder, and trying to look at his averted face. "I never,
never believed it, dear. But no one else must believe it
either; you must make them not believe it."

"My dearest," said Paul, almost sternly, but not unkindly, "this thing has pursued me for a long time. I
thought it was dead. It has come between you and me on
the very day of our happiness. You say you believe in me.
I say you shall not believe in me without proof. Good-by,
love, — good-by!"

He drew her to him and kissed her once; then he tried
to go.

"Paul," she cried, holding him, "where are you going?"
She was terrified by his manner.

"I am going away," he said slowly. "I will find my
brother, or his body, and I will not come back until then."

"But you must not go! I cannot bear to let you go!"
she cried, in agonized tones.

"You must," he answered, and the color left his cheeks.
"You cannot marry a man who is suspected. Good-by, my
beloved!"

Once more he kissed her, and then he turned quickly
away and left the hall. Hermione stood still one moment,
staring at his retreating figure. Then she sank into the
deep chair by the side of the great fire and burst into tears.
She had good cause for sorrow, for she had sent Paul Patoff away, she knew not whither. She had not even the
satisfaction of feeling that she had been quite right in speak-

ing to him as she had spoken, and above all she feared lest
he should believe, in spite of her words, that in her own
mind there was some shadow of suspicion left. But he was
gone. He would probably leave the house early in the
morning, and she might never see him again. What could
she do but let her tears flow down as freely as they could ?

Late at night I sat in my room, reading by the light of
the candles, and watching the fire as it gradually died away
in the grate. It was very late, and I was beginning to think
of going to bed, when some one knocked at the door. It
was Paul Patoff. I was very much surprised to see him,
and I suppose my face showed it, for he apologized for the
intrusion.

"Excuse me," he said. "It is very late, but could you
spare me half an hour before going to bed ? "

"Certainly," I answered, noticing his pallor, and fancying that something had happened.

"Thank you," said he. "I believe I have heard you
say that you know Constantinople very well ? "

"Tolerably well — yes. I know many of the natives. I
have been there very often."

"I am going back there," said Patoff. "They sent me
to Persia for a year and more, and now I am to return to
my old post. I want to ask your advice about a very delicate matter. You know — or perhaps you do not know —
that my brother disappeared in Stamboul, a year ago last
summer, under very strange circumstances. I did all I
could to find him, and the ambassador did more. But we
never discovered any trace of him. I have made up my
mind that I will not be disappointed this time."

"Could you tell me any of the details ? " I asked.

Paul looked at me once, and hesitated. Then he settled
himself in his chair, and told me his story very much as I
have told it, from the afternoon of the day on which Alexander disappeared to the moment when Paul left his mother
at Teinach in the Black Forest. He told me also how Pro-

fessor Cutter had written to him his account of the accident at Weissenstein, when Madame Patoff, as he said, had attempted to commit suicide.

"Pardon me," I said, when he had reached this stage. "I do not believe she tried to kill herself."

"Why not?" asked Patoff, in some surprise.

"I was the man with the rope. Cutter has never realized that you did not know it."

Paul was very much astonished at the news, and looked at me as though hardly believing his senses.

"Yes," I continued. "I happened to be leaning out of the window immediately over the balcony, and I saw your mother fall. I do not believe she threw herself over; if she had done that, she would probably not have been caught on the tree. The parapet was very low, and she is very tall. I heard her say to Professor Cutter, 'I am coming;' then she stood up. Suddenly she grew red in the face, tottered, tried to save herself, but missed the parapet, and fell over with a loud scream of terror."

"I am very much surprised," said Paul, "very grateful to you, of course, for saving her life. I do not know how to thank you; but how strange that Cutter should never have told me!"

"He saw that we knew each other," I remarked. "He supposed that I had told you."

"So it was not an attempt at suicide, after all. It is amazing to think how one may be deceived in this world."

For some minutes he sat silent in his chair, evidently in deep thought. I did not disturb him, though I watched the melancholy expression of his face, thinking of the great misfortunes which had overtaken him, and pitying him, perhaps, more than he would have liked.

"Griggs," he said at last, "do you know of any one in Constantinople who would help me, — who could help me if he would?"

"To find your brother? It is a serious affair. Yes, I

do know of one man; if he could be induced to take an interest in the matter, he might do a great deal."

"What is his name?"

"Balsamides Bey," I answered.

"I have seen him, but I do not know him," said Paul. "Could you give me a letter?"

"It would not be of the slightest use. You can easily make his acquaintance, but it will be a very different matter to get him to help you. He is one of the strangest men in the world. If he takes a fancy to you, he will do anything imaginable to oblige you."

"And if not?"

"If not, he will laugh at you. He is a queer fellow."

"Eccentric, I should think. I am not prepared to be laughed at, but I will risk it, if there is any chance."

"Look here, Patoff," I said. "I have nothing to do this spring, and the devil of unrest is on me again. I will go to Constantinople with you, and we will see what can be done. You are a Russian, and those people will not trust you; your nationality will be against you at every turn. Balsamides himself hates Russians, having fought against them ten years ago, in the last war."

Paul started up in his chair, and stretched out his hand. "Will you really go with me?" he cried in great excitement. "That would be too good of you. Shall we start to-morrow?"

"Let me see, — we must have an excuse. Could you not telegraph to your chief to recall you at once? You must have something to show to Carvel. He will be startled at our leaving so suddenly."

"Will he?" said Paul, absently. "I suppose so. Perhaps I can manage it."

It was very late when he left my room. I went to bed, but slept little, thinking over all he had told me, but knowing that he had not told me all. I guessed then what I knew later, — that he had asked Hermione to marry him, and that, in consequence of Chrysophrasia's remark at dinner, she had asked him about his brother. It was easy to understand that the question, coming from her, would produce a revival of his former energy in the search for Alexander. But it was long before I knew all the details of Hermione's visit to Madame Patoff.

The matter was arranged without much difficulty. Paul received a despatch the next day from Count Ananoff, requesting him to return as soon as possible, and I announced my determination to accompany him. The news was received by the different members of the household in different ways, according to the views of each. Poor Hermione was pale and silent. Chrysophrasia's disagreeable eyes wore a greenish air of cat-like satisfaction. Mrs. Carvel herself was sincerely distressed, and John opened his eyes in astonishment. Professor Cutter looked about with an inquiring air, and Macaulay expressed a hope that he might be appointed to Constantinople very soon, adding that he should take pains to learn Turkish as quickly as possible. That fellow regards everything in life as a sort of lesson, and takes part in events as a highly moral and studious undergraduate would attend a course of lectures.

I think Paul and I both breathed more freely when we had announced our departure. He looked ill, and it was evident that he was sorry to go, but it was also quite clear that nothing could move him from his determination. Even at the last minute he kept himself calm, and though he was obliged to part from Hermione in the presence of all the rest, he did not wince. Every one joined in saying that they hoped he would pay them another visit, and even Chrysophrasia drawled out something to that effect, though I have no doubt she was inwardly rejoicing at his going away; and just as we were starting she ostentatiously kissed poor Hermione, as though to reassert her protectorate, and to show that Hermione's safety was due entirely to her aunt Chrysophrasia's exertions on her behalf.

Paul would have been willing to go to his mother once again before parting, but Cutter thought it better not to let him do so, as his presence irritated her beyond measure. Hermione looked as though she would have said something, but seemed to think better of it. At last we drove away from the old place in the chilly February afternoon, and I confess that for a moment I half repented of my sudden resolution to go to the East. But in a few minutes the old longing for some active occupation came back, and though I thought gratefully of John Carvel's friendly ways and pleasant conversation, I found myself looking forward to the sight of the crowded bazaars and the solemn Turks, smelling already the indescribable atmosphere of the Levant, and enjoying the prospect almost as keenly as when I first set my face eastwards, many years ago.

These were the circumstances which brought me back to Constantinople last year. If, in telling my story, I have dwelt long upon what happened in England, I must beg you to remember that it is one thing to construct a drama with all possible regard for the unities and no regard whatever for probability, whereas it is quite another to tell the story of a man's life, or even of those years which have been to him the most important part of it.

XII.

It was not an easy matter to make Balsamides Bey take a fancy to Paul, for he was, and still is, a man full of prejudice, if also full of wit. In his well-shaped head resides an intelligence of no mean order, and the lines graven in his pale face express thought and study, while suggesting also an extreme love of sarcasm and a caustic, incredulous humor. His large and deep-set blue eyes seem to look at things only to criticise them, never to enjoy them, and his arched eyebrows bristle like defenses set up between the world with its interests on the one side and the inner man Balsamides on the other. Though he wears a heavy brown mustache, it is easy to see that underneath it his thin lips curl scornfully, and are drawn down at the extremities of his mouth. He is very scrupulous in his appearance, whether he wears the uniform of a Sultan's adjutant, or the morning dress of an ordinary man of the world, or the official evening coat of the Turks, made like that of an English clergyman, but ornamented by a string of tiny decorations attached to the buttonhole on the left side. Gregorios Balsamides is of middle height, slender and well built, a matchless horseman, and long inured to every kind of hardship, though his pallor and his delicate white hands suggest a constitution anything but hardy.

He is the natural outcome of the present state of civilization in Turkey ; and as it is not easy for the ordinary mind to understand the state of the Ottoman Empire without long study, so it is not by any means a simple matter to comprehend the characters produced by the modern condition of things in the East. Balsamides Bey is a man who seems to unite in himself as many contradictory qualities and characteristics as are to be found in any one living man. He is a thorough Turk in principle, but also a thorough Western Frank in education. He has read immensely in many languages, and speaks French and English with remarkable fluency. He has made an especial study of modern history, and can give an important date, a short account of a great battle, or a brief notice of a living celebrity, with an ease and accuracy that many a student might envy. He reads French and English novels, and probably possesses a contraband copy of Byron, whose works are proscribed in Turkey and confiscated by the custom-house. He goes into European society as well as among Turks, Greeks, and Armenians. Although a Greek by descent, he loves the Turks and is profoundly attached to the reigning dynasty, under whom his father and grandfather lived and prospered. A Christian by birth and education, he has a profound respect for the Mussulman faith, as being the religion of the government he serves, and a profound hatred of the Armenian, whom he regards as the evil genius of the Osmanli. He is a man whom many trust, but whose chief desire seems to be to avoid all show of power. He is often consulted on important matters, but his discretion is proof against all attacks, and there is not a journalist nor correspondent in Pera who can boast of ever having extracted the smallest item of information from Balsamides Bey.

These are his good qualities, and they are solid ones, for he is a thoroughly well-informed man, exceedingly clever, and absolutely trustworthy. On the other hand, he is cold, sarcastic, and possibly cruel, and occasionally he is frank almost to brutality.

On the very evening of our arrival in Pera I went to see him, for he is an old friend of mine. I found him alone in his small lodgings in the Grande Rue, reading a yellow-covered French novel by the light of a German student-lamp. The room was simply furnished with a table, a divan, three or four stiff, straight-backed chairs, and a book-case. But on the matted floor and divan there were two or three fine Siné carpets; a couple of trophies of splendidly ornamented weapons adorned the wall; by his side, upon a small eight-sided table inlaid with tortoise-shell and mother-of-pearl, stood a silver salver with an empty coffee-cup of beautiful workmanship, — the stand of beaten gold, and the delicate shell of the most exquisite transparent china. He had evidently been on duty at the palace, for he was in uniform, and had removed only his long riding-boots, throwing himself down in his chair to read the book in which he was interested.

On seeing me, he rose suddenly and put out his hand.

"Is it you? Where have you come from?" he cried.

"From England, to see you," I answered.

"You must stay with me," he said at once. "The spare room is ready," he added, leading me to the door. Then he clapped his hands to call the servant, before I could prevent him.

"But I have already been to the hotel," I protested.

"Go to Missiri's with a hamál, and bring the Effendi's luggage," he said to the servant, who instantly disappeared.

"Caught," he exclaimed, laughing, as he opened the door and showed me my little room. I had slept there many a night in former times, and I loved his simple hospitality.

"You are the same as ever," I said. "A man cannot put his nose inside your door without being caught, as you call it."

"Many a man may," he answered. "But not you, my dear fellow. Now — you will have coffee and a cigarette. We will dine at home. There is piláff and kebabi and a bottle of champagne. How are you? I forgot to ask."

"Very well, thanks," said I, as we came back to the sitting-room. "I am always well, you know. You look pale, but that is nothing new. You have been on duty at the palace?"

"Friday," he answered laconically, which meant that he had been at the Selamlek, attending the Sultan to the weekly service at the mosque.

"You used to get back early in the day. Have the hours changed?"

"Man of Belial," he replied, "with us nothing changes. I was detained at the palace. So you have come all the way from England to see me?"

"Yes, — and to ask you a question and a favor."

"You shall have the answer and my services."

"Do not promise before you have heard. 'Two acrobats cannot always dance on the same rope,' as your proverb says."

"And 'Every sheep hangs by its own heels,'" said he. "I will take my chance with you. First, the question, please."

"Did you ever hear of Alexander Patoff?"

Balsamides looked at me a moment, with the air of a man who is asked an exceedingly foolish question.

"Hear of him? I have heard of nothing else for the last eighteen months. I have an indigestion brought on by too much Alexander Patoff. Is that your errand, Griggs? How in the world did you come to take up that question?"

"You have been asked about him before?" I inquired.

"I tell you there is not a dog in Constantinople that has not been kicked for not knowing where that fellow is. I am sick of him, alive or dead. What do I care about your Patoffs? The fool could not take care of himself when he was alive, and now the universe is turned upside down to find his silly body. Where is he? At the bottom of the Bosphorus. How did he get there? By the kind exertions of his brother, who then played the comedy of tearing his hair so cleverly that his ambassador believed him. Very simple: if you want to find his body, I can tell you how to do it."

"How?" I asked eagerly.

"Drain the Bosphorus," he answered, with a sneer. "You will find plenty of skulls at the bottom of it. The smallest will be his, to a dead certainty."

"My dear fellow," I protested, "his brother did not kill him. The proof is that Paul Patoff has come back swearing that he will find some trace of Alexander. He came with me, and I believe his story."

"He is only renewing the comedy, — tearing his hair on the anniversary of the death, like a well-paid mourner. Of course, somebody has accused him again of the murder. He will have to tear his hair every time he is accused, in order to keep up appearances. He knows, and he alone knows, where the dead man is."

"But if he killed him the kaváss must have known it — must have helped him. You remember the story?"

"I should think so. What does the kaváss prove? Nothing. He was probably told to go off for a moment, and now will not confess it. Money will do anything."

"There remains the driver of the carriage," I objected. "He saw Alexander go into Agia Sophia, but he never saw him come out."

"And is anything easier than that? A man might learn those few words in three minutes. That proves nothing."

"There is the probability," I argued. "Many persons have disappeared in Stamboul before now."

"Nonsense, Griggs," he answered. "You know that when anything of the kind has occurred it has generally turned out that the missing man was bankrupt. He disappeared to reappear somewhere else under another name. I do not believe a word of all those romances. To you Franks we are a nation of robbers, murderers, and thieves; we are the Turkey of Byron, always thirsting for blood, spilling it senselessly, and crying out for more. If that idiot allowed his brother to kill him without attracting a crowd, — in Stamboul, in the last week of Ramazán, when everybody is out of doors, — he deserved his fate, that is all."

"I do not believe he is dead," I said, "and I have come here to ask you to make the acquaintance of Paul Patoff. If you still believe him to be a murderer when you have heard him tell his story, I shall be very much surprised."

"I should tear him to pieces if I met him," said Balsamides, with a laugh. "The mere sight of anybody called Patoff would bring on an attack of the nerves."

"Be serious," said I. "Do you think I would be so foolish as to interest myself in this business unless I believed that it could be cleared of all mystery and explained?"

"You have been in England," retorted Gregorios. "That will explain any kind of insanity. Do you want me to pester every office in the government with new inquiries? It will do no good. Everything has been tried. The man is gone without leaving a trace. No amount of money will produce information. Can I say more? Where money fails, a man need not be so foolish as to hope anything from his intelligence."

"I am foolish enough to hope something," I replied. "If you will not help me, I must go elsewhere. I will not give up the thing at the start."

"Well, if I say I will help you, what do you expect me to do? Can I do anything which has not been done already? If so, I will do it. But I will not harness myself to a rotten cart, as the proverb says. It is quite useless to expect anything more from the police."

"I expect nothing from them. I believe that Alexander is alive, and has been hidden by somebody rich enough and strong enough to baffle pursuit."

"What put that into your head?" asked my companion, looking at me with sudden curiosity.

"Nothing but the reduction of the thing to the last analysis. Either he is dead, or he is alive. As you say, he could hardly have been killed on such a night without attracting attention. Besides, the motives for Paul's killing him were wholly inadequate. No, let me go on. Therefore I say that he was taken alive."

" Where ? "

" In Santa Sophia."

" But then," argued Balsamides, " the driver would have seen him carried out."

" Yes," I admitted. " That is the difficulty. But he might perhaps have been taken through the porch ; at all events, he must have gone down the stairs alone, taking the lantern."

" They found the lantern," said Gregorios. " You did not know that ? A long time afterwards the man who opens the towers confessed that when he had gone up with the brothers and the kaváss he had found that his taper was burnt out. He picked up the kaváss's lantern and carried it down, meaning to return with the next party of foreigners. No other foreigners came, and when he went up to find the Patoffs they were gone and the carriage was gone. He kept the lantern, until the offers of reward induced him to give it up and tell his story."

" That proves nothing, except that Alexander went down-stairs in the dark."

" I have an idea, Griggs ! " cried Balsamides, suddenly changing his tone. " It proves this, — that Alexander did not necessarily go down the steps at all."

" I do not understand."

" There is another way out of that gallery. Did you know that ? At the other end, in exactly the same position, hidden in the deep arch, there is a second door. There is also a winding staircase, which leads to the street on the opposite side of the mosque. Foreigners are never ad-mitted by that side, but it is barely possible that the door may have been open. Alexander Patoff may have gone down that way, thinking it was the staircase by which he had come up."

" You see," I said, delighted at this information, " every-thing is not exhausted yet."

"No, I begin to think we are nearer to an explanation. If that door was open, — which, however, is very improbable, — he could have gone down and have got into the street without passing the carriage, which stood on the other side of the mosque. But, after all, we are no nearer to knowing what ultimately became of him."

"Would it be possible to find out whether the door was really open, and, if so, who passed that way?" I inquired.

"We shall see," said Gregorios. "I will change my mind. I will make the acquaintance of your Russian friend. I know him by sight, though I never spoke to him. When I have talked the matter over with him I will tell you what I think about it. Let us go to dinner."

I felt that I had overcome the first great difficulty in persuading Balsamides to take some interest in my errand. He is one of those men who are very hard to move, but who, when once they are disposed to act at all, are ready to do their best. Moreover, the existence of the second staircase, leading from the gallery to the street, at once explained how Alexander might have left the church unobserved by the coachman. I wondered why no one had thought of this. It had probably not suggested itself to any one, because strangers are never admitted from that side, and because the door is almost always closed.

Gregorios did not refer to the subject again that evening, but amused himself by asking me all manner of questions about the state of England. We fell to talking about European politics, and the hours passed very pleasantly until midnight.

On the next day I went to see Paul, and told him the result of my first step. He appeared very grateful.

"It seems hard that my life should be ruined by this thing," he said wearily. "Any prospect of news is delightful, however small. I am under a sort of curse, — as much as though I had really had something to do with poor Alexander's death. It comes up in all sorts of ways. Unless we can solve the mystery, I shall never be really free."

"We will solve it," I said, in order to reassure him. "Nothing shall be left undone, and I hope that in a few weeks you may feel relieved from all this anxiety."

"It is more than anxiety; it is pain," he answered. I supposed that he was thinking of Hermione, and was silent. Presently he proposed to go out. It was a fine day in February, though the snow was on the ground and filled the ruts in the pavement of the Grande Rue de Pera. Every one was wrapped in furs and every one wore overshoes, without which it is impossible to go out in winter in Constantinople. The streets were crowded with that strange multitude seen nowhere else in the world ; the shops were full of people of all sorts, from the ladies of the embassies to the veiled Turkish ladies, who have small respect for the regulation forbidding them to buy in Frank establishments. At Galata Serai the huge Kurdish hamáls loitered in the sun, waiting for a job, their ropes and the heavy pillows on which they carry their burdens lying at their feet. The lean dogs sat up and glared hungrily at the huge joints of meat which the butchers' lads carried through the crowd, forcing their way past the delicate Western ladies, who drew back in horror at the sight of so much raw beef, and through knots of well-dressed men standing before the cafés in the narrow street. Numberless soldiers moved in the crowd, tall, fair Turks, with broad shoulders and blue eyes, in the shabby uniform of the foot-guards, but looking as though they could fight as well as any smart Prussian grenadier, as indeed they can when they get enough to eat. Now and then a closed sedan-chair moved rapidly along, borne by sturdy Kurds, and occasionally a considerable disturbance was caused by the appearance of a carriage. Paul and I strolled down the steep street, past Galata Tower and down into Galata itself.

"Shall we cross ?" asked Paul, as we reached the bridge.

"Let us go up the Bosphorus," I said. "There will probably be a steamer before long."

He assented readily enough.   It was about eleven o'clock
in the morning, — five by the Turkish clocks, — and the
day was magnificent.   The sun was high, and illuminated
everything in the bright, cold air, so that the domes and
minarets of the city were white as snow, with bluish shadows, while the gilded crescents and spires glistened with unnatural brilliancy in the clear winter's daylight.   It is hard
to say whether Stamboul is more beautiful at any one season
of the year than during the other three, for every season
brings with it some especial loveliness, some new phase of
color.   You may reach Serai point on a winter's morning in
a driving snow-storm, so that everything is hidden in the
gray veil of the falling flakes ; suddenly the clouds will part
and the sunlight will fall full upon the city, so that it seems
as if every mosque and spire were built of diamonds.   Or
you may cross to Scutari in the early dawn of a morning in
June, when the sky is like a vast Eastern flower, dark blue
in the midst overhead, the petals shaded with every tint
to the faint purple on the horizon ; and every hue in turn
passes over the fantastic buildings, as the shadows gradually
take color from the sky, and the soft velvety water laps up
the light in broad pools and delicate streaks of tinted reflection.   It is always beautiful, always new ; but of all times,
I think the hour when the high sun illuminates most distinctly everything on land and sea is the time when Stamboul is most splendid and queenly.

The great ferry-boat heaved and thumped the water,
and swung slowly off the wooden pier, while we stood on
the upper deck watching the scene before us.   For two men
as familiar with Constantinople in all its aspects as we were,
it seemed almost ridiculous to go on board a steamer merely
for the sake of being carried to the mouth of the Black Sea
and back again.   But I have always loved the Bosphorus,
and I thought it would amuse Paul to pass the many landings, and to see the crowds of passengers, and to walk
about the empty deck.   He was tired with the journey and

harassed in mind, and for those ills the open air is the best medicine.

He appeared to enjoy it, and asked me many questions about the palaces and villas on both shores, for I was better acquainted with the place than he. It seemed to interest him to know that such a villa belonged to such a Pasha, that such another was the property of an old princess of evil fame, while the third had seen strange doings in the days of Mehemet Ali, and was now deserted or inhabited only by ghosts of the past, — the resort of ghouls and jins from the neighboring grave-yards. As we lay a moment at the pier of Yeni Köj, — "New town" sounds less interesting, — we watched the stream of passengers, and I thought Paul started slightly as a tall, smooth-faced, and hideous negro suddenly turned and looked up to where we stood on the deck, as he left the steamer. I might have been mistaken, but it was the only approach to an incident of interest which occurred that day. We reached the upper part of the Bosphorus, and at Yeni Mahalle, within sight of the Black Sea, the ferry-boat described a wide circle and turned once more in the direction of Stamboul.

"I feel better," said Paul, as we reached Galata bridge and elbowed our way ashore through the crowd. "We will go again."

"By all means," I answered.

From that time during several weeks we frequently made excursions into Stamboul and up the Bosphorus, and the constant enjoyment of the open air did Paul good. But I could see that wherever we went he watched the people with intense interest; following some individual with his eyes in silence, or trying to see into dark archways and through latticed windows, staring at the files of passengers who came on board the boats or went ashore at the different landings, and apparently never relaxing his attention. The people grew familiar to me, too, and gradually it appeared that Paul was constructing a method for our peregrinations.　It was he, and not I, who suggested the direction of our expeditions, and I noticed that he chose certain places on certain days.　On Monday, for instance, he never failed to propose a visit to the bazaars, on Tuesday we generally went up the Bosphorus, on Wednesday into Stamboul. On Friday afternoons, when the weather was fine, we used to ride out to the Sweet Waters of Europe ; for Friday is the Mussulman's day of rest, and on that day all who are able love to go out to the Kiat-hané — the " paper-mill," — where they pass the afternoon in driving and walking, eating sweetmeats, smoking, drinking coffee, watching gypsy girls dance, or listening to the long-winded tales of professional storytellers.　Almost every day had its regular excursion, and it was clear to me that he always chose the place where on that day of the week there was likely to be the greatest crowd.

Meanwhile Balsamides, in whose house I continued to live, alternately laughed at me for believing Paul's story, and expressed in the next breath a hope that Alexander might yet be found.　He had been to Santa Sophia, and had ascertained that the other staircase was usually opened on the nights when the mosque was illuminated, for the convenience of the men employed in lighting the lamps, and this confirmed his theory about the direction taken by Alexander when he left the gallery.　But here all trace ceased again, and Balsamides was almost ready to give up the search, when an incident occurred which renewed our energy and hope, and which had the effect of rousing Paul to the greatest excitement.

We were wandering under the gloomy arches of the vast bazaar one day, and had reached the quarter where the Spanish Jews have their shops and collect their wonderful mass of valuables, chiefly antiquities, offering them for sale in their little dens, and ever hungry for a bargain.　We strolled along, smoking and chatting as we went, when a Jew named Marchetto, with whom I had had dealings in former days and who knew me very well, came suddenly out into the broad covered way, and invited us into his shop. He said he had an object of rare beauty which he was sure I would buy. We went in, and sat down on a low divan against the wall. The sides of the little shop were piled to the ceiling with neatly folded packages of stuffs, embroideries, and prayer carpets. In one corner stood a shabby old table with a glass case, under which various objects of gold and silver were exposed for sale. The whole place smelled strongly of Greek tobacco, but otherwise it was clean and neat. A little raised dome in the middle of the ceiling admitted light and air.

Marchetto disappeared for a moment, and instantly returned with two cups of Turkish coffee on a pewter salver, which he deposited on a stool before us. He evidently meant business, for he began to talk of the weather, and seemed in no hurry to show us the object he had vaguely mentioned. At last I asked for it, which I would certainly not have done had I meant to buy it. It proved to be a magnificent strip of Rhodes tapestry, of the kind formerly made for the Knights of Malta, but not manufactured since the last century. It consists always of Maltese crosses, of various sizes and designs, embroidered in heavy dark red silk upon strips of coarse strong linen about two feet wide, or of the same design worked upon square pieces for cushions. The value of this tapestry is very great, and is principally determined by the fineness of the stitch and the shade of red in the silk used.

Marchetto's face fell as we admired his tapestry, for he knew that we would not begin a bargain by conceding the smallest merit to the object offered. But he put a brave face on the matter, and began to show us other things: a Giordès carpet, a magnificent piece of old Broussa gold embroidery on pale blue satin, curious embroideries on towels, known as Persian lace, — indeed, every variety of ancient stuff. Tired of sitting still, I rose and turned over some of the things myself. In doing so I struck my elbow against

the old glass case in the corner, and looked to see whether
I had broken it. In so doing my eye naturally fell upon
the things laid out on white paper beneath the glazed frame.
Among them I saw a watch which attracted my attention.
It was of silver, but very beautifully engraved and adorned
in Russian *niello*. The ribbed knob which served to wind
it was of gold. Altogether the workmanship was very fine,
and the watch looked new.

"Here is a Russian watch, Patoff," I said, tapping the
glass pane with my finger. Paul rose languidly and came
to the table. When he saw the thing he turned pale, and
gripped my arm in sudden excitement.

"It is his," he said, in a low voice, trying to raise the lid.

"Alexander's?" Paul nodded. "Pretend to be indifferent," I said in Russian, fearing lest Marchetto should
understand.

The Jew unclosed the case and handed us the watch.
Paul took it with trembling fingers and opened it at the
back. There in Russian letters were engraved the words
Alexander Paulovitch, from his father; the date followed.
There was no doubt about it. The watch had belonged to
the lost man; he had, therefore, been robbed.

"You got this from some bankrupt Pasha, Marchetto?"
I inquired. Everything offered for sale in the bazaar at
second hand is said to come from the establishment of a
Pasha; the statement is supposed to attract foreigners.

Marchetto nodded and smiled.

"A Russian Pasha," I continued. "Did you ever hear
of a Russian Pasha, Marchetto? The fellow who sold it to
you lied."

"He who lies on the first day of Ramazán repents on the
day of Bairam," returned the Jew, quoting a Turkish proverb, and grinning. I was struck by the words. Somehow
the mention of Bairam made me think of Alexander's uncertain fate, and suggested the idea that Marchetto knew
something about it.

"Yes," I answered, looking sharply at him; "and another proverb says that the fox ends his days in the furrier's shop. Where did you buy the watch?"

"Allah bilir! I have forgotten."

"Allah knows, undoubtedly. But you know too," I said, laughing, and pretending to be amused. Paul had resumed his seat upon the small divan, and was listening with intense interest; but he knew it was best to leave the thing to me. Marchetto was a fat man, with red hair and red-brown eyes. He looked at me doubtfully for a moment.

"I will buy it if you will tell me where you got it," I said.

"I got it" — He hesitated. "It came out of a harem," he added suddenly, with a sort of chuckle.

"Out of a harem!" I exclaimed, in utter incredulity. "What harem?"

"I will not tell you," he answered, gravely, the smile fading from his face. "I swore that I would not tell."

"Will you swear that it really came from a harem?" I asked.

"I give you my word of honor," asseverated Marchetto. "I swear by my head, by your beard" —

"I do not mean that," I said quietly. "Will you swear to me, solemnly, before God, that you are telling the truth?"

Marchetto looked at me in surprise, for no people in the world are so averse to making a solemn oath as the Hebrews, as, perhaps, no people are more exact in regard to the truth when so made to bind themselves. The man looked at me for a moment.

"You seem very curious about that watch," he said at last, turning away and busying himself with his stuffs.

"Then you will not swear?" I asked, putting the watch back in its place.

"I cannot swear to what I do not know. But I know the man who sold it to me. He is the Lala of a harem,

that is certain.   I will not tell you his name, nor the name
of the Effendi to whose harem he belongs.   Will you buy
my watch ? — birindjí — first quality — it is a beautiful
thing.   On my honor, I have never seen a finer one, though
it is of silver."

"Not unless you will tell me where it came from," I said
firmly.   "Besides, I must show it to Vartan in Pera before
I buy it.   Perhaps the works are not good."

"It is yours," said Marchetto.   "Take it.   When you
have had it two days you will buy it."

"How much ?"

"Twenty liras, — twenty Turkish pounds," answered the
Jew promptly.

"You mean five," I said.   The watch was worth ten, I
thought, about two hundred and thirty francs.

"Impossible.   I would rather let you take it as a gift.   It
is birindjí — first quality — upon my honor.   I never
saw " —

"Rubbish, Marchetto !" I exclaimed.   "Let me take it
to Vartan to be examined.   Then we will bargain."

"Take it," he answered.   "Keep it as long as you like.
I know you very well, and I thank Heaven I have profited
a little with you.   But the price of the watch is twenty
pounds.   You will pay it, and all your life you will look at
it and say, 'What an honest man Marchetto is !'   By my
head — it is birindjí — first quality — I never " —

"I have no doubt," I answered, cutting him short.   I
motioned to Paul that we had better go : he rose without a
word.

"Good-by, Marchetto," I said.   "I will come back in a
day or two and bargain with you."

"It is birindjí — by my head — first quality " — were
the last words we heard as we left the Jew amongst his
stuffs.   Then we threaded the subterranean passages of the
bazaar, and soon afterwards were walking in the direction
of Galata bridge, on our way back to Pera.   At last Paul
spoke.

"We are on the scent," he said. "That fellow was speaking the truth when he said the watch came from a harem. I could see it in his face. I begin to think that Alexander did some absurdly rash thing, — followed some veiled Turkish woman, as he would have done before if I had not stopped him, — was seized, imprisoned in some cellar or other, and ultimately murdered."

"It looks like it," I answered. "Of course I would not buy the watch outright, because as long as it is not paid for I have a hold upon Marchetto. I will talk to Balsamides to-night. He is very clever about those things, and he will find out the name of the black man who sold it."

We separated, and I went to find my friend; but he was on duty and would not return until evening. I spent the rest of the day in making visits, trying to get rid of the time. On returning to the house of Gregorios I found a letter from John Carvel, the first I had received from him since I had left England. It ran as follows : —

MY DEAR GRIGGS : Since you left us something very extraordinary and unexpected has taken place, and considering the part you took in our household affairs, you should not be kept in the dark. I have suffered more annoyance in connection with my unfortunate sister-in-law than I can ever tell you; and the thing has culminated in a sort of transformation scene, such as you certainly never expected any more than I did. What will you say when I tell you that Madame Patoff has suddenly emerged from her rooms in all respects a sane woman? You will not be any less surprised — unless Paul has confided in you — to hear that he asked Hermione to marry him before leaving us, and that Hermione did not refuse him! I am so nervous that I have cut three meets in the last month.

Of course you will want to know how all this came out. I do not see how I can manage to write so long a letter as this must be. But the *labor improbus* knocks the stuffing out of all difficulties, as you put it in your neat American way. I dare say I shall survive. If I do not, the directions for my epitaph are, "Here lies the body of Anne Patoff's brother-in-law." If you could see me, you would appreciate the justice of the inscription.

Madame Patoff is perfectly sane; dines with us, drives out, walks, talks, and reads like any other human being, — in which she differs materially from Chrysophrasia, who does all these things as they were never done, before or after the flood. We do not know what to make of the situation, but we try to make the best of it. It came about in this way. Hermione had taken a fancy to pay her aunt a visit, a day or two after you had left. Mrs. North was outside, as usual, reading or working in the next room. It chanced that the door was left open, or not quite closed. Mrs. North had the habit of listening to what went on, professionally, because it was her business to watch the case. As she sat there working, she heard Madame Patoff's voice, talking consecutively. She had never heard her talk before, more than to say "Yes," or "No," or "It is a fine day," or "It rains." She rose and went near the door. Her patient was talking very connectedly about a book she had been reading, and Hermione was answering her as though not at all surprised at the conversation. Then, presently, Hermione began to beg her to come out into the house and to live with the rest of us, since she was now perfectly sane. Mrs. North was thunderstruck, but did not lose her head. She probably did the best thing she could have done, as the event proved. She entered the room very quietly, — she is always so quiet, — and said in the most natural way in the world, "I am so glad you are better, Madame Patoff. Excuse me, Miss Hermione left the door open and I heard you talking." The old lady started and looked at her a moment. Then she turned away, and presently, looking rather white, she answered the nurse: "Thank you, Mrs. North, I am quite well. Will you send for Professor Cutter?" So Cutter was sent for, and when he had seen her he sent for me, and told me that my sister-in-law was in a lucid state, but that it would be just as well not to excite her. If she chose to leave her room she might, he said, but she ought to be watched. "The deuce!" said I, "this is most extraordinary!" "Exactly," said he, "most extraordinary."

The lucid moment lasted, and she has been perfectly sane ever since. She goes about the house, touching everything and admiring everything, and enjoys driving with me in the dog-cart. I do not know what to make of it. I asked Hermione how it began. She only said that she thought her aunt had been better when she was with her, and then it had come very suddenly. The other day Madame Patoff asked about Paul, and I told her he had gone to the East with you. But she did not seem to know anything about you, though I told her you had seen her. "Poor Paul," she said, "I should like to see him so much. He is the only one left." She was sad for a moment, but that was all. Cutter said it was very strange; that her insanity must have been caused in some way by the shock she had when she threw herself out of the window in Germany. Perhaps so. At all events she is sane now, and Cutter says she will not be crazy again. I hope he is right. She appeared very grateful for all I had done for her, and I believe she has written to Paul. Queer story, is it not?

Now for the sequel. Hermione came to me one morning in the library, and confessed that Paul had asked her to marry him, and that she had not exactly refused. Girls' ideas about those things are apt to be very inexact when they are in love with a man and do not want to own it. Of course I said I was glad she had not accepted him; but when I put it to her in that way she seemed more uncertain than ever. The end of it was that she said she could not marry him, however much she liked him, unless he could put an end to a certain foolish tale which is told against him.

I dare say you have heard that he had been half suspected of helping his brother out of the world. Was there ever such nonsense? That was what Chrysophrasia meant with her disgusting personalities about Cain and Abel. I dare say you remember. I do not mind telling you that I like Paul very much more than I expected to when he first came. He has a hard shell, but he is a good fellow, and as innocent of his brother's death as I am. But — they are cousins, and Paul's mother has certainly been insane. Of course insanity brought on by an accident can never be hereditary; but then, there is Chrysophrasia, who is certainly very odd. However, Paul is a fine fellow, and I will think of it. Mrs. Carvel likes him even better than I do. I would have preferred that Hermione should marry an out-and-out Englishman, but I always said she should marry the man she loved, if he were a gentleman, and I will not go back on my word. They will not have much to live on, for I believe Paul has refused to touch a penny of his brother's fortune, believing that he may yet be found.

But the plot thickens. What do you suppose Macaulay has been doing? He has written a letter to his old chief, Lord Mavourneen, who always liked him so much, begging to be sent to Constantinople. The ambassador had a secretary out there of the same standing who wanted to go to Paris, so the matter was arranged at the Foreign Office, and Macaulay is going out at once. Naturally the female establishment set up a howl that they must spend the summer on the Bosphorus; that I had taken them everywhere else, and that no one of them could die happy without having seen Constantinople. The howl lasted a week. Then I went the way of all flesh, and gave in. Mrs. Carvel wanted to see Macaulay, Madame Patoff wanted to see the place where poor Alexander disappeared, Hermione wanted to see Paul, and Chrysophrasia wanted to see the Golden Horn and dance upon the glad waters of the joyous Bosphorus in the light caïque of commerce. I am rather glad

I have submitted. I think that Hermione's affection is serious, — she looks ill, poor child, — and I want to see more
of Paul before deciding. Of course, with Macaulay in one
embassy and Paul in another, we shall see everything; and
Mary says I am growing crusty over my books. You understand now how all this has occurred.

Now I want your advice, for you not only know Constantinople, but you are living there. Do you advise us to come
at once and spend the spring, or to come later and stay all
summer? Is there anything to eat? Must I bring a cook?
Can I get a house, or must we encamp in a hotel? What
clothes does one wear? In short, tell me everything you
know, on a series of post cards or by telegraph, — for you
hate writing letters more than I do. I await your answer
with anxiety, as we shall regulate our movements by what
you say. All send affectionate messages to you and to
Paul, to whom please read this letter.

Yours ever,   JOHN CARVEL.

I had not recovered from my astonishment in reading
this long epistle, when Gregorios came in and sat down by
the fire. His entrance reminded me of the watch, and for
the moment banished John Carvel and his family from my
thoughts. I showed him the thing, and told him what
Marchetto had said.

"We have him now!" he exclaimed, examining the
name and date with interest, though he could not read the
Russian characters.

"It is not so sure," I said. "He will never tell the name
of the negro."

"No; but we can see the fellow easily enough, I fancy,"
returned Balsamides. "You do not know how these things
are done. It is most probable that Marchetto has not paid
him for the watch. Things of that sort are generally not
paid for until they have been sold out of the shop. Marchetto would not give him a good price for the watch until

he knew what it would fetch, and the man would not take a small sum because he believes it to be valuable. The chances are that the Lala comes from time to time to inquire if it is sold, and Marchetto shows it to him to prove that he has not got any money for it."

"That sounds rather far-fetched," I observed. "Marchetto may have had it in his keeping ever since Alexander disappeared. The Lala would not wait as long as that. He would take it to some one else."

"No, I do not believe so," said Gregorios thoughtfully. "Besides, it may not have been brought to the Jew more than a week ago. Those fellows do not part with jewelry unless they need money. It is a pretty thing, too, and would attract the attention of any foreigner."

"How can you manage to watch Marchetto so closely as to get a sight of the man?"

"Bribe the Jew in the next shop; or, still better, pay a hamál to spend his time in the neighborhood. The man probably comes once a week on a certain day. Keep the watch. The next time he comes it will be gone, but Marchetto will not have been paid for it and will refuse to pay the Lala. There will inevitably be a hubbub and a noise over it. The hamál can easily find out the name of the negro, who is probably well known in the bazaar."

"But suppose that I am right, and it is already paid for?" I objected.

"It is very unlikely. I know these people better than you do. At all events, we will put the hamál there to watch for the row. If it does not come off in a month, I will begin to think you are right."

Gregorios is a true Oriental. He possesses the inborn instinct of the bazaar.

XIII.

THAT night I went in search of Paul, and found him standing silent and alone in the corner of a drawing-room at one of the embassies. There was a great reception and a dance, and all the diplomats had turned out officially to see that portion of the native Pera society which is invited on such occasions.

There is a brilliancy about such affairs in Constantinople which is hardly rivaled elsewhere. The display of jewels is something wonderful, for the great Fanariote families are still rich, in spite of the devastations of the late war, and the light of their hereditary diamonds and pearls is not hidden under a bushel. There is beauty, too, of the Oriental and Western kind, and plenty of it. The black eyes and transparently white complexions of the Greek ladies, their raven hair and heavy brows, their magnificent calm and their languid attitudes, contrast strangely with the fair women of many countries, whose husbands, or fathers, or brothers, or uncles are attached to the different embassies. The uniforms, too, are often superb, and the display of decorations is amazing. The conversation is an enlargement on the ordinary idea of Babel, for almost every known language is spoken within the limits of the ball-room.

I found Paul alone, with an abstracted expression on his face, as he stood aside from the crowd, unnoticed in his corner.

"My dear fellow," I said, "I believe I may congratulate you."

"Upon what?" he asked, in some surprise.

"Let us get out of this crowd," I answered. "I have a letter from John Carvel, which you ought to read."

We threaded the rooms till we reached a small boudoir, occupied only by one or two couples, exceedingly interested in each other.

"Read that," said I. It was the best thing I could do for him, I thought. He might be annoyed to find that I knew his secret, but he could not fail to rejoice at the view John took of the engagement. His face changed many times in expression, as he read the letter carefully. When he had finished he was silent and held it in his hand.

"What do you think of all this?" I asked.

"She never was mad. Or if she was, this is the strangest recovery I ever heard of. So she is coming here with the rest! And uncle John thinks me a very fine fellow," he added with a laugh, meant to be a little sarcastic, but which ended with the irrepressible ring of genuine happiness.

"I congratulate you," I said. "I think the affair is as good as settled. You have only to wait a few weeks, and they will be here. By the by, I hope you do not mind Carvel's frankness in telling me all about it?"

"Not in the least," answered Paul, with a smile. "I believe you are the best friend I have in the world, and you are his friend. You will do good rather than harm."

"I hope so," said I. "But if any one had foretold a month ago that we should all be together again so soon, — and here, too, — I could have laughed at him."

"It is fate," answered Paul. "It would be better if it could be put off until we reach the end of our search, especially as we seem to be nearer the track than ever before. I am afraid that their arrival will hinder us — or, at least, me — from working as hard as I would like."

"On the contrary," I replied, "I fancy you will work all the harder. I have been talking to Balsamides about the watch. He feels sure that he can catch the man who took it to Marchetto."

I explained to Paul the course Gregorios proposed to follow. He seemed to think the chance was a poor one.

"I have been pursued by an idea ever since this morning," he said at last. "I dare say you will think it very foolish, but I cannot get rid of it. Do you remember the adventure in the Valley of Roses? I told you about it at Carvel Place. Very well. I cannot help thinking that the negro who took the watch to Marchetto was the one who accompanied those two Turkish women. The man was exasperated. He probably knew us by sight, for we had constantly met him and the lady with the thick yashmak. They had often seen us come out of the Russian embassy. No complaint was ever made against Alexander. It looks to me like a piece of private vengeance."

"Yes," I assented, struck by the idea. "Besides, if the fellow had succeeded in making away with your brother, it is natural that he should have waited a long time before disposing of his jewelry."

"I wonder what became of the other things," said Patoff. "Alexander had with him his Moscow cigarette case, he wore a gold chain with the watch, and he had on his finger a ring with a sapphire and two diamonds in a heavy gold band. If all those things have been disposed of, they must have passed through the bazaar, probably through Marchetto's hands."

At this moment Balsamides Bey's pale, intelligent face showed itself at the door. He came quickly forward on seeing us, and drew up a chair. I told him in a few words what we had said. He smiled and twirled the end of his brown mustache.

"There is something in that," he answered. "I fancy, too, that such a fellow would first part with the chain, then with the cigarette case, thirdly with the watch, and last of all with the ring, which he probably wears."

"We must find out if Marchetto has sold the chain and the case for him," I said.

"Leave Marchetto to me," said Gregorios, confidently. "I will spend the day with him to-morrow. Have you ever seen the negro since.that affair in the Valley of Roses ?"

" Often," replied Paul, somewhat to my surprise. " He goes to Yeni Köj every Thursday."

" You seem to have watched his movements," observed Balsamides, with a smile of admiration. " Did you never tell Griggs ?"

" No," said I, rather amazed.

"What would have been the use? I only watched the man because I fancied he might be in some way connected with the matter, but it seemed so absurd, until the finding of the watch made it look more probable, that I never spoke of it."

" I am glad you have spoken of it now," said Gregorios. " It is probably the key to the whole affair."

We talked on for a few minutes, and Paul told Balsamides that his mother and the Carvels were coming, explaining his anxiety to hasten the search so as to have something positive to show when they arrived. Then Paul left us, and went to fulfill such social obligations as his position imposed upon him. He was not a man to forget such things, even in times of great excitement; and when he returned to Constantinople, his chief had expressed the hope that Paul would not shut himself up, but would go everywhere, as he had formerly done.

" This thing is beginning to interest me, Griggs," said Gregorios, arching his eyebrows, and looking at me with a peculiar expression. " You are doing more than I am, and I will not bear it," he added, with a laugh. " What is my little bit of evidence about the staircase in Santa Sophia compared to your discovery of the watch? I believe that in the end Marchetto will be the *deus ex machina* who will pull us out of all our difficulties. I believe, too, that the best thing to do is to confide the matter to him. I will go and see him to-morrow."

" He will never break his oath to the Lala," I answered.

"Perhaps not. But he has only sworn that he will not tell his name. He has not sworn that he will not let me see him. So the fellow goes to Yeni Köj on Thursday. Then he probably lives there, and chooses that day to come to Stamboul. You have seen him going home. If he goes to Stamboul, he most likely visits the bazaar early in the morning. If so, I will catch him to-morrow, and to-morrow night I will tell you whether he is the man or not. I will come upon Marchetto by accident, and he will of course want to show me the Rhodes tapestry; then I will spend the whole morning over the bargain, and I shall not miss the Lala if he comes."

Balsamides was evidently fully roused, and as we smoked a last cigarette in his rooms that night he talked enthusiastically of what he hoped to accomplish on the next day. He kept his word, and very early in the morning I heard him go out. From the sound of his walk I could tell that he had no spurs, and was therefore in civilian's dress. He told me afterwards what occurred.

At half past eight o'clock he was drinking a cup of coffee in Marchetto's shop in the bazaar, and the Jew was displaying his tapestry, and swearing that it was birindjí, first quality. Balsamides wanted to produce the impression that he intended to make a bargain.

"Kaldyr! Take it away!" he exclaimed. "It is rubbish."

Marchetto held the stuff up over his customer's head so that the light from the little dome could fall upon it.

"There is not a hole in the whole length of it," he cried enthusiastically. "It is perfect; not a thread loose. Examine it; is there a patch? By my head, if you can find such another piece I will give you a present."

"Is that a color?" asked Balsamides contemptuously. "Is that red? It is pink. It is magenta. How much did you pay to have it made?"

"If I could make Rhodes tapestry, I should be as rich as

the Hunkyar," retorted Marchetto, squatting on the matted
floor and slowly drawing the magnificent tapestry across his
knees, so that Gregorios could see it to advantage.

"Do you take me for a madman?" asked the aid-de-
camp. "I do not care for Rhodes tapestry. Kaldyr! If
it were old, it would have holes in it."

"I have Rhodes full of holes, beautiful holes," observed
Marchetto, with a grin.

"Fox!" retorted Gregorios. "Do you think when I
buy tapestry I want to buy holes?"

"But this piece has none," argued the Jew.

"You want me to buy it. I can see you do. You are
laughing at my beard. You think I will give a thousand
pounds for your rubbish?"

"Not a thousand pounds," said Marchetto. "It is worth
a hundred and fifty pounds, neither more nor less. Marchetto is an honest man. He is not a Persian fox."

"No," answered Balsamides, "he is an Israelite of Saloniki. What have I to do with such a fellow as you, who
have the impudence to ask a hundred and fifty liras for that
rag?"

"How shall the lion and the lamb lie down together?"
inquired Marchetto. "And is it a rag?"

"I will tell you, Marchetto," said Gregorios, gravely.
"The lion and the lamb shall lie down together, when the
lion lies down with the lamb inside of him."

"Take, and eat!" exclaimed the ready Jew, holding out
the Rhodes tapestry to Balsamides.

"A man who has fasted throughout Ramazán shall not
break his fast with an onion," retorted Gregorios, laughing.

"Who eats little earns much," replied Marchetto. "Is
it not the most beautiful piece of Rhodes you ever saw, Effendim? There is not a Pasha in Stamboul, nor in Pera,
nor in Scutari, who possesses the like of it. Only a hundred
and fifty pounds; it is very cheap."

"I will give you ten pounds for it, if you will give me

a good backsheesh," said Gregorios at last. In Stamboul it is customary, when a bargain of any importance is completed, for the seller to make the buyer a present of some small object, which is called the backsheesh, or gift.

On hearing the offer, Marchetto looked slyly at Gregorios and laughed, without saying anything. Then he slowly began to fold the tapestry together.

"Ten pounds," said Balsamides. "Pek chok, — that is quite enough, and too much."

"Yes, of course it is," answered the Jew, ironically. "I paid a hundred and nineteen pounds and eighty-five piastres for it. I only ask fifteen piastres profit. Small profits. Get rid of everything quickly. Who sells cheaply sells soon ; who sells soon earns much."

"I told you from the first that I did not want your Rhodes," said Balsamides. "I came here to see what you had. Have you nothing else that is good ?"

"Everything Marchetto has is good. His carpets are all of silk, and of the finest colors. His embroideries are the envy of the bazaar. Marchetto has everything."

He did not finish folding the Rhodes, but thrust it aside upon the matting, and began to pull down other stuffs and carpets from the shelves. From the obstinacy Gregorios displayed, he really judged that he meant to buy the tapestry, and to make a good bargain he would willingly have turned everything in his little shop upside down.

Gregorios admired several pieces very much, whereupon the Jew threw them aside in disgust, well knowing that his customer would not buy them. The latter had now been an hour in the shop, and showed no signs of going away. Marchetto returned to the original question.

"If it is worth so much, why do you not take it to one of the embassies ?" asked Balsamides at last. He had resolved that he would prolong the discussion until twelve o'clock, judging that by midday the negro would be on his way back to Yeni Köj, and that there would be no further

chance of seeing him.   He therefore broached the subject
of Marchetto's trade with the foreigners, knowing that once
upon this tack the Jew would have endless stories and anecdotes to relate.   But Gregorios was not destined to stand in
need of so much ingenuity.   He would never have made the
attempt in which he was now engaged unless he had antici-
pated success, and he was not surprised when a tall, smooth-
faced negro, of hideous countenance but exceedingly well
dressed, put his head into the shop.   He saluted Gregorios
and entered.   Marchetto touched his mouth and his fez
with his right hand, but did not at first rise from his seat
upon the floor.   Balsamides watched the man.   He looked
about the shop, and then approached the old glass case in
the corner.   He had hardly glanced at it when he turned
and tried to catch Marchetto's eye.   The latter made an
almost imperceptible motion of the head.   Gregorios was
satisfied that the pantomime referred to the watch, which
was no longer in its place.   He continued to talk with the
Jew for a few minutes, and then slowly rose from his seat.

"I see you have business with this gentleman," he said.
"I have something to do in the bazaar.   I will return in
half an hour."

The Lala seemed delighted, and politely made way for
Gregorios to pass, but Marchetto of course protested loudly
that the negro's business could wait.   He accompanied
Gregorios to the door, and with many inclinations stood
looking after him for a few moments.   At a little distance
Gregorios pretended to be attracted by something exposed
for sale, and, pausing, looked furtively back.   The Jew had
gone in again.   Then Balsamides returned and entered a
shop almost opposite to Marchetto's, kept by another Spanish Hebrew of Saloniki, who made a specialty of selling
shawls, — a smart young fellow, with beady black eyes.

"Good morning, Abraham," he said.   "Have you manufactured any new Kashmir shawls out of old rags of borders and French imitations since I saw you?"

Abraham smiled pleasantly, and began to unfold his wares. Before many minutes the sound of angry voices was heard outside. Gregorios had ensconced himself in a corner, whence he could see what went on without being seen. The quarrelers were Marchetto and the Lala.

"Dog of a Jew!" screamed the black man in his high, cracked voice. "Will you rob me, and then turn me out of your filthy den? You shall suffer for it, you Saloniki beast!"

"Dog yourself, and son of a dog!" bellowed Marchetto, his big face growing fiery red as he blocked the doorway with his bulky shoulders. "Behold the gratitude of this vile wretch!" he cried, as though addressing an audience. "Look at this insatiate jackal, this pork-eater, this defiler of his father's grave! Oh! beware of touching what is black, for the filth will surely rub off!"

Exasperated at the Jew's eloquent abuse, the Lala tried to push him back into the shop, flourishing his light cane in his right hand. In a moment a crowd collected, and the epithets of the combatants were drowned amidst the jeers and laughter of the by-standers, delighted at seeing the dandy keeper of a great harem in the clutches of the sturdy Marchetto.

Abraham looked out, and then turned back to his customer.

"It is Selim," he said with a chuckle. "He has been trying to cheat Marchetto again."

"Again?" repeated Gregorios, who had at last attained his end. "And who is Selim, Abraham?"

"Selim? Everybody in the bazaar knows Selim, the most insolent, avaricious, money-grabbing Lala in Stamboul. He is more like a Persian than anything else. He is the Lala of Laleli Khanum Effendi, who lives at Yeni Köj. They say she is a witch since her husband died," added Abraham, lowering his voice.

"I have heard so," said Gregorios calmly. But in real-

ity he was triumphant. He knew now what had become of
Alexander Patoff.

The noise outside was rapidly growing to an uproar.
Gregorios slipped quickly out of the shop and made his way
through the crowd, for he felt that it was time to put a stop
to the quarrel. Many of the people knew him, and knew
that he was an officer and a man in authority ; recognizing
him, they stopped yelling and made way for him.

" What is this ? " he cried, violently separating Marchetto
and the negro, who were screaming insults at each other and
shaking their fists in each other's faces. " Stop this noise,"
he continued, " or I will send a score of soldiers down to
keep you in order. If the Lala is not satisfied, he can go
before the magistrate. So can Marchetto, if he likes. —
Go ! " he said to the negro, pushing him away and scatter-
ing the crowd. " If you have any complaints to make, go
to the magistrate."

" Who are you ? " asked the fellow, insolently.

" It is none of your business," answered Gregorios, dragging the man away in the nervous grip of his white hand ;
then lowering his voice, he spoke quickly in the man's ear :
" Do you remember the Bairam, a year ago last summer ?
If you are not quiet, I will ask you what became of the
chain of that watch, of the silver box, and especially of that
beautiful ring with the sapphire and two diamonds. Moreover, I may ask you what became of a certain Frank Effendi, to whom they belonged, — do you understand ? "

The man trembled in every joint, and a greenish livid hue
seemed to drive the blackness out of his face.

" I know nothing ! " he gasped hysterically. But Balsamides let him go.

" Be quick," he said. " The watch will be paid for, but
do not venture to come to the bazaar again for some time.
Fear nothing, — I have an eye to your safety."

The last speech was perhaps somewhat ambiguous, but
the man, being once released, dived into a narrow passage

and disappeared. The crowd of Jews had shrunk into their shops again. Gregorios hastily concluded a bargain with Abraham, and then returned to finish his conversation with Marchetto. He found the latter mopping his forehead, and talking excitedly to a couple of sympathetic Hebrews who had entered his place of business. On seeing Balsamides they immediately left the shop.

"I have sent him away," said Gregorios. "He will not trouble you again."

"It is not my fault if the dog of a Turk is angry," answered Marchetto.

"I hardly know. He says he had left a watch with you to be sold, and that now he can get neither the watch nor the money. You like to keep your customers waiting when they have anything to sell, Marchetto. How long is it since he gave you the watch?"

"On my head, it is only three weeks," answered the Jew. "How can I sell a watch in three weeks and get the money for it? An Effendi took the watch yesterday to show it to Vartan, the jeweler. He is a friend of yours, Effendim; you first brought him here a long time ago. His name is a strange name, — Cricks, — a very strange name, like the creaking of an ungreased cart-wheel."

"Oh, did he take the watch? I will speak to him about it. He will pay you immediately. How did the Lala come to have a watch to sell?"

"Allah bilir. He is always bringing me things to sell."

"Other things?"

"He showed me a gold chain one day in the winter. But it was not curious, so he took it to a jeweler in the jeweler's tcharshee, who gave him the value of the gold by weight."

"Who is he?" asked Gregorios, judging that he ought to show some curiosity about the man.

"I cannot tell," answered the Jew.

"That means that you will not, of course. Very well.

It is your affair. Curiosity is the mother of deception. Will you give me the Rhodes for ten pounds ? "

They began to bargain again, but nothing was concluded on that day, for Gregorios had got what he wanted, and was anxious to reach home and to see me.

Patoff and I, as usual on Thursday, had made a trip up the Bosphorus, and it was on this occasion that he first pointed out to me the hideous negro. He proved to be the same man I had seen once before, on our very first excursion. To-day he looked more ugly than ever, as he went ashore at Yeni Köj. There was a malignity in his face such as I have never seen equaled in the expression of any human being.

"I wonder what we shall find out," said Paul thoughtfully. "I have a very strong belief that he is the fellow who sold the watch. If he is, poor Alexander can have had but small chance of escape. Did you ever see such a diabolical face ? Of course it may be a mere fancy, but I cannot rid myself of the thought."

"Balsamides will find out," I replied. "He can handle those fellows in the bazaar as only an Oriental can."

It was not long before I heard the story of the morning's adventure from Gregorios. I found him waiting for me and very impatient. He told his tale triumphantly, dwelling on the fact that Marchetto himself had never suspected that he was interested in the matter.

"And who is Laleli Khanum Effendi ? " I inquired when he had finished. "And how are we to get into her house ?"

"You never heard of Laleli ? You Franks think you know Constantinople, but you know very little in reality. Laleli means ' a tulip.' A pretty name, Tulip. Why not ' cabbage rose,' or ' artichoke,' or ' asparagus ' ? Laleli is an extraordinary woman, my friend, and has been in the habit of doing extraordinary things, ever since she poisoned her husband. She is the sister of a very high and mighty personage, who has been dead some time. She was married to an important officer in the government. She was concerned in the conspiracy against Abdul Azis ; she is said to have poisoned her husband ; she fell in her turn a victim to the conspiracy against Murad, and, though not banished, lost all favor. She managed to keep her fortune, however, which is very large, and she has lived for many years in Yeni Köj. There are all sorts of legends about her. Some say she is old and hideous, others declare that she has preserved her beauty by witchcraft. There is nothing absurd which has not been said of her. She certainly at one time exercised considerable influence in politics. That is all I know of her except this, which I have never believed : it has been said that more than one person has been seen to enter her house, but has never been seen to leave it."

"How can one believe that ? " I asked skeptically. "If it were really known, her house would have been searched, especially as she is out of favor."

"It is curious, however," said Gregorios, without contradicting me, "that we should have traced Alexander Patoff's personal possessions to her house."

"What shall we do next ? " I asked.

"There are only two courses open. In the first place, we can easily catch the Lala who sold the watch, and take him to a quiet place."

"Well, do you suppose he will tell us what he knows ? "

"We will torture him," said Balsamides, coolly. I confess that I was rather startled by the calm way in which he made the proposition. I inwardly determined that we should do nothing of the kind.

"What is the other alternative ? " I inquired, without showing any surprise.

"To break into the house and make a search, I suppose," answered my friend, still quite unmoved, and speaking as though he were proposing a picnic on the Bosphorus.

"That is not an easy matter," I remarked, " besides being slightly illegal."

" Whatever we do must be illegal," answered Gregorios. " If we begin to use the law, the Khanum will have timely warning. If Alexander is still alive and imprisoned in her house, it would be the work of a moment to drop him into the Bosphorus. If he is dead already, we should have less chance of getting evidence of the fact by using legal means than by extracting a confession by bribery or violence."

" In other words, you think it is indispensable that we should undertake a burglary ? "

" Unless we succeed in persuading the Lala to confess," said Balsamides.

" This is a very unpleasant business," I remarked, with a pardonable hesitation. " I do not quite see where it will end. If we break into the house and find nothing, we shall be amenable to the law. I object to that."

" Very well. What do you propose ? "

" I cannot say what would be best. In my opinion, Paul should consult with his ambassador, and take his advice. But before all else it is necessary to find out whether Alexander is dead or alive."

" Of course. That is precisely what I want to find out," answered Balsamides, rather impatiently. " The person who can best answer the question is Selim, the Lala."

" I object to using violence," I said, boldly. " I fancy he might be bribed. Those fellows will do anything for money."

" You do not know them. They will commit any baseness for money, except betraying their masters. It has been tried a hundred times. We may avoid using violence, as you call it, but the man must be frightened with the show of it. The people who can be bribed are the women slaves of the harem. But they are not easily reached."

" It is not impossible, though," I answered. " Nevertheless, if I were acting alone, I would put the matter in the hands of the Russian embassy."

" Do you think they would hesitate at any means of getting information, any more than I would?" inquired Gregorios, scornfully.

"We shall see," I said. "We must discuss the matter thoroughly before doing anything more. I have no experience of affairs of this sort; your knowledge of them is very great. On the other hand, I am more prudent than you are, and I do not like to risk everything on one throw of the dice."

"We might set fire to the house and burn them out," said Gregorios, thoughtfully. "The danger would be that we might burn Alexander alive."

My friend did not stick at trifles. Under his cold exterior lurked the desperate rashness of the true Oriental, ready to blaze out at any moment.

"No," I said, laughing; "that would not do, either. Is it not possible to send a spy into the house? It seems to me that the thing might be done. What sort of women are they who gain access to the harems?"

"Women who sell finery and sweetmeats; women who amuse the Khanums by dressing their hair, when they have any, in the Frank style; women who tell stories" —

"A story-teller would do," I said. "They are often admitted, are they not? It is almost the only amusement those poor creatures have. I fancy that one who could interest them might be admitted again and again."

Balsamides was silent, and smoked meditatively for some minutes.

"That is an idea," he said at last. "I know of such a woman, and I dare say she could get in. But if she did, she might go to the house twenty times, and get no information worth having."

"Never mind. It would be a great step to establish a means of communication with the interior of the house. You could easily force the Lala to recommend the story-teller to his Khanum. She could tell us about the internal arrangement of the place, at all events, which would make it easier for us to search the house, if we ever got a chance."

"If one could get as far as that, it would be a wise precaution and a benefit to the human race to convey a little strychnine to the Khanum in a sweetmeat," said Gregorios, with a laugh.

"How horribly bloodthirsty you are!" I answered, laughing in my turn. "I believe you would massacre half of Stamboul to find a man who may be dead already."

"It is our way of looking at things, I suppose," returned Balsamides. "I will see the story-teller, and explain as much as possible of the situation. What I most fear is that we may have to take somebody else into our confidence."

"Do none of the ladies in the embassies know this Laleli, as you call her?" I asked.

"Yes. Many Frank ladies have been to see her. But their visits are merely the satisfaction of curiosity on the one side, and of formality on the other."

"I was wondering whether one of them would not be the best person in whom to confide."

"Not yet," said Balsamides.

And so our interview ended. When I saw Paul and told him the news, he seemed to think that the search was already at an end. I found it hard to persuade him that a week or two might elapse before anything definite was known. In his enthusiasm he insisted that I should answer John Carvel's letter by begging him to come at once. As he was the person most concerned, I yielded, and wrote.

"It is strange," said Paul, "that we should have accomplished more in a single month than has been done by all the official searching in a year and a half."

"The reason is very simple," I answered. "The Lala did not chance to be in want of money until lately. Everything we have discovered has been found out by means of that watch."

"Griggs," said Paul, "Balsamides is a very clever fellow, but he has not thought of asking one question. Why was the Lala never in want of money before?"

" I do not know."

" Because, in some way or other, he is out of favor with his Khanum. If that is the case, this is the time to bribe him."

" Very true," I said. " In any case, if he is trying to get money, it is a sign that he needs it, in spite of our friend's declaration that he and his kind cannot be bribed."

XIV.

It often happens, when our hopes are raised to the highest pitch of expectation, and when we think we are on the eve of realizing our well-considered plans, that an unexpected obstacle arises in our path, like the impenetrable wall which so often in our dreams suddenly interposes itself between us and the enemy we are pursuing. At such moments we are apt to despair of ourselves, and it is the inability to rise above this dejection at the important crisis which too often causes failure. After we had discovered the watch, and after Balsamides had traced it to the house of Laleli Khanum Effendi, it seemed to me that the end could not be far. It could not be an operation of superhuman difficulty to bribe some one in the harem to tell us what we wanted to know. In a few days this might be accomplished, and we should learn the fate of Alexander Patoff.

It was at this point, however, that failure awaited us. The house of Laleli was impenetrable. The scheme to establish communication by means of the story-teller did not succeed. The old woman was received once, but saw nothing, and never succeeded in gaining admittance again. Selim, the Lala, ceased at that time to pay regular visits to Stamboul on Thursday, and Balsamides realized that he had perhaps not done wisely in letting him go free from the bazaar. We paid several visits to Yeni Köj, and contemplated the dismal exterior of the Khanum's villa. High walls of mud and stone surrounded it on all sides except the front, and there the long, low wooden facade exhibited only its double row of latticed windows, overlooking the water, while two small doors, which were always closed, constituted the entrance from the narrow stone quay. Nothing could penetrate those lattices, nor surmount the blank steepness of those walls. Our only means of reaching the interior of the dwelling and the secrets which perhaps were hidden there lay in our power over Selim; but the Lala had no difficulty in eluding us, and either kept resolutely within doors, or sallied out in company with his mistress. It was remarkable, however, that we had never met him in charge of the ladies of the harem, as Paul had so often met him during the summer when Alexander had made his visit to his brother. We went to every place where Turkish ladies are wont to resort in their carriages during the winter, but we never saw Selim nor the lady with the thick veil.

Meanwhile, Paul grew nervous, and his anxiety for the result of our operations began to show itself in his face. I had written to John Carvel, and he had replied that he was making his preparations, and would soon join us. Then Macaulay Carvel arrived, and, having found Paul, came with him to see me. The young man's delight at being at last appointed to Constantinople knew no bounds, and he almost became enthusiastic in his praises of the city and the scenery. He smiled perpetually, and was smoother than ever in speech and manner. Balsamides conceived a strong dislike for him, but condescended to treat him with civility in consideration of the fact that he was Paul's cousin and the son of my old friend.

Indeed, Macaulay had every reason to be happy. He had succeeded in getting transferred to the East, where he could see his cousin every day; he was under one of the most agreeable and kind-hearted chiefs in the service; and now his whole family had determined to spend the summer with him. What more could the heart of a good boy desire? It was rather odd that Paul should like him so much, I thought. It seemed as though Patoff, who was inclined to repel all attempts at intimacy, and who at four-and-thirty years of age was comparatively friendless, were touched by the admiration of his younger cousin, and had for him a sort of half-paternal affection, which was quite enough to satisfy the modest expectations of the quiet young man. Yet Macaulay was far from being a match for Paul in any respect. Where Paul exhibited the force of his determination by intelligent hard work, Macaulay showed his desire for excellence by doggedly memorizing in a parrot-like way everything which he wished to know. Where Paul was enthusiastic, Macaulay was conscientious. Where Paul was original, Macaulay was a studious but dull imitator of the originality of others. Instead of Paul's indescribable air of good-breeding, Macaulay possessed what might be called a well-bred respectability. Where Paul was bold, Macaulay exhibited a laudable desire to do his duty.

Yet Macaulay Carvel was not to be despised on account of his high-class mediocrity. He did his best, according to his lights. He endeavored to improve the shining hour, and admired the busy little bee, as he had been taught to do in the nursery. If he had not the air of a thoroughbred, he had none of the plebeian clumsiness of the cart-horse. Though he was not the man to lead a forlorn hope, he was no coward; and though he had not invented gunpowder, he had the requisite intelligence to make use of already existing inventions under the direction of others. He had a way of remembering what he had learned laboriously which his brilliant chief found to be very convenient, and he was a useful secretary. His admiration for Paul was the honest admiration which many a young man feels for those qualities which he does not possess, but which he believes he can create in himself by closely imitating the actions of others.

It is unnecessary to add that Macaulay was discreet, and that in the course of a few days he was put in possession of the details of what had occurred. I had feared at first that his presence might irritate Paul, in the present state of affairs, but I soon found out that the younger man's uniformly cheerful, if rather colorless, disposition seemed to act like a sort of calming medicine upon his cousin's anxious moods.

"That fellow Carvel," Balsamides would say, "is the ultimate expression of your Western civilization, which tends to make all men alike. I cannot understand why you are both so fond of him. To me he is insipid as boiled cucumber. He ought to be a banker's clerk instead of a diplomatist. The idea of his serving his country is about as absurd as hunting bears with toy spaniels."

"You do not do him justice," I always answered. "You forget that the days of original and personal diplomacy are over, or very nearly over. Plenipotentiaries now are merely persons who have an unlimited credit at the telegraph office. The clever ones complain that they can do nothing without authority; the painstaking ones, like Macaulay Carvel, congratulate themselves that they need not use their own judgment in any case whatever. They make the best government servants, after all."

"When servants begin to think, they are dangerous. That is quite true," was Gregorios' scornful retort; and I knew how useless it was to attempt to convince him. Nevertheless, I believe that as time proceeded he began to respect Macaulay on account of his extreme calmness. The young man had made up his mind that he would not be astonished in life, and had therefore systematically deadened his mental organs of astonishment, or the capacity of his mental organs for being astonished. As no one has the least idea what a mental organ is, one phrase is about as good as another.

We had not advanced another step in our investigations, in spite of all our efforts, when we received news that the Carvels, accompanied by Madame Patoff and Chrysophrasia Dabstreak, were on their way to Constantinople. We had looked at several houses which we thought might suit them, but as the season was advancing we supposed that John would prefer to spend the remainder of the spring in a hotel,

and then engage a villa on the Bosphorus, at Therapia or
Buyukdere.   At last the day came for their arrival, and
Macaulay took the kaváss of his embassy with him to facili-
tate the operations of the custom-house.   Paul did not go
with him, thinking it best not to meet his mother, for the
first time since her recovery, in the hubbub of landing.   I,
however, went with Macaulay Carvel on board the Varna
boat.   In a few minutes we were exchanging happy greetings on the deck of the steamer, and in the midst of the confusion I was presented to Madame Patoff.

She was not changed since I had seen her last, except
that she now looked quietly at me and offered her hand.
Her fine features were perhaps a little less pale, her dark
eyes were a little less cold, and her small traveling-bonnet
concealed most of her thick gray hair.   She was dressed in
a simple costume of some neutral tint which I cannot remember, and she wore those long loose gauntlets commonly
known as Biarritz gloves.   I thought her less tall and less
imposing than when I had seen her in the black velvet
which it was her caprice to wear during the period of her
insanity; but she looked more natural, too, and at first sight
one would have merely said that she was a woman of sixty,
who had once been beautiful, and who had not lost the
youthful proportions of her figure.   As I observed her more
closely in the broad daylight, on the deck of the steamer,
however, I began to see that her face was marked by innu-
merable small lines, which followed the shape of her features like the carefully traced shadows of an engraving;
they crossed her forehead, they made labyrinths of infini-
tesimal wrinkles about her eyes, they curved along the high
cheekbones and the somewhat sunken cheeks, and they surrounded the mouth and made shadings on her chin.   They
were not like ordinary wrinkles.   They looked as though
they had been drawn with infinite precision and care by the
hand of a cunning workman.   To me they betrayed an ab-
normally nervous temperament, such as I had not suspected

that Madame Patoff possessed, when in the yellow lamp-light of her apartment her white skin had seemed so smooth and even. But she was evidently in her right mind, and very quiet, as she gave me her hand, with the conventional smile which we use to convey the idea of an equally conventional satisfaction when a stranger is introduced to us.

John was delighted to see me, and was more like his old self than when I had last seen him. Mrs. Carvel's gentle temper was not ruffled by the confusion of landing, and she greeted me as ever, with her sweet smile and air of sympathetic inquiry. Chrysophrasia held out her hand, a very forlorn hope of anatomy cased in flabby kid. She also smiled, as one may fancy that a mosquito smiles in the dark when it settles upon the nose of some happy sleeper. I am sure that mosquitoes have green eyes, exactly of the hue of Chrysophrasia's.

"So deliciously barbarous, is it not, Mr. Griggs?" she murmured, subduing the creaking of her thin voice.

"Dear Mr. Griggs, I am so awfully glad to see you again," said Hermione with genuine pleasure, as she laid her little hand in mine.

It seemed to me that Hermione was taller and thinner than she had been in the winter. But there was something womanly in her lovely face, as she looked at me, which I had not seen before. Her soft blue eyes were more shaded, — not more sad, but less carelessly happy than they used to be, — and the delicate color was fainter in her transparent skin. There was an indescribable look of gravity about her, something which made me think that she was very much in earnest with her life.

"Paul is at the hotel," I said, rather loudly, when the first meeting was over. "He has made everything comfortable for you up there. The kaváss will see to your things. Let us go ashore at once, out of all this din."

We left the steamer, and landed where the carriages were waiting. John talked all the time, recounting the incidents

of the journey, the annoyance they had had in crossing the
Danube at Rustchuk, the rough night in the Black Sea, the
delight of watching the shores of the Bosphorus in the
morning. When we landed, Chrysophrasia turned suddenly
round and surveyed the scene.

"We are not in Constantinople at all," she said, in a
tone of bitter disappointment.

"No," said Macaulay; "nobody lives in Stamboul. This
is Galata, and we are going up to Pera, which is the European town, formerly occupied by the Genoese, who built
that remarkable tower you may have observed from the
harbor. The place was formerly fortified, and the tower
has now been applied to the use of the fire brigade. Much
interest is attached " —

How long Macaulay would have continued his lecture on
Galata Tower is uncertain. Chrysophrasia interrupted him
in disgust.

"A fire brigade!" she exclaimed. "We might as well
be in America at once. Really, John, this is a terrible disappointment. A fire brigade! Do not tell me that the
people here understand the steam-engine, — pray do not!
All the delicacy of my illusions is vanishing like a dream!"

Chrysophrasia sometimes reminds me of a certain imperial sportsman who once shot an eagle in the Tyrol.

"An eagle!" he cried contemptuously, when told what
it was. "Gentlemen, do not trifle with me, — an eagle
always has two heads. This must be some other bird."

In due time we reached the hotel. Paul was standing in
the doorway, and came forward to help the ladies as they
descended from the carriage, greeting them one by one.
When his mother got out, he respectfully kissed her hand.
To the surprise of most of us, Madame Patoff threw her
arms round his neck, and embraced him with considerable
emotion.

"Dear, dear Paul, — my dear son!" she cried. "What
a happy meeting!"

Paul was evidently very much astonished, but I will do
him the credit to say that he seemed moved as he kissed
his mother on both cheeks, for his face was pale and he appeared to tremble a little.

The travelers were conducted to their rooms by Macaulay,
and I saw no more of them. But John insisted that I should
dine with them in the evening. In the mean while I went
home, and found Gregorios reading, as usual when he was
not on duty at Yildiz-Kiösk, — the " Star-Palace," where
the Sultan resides.

" Have you deposited your friends in a place of safety ? "
he asked, looking up from his book. " Have they all come,
— even the old maid with the green eyes, and the mad lady
whom Patoff is so unfortunate as to call his mother ? "

" All," I answered. " They are real English people, and
my old friend John Carvel is the patriarch of the establishment. There are maid-servants and men-servants, and
more boxes than any house in Pera will hold. The old lady
seems perfectly sane again."

" Then she will probably die," said Gregorios, reassuringly. " Crazy people almost always have a lucid interval
before death."

" You take a cheerful view," I observed.

" Fate would confer a great benefit on Patoff by remov-
ing his mother from this valley of tears," returned my
friend. " Besides, as our proverb says, mad people are the
only happy people. Madame Patoff, in passing from insanity to sanity, has therefore fallen from happiness to unhappiness."

" If all your proverbs were true, the world would be a
strange place."

" I will not discuss the inexhaustible subject of the truth
of proverbs," answered Balsamides. " I only doubt whether
Madame Patoff will be happy now that she is sane, and
whether the uncertainty of the issue of our search may not
drive her mad again. She will probably spoil everything

by chattering at all the embassies. By the by, since we are on the subject of death, lunacy, and other similar annoyances, I may as well tell you that Laleli is very ill, and it is not expected that she can live. I heard it this morning on very good authority."

"That is rather startling," I said.

"Very. Dying people sometimes make confessions of their crimes, but to hear the confession you must be there when they are about to give up the ghost."

"That is impossible in this case, unless you can get into the harem as a doctor."

"Who knows? We must make a desperate attempt of some kind. Leave it to me, and do not be surprised if I do not appear for a day or two. I have made up my mind to strike a blow. You are too evidently a Frank to be of any use. I wish you were a Turk, Griggs. You have such an enviably sober appearance. You speak Turkish just well enough to make me wish you would never betray yourself by little slips in the verbs and mistakes in using Arabic words. Only educated Osmanlis can detect those errors: just now they are the very people we want to deceive."

"I can pass for anything else here without being found out," I answered. "I can pass for a Persian when there are no Persians about, or for a Panjabí Mussulman, if necessary."

"That is an idea. You might be an Indian Hadji. I will think of it."

"What in the world do you intend to do?" I asked, suspecting my friend of some rash or violent project.

"A very sly trick," he replied, with his usual sarcastic smile. "There need not necessarily be any violence about it, unless we find Alexander alive, in which case you and I must manage to get him out of the house."

"Tell me your plan," I said. "Let me hear what it is like."

"No; I will tell you to-night, when I know whether it is

possible or not. You are going to dine with your friends? Yes; very well, when you have finished, come here, and we will see what can be done. We must only pray that the iniquitous old woman may live till morning."

It was clear that Gregorios was not ready, and that nothing would induce him to speak what was in his mind. I showed no further curiosity, and at the appointed time I left the house to go and dine with the Carvels.

"Say nothing to Patoff," said Balsamides, as I went out.

I found the Carvels assembled in their sitting-room, and we went to dinner. I could not help looking from time to time at Paul's mother, who surprised me by her fluent conversation and perfect self-possession. With the exception that she was present and that Professor Cutter was absent, the dinner was very much like the meals at Carvel Place. I noticed that Paul was placed between Mrs. Carvel and his mother, while Hermione was on the opposite side of the table. But their eyes met constantly, and there was evidently a perfect understanding between them. Paul looked once more as I had seen him when he was talking to Hermione in England, and the coldness I so much disliked had temporarily disappeared from his face. I did not know what had occurred during the afternoon, since I had left the hotel, and it was not until later that I learned some of the details of the meeting.

When the members of the party retired to their rooms, on arriving at Missiri's, Macaulay had gone off with his father, and Paul had been left alone for a few minutes in the sitting-room. When all was quiet, Hermione opened her door softly and looked in. Paul was standing by the chimney-piece, contemplating the smouldering logs with the interest of a man who has nothing to do. He raised his head suddenly, and saw that Hermione had entered the room and was standing near him. She had taken off her traveling-hat, and her golden hair was in some disorder, but the tangled coils and waves of it only showed more perfectly how beautiful she was. She came forward, and he, too, left his place. She took his hands rather timidly in hers.

"Paul — I never meant that you should go!" she exclaimed, while the tears stood in her eyes. "Why did you take me so literally at my word?"

"It was better, darling," said he, drawing her nearer to him. "You were quite right. I could not bear the idea of any one being free to speak to me as your aunt did ; but I was very unhappy. How could I know that you were coming here so soon?"

"I did not know," she said simply. "But I was very unhappy, too, and the days seemed so long. I could worship my brother for bringing it about."

"So could I," answered Paul, rather absently. He was looking down into her eyes that met his so trustfully. "Do you really and truly believe in me, Hermione?" he asked.

"Indeed I do ; I always did!" she cried passionately. Then he kissed her very tenderly, and held her in his arms.

"Thank you, — thank you, my darling," he murmured in her ear.

Presently they stood by the chimney-piece, still holding each other's hands.

"I must speak to your father," he said. "You know his way. He wrote all about it to Griggs, telling him to show me the letter."

"I could not keep the secret to myself any longer," she answered. "And I knew that papa loved me and liked you."

"Yes, dear, you were quite right," said Paul. "But I did not mean to tell him, after what happened that evening, until I had found my brother. Do you know? I have almost found him. I hope to reach the end in a day or two."

"Oh, Paul! that is splendid!" cried Hermione. "I knew you would. You must tell me all about it."

There was a sound of footsteps in one of the rooms. Hermione slipped quickly away, and throwing a kiss towards Paul with her fingers, disappeared through the door by which she had entered, leaving him once more alone. The moments of their meeting had been few and short, but they had more than sufficed to show that these two loved each other as much as ever. Some time afterwards Paul had been alone with his mother for half an hour and had frankly asked her whether she was able to hear him speak of Alexander or not. Her face twitched nervously, but she answered calmly enough that she wished to hear all he had to tell. But when he had finished she shook her head sadly.

"You may find out how he died, but you will never find him," she said. Then, with a sudden energy which startled Paul, she gazed straight into his eyes. "You know that you cannot," she added, almost savagely.

"I do not know, mother," he answered, calmly. "I still have hope."

Madame Patoff looked down, and seemed to regain her self-control almost immediately. The long habit of concealing her feelings, which she had acquired when deceiving Professor Cutter, stood her in good stead, and she had not forgotten what she had studied so carefully. But Paul had seen the angry glance of her eyes, and the excited tone of her voice still rang in his ears. He guessed that, although she had come to Constantinople with the full intention of forgetting the accusations she had once uttered, the mere sight of him was enough to bring back all her virulent hatred. She still believed that he had killed his brother. That was clear from her words, and from the tone in which they were spoken. Whether the thought was a delusion, or whether she sanely believed Paul to be a murderer, made little difference. Her mind was evidently still under the influence of the idea. But Paul determined that he would hold his peace, and it was not until later, when all necessity for concealment was removed, that I learned what had passed. Paul believed that in a few days he should certainly solve the mystery of Alexander's disappearance, and thus effectually root out his mother's suspicions.

All this had occurred before dinner, and without my knowledge. Madame Patoff seemed determined to be agreeable and to make everything go smoothly. Even Chrysophrasia relaxed a little, as we talked of the city and of what the party must see.

"I am afraid," said I, "that you do not find all this as Oriental as you expected, Miss Dabstreak."

"Ah, no!" she sighed. "If by 'this' you mean the hotel, it is European, and unpleasantly so at that."

"I think it is a very good hotel; and this rice — what do you call it? — is very good, too," said John Carvel, who was tasting pilaff for the first time.

"Your carnal love of food always shocks me, John," murmured Chrysophrasia. "But I dare say there is a good deal that is Oriental on the other side. There, I am sure, we should be sitting on very precious carpets, and eating sweetmeats with golden spoons, while some fair young Circassian slave sang wild melodies and played upon a rare old inlaid lute."

"Yes," I answered. "I have dined with Turks in Stamboul."

"Oh, do describe it!" exclaimed Miss Dabstreak.

"We squatted on the floor around a tiny table, and we devoured ragouts of mutton and onions with our fingers," I said.

"How very disgusting!" Miss Dabstreak made an unæsthetic grimace, and looked at me with profound contempt.

"But I suppose they eat other things, Griggs?" asked John, laughing.

"Yes. But mutton and onions and pilaff are the staple of their consumption. They eat jams of all sorts. Sometimes soup is brought in in a huge bowl, and put down in the middle of the table. Then each one dips in his spoon in the order of precedence, and eats as much as he can.

They will give you a dozen courses in half an hour, and they never speak at their meals if they can help it."

"Pigs!" exclaimed Chrysophrasia, whose delicacy did not always assert itself in her selection of epithets.

"No; I assure you," I objected, "they are nothing of the kind. They consider it cleaner to eat with their fingers, which they can wash themselves, than with forks, which are washed in a common bath of soapsuds by the grimy hands of a scullery maid. It is not so unreasonable."

"You have such a terrible way of putting things, Mr. Griggs!" exclaimed Mrs. Carvel in a tone of gentle protest. "But I dare say," she added, as though fearing lest her mild rebuke should have hurt my feelings, — "I dare say you are quite right."

"To tell the truth," I answered, "I am rather fond of the Turks."

"I have always noticed," remarked Madame Patoff, "that you Americans generally admire people who live under a despotic government. Americans all like Russia and Russians."

"Our government is not quite despotic," observed Paul, who felt bound to defend his country. "We have laws, and the laws are respected. The Czar would not think of acting against the established law, even though in theory he might."

"The Turks must have laws, too," objected Madame Patoff.

"I don't know," said Chrysophrasia. "I already feel a delicious sensation, as though I might be strangled with a bow-string at any moment and dropped into the Bosphorus."

John Carvel looked very grave. Perhaps he was offering up a silent prayer to the end that such a consummation might soon be reached; but more probably he considered the topic of sudden death by violence as one to be avoided. Macaulay Carvel came to the rescue.

"The Turks have laws," he said, fluently. "All their law is founded upon the Koran, and they are most ingenious in making the Koran answer the purpose of our more learned and therefore more efficacious codes. The Supreme Court really exists in the person of the Sheik ul Islam, who may be called the High Pontiff, a sort of Pontifex Maximus with judicial powers. All important cases are ultimately referred to him, and as most of these important cases are connected with the Vakuf, the real estate held by the mosques, like our glebe lands at home, it follows that the Sheik ul Islam generally decides in favor of his own class, who are the Ulema, or priests. The consequences of this mode of administering the laws are very " —

"Capital!" exclaimed John Carvel. "Where on earth did you learn all that, my boy?"

"I began to coach the East when I saw there was a chance of my coming here," answered Macaulay, much pleased at his father's acknowledgment of his learning. It struck me that the young man had got his information out of some rather antiquated book, in which no mention was made of the present division of the civil and criminal courts under the Ministry of Justice, and of the ecclesiastical courts under the Sheik ul Islam. But I held my peace, being grateful to Macaulay for delivering his lecture at the right moment. Mrs. Carvel looked with undisguised admiration at her son, and even Hermione smiled and felt proud of her brother.

"Wonderful, this modern education, is it not?" said John Carvel, turning to me.

"Amazing," I replied.

"I want to see all those delightful creatures, you know," said Chrysophrasia. "The Sultan and the Sheik — what do you call him?"

"Sheik ul Islam," said the ready Macaulay.

"Sheik Ool is lamb!" repeated Chrysophrasia, thoughtfully. "Lamb, — so symbolical in our own very symbolic religion. It means so much, you know."

"Chrysophrasia!" ejaculated Mary Carvel, in a tone of gentle reproach. She thought she detected the far-off shadow of a possible irreverence in her sister's tone. Macaulay again interposed, while Paul and I endeavored to avoid each other's eyes, lest we should be overtaken by an explosion of laughter.

"It is '*Islam*,' not '*is lamb*,' aunt Chrysophrasia," said Macaulay, mildly.

"I don't see much difference," retorted Miss Dabstreak, "except that you say it *is* lamb, and I say it is *lamb*. Oh! you mean it is one word, — yes, I dare say," she added quickly, in some confusion. "Of course, I don't speak Turkish."

"It is Arabic," observed the implacable Macaulay.

"John," said Chrysophrasia, ignoring the correction with a fine indifference, "we must see everything at once. When shall we begin?"

The question effectually turned the conversation, for all the party were anxious to see what Macaulay was equally anxious to show, having himself only seen each sight once. The remainder of the time while we sat at table was occupied in discussing the various expeditions which the party must undertake in order to see the city and its surroundings systematically. After dinner John and I remained behind for a while. Paul wanted to talk to Hermione, and Macaulay, who was the most domestic of young men, preferred the society of his mother and aunts, whom he had not seen for several months, to the smell of cigars and Turkish coffee.

"What do you think of her?" asked John Carvel when we were alone. "She seems perfectly sane, does she not?"

"Perfectly. What proves it best is the way she treats Paul. She is very affectionate. I suppose there is no fear of a relapse?"

"I hope not, I hope not!" repeated John fervently. "She has behaved admirably during the journey. Now, about Paul," he continued, lowering his voice a little : "how does he strike you since you have known him better ? You have seen him every day for some time. What sort of a fellow is he ? "

"I think he is very much in earnest," I answered.

"Yes, yes, — no doubt. But you know what I mean, Griggs : is he the kind of man to whom I can give my daughter ? That is what I am thinking of. I know that he works hard and will succeed, and all that."

"I can tell you what I think," said I, "but you must form your own judgment as well. I like Paul very much, but you must like him too, before you decide. In my opinion he is a man of fine character, scrupulously honest, and not at all capricious. I cannot say more."

"A little wild when he was younger ? " suggested John.

"Not very, I am sure. He was unhappy in his childhood ; he was one of those boys who make up their minds to work, and who grow so fond of it that they go on working when other boys begin to play."

"Very odd," observed John. "He is not at all a prig."

"No, indeed. He is as manly a fellow as you could meet, and at first sight he does not produce the impression of being so serious as he is. I think that is put on. He once told me that he had made a study of small talk and of the art of appearing well, because he thinks it so important in his career. I dare say he is right. He knows a great deal, and knows it thoroughly."

"He does not know any more than Macaulay," said John, as though in praising Paul I had attacked his son. "What a clever fellow he is ! I only wish he were a little tougher, — just a little more shell to him, I mean."

"He will get that," I answered. "He is younger than Paul, and has not seen so much of the world."

"You say you like Paul. Do you think he would make a good husband ? "

"Yes, I really believe he would," I replied. "But do

not take him on my recommendation. You must know him better yourself. You will meet many people here who know him, and some who know him well."

"What do you think of that story about his brother?" asked John, looking at me very earnestly.

"I believe he is as innocent as you or I. But we are getting near the truth, and have made some valuable discoveries."

I explained to Carvel what we had found, and without mentioning the name of Laleli Khanum I told him how far we had traced the mystery, and he listened with profound interest to my account.

"I hope you may find him alive," he said, as we rose from the table. "For my part, I do not believe we shall ever see him. Paul was alone with his mother this afternoon, and I dare say he told her what you have told me. She does not seem to object to the subject, though of course we generally avoid it."

I stayed an hour longer with the party, during which time Paul talked a great deal to Hermione, occasionally joining in the general conversation, and certainly not trying to prevent what he said to the young girl from being heard. At last I took my leave and went home, for I was anxious to see Gregorios, and to hear from him what plan he proposed to adopt for the solution of our difficulties at this critical moment. I found him waiting for me.

"Have you made up your mind?" I asked.

Balsamides was sitting beside his table with a book. He looked even paler than usual, and was evidently more excited than he liked to own. He is eminently a man who loves danger, and his nature never warms so genially as when something desperate is to be done. A Christian by race and belief, he has absorbed much of the fatalism of the Oriental races, and his courage is of the fatalist kind, reckless and devoted.

"Yes," he answered. "I have made up my mind. One

must either be the camel or the camel-driver. One must either submit to the course of events, or do something to violently change their direction. If we submit much longer, we shall lose the game. The old woman will die, — the Turkish women always die when they are ill; and if she is once dead without confessing, we may give up all hope."

"We should always have Selim to examine," I remarked.

"If Laleli Khanum dies, Selim will disappear the same hour, — laying hands on everything within reach, of course. How could we catch him? He would cross the Bosphorus, put on a disguise of some sort, and make his way to Egypt in no time. Those fellows are very cunning."

"Then you mean to try and extort a confession from Laleli herself? How in the world do you mean to do it? It is a case of life or death."

"I have got life and death in my pocket," answered Gregorios, his eyes beginning to sparkle. "Can you read Turkish? Of course you can. Read that."

I took the folded document and examined it.

"This is an Iradè!" I exclaimed, in great surprise; "an imperial order to arrest Laleli Khanum Effendi, — good heavens! Balsamides, I had no idea that you possessed such tools as this!"

"To tell you how I got it would be to tell you my own history during the last ten years," he answered, in low tones. "I trust you, Griggs, but there are other reasons why I cannot tell you all that. You see the result, at all events, and a result very dearly paid for," he added gravely. "But I have got the thing, and what is more, I have permission to personate the Sultan's private physician."

"What is that for? I should think the Iradè were quite enough."

"Laleli might die of fright, if I merely presented myself and threatened to arrest her. But I shall see her in the assumed character of the court physician. Laleli is a Turkish

woman, who understands no other language but her own
and Greek. She is very superstitious, and believes in all
manner of charms and spells; for she has no ideas at all
concerning Western science, except that it is all contrary to
the Koran. I can talk the jargon of an old Hadji well
enough, and besides I know something of medicine; very
little, but enough to tell me whether she is absolutely in a
dying state. It is a great compliment for the Sultan to send
his private physician, and if she is in a conscious state she
will be flattered and thrown off her guard. If I can manage to get her slaves out of the way, I may induce her to
confess. If I fail in this, I have the means to frighten her.
If she dies, I have the means of arresting Selim before he
can escape. It is all very well arranged, and there is nothing to be done but to put the plan into execution. When
you left me I had not got the Iradè; it came about an hour
ago."

"How can I help you?" I asked.

"You must have a disguise, too. When the court physician is sent to visit a person of consequence, he is always
accompanied by an adjutant from the palace. You must
play this part. I have borrowed a uniform from a brother
officer which will fit you. It is in your room, and I will
help you to put it on. You need say nothing, nor answer
any questions the slaves may put to you unless you are quite
sure of your words. You have a very military figure, and
the sight of a uniform acts like magic on fellows like the
Lala and his companions. As I am an adjutant myself, I
can tell you exactly what to do, so that no one could detect
you. Are you willing to try?"

"Of course," I said, rising and going towards my room.
"How are we to go to Yeni Köj?"

"A carriage from the palace will be at the door in half
an hour," answered Gregorios, looking at his watch. "Now,
then, we must turn you into a Turkish officer," he added,
with a laugh.

In ten minutes the change was complete, and I do not believe that my best friend would have recognized me in the
close-fitting dress, cut like that of a Prussian dragoon's pa-
rade uniform, but made of dark cloth with red facings. I
buckled on the sabre, and Gregorios set the fez carefully on
my head. I looked at myself in the glass. The costume
fitted as though it were made for me.

"I feel as though I were going to a masked ball," I said,
laughing. "I never was so disguised before in my life."

"I hope you may feel so when you come home," answered
Balsamides, with a smile. "Now you must take some of
your own clothes in a bag. We may not get home before
morning, and we might meet some one of the adjutants
when we come back. They would know that you are not
one of us, and there might be trouble. We must take some
money, too. We may need to hire a boat or horses; one
can never tell."

Balsamides stood a moment and looked at me, apparently
well satisfied with my appearance. Then he opened the
window to see whether the carriage was below, but it had
not yet come.

"While we are waiting, I will explain our plan of action,"
he said, as he opened his writing-desk and took a small roll of
gold pieces and a handful of silver. "We shall be driven
to the door of the house, and when we knock, Selim or some
other Lala, if there are others, will open the door. He will
see you and recognize your uniform, as well as the livery
of the palace carriage. He will salute us, and you must of
course return the salutation. I will then explain that I am
the court physician, and that his majesty, having just heard
of the Khanum Effendi's illness, has sent me down to attend her. Selim will salute us again, and show us into the
house. You will be left in the *salamlek*, the lower hall, and
I shall be shown into the harem, after a few minutes have
elapsed to give time for preparation. Then you will have
to wait, but you will probably not be disturbed, unless a

slave brings you coffee and cigarettes. Selim will probably remain in the harem all the time I am there. But if you hear anything like a scuffle, you must come when you recognize my voice. This will not occur unless Selim hears something which frightens him, and tries to get away. Of course you are supposed to be present for my protection, and you must affect a certain deference towards me."

" I will be humility itself," I answered.

" No, not too much humility. A mere show of respect for my position will do. We adjutants about the palace are not much given to self-abasement of any sort. There is one catastrophe which may occur. If the old woman is really dying, as they say she is, she may die while we are there. We must then take possession of the person of Selim and carry him off. There will not be much trouble about that. The house is in a lonely place, and the driver of the carriage knows his orders. He will obey instantly, no matter what I tell him to do."

" And if we should, by any chance, find Alexander in the house," I asked, " shall we be able to get him out without trouble ? "

" Not without trouble," answered Gregorios, with a grim smile. " But we will not stick at trifles so long as we have the imperial Iradè with us. I hear the carriage. Let us be off."

So we left the house on our errand without further words.

XV.

PAUL stayed at the hotel until a late hour, and went home, feeling lighter at heart than he had felt for many days. He was in love, and the passion had a very salutary effect upon his nature. His heart had been crushed down when he was a child, until he doubted whether he had any heart at all. His early sufferings had hardened his nature, and his cool strong mind had approved the process, so that he was well satisfied with his solitary condition and his loveless life. He had seen much of the world, and had known many women of all nations, but his immovable indifference was proverbial among his colleagues, and if he had ever entertained a passing fancy for any one, the fact was unknown to gossip. It might be supposed that this very coldness would have rendered him attractive to women, for it is commonly said, and with some truth, that they are sometimes drawn to those men who show them no manner of attention. But I think that the case is not always the same, and admits of very subtle distinctions. It is not a man's coldness that attracts a woman, but the belief that, though he is cold to others, he may soften towards herself; and this belief often rests on mere vanity, and often on the truth of the supposition. There are many men who systematically affect outward indifference in order to make themselves interesting in the eyes of the other sex, allowing a word, a look, a gesture, to betray at stated intervals that they are not indifferent to the one woman whose love they covet. They give these signs with the utmost skill and with a strange, calculating avarice. Women watch such men jealously from a distance, to see if they can detect the slightest softening of manner towards other women; and when they have convinced themselves that they alone have the power to influence the frozen nature they admire, they very easily fall wholly in love. In general a man who is very cold and indifferent is not to be trusted. The chances are ten to one that he is playing the old and time-honored part for a definite purpose.

But there are those who play no part, nor need to affect any characteristic not theirs. When women find out that a man is really indifferent to all women, their disgust knows no bounds. So long as he is known to have loved any one in the past, or to love any one in the present, or to be even likely to love any one in the future, he may be pardoned. But if it is firmly believed that he is incapable of love, womankind arises in a body and abuses him in unmeasured terms. He is selfish. He is arrogant. He is so conceited that he thinks no one good enough for him. He is a stone, a prig, a hypocrite, a maniac, a monster, a statue, and especially he is a bore. In other words, he is a man's man, and not a woman's man; and unless it can be proved that his madness proceeds from disappointed love, even Dives in hell is not further removed from forgiveness than he. Men may admire his strength, his talents, his perseverance, and some friend will be found foolish enough to sing his praises to some woman of the world. She will answer the panegyrist with a blank stare, and will very likely say coldly, that he is a bore, or that he is very rude. No amount of praise or ingenious argument will extort an admission that the unfortunate man is worthy of human sympathy. And yet, he may be very human, after all. At all events, if we say with the Greek philosopher that a man shall not be called happy until he be dead, we should not allow that he is beyond the

reach of love until the life has gone out of him, certainly
not until he is sixty years of age at the very least.

Now Paul Patoff was not sixty years old when he found
himself in the quiet English country house, and looked on
his fair English cousin and loved her. He was, as the times
go, a young man, just entered upon the prime of his life,
just past the age when youth is considered foolish, and
just reaching the time when it is considered desirable.
The fact that he had not loved before was not likely to
make his passion less strong now that it had come at last,
and he knew it, as men generally understand themselves
better when they are in love with a good woman. He asked
himself, indeed, why he had so suddenly given himself up,
heart and soul, to the lovely girl he had known only for a
month; but such questions are necessarily futile, because
the heart does not always go through the formality of asking the mind's consent before acting, and the mind consequently refuses to be called to account in a matter for
which it is in no way responsible. It seemed to Paul very
strange that after so many years of a busy life, in which no
passion but ambition had played any part, he should all at
once find his whole existence involved in a new and un-
dreamed-of labyrinth of feeling. But though it was indeed
a labyrinth, from which he did not even desire to escape,
he acknowledged that the paths of it were full of roses, and
that life in its winding walks was pleasanter than life outside.

The uncertainty of his position, however, disturbed his
dreams, and even the pleasant hours he spent with Hermione, listening to her rippling laughter and gentle voice,
were somewhat disturbed by the thought of the morrow, and
of what the end would be. His own instinct would have led
him to speak to Carvel at once and to have the matter settled,
but another set of ideas argued that he should wait and see
what happened, and if possible put off asking the fatal ques-

tion until he had unraveled the mystery of his brother's disappearance. That Carvel could have believed him in any way implicated in the tragedy, and yet have asked him to his house, he knew to be impossible; but he knew also that the shadow of Alexander's fate hung over him, and now that there existed a chance of completely and brilliantly establishing his innocence before the world, he was unwilling to take so serious a step as formally · proposing for Hermione's hand, until the long desired result should be reached. He had deeply felt the truth of what she had said to him in England, — that he should be able to silence hints like those Chrysophrasia had let fall, that he should place himself in such a position as to defy insults instead of being obliged to bear them quietly; and the conviction brought home to him by Hermione's words had resulted in his immediate departure, with the determination to fathom the mystery, and to clear himself forever, or to sacrifice his love in case of failure.

But he had not counted upon the visit of the Carvels to Constantinople. So long as he could not see Hermione, he had felt that it was possible to contemplate with some calmness the prospect of giving her up if he failed in his search. When Carvel had proposed to come out and had asked my advice, we had fancied ourselves on the verge of the final discovery, and with natural and pardonable enthusiasm Paul had joined me in urging John to bring his family at once. He had felt sure that the end was near, and he had wished that Hermione might arrive at the moment of his triumph. It would not be a complete triumph, he thought, unless she were there, and this idea showed how the man had changed under the influence of his love. In former times Paul Patoff would never have thought of anticipating success until he held it securely in his own hands; he would have worked silently, giving no sign, and when the result was obtained he would have presented it to the world with his coldest and most sarcastic stare, content in the thought that he had satisfied himself, and demanding no appreciation from others. To feel that he had succeeded was then the most delicious part of success. Now, he was so changed that he could not imagine success as being at all worth having unless Hermione were there to share it. No one else would do, and something of his exclusiveness might still be found in his desire for her sympathy, and for that of no one else. But the transformation was very great, and as he had realized it, he had understood the extent of his love for his cousin. The sensation was wholly novel, and he again asked himself what it meant, half doubting its reality, but never doubting that it would last forever, — in the highly contradictory spirit of a man who is in love for the first time.

Then Hermione arrived, and Paul awoke to find himself between two fires. To contemplate the possibility of not marrying Hermione, when she was in the same city, when he must see her and hear her voice every day of his life, was now out of the question. His love had grown ten times stronger in the separation of the last months, and he knew that it was now useless to think of putting it away. With a modesty not found in men who have loved many women, Paul discarded the idea that Hermione's happiness was as deeply concerned as his own. He did not understand how very much she loved him, and it would have seemed to his softened soul an outrageous piece of arrogance to suppose that she could not be quite as happy with some one else as with himself. But of his own feelings he had no doubt. It was perfectly clear that without Hermione life could never be worth living, and he found himself face to face with a most difficult question, — a true dilemma, from which there could be no issue unless he found his brother, or the evidences of his brother's death.

If the search proved fruitless, he was still in the position of a man who is liable to suspicion, and he had firmly resolved that he would not permit the woman he loved to marry a man who could be accused, however unjustly, of the crime of murder. On the other hand, he knew that while she was present in Constantinople he was not master of his feelings, hardly of his words; and he could not go away : first, because to go away would be to leave the search wholly in the hands of others ; and secondly, because his presence was required at the embassy and his services were constantly in requisition. To abandon his career was a course he never contemplated for a moment. His personal resources were small, and his pay was now considerable, so that he depended upon it for the necessities of life. He had never been willing to touch his brother's money, either, and this honorable refusal had practically crushed all gossip about Alexander's disappearance ; so that at the present time he was dependent upon himself. With the prospect of being a *chargé d'affaires* in a short time, and of being chancellor of an embassy at forty, he believed that he could fairly propose to marry Hermione. But to do this he must abide by his career, a conclusion which effectually prevented his flying from danger and giving the inquiry entirely into my hands. With a keen sense of honor and a very strong determination on the one side, and all the force of his love for Hermione on the other, Paul's position was not an easy one, and he knew it.

Nor was his mind wholly at rest concerning his mother. He had seen her that afternoon, and had recognized that in the ordinary sense of the word, and in the common opinion of people on the subject, she was perfectly sane. She looked, moved, talked, ate, and dressed as though she were wholly in her right mind ; but Paul was not satisfied. He had seen the old gleam of unreasoning anger in her eyes, when she had said that he knew Alexander could never be found ; meaning, as Paul supposed, that he knew how the unfortunate man had come to his end. That this belief had been the cause and first beginning of her madness, he was convinced ; and if the disturbing element was still present in her mind, it might assert itself again at any moment with direful results. He was willing, for the sake of argument, to believe that her idea was a delusion, and indeed he preferred to think so. He did not like the thought that his mother could seriously and sanely believe him to be a murderer, though she had given him reason enough for knowing how she had always disliked him. There was no affection between the mother and the son, there was not even much respect ; but beyond respect and affection we recognize in the relations of a mother with her children a sort of universal law of fitness, embracing the few conditions without which there can be no relations at all between them. That a mother should dislike her child offends our feelings and our conceptions of human sympathy ; but that a mother should wantonly and without evidence accuse her son of a fearful crime, and be his only accuser, is a sin against humanity itself, and our reason revolts against it as much as our heart.

It was hopeless to attempt an explanation of Madame Patoff's state of mind. Paul might have understood her better had he known how she talked and behaved when he was not present. John Carvel and his wife had indeed assured Paul that his mother was entirely sane, and had forgotten her resentment against him, speaking of him affectionately, and showing herself anxious to see him during the long journey. But there was one of the party who could have told a different story ; who could have repeated some of her aunt's utterances, and could have described certain phases in her temper in such a way as would have surprised the rest. Madame Patoff had naturally chosen to confide in Hermione, for Hermione had first startled her into a confession of her sanity, and with her rested the secret of the last two years. On the occasion which Carvel had mentioned in his letter to me, when Madame Patoff had been surprised in a sensible conversation by her nurse, the old lady had shown very great presence of mind. She had recognized immediately that she was detected, and that she would find it extremely difficult in future to deceive the practiced eye of the vigilant Mrs. North. She was tired, too, in spite of what she said to Hermione, of the absolute seclusion in which she lived; not that she was wearied of mourning for Alexander, but because she had exhausted one way of expressing her grief. So, at least, it seemed to Hermione. Madame Patoff had therefore accepted the situation and made the best of it, declaring herself sane and entirely recovered. She had always contemplated the possibility of some such termination to her pretended madness, and was perhaps glad that it had come at last. She even found at first a pleasant relaxation in leading the life of an ordinary person, and she tried to join in the life of the family in such a way as to be no longer a burden or a source of anxiety to those she had capriciously sacrificed during a year and a half. But with Hermione she was not the same as with the rest. She was with her what she had been on the first day when Hermione had declared her love for Paul, and it appeared to the young girl that her aunt was in reality leading a double existence, being in one state when with the assembled family, and in quite another when she was alone with Hermione.

Madame Patoff was able to force herself upon her niece, for the young girl had given a promise not to betray her secret, and though often in hard straits to elude her father's questions without falling into falsehood, felt herself bound to her aunt, and obliged to submit to long conversations with her. It was a difficult position, and any one less honest than Hermione and less sensitively tactful would have found it hard to maintain the balance. She herself avoided carefully all mention of Paul, but her aunt delighted in talking of him. One of these conversations took place on the evening of their arrival in Constantinople, and may well serve as a specimen of the rest. When all the party had retired for the night, Madame Patoff came into Hermione's room and sat down, evidently with the intention of staying at least an hour. Hermione looked at her with a deprecating expression, being indeed very tired, and wishing that her aunt would put off her visit until the next day. She saw, however, that there was no hope of this, and submitted herself with a good grace.

"Are you not tired, aunt Annie?" asked the young girl.

"No, no, not very, my dear," said the old lady, smoothing her thick gray hair with her hand, and fixing her dark eyes on her niece's face. "Oh, Hermy, what a meeting!" she suddenly exclaimed. "If you knew how hard I tried to be kind to him, I am sure you would pity me. It is so hard, so hard!"

"It is the least you can do, — to treat him kindly," answered Hermione, somewhat coldly. "But I was very glad to see that you kissed him when we arrived."

"It was dreadfully hard to do it. The very sight of him freezes my blood. Oh, Hermy dear, how can you love him so much, when I love you as I do? It frightens me" —

"It does not frighten me, aunt Annie," said her niece. "I can say, when you love me as you do, how can you not love him?"

"It is not the same, my dear. How could I love him, knowing what I know?"

"You do not know it," answered Hermione very firmly, "and you must not suggest it to me. Sometimes I could almost think you were really mad, aunt Annie, — forgive me, I must say it. Not mad as you pretended to be, but mad on this one point. You have always hated poor Paul since he was a child, and you have treated him very unkindly. But you have no right to accuse him now, and I would not listen to you unless I believed that I could help to make you see him as you should."

Madame Patoff bent her head and hid her eyes in her hand, as though greatly distressed.

"I love you so much, dear Hermy — I cannot bear to think of your marrying him. You cannot understand me — I know — and you think me very unkind. But I hate him!" she cried, with a burst of uncontrollable anger. "Oh, how I hate him!"

Her hands had dropped from her face, and her dark eyes flashed wickedly as she stared at the young girl. Hermione was startled for a moment, but she also had learned a lesson of self-possession.

"Do you think that I am afraid when you look at me like that, aunt Annie?" she asked, very quietly.

Madame Patoff's features relaxed, and she laughed a little foolishly, as though ashamed of herself.

"No, child; why should you be afraid? I am only an unhappy old woman. I cannot speak to any one else."

"And you must not speak to me in that way," answered Hermione, in a gentle tone. "I love Paul with all my heart, and I cannot hear him abused by you, even though I know you are out of your mind when you say such things. I should be despicable if I listened to you."

"If I loved you less, dear," returned the old lady, "I might hate him less. Ah, if you could only have married Alexis, — if it could only have been the other way!"

"Hush!" exclaimed Hermione, almost roughly. "You are wishing that Paul were dead, instead of his brother. I will go away, if you talk like that."

She suited the action to the word, and rose to go towards the door. She knew her aunt very well. Madame Patoff changed her tone at once.

"Oh, don't go away, don't go away!" she cried nervously. "I will never speak of him again, if you will only stay with me."

Hermione turned and came back, and saw that her threat had for the present produced its effect, as it usually did.

Madame Patoff had indeed a strange affection for her niece,
and the latter knew how to manage her by means of it. **At**
the mere idea of Hermione's leaving her in anger, the aunt
softened and became docile.

"I did not mean it, child," she said, dolefully. "I am
always so unhappy, so dreadfully wretched, that I say
things I do not altogether mean. I am not quite myself
to-night, either. Coming here, to the place where my
poor boy was lost, has upset my nerves; and, really, your
aunt Chrysophrasia is so very tactless. She always was
like that. I remember the way in which she treated my
poor husband before we were married. It was she who
made all the quarrel, you know. It broke up my life at
the very beginning, and we two sisters never saw each other
again. I do not know what would have become of me if
my husband had not loved me as he did. He was so kind
to me, always, and he sympathized in all my feelings and
ideas. If he had only lived, how different it might all have
been!"

Hermione thought so, too; reflecting that if Paul's father
had been alive during the time when he was growing up,
the unfortunate boy would have been spared a vast deal of
suffering, and Madame Patoff would perhaps have been
held in check. Her character was not of the kind which
could safely be left to its own development, for she called
her caprices justice and her obstinacy principle, a mode of
viewing life not conducive to much permanent satisfaction
when not modified by the salutary restraint of a more sensible companion. But Hermione was glad that her aunt
was willing to talk of anything except Paul, and encouraged
her to continue, though she had heard again and again Madame Patoff's account of her own life and of the family
quarrels. By carefully listening and watching her, it was
possible to keep her from reaching the point at which Hermione was always obliged to protest that she would not hear
more.

It may be judged from this scene that the young girl's position was not an easy one. She was beginning to feel that Madame Patoff's hatred for Paul approached in reality much nearer to insanity than the affected apathy she had assumed before Hermione discovered the imposition; but, nevertheless, the young girl felt that, sane or not sane, she could allow no one to cast a slur on the name of the man she loved. She was glad, indeed, that Madame Patoff did not make her hatred and her suspicion topics for conversation with the rest of the family, and she was willing to suffer much in order that her aunt might confide in her alone, and behave herself with propriety and dignity before the others. But when Madame Patoff overstepped the limits Hermione had set for her, the old lady invariably found herself checked and even frightened by the authoritative manner of her niece. The anxiety, however, and the constant annoyance to which she was subjected, together with the sorrow of the separation from Paul, had told upon the girl's strength, and it was no wonder that she had grown thinner during the last months. Her young character was forming itself under terrible difficulties, and it was well that she inherited more of her father's good sense and courage than of her mother's meekness and gentleness under all circumstances. Hermione looked back and tried to remember what she had been six months ago, but she hardly recognized herself in the picture called up by her memories. She thought of her ignorance about her aunt's state, and of how she had sometimes felt sad and sorry for the old lady, but had on the whole not found that her presence in the house materially changed her own smooth life. She looked further back, and remembered as in a dream her first London season. She had not enjoyed herself; she had been oppressed rather than delighted by the crowds, the lights, the whirl of a life she could not understand, the terrors of presentation, the men suddenly brought up to her, who bowed and immediately whirled her away amongst a crowd of young people, all spinning madly round, and knowing each other probably as little as she knew her partner of the moment. It had all been strange to her, and she realized with pleasure that she should not be obliged to go through it again this year. Her mother was not a worldly woman, and had not inspired her, while still in the schoolroom, with a mad desire for the world. Hermione was an only daughter, and there was no reason for hastening her marriage; nor had she ever been told, as many young girls are, that she must marry well, and if possible in her first season. She saw many men in the round of parties to which she was taken, but she found it hard to remember the names of even a few of them. They had been presented, had danced with her, had perhaps danced with her again somewhere else, and had dropped out of her existence without inspiring in her the smallest interest. Now, after nearly a year, she would not have known their faces. Some had talked to her, but their language was not hers; it was the jargon of society, the petty gossip, the eternal chatter of people and people's doings. Her answers were vague, and when she asked a question about a book, about an idea, about a fact, the faultlessly correct young men smiled sweetly, and answered that they did not understand that sort of thing. Towards the end of the season, when the first surprise of watching the moving crowds, the dancing, the women's gowns, and the men's faces, had worn out, Hermione had regarded the whole thing as an inexpressible bore, and had returned with delight to the quiet life at Carvel Place, glad that her father's position and tastes did not lead him to keep open house, as some of his neighbors did, and that she was allowed to read and to be quiet, and to do everything she liked.

Then her real life had begun, and her character, untouched and unchanged by what she had seen in a London season, had suddenly come under the influence of another character, strong, dominant, and apparently good, but in the eyes of the young girl eminently mysterious. She had known

Paul Patoff as one knows people in the midst of a small family party in a country house, and he had at first repelled her, as he repelled many people ; but soon, very soon, she thought, the feeling of repulsion had grown to be a curiosity to know the man's history, the secret of his coldness towards his mother, and of his hard and cynical expression. From such interest as she felt for him, it was but a step to love, and the step was soon taken. The nearer she came to him, the more she felt the power of his fascination, and the more she wondered that every one else did not see it as she saw it, and yield to it as she yielded to it. Then had come the afternoon in the park ; the joy of those few hours ; the scene at dinner on the same evening ; the revelation she had extracted from Cutter ; the discovery that her aunt was sane ; her interview with Paul, and his sudden departure, wounded by her speech ; — all these events following on each other in less than four-and-twenty hours. From that day she knew that she had changed much, and she realized the strength of her love for Paul. And on that day, also, had begun her annoyances with Madame Patoff, her constant defense of the son against the accusations of the mother, and her own fears lest she should be playing a double part. She had suffered much by the separation from Paul ; she suffered more whenever her aunt fell into her passionate way of abusing him, and she felt that her faculties were over-strained when she was in the society of her strange relative. But Madame Patoff loved her, and her affection was so evident to Hermione that she found it hard to cut her speeches short with a sharp word, however painful it might be to her to listen to them. Of late she had adopted the practice of· treating her as she did on the first night, assuming that her hatred was very nearly an insanity in itself, and managing her almost like a child, threatening to leave her when she said too much, and bringing her to her senses by seeming to withdraw her affection. Indeed, there was something exaggerated in Madame Patoff's love for the girl, as there appeared to be in everything she really felt. With the other members of the household she behaved with perfect self-possession, but when she was alone with Hermione she laid aside all her assumed calm, and spoke unreasonably about her son, as though it gave her pleasure ; always submitting, however, to the rebuke which Hermione invariably administered on such occasions. But the idea that whenever she was alone with her aunt something of the kind was sure to occur made Hermione nervous, so that she avoided an interview whenever she could.

XVI.

IF any of the party could have guessed what Gregorios Balsamides and I were doing on that dark night, they would not have slept as soundly as they did. It was an evil night, a night for a bad deed, I thought, as I looked out of the carriage-window, when we were clear of the houses and streets of Pera. The black clouds drove angrily down before the north wind, seeming to tear themselves in pieces on the stars, as one might tear a black veil upon steel nails. The wind swept the desolate country, and made the panes of the windows rattle even more loudly than did the hoofs and wheels upon the stony road. But the horses were strong, and the driver was not a shivering Greek, but a sturdy Turk, who could laugh at the wind as it whistled past his ears, striking full upon his broad chest. He drove fast along the rising ground, and faster as he reached the high bend which the road follows above the Bosphorus, winding in and out among the hills till it descends at last to Therapia.

"The clouds look like the souls of the lost, to-night," said Balsamides, drawing his fur coat closely around him. "One can imagine how Dante conceived the idea of the scene in hell, when the souls stream down the wind."

"You seem poetically inclined," I answered.

"Why not? We are out upon a romantic errand. Our lives are not often romantic. We may as well make the best of it, as a beggar does when he gets a bowl of rice."

"I should fancy you had led a very romantic life," said I, lighting a cigarette in the dark, and leaning back against the cushions.

"That is what women always say when they want a man to make confidences," laughed Balsamides. "No, I have not led a romantic life. I pass most of my time sitting on my horse in the hot sun, or the driving snow, preserving, or pretending to preserve, the life of his Majesty from real or imaginary dangers. Or else I sit eight or nine hours a day chatting and smoking with the other adjutants. It is not a healthy life. It is certainly not romantic."

"Not as you describe it. But I judged from the ease with which you made the preparations for this expedition that you had done things of the sort before."

My friend laughed again, but turned the subject.

"I hope that when we meet your friends to-morrow morning, we may have something to show for our night's work," he said. "Fancy what an excitement there would be if we brought Alexander Patoff back with us! Not that it is at all probable. We may bring back nothing but broken bones."

"I do not think Selim will hurt us much," I answered. "He is not exactly an athlete. I would risk a fight with him."

"I dare say. But there may be plenty of strong fellows about the premises. There are the four caïdjs, the boatmen, to begin with. There is a coachman and probably two grooms. Very likely there are half a dozen big hamáls about."

"That makes thirteen," I said. "Six and a half to one, or four and a third to one, if we count upon our own driver."

"You may count upon him," replied Gregorios. "He is an old soldier, and as strong as a lion. In case of necessity he will call the watch from Yeni Köj. There is a small detachment of infantry there. But we shall not have to resort to such measures. I believe that I can make the Khanum confess. If so, I can make her order Selim to give up Patoff, if he is alive."

"And if he is dead?"

"It will be the worse for the Khanum and her people. She is not in good odor at the palace. It would not take much to have her exiled to Arabia, even though she be dying, as they say she is. That is the question. Let me only find her alive, and I will answer for the rest."

"She might very well refuse to confess, I fancy," I remarked, surprised at my friend's tone of conviction.

"I believe not," he said shortly. Then he remained silent for some time.

My nerves are good; but I did not like the business, though I knew it was undertaken for a good purpose, and that if we were successful we should be conferring great and lasting happiness upon more than one of my friends. I had heard many queer stories of wild deeds in the East, and in my own experience had been concerned in at least one strange and unhappy story, which had ended in my losing sight forever of a man who was very dear to me. I do not think that the fact of having been in danger necessarily brings with it a liking for dangerous adventures, though it undoubtedly makes a man more fit to encounter perils of all kinds. Few men are absolutely careless of life, and those who are, do not of necessity court death. It is one thing to say that one would readily die at any moment; it is quite another to seek risks and to incur them voluntarily. The brave man, as a general rule, does not feel a thrill of pleasure until the struggle has actually begun; when he is expecting it he is grave and cautious, lest it should come upon him unawares. This, at least, I believe to be the character of the Northern man, and I think it constitutes one of his elements of superiority.

Balsamides is an Oriental, and looks at things very differently. In his belief death will come at its appointed time, whether a man stay at home and nurse his safety, or whether he lead the front in battle. The essence of fatalism is the conviction that death must come at a certain time, no matter what a man is doing, nor how he may try to protect himself. This is the reason why the fanatic Mussulman is absolutely indifferent to danger. He firmly believes that if he is to die, death will overtake him at the plow as surely as in storming an enemy's battery. But he believes also that if he dies fighting against unbelievers his place in Paradise will be far higher than if he dies upon his farm, his ambrosial refreshment more abundant, and the dark-eyed houris who will soothe his eternal repose more beautiful and more numerous. The low-born hamál in the street will march up to the mouth of the guns without so much as a cup of coffee to animate him, with an absolute courage not found in men who have not his unswerving faith. To him Paradise is an almost visible reality, and the attainment of it depends only on his individual exertions. But what is most strange is the fact that this indifference to death is contagious, so that Christians who live among Turks unconsciously acquire much of the Moslem belief in fate. The Albanians, who are chiefly Christians, are among the bravest officers in the Turkish army, as they are amongst the most faithfully devoted to the Sultan and to the interests of the Empire.

Balsamides was in a mood which differed widely from mine. As we clattered over the rough road in the face of the north wind, I was thinking of what was before us, anticipating trouble, and determining within myself what I would do. If I were ready to meet danger, it was from an inward conviction of necessity which clearly presented itself to me, and I consequently made the best of it. But Balsamides grew merry as we proceeded. His spirits rose at the mere thought of a fight, until I almost fancied that he would provoke an unnecessary struggle rather than forego the pleasure of dealing a few blows. It was a new phase of his character, and I watched him, or rather listened to him, with interest.

"This is positively delightful," he said in a cheerful voice.

"What?" I inquired, with pardonable curiosity.

"What? In an hour or two we may have strangled the Lala, have forced the old Khanum to confess her iniquities, kicked the retainers into the Bosphorus, and be on our way back, with Alexander Patoff in this very carriage! I cannot imagine a more delightful prospect."

"It is certainly a lively entertainment for a cold night," I replied. "But if you expect me to murder anybody in cold blood, I warn you that I will not do it."

"No; but they may show fight," he said. "A little scuffle would be such a rest after leading this monotonous life. I should think you would be more enthusiastic."

"I shall reserve my enthusiasm until the fight is over."

"Then it will be of no use to you. Where is the pleasure in talking about things when they are past? The real pleasure is in action."

"Action is not necessarily bloodshed," said I. "Active exercise is undoubtedly good for mind and body, but when you take it by strangling your fellow-creatures " —

"Rubbish!" exclaimed Balsamides. "What is the life of one Lala more or less in this world? Besides, he will not be killed unless he deserves it."

"With your ideas about the delight of such amusements, you will be likely to find that he deserves it. I do not think he would be very safe in your keeping."

"No, perhaps not," he answered, with a light laugh. "If he objects to letting me in, I shall take great pleasure in making short work of him. I am rather sorry you have put on that uniform. Your appearance will probably inspire so much respect that they will all act like sheep in a thunderstorm, — huddle together, and bleat or squeal. It is some consolation to think that unless I appeared with an adjutant they would not believe that I came from the palace."

"It is a consolation to me to think that my presence may render it unnecessary for you to strangle, crucify, burn alive, and drown the whole population of Yeni Köj," I answered. "I dare say you have done most of those things at one time or another."

"In insurrections, such as we occasionally have in Albania and Crete, it is imperative sometimes to make an example. But I am not bloodthirsty."

"No; from your conversation I should take you for a lamb," said I.

"I am not bloodthirsty," continued Gregorios. "I should not care to kill a man who was quite defenseless, or who was innocent. Indeed, I would not do such a thing on any account."

"You amaze me," I observed.

"No. But I like fighting. I enter into the spirit of the thing. There is really nothing more exhilarating, — I even believe it is healthy."

"For the survivors it is good exercise. Those who do not survive are, of course, no longer in a condition to appreciate the fun."

"Exactly; the fun consists in surviving."

"One does not always survive," I objected.

"What is the difference?" exclaimed Balsamides, who probably shrugged his shoulders, in his dark corner of the carriage. "A man can die only once, and then it is all over."

"A man can also live only once," said I. "A living dog is better than a dead lion."

"Very little," answered Balsamides, with a laugh. "I would rather have been a living lion for ever so short a time, and be dead, than be a Pera dog forever. The Preacher would have been nearer to the truth if he had said that a living man is better than a dead man. But the Preacher was an Oriental, and naturally had to use a simile to express his meaning."

Suddenly the carriage stopped in the road. Then, after a moment's pause, we turned to the right, and began to descend a steep hill, slowly and cautiously, for the night was very dark and the road bad.

"We are going down to Yeni Köj," said Balsamides.

"In twenty minutes we shall be there. I will get out of the carriage first. Remember that, once there, you must not speak a word of any language but Turkish."

Slowly we crept down the hill, the wheels grinding in the drag, and jolting heavily from time to time. There were trees by the roadside, — indeed, we were on the outskirts of the Belgrade forest. The bare boughs swayed and creaked in the bitter March wind, and as I peered out through the window the night seemed more hideous than ever.

"By the by," said I, suddenly, "we have no names. What am I to call you, if I have to speak to you?"

"Anything," said Balsamides. "She does not know the name of the court physician, I suppose. However, you had better call me by his name. She might know, after all. Call me Kalopithaki Bey. You are Mehemet Bey. That is simple enough. Here we are coming to the house; be ready, they will open the door if they recognize the palace carriage through the lattice. Of course every one will be up if the old lady is dying, and it is not much past twelve. The man has driven fast."

The wheels rattled over the pavement, and we drew up before the door of Laleli's house. We both descended quickly, and Balsamides went up the broad steps which led to the door and knocked. Some one opened almost immediately, and a harsh voice — not Selim's — called out, —

"Who is there?"

"From the palace, by order of his Majesty," answered Balsamides, promptly. I showed myself by his side, and, as he had predicted, the effect produced by the adjutant's uniform was instantaneous. The man made a low salute, which we hastily returned, and held the door wide open for us to pass; closing it and bolting it, however, when we had entered. I noticed that the bolts slid easily and noiselessly in their sockets. The man was a sturdy and military Turk, I observed, with grizzled mustaches and a face deeply marked with small-pox.

We entered a lofty vestibule, lighted by two hanging lamps. The floor was matted, but there was no furniture of any description. At the opposite end a high doorway was closed by a heavy curtain. A large Turkish mangál, or brazier, stood in the middle of the wide hall. The man turned to the right and led us into a smaller apartment, of which the walls were ornamented with mirrors in gilt frames. A low divan, covered with satin of the disagreeable color known as magenta, surrounded the róom on all sides. Two small tables, inlaid with tortoise-shell and mother-of-pearl, stood side by side in the middle of the apartment.

"Buyurun, be seated, Effendimlir," said the man, who then left the room. A moment later we heard his harsh voice at some distance : —

"Selim, Selim ! There are two Effendilir from Yildiz-Kiöshk in the selamlek ! "

We sat down to wait.

"The porter is a genuine Turk, and not a Circassian. A Circassian would have said ' Effendilir,' without the ' m,' in the vocative when he spoke to us, as he did when he used it in the nominative to Selim."

I reflected that Balsamides had good nerves if he could notice grammatical niceties at such a moment.

XVII.

In a few moments Selim, the hideous Lala, entered the room, making the usual salutation as he advanced. He must have recognized Balsamides at once, for he started and stood still when he saw him, and seemed about to speak. But my appearance probably prevented him from saying what was on his lips, and he stood motionless before us. Balsamides assumed a suave manner, and informed him that he was sent by his Majesty to afford relief, if possible, to Laleli Khanum Effendi. His Majesty, said Gregorios, was deeply grieved at hearing of the Khanum's illness, and desired that every means should be employed to alleviate her sufferings. He begged that Selim would at once inform the Khanum of the physician's presence, as every moment might be of importance at such a juncture.

Selim could hardly have guessed the truth. He did not know the court doctor by sight, and Balsamides played his part with consummate coolness. The negro could never have imagined that a Frank and a foreigner would dare to assume the uniform of one of the Sultan's adjutants, — a uniform which he knew very well, and which he knew that he must respect. He was terrified when he recognized in the Sultan's medical adviser the man who had scattered the crowd in the bazaar, and who had so startled him by his references to the ring, the box, and the chain. He was frightened, but he knew he could not attempt to resist the imperial order, and after a moment's hesitation he answered.

" The Khanum Effendi," he said, " is indeed very ill. It is past midnight, and no one in the harem thinks of sleep. I will prepare the Khanum for the Effendi's visit."

Thereupon he withdrew, and we were once more left alone. I confess that my courage rose as I grew more confident of the excellence of my disguise. If the Lala himself had no doubts concerning me, it was not likely that any one else would venture to question my identity. As for Balsamides, he seemed as calm as though he were making an ordinary visit.

"They will make us wait," he said. "It will take half an hour to prepare the harem for my entrance. The old lady may be dying, but she will not sacrifice the formalities. It is no light thing with such as she to receive a visit from a Frank doctor."

He spoke in a low voice, lest the porter in the hall should hear us. But he did not speak again. I fancied he was framing his speech to the Khanum. The preparations within did not take so long as he had expected, for scarcely ten minutes had elapsed when Selim returned.

"Buyurun," said the negro, shortly. The word is the universal formula in Turkey for "walk in," "sit down," "make yourself comfortable," "help yourself."

Balsamides glanced at me, as we both rose from our seats, and I saw that he was perfectly calm and confident. A moment later I was alone.

Gregorios followed Selim into the hall; then, passing under the heavy curtain and through a door which the Lala opened on the other side, he found himself within the precincts of the harem, in a wide vestibule not unlike the one he had just quitted, though more brilliantly lighted, and furnished with low divans covered with pale blue satin. There was no one to be seen, however, and Balsamides followed the negro, who entered a door on the right-hand side, at the end of the hall. They passed through a narrow passage, entirely hung with rose-colored silk and matted, but devoid of furniture, and then Selim raised a curtain and admitted Gregorios to the presence of the sick lady.

The apartment was vast and brilliantly illuminated with

lamps. Huge mirrors in gilt frames of the fashion of the last century filled the panels from the ceiling to the wainscoting. In the corners, and in every available space between the larger ones, small mirrors bearing branches of lights were hung, and groups of lamps were suspended from the ceiling. The whole effect was as though the room had been lighted for a ball. The Khanum had always loved lights, and feeling her sight dimmed by illness she had ordered every lamp in the house to be lighted, producing a fictitious daylight, and perhaps in some measure the exhilaration which daylight brings with it.

The floor of the hall was of highly polished wood, and the everlasting divans of disagreeable magenta satin, so dear to the modern Turkish woman, lined the walls on three sides. At the upper end, however, a dais was raised about a foot from the floor. Here rich Siné and Giordès carpets were spread, and a broad divan extended across the whole width of the apartment, covered with silk of a very delicate hue, such as in the last century was called " bloom " in England. The long stiff cushions, of the same material, leaned stiffly against the wall at the back of the low seat, in an even row. Several dwarf tables, of the inlaid sort, stood within arm's-length of the divan, and on one of them lay a golden salver, bearing a crystal jar of strawberry preserves, and a glass half full of water, with a gold spoon in it. In the right-hand corner of the divan was the Khanum herself.

The old lady's dress was in striking contrast to her surroundings. She wore a shapeless, snuff-colored gown, very loose and only slightly gathered at the waist. As she sat propped among her cushions, her feet entirely concealed beneath her, she seemed to be inclosed in a brown bag, from which emerged her head and hands. The latter were very small and white, and might well have belonged to a young woman, but her head was that of an aged crone. Balsamides was amazed at her ugliness and the extraordinary expression of her features. She wore no head-dress, and the bit of gauze about her throat, which properly speaking should have concealed her face, did not even cover her chin. Her hair was perfectly black in spite of her age, and being cut so short as only to reach the collar of her gown, hung straight down like that of an American Indian, brushed back from the high yellow forehead, and falling like stiff horse-hair over her ears and cheeks when she bent forward. Her eyes, too, were black, and were set so near together as to give her a very disagreeable expression, while the heavy eyebrows rose slightly from the nose towards the temples. The nose was long, straight, and pointed, but very thin; and the nostrils, which had once been broad and sensitive, were pinched and wrinkled by old age and the play of strong emotions. Her cheeks were hollowed and yellow, as the warped parchment cover of an old manuscript, seamed with furrows in all directions, so that the slightest motion of her face destroyed one set of deep-traced lines only to exhibit another new and unexpected network of wrinkles. The upper lip was long and drawn down, while the thin mouth curved upwards at the corners in a disagreeable smile, something like that which seems to play about the long, slit lips of a dead viper. This unpleasant combination of features was terminated by a short but prominent chin, indicating a determined and undeviating will. The ghastly yellow color of her face made the unnatural brightness of her beady eyes more extraordinary still.

To judge from her appearance, she had not long to live, and Balsamides realized the fact as soon as he was in her presence. It was not a fever; it was no sudden illness which had attacked her, depriving her of strength, speech, and consciousness. She was dying of a slow and incurable disease, which fed upon the body without weakening the energies of the brain, and which had now reached its last stage. She might live a month, or she might die that very night, but her end was close at hand. With the iron determination of a tyrannical old woman, she kept up appearances to the last, and had insisted on being carried to the great hall and set in the place of honor upon the divan to receive the visit of the physician. Indeed, for many days she had given the slaves of her harem no rest, causing herself to be carried from one part of the house to another, in the vain hope of finding some relief from the pain which devoured her. All night the great rooms were illuminated. Day and night the slaves exhausted themselves in the attempt to amuse her: the trained and educated Circassian girl translated the newspapers to her, or read aloud whole chapters of Victor Hugo's Misérables, one of the few foreign novels which have been translated into Turkish; the almehs danced and sang to their small lutes; the black slaves succeeded each other in bringing every kind of refreshment which the ingenuity of the Dalmatian cook could devise; the whole establishment was in perpetual motion, and had rarely in the last few days snatched a few minutes of uneasy rest when the Khanum slept her short and broken sleep. It chanced that Laleli had all her life detested opium, and was so quick to detect its presence in a sweetmeat or in a sherbet, that now, when its use might have soothed her agonies, no member of her household had the courage to offer it to her. Her sleepless days and nights passed in the perpetual effort to obtain some diversion from her pain, and with every hour it became more difficult to satisfy her craving for change and amusement.

Balsamides came forward, touching his hand to his mouth and forehead; and then approaching nearer, he awaited her invitation to sit down. The old woman made a feeble, almost palsied gesture with her thin white hand, and Gregorios advanced and seated himself upon the divan at some distance from his patient.

"His Majesty has sent you?" she inquired presently, slowly turning her head and fixing her beady eyes upon his face. Her voice was weak and hoarse, scarcely rising above a whisper.

"It is his Majesty's pleasure that I should use my art to stay the hand of death," replied Balsamides. "His Majesty is deeply grieved to hear of the Khanum Effendi's illness."

"My gratitude is profound as the sea," said Laleli Khanum, but as she spoke the viper smile wreathed and curled upon her seamed lips. "I thank his Majesty. My time is come, — it is my kadèr, my fate. Allah alone can save. None else can help me."

"Nevertheless, though it be in vain, I must try my arts, Khanum Effendim," said Balsamides.

"What are your arts?" asked the sick woman, scornfully. "Can you burn me with fire, and make a new Laleli out of the ashes of my bones?"

"No," said Gregorios, "I cannot do that, but I can ease your pain, and perhaps you may recover."

"If you can ease my pain, you shall be rich. But you can not. Only Allah is great!"

"If the Khanum will permit her servant to approach her and to touch her hand" — suggested Balsamides, humbly.

"Gelinis, come," muttered Laleli. But she drew the pale green veil that was round her throat a little higher, so as to cover her mouth. "What is this vile body that it should be any longer withheld from the touch of the unbeliever? What is your medicine, Giaour? Shall the touch of your unbelieving hand, wherewith you daily make signs before images, heal the sickness of her who is a daughter of the prophet of the Most High?"

Balsamides rose from his seat and came to her side. She shrank together in her snuff-colored, bag-shaped gown, and hesitated before she would put out her small hand, and her eyes expressed ineffable disgust. But at last she held out her fingers, and Gregorios succeeded in getting at her wrist. The pulse was very quick, and fluttered and sank at every fourth or fifth beat.

"The Khanum is in great pain," said Gregorios. He saw

indeed that she was in a very weak state, and he fancied she could not last long.

"Ay, the pains of Gehennam are upon me," she answered in her hoarse whisper, and at the same time she trembled violently, while the perspiration broke out in a clammy moisture on her yellow forehead.

Gregorios produced a small case from his pocket. It is the magical transformer of the modern physician.

"The prick of a pin," said he, "and your pain will cease. If the Khanum will consent?"

She was in an access of terrible agony, and could not speak. Gregorios took from his case a tiny syringe and a small bottle containing a colorless liquid. It was the work of an instant to puncture the skin of Laleli's hand, and to inject a small dose of morphine, — a very small dose indeed, for the solution was weak. But the effect was almost instantaneous. The Khanum opened her small black eyes, the contortion of her wrinkled face gave way to a more natural expression, and she gradually assumed a look of peace and relief which told Gregorios that the drug had done its work. Even her voice sounded less hoarse and indistinct when she spoke again.

"I am cured!" she exclaimed in sudden delight. "The pain is gone, — Allah be praised, the pain is gone, the fire is put out! I shall live! I shall live!"

Not one word of thanks to Gregorios escaped her lips. It was characteristic of the woman that she expressed only her own satisfaction at the relief she experienced, feeling not the smallest gratitude towards the physician. She clapped her thin hands, and a black slave girl appeared, one of those called halaïk, or "creatures." The Khanum ordered coffee and chibouques. She had never accepted the modern cigarette.

"The relief is instantaneous," remarked Balsamides, carefully putting back the syringe and the bottle in the little case, which he returned to his pocket.

"Tell me," said the old woman, lowering her voice, "is it the magic of the Franks?"

"It is, and it is not," answered Gregorios, willing to play upon her superstition. "It is, truly, very mysterious, and a man who employs it must have clean hands and a brave heart. And so, indeed, must the person who benefits by the cure. Otherwise it cannot be permanent. The sins which burden the soul have power to consume the body, and if there is no repentance, no device to undo the harm done, the magic properties of the fluid are soon destroyed by the more powerful arts of Satan."

The Khanum looked anxiously at Balsamides as he spoke. At that moment the black slave girl returned, bearing two little cups of coffee, while two other girls, exactly like the first, followed with two lighted chibouques, a mangál filled with coals, two small rass dishes upon which the bowls of the pipes were to rest, so as not to burn the carpet, and a little pair of steel firetongs inlaid with gold. At a sign the three slaves silently retired. The Khanum drank the hot coffee eagerly, and, placing the huge amber mouthpiece against her lips, began to inhale the smoke. Gregorios followed her example.

"What is this you say of Satan destroying the power of your medicine?" asked Laleli, presently.

"It is the truth, Khanum Effendim," answered Balsamides, solemnly. "If, therefore, you would be healed, repent of sin, and if you have done anything that is sinful, command that be undone, if possible. If not, your pain will return, and I cannot save you."

"How do you, a Giaour, talk to me of repentance?" asked Laleli, in scornful tones. "While you try to extract the eyelash from my eye, you do not see the beam which has entered your own."

"Nevertheless, unless you repent my medicine will not heal you," returned Gregorios, calmly.

"What have I to repent? Shall you find out my sin?"

"That I be unable to find it out does not destroy the necessity for your repenting it. The time is short. If your heart is not clean you will soon be writhing in a worse agony than when I charmed away your pain."

"We shall see," retorted the Khanum, her features wrinkling in a contemptuous smile. "I tell you I feel perfectly well. I have recovered."

But she had hardly spoken, and puffed a great cloud of aromatic smoke into the still air of the illuminated room, when the smile began to fade. Balsamides watched her narrowly, and saw the former expression of pain slowly returning to her face. He had not expected it so soon, but in his fear of producing death he had administered a very small dose of morphine, and the disease was far advanced. Laleli, however, though terrified as she felt that the agony she had so long endured was returning after so brief a respite, endeavored bravely to hide her sufferings, lest she should seem to confess that the Giaour was right, and that it was the presence of the devil in her heart which prevented the medicine from having its full effect. Gradually, as she smoked on in silence, Gregorios saw that the disease had got the mastery over her again, and that she was struggling to control her features. He pretended not to observe the change, and waited philosophically for the inevitable result. At last the unfortunate woman could bear it no longer; the pipe dropped from her trembling hand, and the sweat stood upon her brow.

"I wonder whether there is any truth in what you say!" she exclaimed, in a voice broken with the pain she would not confess.

"It is useless to deny it," answered Balsamides. "The Khanum Effendim is already suffering."

"No, I am not!" she said between her teeth. But the perspiration trickled down her hollow cheeks. Suddenly, unable to hide the horrible agony which was gnawing in her bosom, she uttered a short, harsh cry, and rocked herself backwards and forwards.

"It is even so," said Balsamides, eying her coldly, and not moving from his place as he blew the clouds of smoke into the warm air. "My medicine is of no use when the soul is dark and diseased by a black deed."

"Where is the medicine?" cried the wretched woman, swaying from side to side in her agony. "Where is it? Give it to me again, or I shall die!"

"It cannot help you unless you confess your sin," returned her torturer indifferently.

"In the name of Allah! I will confess all, even to you an unbeliever, if you will only give me rest again!" cried Laleli. From the momentary respite the pain seemed far greater than before.

"If you will do that, I will try and save you," answered Balsamides, producing the case from his pocket. He had been very far from expecting the advantage he had obtained through the combination of the old woman's credulity and extreme suffering; but in his usual cold fashion he now resolved to use it to the utmost. Laleli saw him take the syringe from the case, and her eyes glittered with the anticipation of immediate relief.

"Speak," said Gregorios, — "confess your sin, and you shall have rest."

"What am I to confess?" asked the old woman, hungrily watching the tiny instrument in his fingers.

"This," answered Balsamides, lowering his voice. "You must tell me what became of a Russian Effendi, whose name was Alexander, whom you caused to be seized one night in the last week of" —

Again Laleli cried out, and rocked her body, apparently suffering more than ever.

"The medicine!" she whispered almost inaudibly. — "Quick — I cannot speak — am dying of the pain." The perspiration streamed down her yellow wrinkled face, and Balsamides feared the end was come.

"You must tell me first, or it will be of no use," he said.

But he quickly filled the syringe, and prepared to repeat the former operation.

"I cannot," groaned Laleli. "I die! — quick! Then I will tell."

A physician might have known whether the woman were really dying or not, but Balsamides' science did not go so far as that. Without further hesitation he pricked the skin of her hand and injected a small quantity, a very little more than the first time. The effect was not quite so sudden as before, but it followed after a few seconds. The signs of extreme suffering disappeared from the Khanum's face, and she once more looked up.

"Your medicine is good, Giaour," she said, with the ghost of a disdainful laugh. But her voice was still very weak and hoarse.

"It will not save you unless you confess what became of the Frank," said Gregorios, again putting his instrument into the case, and the case into his pocket.

"It is very easy for me to have you kept here, and to force you to cure me," she answered with a wicked smile. "Do you think you can leave my house without my permission?"

"Easily," returned Balsamides, coolly. "I have not come here unprotected. His Majesty's adjutant is outside. You will not find it easy to take him prisoner."

"Who knows?" exclaimed Laleli. "The only thing which prevents me from keeping you is, that I see you have very little of your medicine. It is a good medicine. But I do not believe your story about repentance. It may serve for Franks; it is not enough for a daughter of the true Prophet."

"You shall see. If you wish to avoid further suffering, I advise you to tell me what became of Alexander Patoff, and to tell me quickly. I was wrong to give you the medicine until you had confessed, but if you refuse I have another medicine ready which may persuade you."

"What do I know of your unbelieving dogs of Russians?" retorted the old woman, fiercely.

"You know the answer to my question well enough. If you do not tell me within five minutes what I want to know, I will tell you what the other medicine is."

Laleli relapsed into a scornful silence. She was better of her pain, but she was angry at the physician's manner. Balsamides took out his watch, and began to count the minutes. There was a dead silence in the spacious hall, where the lights burned as brightly as ever, while the heavy clouds of tobacco smoke slowly wreathed themselves around the chandeliers and mirrors. The two sat watching each other. It seemed an eternity to the old woman, but the dose had been stronger this time, and she was free from pain. At last Balsamides shut his watch and returned it to his pocket.

"Will you, or will you not, tell me what became of Alexander Patoff, whom you caused to be seized in or near Agia Sophia, one night in the last week of the month of Ramazán before the last?"

Laleli's beady eyes were fixed on his as he spoke, with an air of surprise, not unmingled with curiosity, and strongly tinged with contempt.

"I know nothing about him," she answered steadily. "I never caused him to be seized. I never heard of him."

"Then here is my medicine," said Gregorios, coldly. "It is a terrible medicine. Listen to the pleasure of his Majesty the Hunkyar." He rose, and pressed the document to his lips and forehead.

"What!" cried Laleli, in sudden terror, her voice gathering strength from her fright.

"It is an order, dated to-day, to arrest Laleli Khanum Effendi, and to convey her to a place of safety, where she shall await the further commands of his Majesty."

"It is false," murmured the Khanum. But her white fingers twisted each other nervously. "It is a forgery."

"So false," replied Balsamides, with cold contempt,

"that the adjutant is waiting outside, and a troop of horse is stationed within call to conduct you to the place of safety aforesaid. I can force you to lay his Majesty's signature on your forehead and to follow me to my carriage, if I please."

"Allah alone is great!" groaned the Khanum, her head sinking on her breast in despair. "Kadèr, — it is my fate."

"But if you will deliver me this man alive, I will save you out of the hands even of the Hunkyar. I will say that you are too ill to be removed from your house, — unless I give you my medicine," he added, flattering her hopes to the last.

"Give me time. I know nothing — what shall I say?" muttered Laleli incoherently, her thin fingers twitching at the stuff of her snuff-colored gown, while as she beat her head her short, coarse, black hair fell over her yellow cheeks, and concealed her expression from Gregorios.

"You have not much time," he answered. "The pain will soon seize you more sharply than before. If I arrest you, your sentence will be banishment to Arabia, — not for this crime, but for that other which you thought was pardoned. If I leave you here without help, my sentence upon you is pain, pain and agony until you die. It is already returning; I can see it in your face."

"I must have time to consider," said Laleli, her old firmness returning, as it generally did in moments of great difficulty. She looked up, tossing back her hair. "How long will you give me?"

"Till the morning light is first gray in the sky above Beikos," replied Gregorios, without hesitation. "But for your own sake you had better decide sooner."

Laleli was silent. She must have had the strongest reasons for refusing to tell the secret of Alexander's fate, for the penalty of silence was a fearful one. She felt herself to be dying, but the morphine had revived in her the hope of life, and she loved life yet. But to live and suffer, to go

through the horrors of an exile to Arabia, to drag her gnawing pain through the sands of the desert, was a prospect too
awful to be contemplated. As the effects of the last dose
administered began to disappear, and her sufferings recom-
menced, she realized her situation with frightful vividness.
Still she strove to be calm and to baffle her tormentor to the
very end. If she had not felt the unspeakable relief she
had gained from his medicine, she would have wished to die,
but she had tasted of life again. The problem was how to
preserve this new life while refusing to answer the question
Gregorios had asked of her. She was so clever, so thoroughly able to deal with difficulties, that if she could but have
relief from her sufferings, so that her mind might be free to
work undisturbed, she still hoped to find the solution. But
the pain was already returning. In a few minutes she
would be writhing in agony again.

"I will wait until morning, — it is not many hours now,"
said Balsamides, after a pause. "But I strongly advise
you to decide at once. You are beginning to suffer, and I
warn you that unless you confess you shall not have the medicine."

"I lived without it until you came," answered Laleli.
"I can live without it now, if it is my fate." Her voice
trembled convulsively, but she finished her sentence by a
great effort.

"It is not your fate," returned Gregorios. "You can
not live without it."

"Then at least I shall die and escape you," she groaned;
but even in her groan there was a sort of scorn. On the
last occasion she had indeed exaggerated her sufferings,
pretending that she was at the point of death in order to
get relief without telling her secret. She had always believed that at the last minute Balsamides would relent, out
of fear lest she should die, and that she could thus obtain a
series of intervals of rest, during which she might think
what was to be done. She did not know the relentless
character of the man with whom she had to deal.

"You cannot escape me," said Balsamides, sternly. "But you can save me trouble by deciding quickly."

"I have decided to die !" she cried at last, with a great effort. She groaned again, and began to rock herself in her seat upon the divan.

"You will not die yet," observed Gregorios, contemptuously. He had understood that he had been deceived the previous time, and had determined to let her suffer.

Indeed, she was suffering, and very terribly. Her groans had a different character now, and it was evident that she was not playing a comedy. A livid hue overspread her face, and she gasped for breath.

"If you are really in pain," said Balsamides, "confess, and I will give you relief."

But Laleli shook her head, and did not look up. He attributed her constancy to an intention to impose upon him a second time by appearing to suffer in silence rather than to sell her secret for the medicine. He looked on, quite unmoved, for some minutes. At last she raised her head and showed the deathly color of her face.

"Medicine !" she gasped.

"Not this time, unless you make a full confession," said Balsamides calmly. "I will not be deceived again."

The wretched woman cast an imploring glance at him, and seemed trying to speak. But he thought she was acting again, and did not move from his seat.

"You understand the price," he said, slowly taking the case from his pocket. "Tell what you know, and you shall have it all, if you like."

The old Khanum's eyes glittered as she saw the receptacle of the coveted medicine. Her lips moved, producing only inarticulate sounds. Then, with a convulsive movement, she suddenly began to try and drag herself along the divan to the place where Gregorios sat. He gazed at her scornfully. She was very weak, and painfully moved on her hands and knees, the straight hair falling about her face, while her eyes gleamed and her lips moved. Occasionally she paused as though exhausted, and groaned heavily in her agony. But Balsamides believed it to be but a comedy to frighten him into administering the dose, and he sat still in his place, holding the case in his hand and keeping his eyes upon her.

"You cannot deceive me," he said coldly. "All these contortions will not prevail upon me. You must tell your secret, or you will get nothing."

Still Laleli dragged herself along, apparently trying to speak, but uttering only inarticulate sounds. As she got nearer to him, still on her hands and knees, Gregorios thought he had never seen so awful a sight. The straight black hair was matted in the moisture upon her clammy face ; a deathly, greenish livid hue had overspread her features ; her chin was extended forward hungrily and her eyes shone dangerously, while her lips chattered perpetually. She was very near to Balsamides. Had she had the strength to stretch out her hand she could almost have touched the small black case he held. He thought she was too near, at last, and his grip tightened on the little box.

"Confess," he said once more, "and you shall have it."

For one moment more she tried to struggle on, still not speaking. Balsamides rose and quietly put the case into his pocket, anticipating a struggle. He little knew what the result would be. The miserable creature uttered a short cry, and a wild look of despair was in her eyes. Suddenly, as she crawled upon the divan, she reared herself up on her knees, stretching out her wasted hands towards him.

"Give — give" — she cried. "I will tell you all — he is alive — he is — a wan— "

Her staring black eyes abruptly seemed to turn white, and instantly her face became ashy pale. One last convulsive effort, — the jaw dropped, the features relaxed, the limbs were unstrung, and Laleli Khanum fell forward to her full length upon her face on the peach-colored satin of the divan.

She was dead, and Gregorios Balsamides knew it, as he turned her limp body so that she lay upon her back. She was quite dead, but he was neither startled nor horrified; he was bitterly disappointed, and again and again he ground his heel into the thick Siné carpet under his feet. What was it to him whether this hideous old hag were dead in one way or another? She had died with her secret. There she lay in her shapeless bag-like gown of snuff-colored stuff, under the brilliant lights and the gorgeous mirrors, upon the delicate satin cushions, her white eyes staring wide, her hands clenched still in the death agony, the coarse hair clinging to her wet temples.

Presently the body moved, and appeared to draw one — two — three convulsive breaths. Gregorios was startled, and bent down. But it was only the very end.

"Bah!" he exclaimed, half aloud, "they often do that." Indeed, he had many times in his life seen men die, on the battlefield, on the hospital pallet, in their beds at home. But he had never seen such a death as this, and for a moment longer he gazed at the dead woman's face. Then the whole sense of disappointment rushed back upon him, and he hastily strode down the long hall, under the lamps, between the mirrors, without once looking behind him.

XVIII.

BALSAMIDES found Selim outside the door at the other end of the passage, sitting disconsolately upon the divan. The Lala turned up his ugly face as Gregorios entered, and then rose from his seat, reluctantly, as though much exhausted. Balsamides laid his hand upon the fellow's arm and looked into his small red eyes.

"The Khanum is dead," said the pretended physician.

The negro trembled violently, and throwing up his arms would have clapped his hands together. But Balsamides stopped him.

"No noise," he said sternly. "Come with me. All may yet be well with you; but you must be quiet, or it will be the worse for you." He held the Lala's arm and led him without resistance to the outer hall.

"Mehemet Bey! Mehemet Bey!" I heard him call, and I hastened from the room where I had waited to join him in the vestibule. He was very pale and grave. On hearing him enter, the porter appeared, and silently opened the outer door. Balsamides addressed him as we prepared to leave the house.

"The Khanum Effendi is dead," he said. "Selim will accompany us to the palace, and will return in the morning."

The man's face, deeply marked with the small-pox and weather-beaten in many a campaign, did not change color. Perhaps he had long expected the news, for he bowed his head as though submitting to a superior order.

"It is the will of Allah," he said in a low voice. In another moment we had descended the steps, Selim walking between us. The coachman was standing at the horses' heads in the light of the bright carriage lamps. Balsamides entered the carriage first, then I made Selim get in, and last of all I took my seat and closed the door.

" Yildiz-Kioshk ! " shouted Balsamides out of the window to the driver, and once more we rattled over the pavement and along the rough road. I imagined that the order had been given only to mislead the porter, who had stood upon the steps until we drove away. I knew well enough that Balsamides would not present himself at the palace with me in my present disguise, and that it was very improbable that he would take Selim there. I hesitated to speak to him, because I did not know whether I was to continue to personate the adjutant or to reveal myself in my true character. I had comprehended the situation when I heard my friend tell the porter that the Khanum was dead, and I congratulated myself that we had secured the person of Selim without the smallest struggle or difficulty of any kind. I argued from this, either that the Khanum had died without telling her story, or else that she had told it all, and that Selim was to accompany us to the place where Alexander was buried or hidden.

At last we turned to the left. Balsamides again put his head out of the window, and called to the coachman to drive on the Belgrade road instead of turning towards Pera. The negro started violently when he heard the order given, and I thought he put out his hand to take the handle of the door ; but my own was in the hanging loop fastened to the inside of the door, and I knew that he could not open it. The road indicated by Gregorios leads through the heart of the Belgrade forest.

The fierce north wind had moderated a little, or rather, as we drove up the thickly wooded valley, we were not exposed to it as we had been upon the shore of the Bosphorus and on the heights above. Overhead, the driving clouds took a silvery-gray tinge, as the last quarter of the waning

moon rose slowly behind the hills of the Asian shore. The
bare trees swayed and moved slowly in the wind with the
rhythmical motion of aquatic plants under moving water. I
looked through the glass as we drove along, recognizing the
well-known turns, the big trees, the occasional low stone cottages by the roadside. Everything was familiar to me,
even in the bleak winter weather ; only the landscape was
inexpressibly wild in its leafless grayness, under the faint
light of the waning moon. From time to time the Lala
moved uneasily, but said nothing. We were ascending the
hill which leads to the huge arch of the lonely aqueduct
which pierces the forest, when Balsamides tapped upon the
window. The carriage stopped in the road and he opened
the door on his side and descended.

"Get down," he said to Selim. I pushed the negro forward, and got out after him. Balsamides seized his arm
firmly.

"Take him on the other side," he said to me in Turkish,
dragging the fellow along the road in the direction of a
stony bridle-path which from this point ascends into the forest. Then Selim's coolness failed him, and he yelled aloud,
struggling in our grip, and turning his head back towards
the coachman.

"Help! help!" he cried. "In the name of Allah!
They will murder me!"

From the lonely road the coachman's careless laugh
echoed after us, as we hurried up the steep way.

"It is a solitary spot," observed Balsamides to the terrified
Selim. "You may yell yourself hoarse, if it pleases you."

We continued to ascend the path, dragging the Lala
between us. He had little chance of escape between two
such men as we, and he seemed to know it, for after a few
minutes he submitted quietly enough. At last we reached
an open space among the rocks and trees, and Balsamides
stopped. We were quite out of earshot from the road, and
it would be hard to imagine a more desolate place than it

appeared, between two and three o'clock on that March night, the bare twigs of the birch-trees wriggling in the bleak wind, the faint light of the decrescent moon, that seemed to be upside down in the sky, falling on the white rocks, and on the whitened branches torn down by the winter's storms, lying like bleached bones upon the ground before us.

"Now," said Balsamides to the negro, "no one can hear us. You have one chance of life. Tell us at once where we can find the Russian Effendi whose property you stole and sold to Marchetto in the bazaar."

In the dim gloom I almost fancied that the black man changed color as Gregorios put this question, but he answered coolly enough.

"You cannot find him," he said. "You need not have brought me here to ask me about him. I would have told you what you wanted to know at Yeni Köj, willingly enough."

"Why can he not be found?"

"Because he has been dead nearly two years, and his body was thrown into the Bosphorus," answered the Lala defiantly.

"You killed him, I suppose?" Balsamides tightened his grip upon the man's arm. But Selim was ready with his reply.

"You need not tear me in pieces. He killed himself."

The news was so unexpected that Balsamides and I both started and looked at each other. The Lala spoke with the greatest decision.

"How did he kill himself?" asked Gregorios sternly.

"I will tell you, as far as I know. The Bekjí of Agia Sophia, the same who admitted the Effendi, took me up by the other staircase. Franks are never allowed to pass that way, as you know. When we were halfway up, holding the tapers before us, we stumbled over the body of a man lying at the foot of one of the flights, with his hand against the wall. We stooped down and examined him. He was quite dead. 'Selim,' said the Bekjí, who knows me very well, 'the Effendi has fallen down the stairs in the dark, and has broken his neck.' 'If we give the alarm,' said I, 'we shall be held responsible for his death.' 'Leave it to me,' answered the Bekjí. 'Behold, the man is dead. It is his fate. He has no further use for valuables.' So the Bekjí took a ring, and a tobacco-box, and the watch and chain, and some money which was in the man's pockets. Then he said we should leave the corpse where it was. And when the prayers in the mosque were over, before it was day, he got a vegetable-seller's cart, and put the body in it and covered it with cabbages. Then we took it down to the point below Top Kapu Serai, where the waters are swift and deep. So we threw him in, for he was but a dog of a Giaour, and had broken his neck in stumbling where it was forbidden to go. Is it my fault that he stumbled?"

"No," answered Balsamides, "it was not your fault if he stumbled, and the Bekjí was a Persian fox. But you robbed his body, and divided the spoil. What share did the Bekjí take?"

"He took the ring and the tobacco-box and the money, for he was the stronger," answered the Lala.

"Selim," said Balsamides quietly, "before the Khanum died to-night she said that Alexander Patoff was alive. If so, you are lying. You are a greater liar than Moseylama, the false prophet, as they say in your country. But if not, you are a robber of dead bodies. Therefore, Selim, say a Fatihah, for your hour is come."

With that, Balsamides drew a short revolver from his pocket and cocked it before the man's eyes. The negro's limbs relaxed, and with a howl he fell upon his knees.

"Mercy! In the name of Allah!" he cried. "I have told all the truth, I swear by the grave of my father" —

"Don't move," said Gregorios, with horrible calmness. "You will do very well in that position. Now — say your Fatihah, and be quick about it. I cannot wait all night."

"You are not in earnest, Gregorios?" I asked in English, for my blood ran cold at the sight.

"Very much in earnest," he answered in Turkish, presenting the muzzle of the pistol to the Lala's head. "This fellow shall not laugh at our beards a second time. I will count three. If you do not wish to say your prayers, I will fire when I have said three. One — two " —

"He is alive!" screamed the Lala, before the fatal "three" was spoken by Balsamides. "I have lied: he is alive! Mercy! and I will tell you all."

"I thought so," said Balsamides, coolly uncocking his pistol and putting it back into his pocket. "Get up, dog, and tell us what you know."

Selim was literally almost frightened to death, as he kneeled on the sharp stones at our feet. He could hardly speak, and I dragged him up and made him sit upon the trunk of a fallen tree. I was indeed glad that he was still alive, for though Balsamides had not yet told me the events of the night, I could see that he was in no humor to be trifled with. Even I, who am peaceably disposed towards all men, felt my blood boil when the fellow told how he and the Bekji had robbed the body of Alexander Patoff, and thrown it into the Bosphorus for fear of being suspected. But the whole story seemed improbable, and I had a strong impression that Selim was lying. Perhaps nothing but the fear of death could have made him confess, after all, and Balsamides had a way of making death seem very real and near.

"I will tell you this, Selim," said Gregorios. "If you will give me Alexander Patoff Effendi to-night, alive, well, and uninjured in any way, you shall go free, and I will engage that you shall not be hurt. You evidently wished to keep the Khanum's secret. The Khanum is dead, and her secrets are the Padishah's, like everything else she possessed. You are bound to deliver those secrets to my keeping. Therefore tell us shortly where the Russian is, that we may liberate him and take him home at once."

"He is alive and well. That is to say, he has been well treated," answered Selim. "If you can take him, you may take him to-night, for all I care. But you must swear that you will then protect me."

"Filthy liquor in a dirty bottle!" exclaimed Balsamides angrily. "Will you make conditions with me, you soul of a dog in a snake's body?"

"Very well," returned the Lala cunningly. "But if you should kill me by mistake before I have taken you to him, you will never find him."

"I have told you that you shall not be hurt, if you will give him up. That is enough. My word is good, and I will keep it. Speak; you are safe."

"In the first place, we must go back to Yeni Köj. You might have saved yourself the trouble of coming up here on such a night as this."

"I want no comments on my doings. Tell me where the man is."

"I will take you to him," said the Lala.

"Well, then, get up and come back to the carriage," said Balsamides, seeing it was useless to bandy words with the fellow. Moreover, it was bitterly cold in the forest, and the idea of being once more in the comfortable carriage was attractive. Again we took Selim between us, and rapidly descended the stony path. In a few moments we were driving swiftly away from the arches of the aqueduct in the direction whence we had come.

Before we had reached the door of Laleli's house, Selim asked Balsamides to stop the carriage. We got out, and he took us up a narrow and filthy lane between two high walls. The feeble light of the moon did not penetrate the blackness, and we stumbled along in the mud as best we could. After climbing in this way for nearly ten minutes, Selim stopped before what appeared to be a small door sunk in a niche in the wall. I heard a bunch of keys jingling in his hand, and in a few seconds he admitted us. Balsamides held him firmly by the sleeve, as he turned to lock the door behind us.

"You shall not lock it," he said in a low voice. "Are we mice to be caught in a trap?"

Having made sure that the door was open, he pushed Selim forward. We seemed to be in a very spacious garden, surrounded by high walls on all sides. The trees were bare, excepting a few tall cypresses, which reared their black spear-like heads against the dim sky. The flower-beds were covered with dark earth, and the gravel in the paths was rough, as though no one had trod upon it for a long time. The walls protected the place from the wind, and a gloomy stillness prevailed, broken only by the distant sighing of trees higher up, which caught the northern gale.

Selim followed the wall for some distance, and at last stood still. We had reached one angle of the garden, and as well as I could see the corner made by the walls was filled by a low stone building with latticed windows, from one of which issued a faint light. Going nearer, I saw that the lattices were not of wood, but were strong iron gratings, such as no man's strength could break. The door in the middle of this stone box was also heavily ironed. Selim went forward, and again I heard the keys rattle in his hands. Almost instantly the shadow of a head appeared at the window whence the light came. While the Lala was unfastening the lock I went close to the grating. I was just tall enough to meet a pair of dark eyes gazing at me intently through the lowest bars.

"Alexander Patoff, is it you?" I asked in Russian.

"Good God!" exclaimed a tremulous voice. "Have the Russians taken Constantinople at last? Who are you?"

"I am Paul Griggs. We have come to set you free."

The heavy door yielded and moved. I rushed in, and in another moment I clasped the lost man's hand. Gregorios, far more prudent than I, held Selim by the collar as a man would hold a dog, for he feared some treachery.

"Is it really you?" I asked, for I could scarcely believe my eyes. Alexander looked at me once, then broke
into hysterical tears, laughing and crying and sobbing all at
once. He was indeed unrecognizable. I remembered the
descriptions I had heard of the young dandy, the gay officer
of a crack regiment, irreproachable in every detail of his
dress, and delicate as a woman in his tastes. I saw before
me a man of good height, wrapped in an old Turkish kaftan
of green cloth lined with fur, his feet thrust into a pair of
worn-out red slippers. His dark brown hair had grown till
it fell upon his shoulders, his beard reached halfway to his
waist, his face was ghastly white and thin to emaciation.
The hand he had given me was like a parcel of bones in a
thin glove. I doubted whether he were the man, after all.

"We must be quick," I said. "Have you anything to
take away?" He cast a piteous glance at his poor clothing.

"This is all I have," he said in a low voice. Then, with
a half-feminine touch of vanity, he added, "You must
excuse me: I am hardly fit to go with you." He looked
wildly at me for a moment, and again laughed and sobbed
hysterically. The apartment was indeed empty enough.
There was a low round table, a wretched old divan at one
end, and a sort of bed spread upon the floor, in the old
Turkish fashion. The whole place seemed to consist of a
single room, lighted by a small oil lamp which hung in one
corner. The stuccoed walls were green with dampness, and
the cold was intense. I wondered how the poor man had
lived so long in such a place. I put my arm under his, and
threw my heavy military cloak over his shoulders. Then
I led him away through the open door. The key was still
in the lock without, and Balsamides held Selim tightly by
the collar. When we had passed, Gregorios, instead of
following us, held the Lala at arm's-length before him.
Then he administered one tremendous kick, and sent the
wretch flying into the empty cell; he locked the door on
him with care, and withdrew the keys.

"I told you I would protect you," he called out through the keyhole. "You will be quite safe there for the present." Then he turned away, laughing to himself, and we all three hurried down the path under the wall, till we reached the small door by which we had entered the garden. Stumbling down the narrow lane, we soon got to the road, and found the carriage where we had left it. There was no time for words as we almost lifted the wretched Russian into the carriage and got in after him.

"To my house in Pera!" cried Balsamides to the patient coachman. "Pek tchabuk! As fast as you can drive!"

"Evvét Effendim," replied the old soldier, and in another moment we were tearing along the road at breakneck speed.

Hitherto Alexander Patoff had been too much surprised and overcome by his emtions to speak connectedly or to ask us any questions. When once we were in the carriage and on our way to Pera, however, he recovered his senses.

"Will you kindl- tell me how all this has happened? Are you a Turkish officer?"

"No," I answered. "This is a disguise. Let me present you to the man who has really liberated you, — Balsamides Bey."

Patoff took the hand Gregorios stretched out towards him in both of his, and would have kissed it had Gregorios allowed him.

"God bless you! God bless you!" he repeated fervently. He was evidently still very much shaken, and in order to give him a little strength I handed him a flask of spirits which I had left in the carriage. He drank eagerly, and grasped even more greedily the case of cigarettes which I offered him.

"Ah!" he cried, in a sort of ecstasy, as he tasted the tobacco. "I feel that I am free."

I began to tell him in a few words what had happened: how we had stumbled upon his watch in the bazaar, had identified Selim, and traced the Lala to Laleli Khanum's house; how the Khanum had died while Balsamides was there, just as she was about to tell the truth; how we had dragged Selim into the forest, and had threatened him with death; and how at last, feeling that since his mistress was dead he was no longer in danger, the fellow had conducted us to Alexander's cell in the garden. I told him that his brother and mother were in Pera, and that he should see them in the morning. I said that Madame Patoff had been very ill in consequence of his disappearance, and that every one had mourned for him as d ad. In short, I endeavored to explain the whole situation as clearly as I could. While I was telling our story Balsamides never spoke a word, but sat smoking in his corner, probably thi king of the single kick in which he had tried to concentrate all his vengeance.

As we drove along, the dawn began to appear, — the cold dawn of a March morning. I asked Balsamides whether it would be necessary to change my clothes before entering the city.

"No," he answered; "we shall be at home at sunrise. The fellow drives well."

"I shall have to ask you to take me in for a few hours," said Alexander. "I am in a pitiable state."

"You must have suffered horribly in that den," observed Balsamides. "Of course you must come home with me. We will send for your brother at once, and when you are rested you can tell us something of your story. It must be even more interesting than ours."

"It would not take so long to tell," answered Patoff, with a melancholy smile. In the gray light of the morning I was horrified to notice how miserably thin and ill he looked; but even in his squalor, and in spite of the long hair and immense beard, I could see traces of the beauty I had so often heard described by Paul, and even by Cutter, who was rarely enthusiastic about the appearance of his fellows. He seemed weak, too, as though he had been half starved in his prison. I asked him how long it was since he had eaten.

"Last night," he said, wearily, "they brought me food, but I could not eat. A man in prison has no appetite." Then suddenly he opened the window beside him, and put his head out into the cold blast, as though to drink in more fully the sense of freedom regained. Balsamides looked at him with a sort of pity which I hardly ever saw in his face.

"Poor devil!" he said, in a low voice. "We were just in time. He could not have lasted much longer."

We reached the outskirts of Pera, and Alexander hastily withdrew his head and sank back in the corner, as though afraid of being seen. He had the startled look of a man who fears pursuit. At last we rattled down the Grande Rue, and stopped before the door of Balsamides' house. It was six o'clock in the morning, and the sun was nearly up. I thought it had been one of the longest nights I ever remembered.

While Balsamides dismissed the coachman, I led Alexander quickly into the house and up the narrow stairs. In a few minutes Gregorios joined us, and coffee was brought.

"I think you could wear my clothes," he said, looking at Alexander with a scarcely perceptible smile. "We are nearly the same height, and I am almost as thin as you."

"If you would be so very kind as to send for a barber," suggested Patoff. "I have never been allowed one, for fear I should get hold of his razor and kill myself or somebody else."

"I will go and send one," said I. "And I will rouse your brother and bring him back with me."

"Stop!" cried Balsamides. "You cannot go like that!" I had forgotten that I still wore the adjutant's uniform. "Take care of our friend," he added, "and I will go myself."

We should probably have felt very tired, after our night's excursion, had we not been sustained by the sense of triumph at having at last succeeded beyond all hope. It was hard to imagine what the effect would be upon Madame Patoff, and I began to fear for her reason as I remembered how improbable it had always seemed to me that we should find her son alive. I was full of curiosity to hear his story, but I knew that he was exhausted with fatigue and emotion, so that I put him in possession of my room and gave him some of my friend's clothes. In a few moments the barber arrived, and while he was performing his operations I myself resumed my ordinary dress.

Balsamides found Paul in bed and fast asleep, but, pushing the servant aside, he walked in and opened the windows.

"Wake up, Patoff!" he shouted, making a great noise with the fastenings.

"Holloa! What is the matter?" cried Paul, opening his sleepy eyes wide with astonishment as he saw Balsamides standing before him, hite as death with the excitement of the night. "Has anything happened?"

"Everything has happened," said Gregorios. "The sun is risen, the birds are singing, the Jews are wrangling in the bazaar, the dogs are fighting at Gal..ta Serai, and, last of all, your brother, Alexander P..toff, is at this moment drinking his coffee in my rooms."

"My brother!" cried Paul, fairly leaping out of bed in his excitement. "Are you in earnest? Come, let us go at once."

"Your costume," remarked Balsamides quietly, "smacks too much of the classic for the Grande Rue de Pera. I will wait while you dress."

"Does my mother know?" asked Patoff.

"No," replied Balsamides. "Your brother had not been five minutes in my house when I came here." Then he told Paul briefly how we had found Alexander.

Paul Patoff was not a man to be easily surprised; but in the present case the issue had been so important, that, being taken utterly unawares by the news, he felt stunned and dazed as he tried to realize the whole truth. He sat down in the midst of dressing, and for one moment buried his face in his hands. Balsamides looked on quietly. He knew how much even that simple action meant in a man of Paul's proud and undemonstrative temper. In a few seconds Paul rose from his seat and completed his toilette.

"You know how grateful I am to you both," he said. "You must guess it, for nothing I could say could express what I feel."

"Do not mention it," answered Balsamides. "No thanks could give me half the pleasure I have in seeing your satisfaction. You must prepare to find your brother much changed, I fancy. He seemed to me to be thin and pale, but I think he is not ill in any way. If you are ready, we will go."

Meanwhile, Alexander had had his hair cut short, in the military fashion, and had been divested of the immense beard which hid half his face. A tub and a suit of civilized clothes did the rest, even though the latter did not fit him as well as Gregorios had expected. Gregorios is a deceptive man and is larger than he looks, for his coat was too broad for Alexander, and hung loosely over the latter's shoulders and chest. But in spite of the imperfect fit, the change in the man's appearance was so great that I started in surprise when he entered the sitting-room, taking him for an intruder who had walked in unannounced.

He was very beautiful; that is the only word which applies to his appearance. His regular features, in their extreme thinness, were ethereal as the face of an angel, but he had not the painful look of emaciation which one so often sees in the faces of those long kept in confinement. He was very thin indeed, but there was a perfect grace in all his movements, an ease and self-possession in his gestures, a quiet, earnest, trustful look in his dark eyes, which seemed almost unearthly. I watched him with the greatest interest, and with the greatest admiration also. Had I been asked at that moment to state what man or woman in the whole world I considered most perfectly beautiful, I should have

answered unhesitatingly, Alexander Patoff. He had that
about him which is scarcely ever met with in men, and which
does not always please others, though it never fails to attract attention. I mean that he had the delicate beauty of
a woman combined with the activity and dash of a man. I
saw how the lightness, the alternate indolence and reckless
excitement, of such a nature must act upon a man of Paul
Patoff's character. Every point and peculiarity of Alexander's temper and bearing would necessarily irritate Paul,
who was stern, cold, and manly before all else, and who
readily despised every species of weakness except pride,
and every demonstration of feeling except physical courage.
Alexander was like his mother; so like her, indeed, that as
soon as I saw him without his beard I realized the cause of
Madame Patoff's singular preference for the older son, and
much which had seemed unnatural before was explained by
this sudden revelation. Paul probably resembled his father's family more than his mother's. Madame Patoff, who
had loved that same cold, determined character in her husband, because she was awed by it, hated it in her child, because she could neither bend it nor influence it, nor make it
express any of that exuberant affection which Alexander so
easily felt. Both boys had inherited from their father a
goodly share of the Slav element, but, finding very different
ground upon which to work in the natures of the two brothers, the strong Russian individuality had developed in
widely different ways. In Alexander were expressed all
the wild extremes of mood of which the true Russian is so
eminently capable; all the overflowing and uncultivated talent and love of art and beauty, which in Russia brings forth
so much that approaches indefinitely near to genius without
ever quite reaching it. In Paul the effect of the Slavonic
blood was totally opposite, and showed itself in that strange
stolidity, that cold and ruthless exercise of force and pursuance of conviction, which have characterized so many Russian generals, so many Russian monarchs, and which have

produced also so many Russian martyrs. There is something fateful in that terrible sternness, something which
very well excites horror while imposing respect, and especially when forced to submit to superior force; and when
vanquished, there is something grand in the capacity such a
character possesses for submitting to destiny, and bearing
the extremest suffering.

It was clear enough that there could never be any love
lost between two such men, and I was curious to see their
meeting. I wondered whether each would fall upon the
other's neck and shed tears of rejoicing, or whether they
would shake hands and express their satisfaction more formally. In looking forward to the scene which was soon to
take place, I almost wished that Paul might have accompanied us in the disguise of a second adjutant, and thus have had
a hand in the final stroke by which we had effected Alexander's liberation. But I knew that he would only have been
in the way, and that, considering the whole situation, we had
done wisely. The least mistake on his part might have led
to a struggle inside the Khanum's house, and we had good
cause to congratulate ourselves upon having freed the prisoner
without shedding blood. There was something pleasantly
ludicrous in the thought that all our anticipations of a fight
had ended in that one solemn kick with which Balsamides
had consigned Selim to the prison whence we had taken Alexander.

I was giving the latter a few more details of the events
of the night, when Paul and Balsamides entered the room
together. Paul showed more emotion than I had expected,
and clasped his brother in his arms in genuine delight at
having found him at last. Then he looked long at his face,
as though trying to see how far Alexander was changed in
the twenty months which had elapsed since they had met.

" You are a little thinner, — you look as though you had
been ill," said Paul.

" No, I have not been ill, but I have suffered horribly in

many ways," answered Alexander, in his smooth, musical voice.

For some minutes they exchanged questions, while they overcame their first excitement at being once more together. It was indeed little less than a resurrection, and Alexander's ethereal face was that of a spirit returning to earth rather than of a living man who had never left it. At last Paul grew calmer.

"Will you tell us how it happened?" he asked, as he sat down upon the divan beside his brother. Balsamides and I established ourselves in chairs, ready to listen with breathless interest to the tale Alexander was about to tell.

"You remember that night at Santa Sophia, Paul?" began the young man, leaning back among the cushions, which showed to strong advantage the extreme beauty of his delicate face. "Yes, of course you remember it, very vividly, for Mr. Griggs has told me how you acted, and all the trouble you took to find me. Very well; you remember, then, that the last time I saw you we were all looking down at those fellows as they went through their prayers and prostrations, and I stood a little apart from you. You were very much absorbed in the sight, and the kaváss, who was a Mussulman, was looking on very devoutly. I thought I should like to see the sight from the other side, and I walked away and turned the corner of the gallery. You did not notice me, I suppose, and the noise of the crowd, rising and falling on their knees, must have drowned my footsteps."

"I had not the slightest idea that you had moved from where you stood," said Paul.

"No. When I reached the corner, I was very much surprised to see a man standing in the shadow of the pillar. I was still more astonished when I recognized the hideous negro who had knocked off my hat in the afternoon. I expected that he would insult me, and I suppose I made as though I would show fight; but he raised his finger to his lips, and with the other hand held out a letter, composing his face into a sort of horrible leer, intended to be attractive. I took the letter without speaking, for I knew he could not understand a word I said, and that I could not understand him. The envelope contained a sheet of pink paper, on which, in an ill-formed hand, but in tolerably good French, were written a few words. It was a declaration of love."

"From Laleli?" asked Balsamides, with a laugh.

"Exactly," replied Alexander. "It was a declaration of love from Laleli. I leave you to imagine what I supposed Laleli to be like at that time, and Paul, who knows me, will tell you that I was not likely to hesitate at such a moment. The note ended by saying that the faithful Selim would conduct me to her presence without delay. I was delighted with the adventure, and crept noiselessly after him in the shadow of the gallery, lest you should see me; for I knew you would prevent my going with the man. We descended the stairs, but it was not until we reached the bottom that I saw we had not come down by the way I had ascended. Selim was most obsequious, and seemed ready to do everything for my comfort. As we walked down a narrow street, he presented me with a new fez, and made signs to me to put it on instead of my hat, which he then carefully wrapped in a handkerchief and carried in his hand. At a place near the bridge several caïques were lying side by side. He invited me to enter one, which I observed was very luxuriously fitted, and which I thought I recognized as the one in which I had so often seen the woman with the impenetrable veil. I lay back among the cushions and smoked, while Selim perched himself on the raised seat behind me, and the four boatmen pulled rapidly away. It was heavy work for them, I dare say, tugging up-stream, but to me the voyage was enchanting. The shores were all illuminated, and the Bosphorus swarmed with boats. It was the last time I was in a caïque. I do not know whether I could bear the sight of one now."

"So they took you to Laleli's house?" said Paul, anxious to hear the rest.

"Yes; I was taken to Laleli's house, and I never got out of it till last night," continued Alexander. "How long is it? I have not the least idea of the European date."

"This is the 29th of March," said I.

"And that was the end of June, — twenty-one months. I have learned Turkish since I was caught, to pass the time, and I always knew the Turkish date after I had learned their way of counting, but I had lost all reckoning by our style. Well, to go on with my story. They brought me to the stone pier before the house. Selim admitted me by a curiously concealed panel at one end of the building, and we found ourselves in a very narrow place, whence half a dozen steps ascended to a small door. A little oil lamp burned in one corner. He led the way, and the door at the top slid back into the wall. We entered, and he closed it again. We were in the corner of a small room, richly furnished in the worst possible taste. I dare say you know the style these natives admire. Selim left me there for a moment. I looked carefully at the wall, and tried to find the panel; but to my surprise, the wainscoting was perfectly smooth and even, and I could not discover the place where it opened, nor detect any spring or sign of a fastening. Laleli, I thought, understood those things. Presently a door opened on one side of the room, and I saw the figure I had often watched, beckoning to me to come. Of course I obeyed, and she retired into the room beyond, which was very high and had no windows, though I noticed that there was a dome at the top, which in the day-time would admit the light."

"The Khanum was waiting for you?" I asked.

"Yes. I was surprised to see her dressed in the clothes she wore out-of-doors, and as thickly veiled as ever. There were lights in the room. She held out her small hand, — you remember noticing that she had small white hands?"

"Like a young woman's," replied Balsamides.

"Yes. I took her hand, and spoke in French. I dare say I looked very sentimental and passionate as I gazed into her black eyes. I could see nothing of her face. She answered me in Turkish, which of course I could not under-stand. All I could say was Pek güzel, very beautiful, which I repeated amidst my French phrases, giving the words as passionate an accent as I could command. At last she seemed to relent, and as she bent towards me I expected that she was about to speak very softly some Turkish love-word. What was my horror when she suddenly screamed into my ear, with a hideous harsh voice, my own words, Pek güzel! In a moment she threw off her black ferigee, and tore the thick veil from her head. I could have yelled with rage, for I saw what a fool I had made of myself, and that the old hag had played a practical joke on me in revenge for the affair in the Valley of Roses. I cursed her in French, I cursed her in Russian, I cursed her in English, and stamped about the room, trying to get out. The hor-rible old witch screamed herself hoarse with laughter, mak-ing hideous grimaces and pointing at me in scorn. What could I do? I tried to force one of the doors, and twisted at the handle, and tugged and pushed with all my might. While I was thus engaged I heard the door at the other end of the room open quickly, and as I turned and sprang towards it I caught sight of her baggy, snuff-colored gown disappearing, as she slammed the door behind her. Before I could reach it the lock was turned, and I was caught in the trap, — caught like a mouse."

"What a spiteful old thing she was!" I exclaimed. "She might have been satisfied with keeping you there a day instead of two years."

"Nearly two years. I did everything humanly possible to escape. I gave all I possessed to Selim to take a mes-sage to Paul, to anybody; but of course that was useless. At first they kept me in the room where I had been caught. My food was brought to me by the Turkish porter, a brawny fellow, who could have brained me with his fist. He was always accompanied by another man, as big as himself, who carried a loaded pistol, in case I attacked the first. I had no chance, and I wished I might go mad. Then, one night, they set upon me suddenly, and tied a handkerchief over my mouth, and bound me hand and foot, in spite of my struggles. I thought I was to be put into a sack and drowned. They carried me like a log out into the garden, and put me into that cell where you found me, which had apparently just been built, for the stones were new and the cement was fresh. There, at least, I could look through the gratings. I even thought at one time that I could make myself heard, having no idea of the desolate position of the place. But I soon gave up the attempt and abandoned myself to despair. There it was that Selim used to come occasionally, and talk to me through the bars. That was better than nothing, and the villain amused his leisure moments by teaching me to speak Turkish. One day he brought me a book, which I hailed with delight. It was an old French method for learning the language. I made great progress, as I studied from morning to night. Selim grew more familiar to me, and I confess with shame that I missed his visits when he did not come. The men who brought my food seemed absolutely mute, and I never succeeded in extracting a word from either of them. Even Selim was a companion, and talking to him saved me from going mad. I asked him all sorts of questions, and at last I guessed from his answers that the Khanum had been terrified by the disturbance my disappearance had created, and was afraid to set me free lest I should take vengeance on her. She was also afraid to kill me, for some reason or other. The result was, that, from having merely wished to revenge upon me the affair in the Valley of Roses by means of a practical joke, she found herself obliged to keep me a prisoner. I used every means of persuasion to move Selim. I told him I was rich, and would make him rich if he would help me to escape. I prom-

ised to take no steps against the Khanum. It was in vain.
I assure you I have conceived a very high opinion of the
fidelity of Lalas in general, and of Selim in particular."

"They are very faithful," said Balsamides gravely. I
have since fancied that he had some reason for knowing.

Alexander afterwards told us many more details of his
confinement; but this was his first account of it, and embraced all that is most important to know. The whole affair
made a very strong impression on me. The unfortunate
man had fallen a victim to a chain of circumstances which
it had been entirely impossible to foresee, all resulting directly from his first imprudent action in addressing the
veiled lady in the Valley of Roses. A little piece of folly
had ruined two years of his life, and subjected him to a
punishment such as a court of justice would have inflicted
for a very considerable crime.

The remainder of the day was occupied by the meeting
of Alexander with his mother and his introduction to his
English relations, upon which it is needless to dwell long.
I never knew what passed between the mother and son, but
the interview must have been a very extraordinary one. It
was necessary, of course, to prepare Madame Patoff for the
news and for the sight of the child she seemed to love better
than anything in the world. Hermione performed the task,
as being the one who understood her best. She began by
hinting vaguely that we had advanced another step in our
search, and that we were now confident of finding Alexander before long, perhaps in a few hours. She gradually,
in talking, spoke of the moment when he would appear,
wondering how he would look, and insensibly accustoming
Madame Patoff to the idea. At last she confessed that he
had been found during the night, and that he was ready to
come to his mother at any moment.

It was well done, and the force of the shock was broken.
The old lady nearly swooned with joy, but the danger was
past when she recovered her consciousness and demanded to

see Alexander at once. He was admitted to her room, and the two were left alone to their happiness.

The rest of the family were mad with delight. John Carvel grew ten years younger, and Mrs. Carvel fairly cried with joy, while Chrysophrasia declared that it was worth while to be disappointed by the first impression of Constantinople, when one was consoled by such a thrilling tale with so joyous a termination, — or happy end, as I should have said. Hermione's face beamed with happiness, and Macaulay literally melted in smiles, as he retired to write down the story in his diary.

"Oh, Paul!" Hermione exclaimed when they were alone, "you never told me he was such a beauty!"

"Yes," he answered quietly, "he is far better-looking than I am. You must not fall in love with him, Hermy."

"The idea of such a thing!" she cried, with a light laugh.

"I should not be surprised if he fell in love with you, dear," said Paul, smiling.

"You only say that because you do not like him," she answered. "But you will like him now, won't you? You are so good, — I am sure you will. But think what a splendid thing it is that you should have found him. If aunt Chrysophrasia says, 'Where is your brother?' you can just answer that he is in the next room."

"Yes; I am a free man now. No one can ever accuse me again. But apart from that, I am really and sincerely glad that he is alive. I wish him no ill. It is not his fault that I have been under a cloud for nearly two years. He was as anxious to be found as I was to find him. After all, it was not I. It was Balsamides and Griggs who did it at last. I dare say that if I had been with them I should have spoiled it all. I could not have dressed myself like a Turkish officer, to begin with. If I had been caught in the uniform, belonging as I do to the embassy, there would have been a terrible fuss. I should have been obliged to go away, very likely without having found my brother at all. I owe everything to those two men."

" If you had not made up your mind that he should be found, they would never have found him ; they would not have thought of taking the trouble."

Hermione spoke in a reassuring tone, as though to comfort Paul for having had no share in the final stroke which had liberated his brother. In reality Paul needed no consolation. In his heart he was glad that Alexander had been set free by others, and need therefore never feel himself under heavy obligations to Paul. It was not in the strong man's nature to wish to revenge himself upon his brother because the latter had been the favored child and the favorite son. Nor, if he had contemplated any kind of vengeance, would he have chosen the Christian method of heaping coals of fire upon his head. He merely thought of Alexander as he would have thought of any other man not his relation at all, and he did not wish to appear in the light of his liberator. It was enough for Paul that he had been found at last, and that his own reputation was now free from stain. Nothing prevented him any longer from marrying Hermione, and he looked forward to the consummation of all his hopes in the immediate future.

The day closed in a great rejoicing. John Carvel insisted that we should all dine with him that night ; and our numbers being now swelled by the addition of Alexander Patoff and Gregorios Balsamides, we were a large party, — ten at table. I shall never forget the genuine happiness which was on every face. The conversation flowed brilliantly, and every one felt as though a weight had been lifted from his or her spirits. Alexander Patoff was of course the most prominent person, and as he turned his beautiful eyes from one to the other of us, and told us his story with many episodes and comments, I think we all fell under his fascination, and understood the intense love his mother felt for him. He had indeed a woman's beauty with a man's energy, when his energy was roused at all; and though the feminine element at 'first seemed out of place in him, it gave him that singular faculty of charming when he pleased, and that brilliancy which no manly beauty can ever have.

It was late when we got home, and *I* went to bed with a profound conviction that Paul Patoff's troubles had come to a happy end, and that he would probably be married to Hermione in the course of the summer. If things had ended thus, my story would end here, and perhaps it would be complete. Unfortunately, events rarely take place as we expect that they will, still more rarely as we hope that they may; and it is generally when our hopes coincide with our expectations, and we feel most sure of ourselves, that fate overtakes us with the most cruel disappointments. Paul Patoff had not yet reached the quiet haven of his hopes, and I have not reached the end of my story. It would indeed be a very easy matter, as I have said before, to collect all the things which happened to him into a neat romance, of which the action should not cover more than four-and-twenty hours of such excitement as no one of the actors could have borne in real life, any more than Salvini could act a tragedy which should begin at noon to-day and end at midday to-morrow. I might have divested Paul of many of his surroundings, have bereaved him of many of his friends, and made him do himself what others did to him; but if he were to read such an account of his life he would laugh scornfully, and say that the real thing was very different indeed, as without doubt it was.

This is the reason why I have not hesitated to bring before you a great number of personages, each of whom, in a great or a small way, affected his life. I do not believe that you could understand his actions in the sequel without knowing the details of those situations through which he had passed before. We are largely influenced by little things and little events. The statement is a truism in the eyes of the moralist, but the truth is, unfortunately, too often forgotten in real life. The man who falls down-stairs and breaks his leg has not noticed the tiny spot of candle grease which made the polished step so slippery just where he trod.

XIX.

THERE were great rejoicings when it was known in Pera that Alexander Patoff had been found. His disappearance had furnished the gossips with a subject of conversation during many weeks, and his coming back revived the whole story, with the addition of a satisfactory ending. In consideration of the fact that Laleli Khanum was dead, Count Ananoff thought it best to take no official notice of the matter. To treat it diplomatically would be useless, he said. Alexander had fallen a victim to his own folly, and though the penalty had been severe, it was impossible to hold the Ottoman government responsible for what Patoff had suffered, now that the Khanum had departed this life. Alexander received permission to take three months' leave to recruit his health before returning to his regiment, and he resolved to spend a part of the time in Constantinople, after which his mother promised to accompany him to St. Petersburg.

The Carvels had very soon made the acquaintance of the small but brilliant society of which the diplomatic corps constituted the chief element; and if anything had been needed to make them thoroughly popular, their near connection with the young man whose story was in every one's mouth would alone have sufficed to surround them with interest. The adventure was told with every conceivable variety of detail, and Alexander was often called upon to settle disputes as to what had happened to him. He was ready enough at all times to play the chief part in a drawing-room, and delighted in being questioned by grave old gentlemen, as well as by inquisitive young women. The women admired him for his beauty, his grace and brilliancy, and especially for the expression of his eyes, which they declared in a variety of languages to be absolutely fascinating. The men were interested in his story, and envied him the additional social success which he obtained as the hero of so strange an adventure. Some people admired and praised his devotion to his mother, which they said was most touching, whatever that may mean. Others said that he had an angelic disposition, flavored by a dash of the devil, which saved him from being goody; and this criticism of his character conveyed some meaning to the minds of those who uttered it. People have a strange way of talking about their favorites, and when the praise they mean to bestow is not faint, the expression of it is apt to be feeble and involved.

Pera is a gay place, for when a set of men and women are temporarily exiled from their homes to a strange country, where they do not find the society of a great capital, they naturally seek amusement and pursue it; creating among themselves those pastimes which in the great European cities others so often provide for them. Politically, also, Constantinople is a very important place to most of the powers, who choose their representatives for the post from among the cleverest men they can find; and I will venture to say that there is scarcely a court in the world where so many first-rate diplomatists are gathered together as are to be met with among the missions to the Sublime Porte. Diplomacy in Constantinople has preserved something of the character it had all over the world fifty years ago. Personal influence is of far greater importance when negotiations are to be undertaken with a half-civilized form of administration, which is carried on chiefly by persons of imperfect education, but of immense natural talent for intrigue. The absence of an hereditary nobility in Turkey, and the extremely democratic nature of the army and the civil service, make it possible for men of the lowest birth to attain to the highest power. The immense and complicated bureaucracy is not in the hands of any one class of the people; its prizes are won by men of all sorts and conditions, who continue to pursue their own interests and fortunes with undiminished energy, when they ought to be devoting their whole powers to the service of the country. Their power is indeed checked by the centralization of all the executive faculties in the person of the sovereign. Without the Sultan's signature the minister of war cannot order a gun to be cast in the arsenal of Tophanè, the minister of marine cannot buy a ton of coal for the ironclads which lie behind Galata bridge in the Golden Horn, the minister of foreign affairs cannot give a reply to an ambassador, nor can the minister of justice avail himself of the machinery of the law. Every smallest act must be justified by the Sultan's own signature, and the chief object of all diplomacy from without, and of all personal intrigue from within, is to obtain this imperial consent to measures suggested by considerations of private advantage or public necessity. The Ottoman Empire may be described as an irregular democracy, whose acts are all subject to the veto of an absolute autocrat. The officials pass their lives in proposing, and his Majesty very generally spends his time in opposing, all manner of schemes, good, bad, and indifferent. The contradictory nature of the system produces the anomalous position occupied by the Ottoman Empire in Europe.

The fact that there is no aristocracy and the seclusion of women among the Mussulmans are the chief reasons why there is no native society, in our sense of the word. A few of the great Greek families still survive, descendants of those Fanariotes whose ancestors had played an important part in the decadence of the Eastern Empire. A certain number of Armenians who have gained wealth and influence follow more or less closely the customs of the West. But beyond these few there cannot be said to be many houses of the social kind. Two or three pashas, of European origin, and Christians by religion, mix with their families in the gayety of Pera and the Bosphorus. A few Turkish officers, and Prussian officers in Turkish service, show their brilliant uniforms in the ball-rooms, and occasionally some high official of the Porte appears at formal receptions; but on the whole the society is diplomatic, and depends almost entirely upon the diplomatists for its existence and for its diversions. The lead once given, the old Greek aristocrats have not been behindhand in following it; but their numbers are small, and the movement and interest in Pera, or on the Bosphorus, centre in the great embassies, as they do nowhere else in the world.

Small as the society is, it is, nevertheless exceedingly brilliant and very amusing. Intimacies grow up quickly, and often become lasting friendships when fostered by such influences. Every one knows every one else, and every one meets everybody else at least once a week. The arrival of a new secretary is expected with unbounded interest. The departure of one who has been long in Constantinople is mourned as a public loss. Occasionally society is convulsed to its foundations by the departure of an ambassador to whom every one has been so long accustomed that he has come to be regarded as one of the fathers of the community, whose hospitality every one has enjoyed, whose tact and knowledge of the world have been a source of satisfaction to his colleagues in many a diplomatic difficulty, and whose palace in Pera is associated in the minds of all with many hours of pleasure and with much delightful intercourse. He goes, and society turns out in a body to see him off. The occasion is like a funeral. People send hundreds of baskets of flowers. There is an address, there are many leave-takings. Once, at least, I remember seeing two thirds of the people shedding tears, — genuine wet tears of sorrow. And there was good reason for their grief. In such communities as the diplomatic colony in Pera, people understand the value of those who not only do more than their share in contributing to the pleasantness of life, but who possess in an abundant degree those talents which delight us in individuals, and those qualities which are dear to us in friends. It would be easy to write a book about society in Pera, and it would be a pleasant book. But these are not the days of Samuel Pepys; we have hardly passed the age of Mr. George Ticknor.

In a short time after their arrival, and after the reappearance of Alexander Patoff, the Carvels knew everybody, and everybody knew them. Each member of the party found something to praise and some one to like. John Carvel was soon lost in admiration of Lord Mavourneen, while Mrs. Carvel talked much with the English missionary bishop of Western Kamtchatka, who happened to be spending a few days at the embassy. She asked him many questions concerning the differences between Armenian orthodox, Armenian catholic, Greek orthodox, and Russian orthodox; and though his lordship found a great deal to say on the subject, I am bound to allow that he was almost as much puzzled as herself when brought face to face in the reality with such a variety of sects. Chrysophrasia had not come to the East for nothing, either. She meant to indulge what John called her fancy for pots and pans and old rags; in other words, she intended to try her luck in the bazaar, and with the bloodhound's scent of the true collector she detected by instinct the bricabrac hunters of society. There is always a goodly number of them wherever antiquities are to be found, and Chrysophrasia was hailed by those of her persuasion with the mingled delight and jealousy which scientific bodies feel when a new scientist appears upon the horizon.

As for Hermione, she created a great sensation, and the hearts of many secretaries palpitated in the most lively manner when she first entered the ballroom of one of the embassies, two days after her arrival. The astonishment was great when it was known that she was Paul Patoff's own cousin; and when it was observed that Paul was very often with her the cry went up that he had fallen in love at last.

Thereupon all the women who had said that he was a bore, a monster, a statue, and a piece of ice, immediately declared that there must be something in him, after all, and began to talk to him whenever they got a chance. Some disappointment was felt, too, when it was observed that Alexander Patoff also showed a manifest preference for the society of his beautiful cousin, and wise old ladies said there would be trouble. Everybody, however, received the addition to society with open arms, and hoped that the Carvels' visit might be prolonged for at least a whole year.

Many of these comments reached my ears, and the remarks concerning Alexander's growing attachment for Hermione startled me, and chilled me with a sense of evil to come. I opened my eyes and watched, as every one else was doing, and in a short time I came to the conclusion that public opinion was right. It was very disagreeable to me to admit it, but I soon saw that there was no doubt that Alexander was falling in love with his cousin. I saw, too, what others who knew them less well did not see : Madame Patoff exercised all her ingenuity in giving her favorite son opportunities of seeing Hermione alone. It was very easy to do this, and she did it in the most natural way ; she affected to repent bitterly of her injustice to Paul, and took delight in calling him to her side, and keeping him with her as long as possible. Sometimes she would make him stay an hour by her side at a party, going over and over the strange story of Alexander's imprisonment, and asking him questions again and again, until he grew weary and absent, and answered her with rather incoherent phrases, or in short monosyllables not always to the point. Then at last, when she saw that she could keep him no longer, she would let him go, asking him to forgive her for being so importunate, and explaining as an excuse that she could never hear enough of a story that had ended so happily. Meanwhile Alexander had found ample opportunity for talking with Hermione, and had made the most of his time.

I have said that I had always been very fond of the young girl, and I thought that I understood her character well enough; but I find it hard to understand the phases through which she passed after she first met Alexander. I believe she loved Paul very sincerely from the first, and I know that she contemplated the prospect of marrying him at no distant time. But I am equally sure that she did not escape the influence of that wonderful fascination which Alexander exercised over everybody. If it is possible to explain it at all, which is more than doubtful, I should think that it might be accounted for on some such theory as this. Hermione was negative as compared with Paul, but in comparison with Alexander she was positive. It is clear that if this were so she must have experienced two totally different sets of impressions, according as she was with the one or the other of the brothers.

To define more clearly what I mean, I will state this theory in other words. Paul Patoff was a very masculine and dominating man. Hermione Carvel was a young girl, who resembled her strong, sensible, and manly father far more than her meek and delicate mother. Though she was still very young, there was much in her which showed the determined will and energetic purpose which a man needs to possess more than a woman. Alexander Patoff, on the other hand, without being effeminate, was intensely feminine. He had fine sensibilities, he had quick intuitions, he was capricious and womanly in his ideas. It follows that, in the scale of characters, Hermione held the mean between the two brothers. Compared with Paul's powerful nature, her qualities were those of a woman; in comparison with Alexander's delicate organization of mind, Hermione's character was more like that of a man. The effect of this singular scale of personalities was, that when she found herself alternately in the society of the two brothers she felt as though she were alternately two different women. To a man entering a house on a bitter winter's night the hall seems comfortably warm; but it seems cold to a man who has been sitting over a fire in a hermetically sealed study.

Now Hermione had loved Paul when he was practically the only man of those she had ever known intimately whom she believed it possible to love at all. But she had seen very little of the world, and had known very few men. Her first recollections of society were indistinct, and no one individual had made any more impression upon her than another, perhaps because she was in reality not very impressionable. But Paul was preëminently a man able to impress himself upon others when he chose. He had come to Carvel Place, had loved his cousin, and she had returned his love with a readiness which had surprised herself. It was genuine in its way, and she knew that it was; nor could she doubt that Paul was in earnest, since a word from her had sufficed to make him curtail his visit, and go to the ends of the earth to find his brother. Hermione more than once wished that she had never spoken that word.

She now entered upon a new phase of her life, she saw a new sort of society, and she met a man who upset in a moment all her convictions about men in general. The result of all this novelty was that she began to look at life from a different point of view. Alexander amused her, and at the same time he made her feel of more importance in her own eyes. He talked well, but he made her fancy that she herself talked better. His thoughts were subtle, though not always logical, and his quick instincts gave him an immense advantage over people of slower intelligence. He knew all this himself, perhaps; at all events, he used his gifts in the cleverest possible way. He possessed the power to attract Hermione without dominating her; in other words, he made her like him of her own free will.

She liked him very much, and she felt that there was no harm in it. He was the brother of her future husband, so that she easily felt it a duty to like him, as well as a pleasure. Alexander himself affected to treat her with a sort of cousinly-brotherly affection, and spoke always of Paul with the greatest respect, when he spoke of him at all; but he manifestly sought opportunities of expressing his affection, and avoided all mention of Paul when not absolutely necessary. The position was certainly a difficult one, but he managed it with the tact of a woman and the daring of a man. I have always believed that he was really fond of Hermione; for I cannot imagine him so vile as to attempt to take her from Paul, when Paul had done so much towards liberating him from his prison. But whatever were his motives or his feelings, it was evident to me that he was making love to her in good earnest, that the girl was more interested in him than she supposed, and that Madame Patoff was cunningly scheming to break off the match with Paul in order to marry Hermione to Alexander.

Balsamides had of course become a friend of the family, after the part he had played in effecting Alexander's escape, and in his own way I think he watched the situation when he got a chance with as much interest as I myself. One evening we were sitting in his rooms, about midnight, talking, as we talked eternally, upon all manner of subjects.

"Griggs," said he, suddenly changing the topic of our conversation, "it is a great pity we ever took the trouble to find Alexander. I often wish he were still lying in that pleasant den in Laleli's garden."

"It would be better for every one concerned, except himself, if he were," I answered.

"I detest the fellow's face. If it were not for his mustache, he might pass for a woman anywhere."

"He is as beautiful as an angel," I said, wishing to give him his due.

"What business have men with such beauty as that?" asked Gregorios, scornfully. "I would rather look like a Kurd hamál than like Alexander Patoff. He is spoiling Paul's life. Not that I care!" he added, shrugging his shoulders.

"No," I said, "it is none of our business. I liked him at first, I confess, and I thought that Alexander and Miss Carvel would make a very pretty couple. But I like him less the more I see of him. However, he will soon be going back to his regiment, and we shall hear no more of him."

"His leave is not over yet," answered my friend. "A fellow like that can do a deal of harm in a few weeks."

Gregorios is a man of violent sympathies and antipathies, though no one would suppose it from his cold manner and general indifference. But I know him better than I have known most men, and he is less reticent with me than with the generality of his friends. It was impossible to say whether he took enough interest in the Carvels or in Paul to attempt to influence their destiny, but I was sure that if he crossed Alexander's path the latter would get the worst of it, and I mentally noted the fact in summing up Paul's chances.

At that time nothing had openly occurred which suggested the possibility of a rupture of the unacknowledged engagement between Paul and Hermione. Paul several times told her that he wished to speak formally to John Carvel, and obtain his consent to the marriage; but Hermione advised him to wait a little longer, arguing that she herself had spoken, and that there was therefore no concealment about the matter. The longer they waited, she said, the more her father would become accustomed to the idea, and the more he would learn to like Paul, so that in another month there would be no doubt but that he would gladly give his consent. But Paul himself was not satisfied. His mother's conduct irritated him beyond measure, and he began seriously to suspect her of wishing to make trouble. He was no longer deceived by her constant show of affection for himself, for she continued always to make it most manifest just when it prevented him from talking with Hermione. Alexander, too, treated him as he had not done before, with a deference and a sort of feline softness which inspired distrust. Two years ago Paul would have been the first to expect foul play from his brother, and would have been upon his guard from the beginning ; but Paul himself was changed, and had grown more merciful in his judgment of others. He found it hard to persuade himself that Alexander really meant to steal Hermione's love; and even when he began to suspect the possibility of such a thing, he believed that he could treat the matter lightly enough. Nevertheless, Hermione continued to dissuade him from going to her father, and he yielded to her advice, though much against his will. He found himself in a situation which to his conscience seemed equivocal. He knew from what John Carvel had written to me that his suit was not likely to meet with any serious opposition; he understood that John expected him to speak, and he began to fancy that his future father-in-law looked at him inquiringly from time to time, as though anticipating a question, and wondering why it was not asked.

One day he came to see me, and found me alone. Gregorios had gone to the palace, and I have no doubt that Paul, who knew his habits, had chosen a morning for his visit when he was certain that Balsamides would not be at home. He looked annoyed and almost nervous, as he sat down in silence and began to smoke.

"Anything wrong ? " I asked.

"I hardly know," he replied. "I am very uncomfortable. I am in a very disagreeable situation."

I was silent. I did not want to invite his confidence, and if he had come to tell me anything about himself, it was better to let him tell it in his own way.

"I am in a very disagreeable position," he repeated slowly. "I want to ask your advice."

"That is always a rash thing to do," I replied.

"I do not care. I must confide in you, as I did once before, but this time I only want your advice. My position is intolerable. I feel every day that I ought to ask Mr. Carvel to give me his daughter, and yet I cannot do it."

" Why not? It is certainly your duty," said I.

" Because Miss Carvel objects," he answered, with sudden energy. His voice sounded almost fierce as he spoke.

" Do you mean that she has not accepted " —

" I do not know what I mean, nor what she means, either ! " exclaimed Paul, rising, and beginning to pace the floor.

" My dear Patoff," I said, " you made a grave mistake in making me find your brother. Excuse my abruptness, but that is my opinion."

He turned suddenly upon me, and his face was very pale, while his eyes gleamed disagreeably and his lip trembled.

" So you have noticed that, too," he said in a low voice. " Well — go on ! What do you advise me to do? How am I to get him out of the way ? "

" There can be no doubt that Balsamides would advise you to cut his throat," I replied. " As for me, I advise you to wait, and see what comes of it. He must soon go home and rejoin his regiment."

" Wait ! " exclaimed Paul impatiently. " Wait ! Yes, — and while I am waiting he will be working, and he will succeed ! With that angel's face of his, he will certainly succeed ! Besides, my mother will help him, as you know."

" Look here," said I. " Either Miss Carvel loves you, or she does not. If she does, she will not love your brother. If she does not love you, you had better not marry her. That is the reasonable view."

" No doubt, — no doubt. But I do not mean to be reasonable in that way. You forget that I love her. The argument might have some weight."

" Not much. After all, why do you love her? You do not know her well."

Paul stared at me as though he thought I were going mad. I dare say that I must have appeared to him to be perfectly insane. But I was disconcerted by the gravity of the situation, and I believed that he had a bad chance against Alexander. It was wiser to accustom his mind to the idea of failure than to flatter him with imaginary hopes of success. A man in love is either a hero or a fool; heroes who fail are generally called fools for their pains, and fools who succeed are sometimes called heroes. Paul stared, and turned away in silence.

"You do not seem to have any answer ready," I observed. "You say you love a certain lady. Is there any reason, in the nature of things, why some one else should not love her at the same time? Then it follows that the most important point is this, — she must love you. If she does not, your affection is wasted. I am not an old man, but I am far from being a young one, and I have seen much in my time. You may analyze your feelings and those of others, when in love, as much as you please, but you will not get at any other result. Unless a woman loves you, it is of very little use that you love her."

"What in the world are you talking about, Griggs?" asked Paul, whose ideas, perhaps, did not coincide with mine. "What can you know about love? You are nothing but a hardened old bachelor; you never loved a woman in your life, I am sure."

I was much struck by the truth of this observation, and I held my peace. A cannibal cannot be expected to understand French cooking.

"I tell you," continued Paul, "that Miss Carvel has promised to marry me, and I constantly speak to her of our marriage."

"But does she speak to you of it?" I asked. "I fancy that she never alludes to it except to tell you not to go to her father."

In his turn Paul was silent, and bent his brows. He must have been half distracted, or he would not have talked to me as he did. I never knew a less communicative man.

" This is a very delicate matter," I said presently. "You ask my advice ; I will give you the best I can. Do one of two things. Either go to Mr. Carvel without his daughter's permission, or else fight it out as you can until your brother goes. Then you will have the field to yourself."

" The difficulty lies in the choice," said Paul.

" The choice depends upon your own state of mind, and upon your strength, or rather upon the strength of your position. If Miss Carvel has promised to marry you, I think you have a right to push matters as fast as you can."

" I will," said Paul. " Good-by."

He left me at once, and I began to reflect upon what had passed. It seemed to me that he was foolish and irrational, altogether unlike himself. He had asked my advice upon a point in which his own judgment would serve him better than mine, and it was contrary to his nature to ask advice at all in such matters. He was evidently hard pressed and unhappy, and I wished I could help him, but it was impossible. He was in a dilemma from which he could issue only by his own efforts ; and although I was curious to see what he would do, I felt that I was not in a position to suggest any very definite line of action. I looked idly out of the window at the people who passed, and I began to wonder whether even my curiosity to see the end could keep me much longer in Pera. The crowd jostled and elbowed itself in the narrow way, as usual. The fez, in every shade of red, and in every condition of newness, shabbiness, and mediocrity, with tassel and without, rocked, swayed, wagged, turned, and moved beneath my window till I grew sick of the sight of it, and longed to see a turban, or a tall hat, or no hat at all, — anything for a change of head-dress. I left the window rather wearily, and took up one of the many novels which lay on the table, pondering on the probable fate of Paul Patoff's love for his cousin.

XX.

HERMIONE found herself placed in quite as embarrassing a position as Paul, and before long she began to feel that she had lost herself in a sort of labyrinth of new sensations. She hardly trusted herself to think or to reflect, so confusing were the questions which constantly presented themselves to her mind. It seems an easy matter for a woman to say, I love this man, or, I love that man, and to know that she speaks truly in so saying. With some natures first love is a fact, a certainty against which there is no appeal, and beside which there is no alternative. To see, with them, is practically to love, and to love once is to love forever. We may laugh over "love at first sight," as we call it, but history and every-day life afford so many instances of its reality that we cannot deny its existence. But the conditions in which it is found are rare. To love each other at first sight, both the persons must be impulsive; each must find in the other exactly what each has long sought and most earnestly desired, and each must recognize the discovery instantaneously. I suppose, also, that unless such love lasts it does not deserve the name; but in order that it may be durable it is necessary that the persons should realize that they have not been deceived in their estimate of each other, that they should possess in themselves the capacity for endurance, that their tastes should change little and their hearts not at all. People who are at once very impulsive and very enduring are few in the world and very hard to mate; wherefore love at first sight, but of a lasting nature, is a rare phenomenon.

Hermione did not belong to this class, and she had certainly not loved Paul during the first few days of their acquaintance. Her nature was relatively slow and hard to rouse. A season in society had produced no impression upon her; and if Paul had stayed only a week, or even a fortnight, at Carvel Place he might have fared no better than all the other men who had been presented to her, had talked and danced with her, and had gone away, leaving her life serenely calm as before. But Paul had been very assiduous, and had lost no time. Moreover, he loved her, and was in earnest about it; so that when, on that memorable day in the park, he had spoken at last, she had accepted his speech and had sealed her answer.

She believed that she loved him with all her heart, but she was new to love, and the waking sentiment was not yet a passion. It was only a sensation, and though its strength was great enough to influence Hermione's life, it had not yet acquired any great stability. A more impulsive nature would have been more suddenly moved, but Hermione's love needed time for its development, and the time had been very short. Since she had admitted that she loved Paul, she had not seen him until the eve of his brother's reappearance; and now, owing to Madame Patoff's skillful management, she talked with Alexander more frequently than with Paul. Alexander was apparently doing his best to make her love him, and the world said that he was succeeding. Hermione herself was startled when she tried to understand her own feelings, for she saw that a great change had taken place in her, and she could neither account for it nor assure herself where it would end. It would be unjust to blame her, or to say that she was unfaithful. She did not waver in her determination to marry Paul, but she tried to put it off as long as possible, struggling to clear away her doubts, and trying hard to feel that she was acting rightly. After all, it is easy to comprehend the confusion which arises in a young girl's mind when placed in such a position. We say too readily that a woman who wavers and hesitates is treating a man badly. Men are so quick to jump at the conclusion that women love them that they resent violently the smallest signs of hesitation in the other sex. They do not see that a woman needs time to decide, just as a man does; and they think it quite enough that they themselves have made up their minds, as if women existed only to submit themselves to the choice of men, and had no manner of right to question that choice when once made.

Paul could not imagine why Hermione hesitated, and she herself would certainly have refused to account for the delay she caused, by admitting that Alexander had made an impression upon her heart. But she felt the charm the man exercised, and her life was really influenced by it. The strange adventure which had so long kept him a prisoner in Laleli's house lent him an atmosphere of romantic interest, and his own nature increased the illusion. The brilliant young officer, with his almost supernatural beauty, his ready tongue, his sweet voice, and his dashing grace, was well calculated to make an impression upon any woman; to a young girl who had grown up in very quiet surroundings, who had hitherto regarded Paul Patoff as the ideal of all that a man should be, the soldier brother seemed like a being from another world. At the same time Hermione was reaching the age when she could enjoy society, because she began to feel at home in it, because the first dazzling impression of it had given way to a quieter appreciation of what it offered, and lastly because she herself was surrounded by many admirers, and had become a personage of more importance than she had ever thought possible before. Under such circumstances a young girl's impressions change very rapidly. She feels the disturbing influence and enjoys the moment, but while it lasts she feels also that she is unfit to decide upon the greatest question of her life. She needs time, because she can employ very little of the time she has in serious thought, and because she doubts whether all her previous convictions are not shaken to their foundations. She dreads a mistake, and is afraid that in speaking too quickly she may speak untruly. It is the desire to be honest which forbids her to continue in the course she had chosen before this new phase of her life began, or to come to any new decision involving immediate action, especially immediate marriage.

Herein lies the great danger to a young girl who has promised to marry a man before she has seen anything of the world, and who suddenly begins to see a great deal of the world before the marriage actually takes place. She is just enough attached to the man to feel that she loves him, but the bonds are not yet so close as to make her know that his love is altogether the dominating influence of her life. Unless this same man whom she has chosen stands out as conspicuously in the new world she has entered as in the quiet home she has left, there is great danger that he may fall in her estimation; and in those early stages of love, estimation is a terribly important element. By estimation I do not mean esteem. There is a subtle difference between the two; for though our estimation may be high or low, our esteem is generally high. When a young girl is old enough to be at home in society, she sets a value on every man, and perhaps on every woman, whom she meets. They take their places in the scale she forms, and their places are not easily changed. Among them the man she has previously promised to marry almost inevitably finds his rank, and she is fortunate if he is among the highest; for if he is not, she will not fail to regret that he does not possess some quality or qualities which she supposes to exist in those men whom she ranks first among her acquaintance. Where criticism begins, sympathy very often ends, and with it love. Then, if she is honest, a woman owns that she has made a mistake, and refuses to abide by her engagement, because she feels that she cannot make the man happy. Or if her ideas of faith forbid her from doing this, she marries him in spite of her convictions, and generally makes him miserable for the rest

of his days. When a girl throws a man over, as the phrase
goes, the world sets up a howl, and vows that she has treated
him very badly; but it always seems to me that by a single
act of courage she has freed herself and the man who loves
her from the fearful consequences of a marriage where all
the love would have been on one side, and all the criticism
on the other. It is not always a girl's own fault when she
does not know her own mind, and when she has discovered
her mistake she is wise if she refuses to persist in it. There
is more to be said in favor of breaking off engagements
than is generally allowed, and there is usually far too much
said against the woman who has the courage to pursue such
a course.

In comparing the two brothers, as she undoubtedly did,
Hermione was not aware that she was making any real
comparison between them. What she felt and understood
was that when she was with Paul she was one person, and
when she was with Alexander she was quite another; and
the knowledge of this fact confused her, and made her uncertain of herself. With Paul she was, in her own feelings,
the Hermione he had known in England; with Alexander
she was some one else, — some one she did not recognize,
and who should have been called by another name. Until she
could unravel this mystery, and explain to herself what she
felt, she was resolved not to take any further steps in regard
to her marriage.

Pera, at this time, was indulging itself in its last gaye-
ties before the beginning of the summer season, when every
one who is able to leave the town goes up the Bosphorus, or
to the islands. The weather was growing warm, but still
the dancing continued with undiminished vigor. Among
other festivities there was to be a masked ball, a species of
amusement which is very rare in Constantinople; but somebody had suggested the idea, one of the great embassies had
taken it up, and at last the day was fixed and the invitations
were issued. It was to be a great affair, and everybody

went secretly about the business of composing costumes and disguises. There was much whispering and plotting and agreeing together in schemes of mystification. The evening came, everybody went, and the ball was a great success.

Hermione had entirely hidden her costume with a black domino, which is certainly the surest disguise which anyone can wear. Its wide folds reached to the ground, and completely hid her figure, while even her hands were rendered unrecognizable by loose black gloves. Paul had been told what she was to wear; but he probably knew her by some sign, agreed upon beforehand, from all the other black dominos; for a number of other ladies had chosen the same overgarment to hide the brilliant costumes until the time came for unmasking. He came up to her immediately, and offered his arm, proposing to walk through the rooms before dancing; but Hermione would not hear of it, saying that if she were seen with him at first she would be found out at once.

"Do not be unreasonable," said she, as she saw the disappointed look on his face. "I want to mystify ever so many people first. Then I will dance with you as much as you like."

"Very well," said Paul, rather coldly. "When you want me, come to me."

Hermione nodded, and moved away, mixing with the crowd under the hundreds of lights in the great ball-room. Paul sighed, and stood by the door, caring little for what went on. He was not a man who really took pleasure in society, though he had cultivated his social faculties to the utmost, as being necessary to his career. The fact that all the ladies were masked dispensed him for the time from the duty of making the round of the room and speaking to all his acquaintances, and he was glad of it. But Hermione was bent upon enjoying her first masked ball, and all the freedom of moving about alone. She spoke to many men whom she knew, using a high, squeaking voice which in no way recalled her natural tones. In the course of half an hour she found Alexander Patoff talking earnestly with a lady in a white domino, whom she recognized, to her surprise, as her aunt Chrysophrasia. Alexander evidently had no idea of her identity, for he was speaking in low and passionate tones, while Miss Dabstreak, who seemed to enter into the spirit of the mystification with amazing readiness, replied in the conventional squeak. She had concealed her hands in the loose sleeves of her domino, and as she was of about the same height as Hermione, it was absolutely impossible to prove that she was not Hermione herself.

"Hermione," exclaimed Alexander, just as the real Hermione came up to him, "I cannot bear to hear you talk in that voice! What is the use of keeping up this ridiculous disguise? Do you not see that I am in earnest?"

"Perfectly," squeaked Chrysophrasia. "So am I. But somebody might hear my natural voice, you know."

Hermione started, and drew back a little. It was a strange position, for Alexander was evidently under the impression that he was making love to herself, and her aunt was amused by drawing him on. She hesitated, not knowing what she ought to do. It was clear that, unless she made herself known to him, he might remain under the impression that she had accepted his love-making. She waited to see what would happen. But Chrysophrasia had probably detected her, for presently the white domino moved quickly away towards the crowd. Alexander sprang forward, and would have followed, but Hermione crossed his path, and laid her hand on his sleeve.

"Will you give me your arm, Alexander?" she said, quietly, in her natural way.

He stopped short, stared at her, and then broke into a short, half-angry laugh. But he gave her his arm, and walked by her side, with an expression of bewilderment and annoyance on his beautiful face. Hermione was too wise to say that she had overheard the conversation, and Alexander was ashamed to own that he had made a mistake, and taken some one else for her. But by making herself known Hermione had effectually annulled whatever false impression Chrysophrasia had made upon him.

" Do you know who that lady in the white domino is, with whom I was talking a moment ago? Did you see her?" he asked, rather nervously.

"It is our beloved aunt Chrysophrasia," said Hermione, calmly.

" Good heavens!. Aunt Chrysophrasia!" exclaimed Alexander, in some horror.

"Why 'good heavens'?" inquired Hermione. "Have you been doing anything foolish? I am sure you have been making love to her. Tell me about it."

" There is nothing to tell. But what a wonderful disguise! How many dances will you give me? May I have the cotillon?"

" You may have a quadrille," answered Hermione.

" A quadrille, two waltzes, and the cotillon. That will do very well. As nobody knows you in that domino, we can dance as often as we please, and you will only be seen with me in the cotillon. What is your costume? I am sure it is something wonderful."

"How you run on!" exclaimed the young girl. " You do not give one the time to refuse one thing before you take another!"

" That is the best way, and you know it," answered Alexander, laughing. " A man should never give a woman time to refuse. It is the greatest mistake that can be imagined."

" Did aunt Chrysophrasia refuse to dance with you?" inquired Hermione.

Alexander bit his lip, and a faint color rose in his transparent skin.

"Aunt Chrysophrasia is a hard-hearted old person," he replied, evasively; but he almost shuddered at the thought that under the white domino there had lurked the green eyes and the faded, sour face of his æsthetic relative.

"To think that even she should have resisted you!" exclaimed Hermione, wickedly.

"Better she than you," said Alexander, lowering his tone as they passed near a group of persons who chattered loudly in feigned voices. "Better she than you, dear cousin," he repeated, gently. "To be refused anything by you" —

"They do things very well here," interrupted Hermione, pretending not to hear. "They have such magnificent rooms, and the floor is so good."

"Hermione, why do you" —

"Because," said Hermione quickly, before he could finish his sentence, "because you say too much, cousin Alexander. I interrupt you because you go too far, and because the only possible way of checking you is to cut you short."

"And why must you check me? Am I rude or rough with you? Do I say anything that you should not hear? You know that I love you; why may I not tell you so? I know. You will say that Paul has spoken before me. But do you love Paul? Hermione, can you own to yourself that you love him, — not as a brother, but as the man you would choose to marry? He does not love you as I love you."

"Hush!" exclaimed the young girl. "You must not. I will go away and leave you."

"I will follow you."

"Why will you torment me so?" Perhaps her tone of voice did not express all the annoyance she meant to show, for Alexander did not desist. He only changed his manner, growing suddenly as soft and yielding as a girl.

"I did not mean to annoy you," he said. "You know that I never mean to. You must forgive me, you must be kind to me, Hermione. You have the stronger position, and you should be merciful. How can I help saying something of what I feel?"

"You should not feel it, to begin with," answered his cousin.

"Will you teach me how I may not love you?" His voice dropped almost to a whisper, as he bent down to her and asked the question. But Hermione was silent for a moment, not having any very satisfactory plan to propose. Half reluctant, she sat down by him upon a sofa in the corner of an almost empty room. There were tall plants in the windows, and the light was softened by rose-colored shades.

"It must be a hard lesson to learn," said Alexander, speaking again. "But if you will teach me, I will try and learn it; for I will do anything you ask me. You say I must not love you, but I love you already. When I am with you I am carried away, like a boat spinning down the Neva in the springtime. Can the river stop itself in order that what lives in it may not move any more? Can it say to the skiff, 'Go no further,' when the skiff is already far from the shore, at the mercy of the water?"

"The boatman must pull hard at his oars," laughed Hermione. "Have you never seen a caïque pull through the Devil's Stream on the Bosphorus, at Bala Hissar? It is hard work, but it generally succeeds."

"A man may fight against the devil, but he cannot struggle against what he worships. Or, if he can, you must teach me how to do it, and give me some weapon to fight with."

"You must rely on yourself for that. You must say, 'I will not,' and it will be very easy. Besides," she added, with another laugh, in which there was a rather nervous ring, — "besides, you know all this is only a comedy, or a pastime. You are not in earnest."

"I wish I were not," answered Alexander, softly. "You tell me to rely upon myself. I rely on you. I love you, and that makes you stronger than me."

Hermione believed him, and perhaps she was right. She felt, and he made her feel, that she dominated him, and could turn him whither she would. Her pride was flattered, and though she promised herself that she would make him give up his love for her by the mere exertion of a superior common sense, she was conscious that the task was not wholly distasteful. She enjoyed the sensation of being the stronger, of realizing that Alexander was wholly at her feet and subject to her commands. That he should have gradually grown so intimate as to speak so freely to her is not altogether surprising. They were own cousins, and called each other by their Christian names. They met daily, and were often together for many consecutive hours, and Madame Patoff did her best to promote this state of things. Hermione had become accustomed to his devotion, for he had advanced by imperceptible stages. When he first said that he loved her, she took it as she might have taken such an expression from her brother, — as the exuberant expression of an affection purely platonic, not to say brotherly. When he had repeated it more earnestly, she had laughed at him, and he had laughed with her in a way which disarmed all her suspicions. But each time that he said it he laughed less, until she realized that he was not jesting. Then she reproached herself a little for having let the intimacy grow, and determined to persuade him by gentle means that he had made a mistake. She felt that she was responsible for his conduct, because she had not been wise enough to stop him at the outset, and she therefore felt also that it would be unjust to make a violent scene, and that it was altogether out of the question to speak to Paul about the matter. To tell the truth, she was not sorry that it was out of the question, and this was the most dangerous element in her intimacy with Alexander. When a young woman who has not a profound experience of the world undertakes to convince a man by sheer argument that he ought not to love her, the result is likely to be unsatisfactory, and she stands less chance of persuading than of being persuaded. A man who persuades a woman that she is able to influence him, and that he is wholly at her mercy, has already succeeded in making himself interesting to her ; and she will not readily abandon the exercise of her power, since she is provided with the too plausible excuse that she is doing him good, and consequently is herself doing right.

"I wish you would really listen to me, and take my advice," said Hermione, after a pause. "There is so much that is good in you, — so much that is far better than this foolish love-making."

Alexander Patoff smiled softly, and his brown eyes gazed dreamily at hers, that just showed through the openings in the black domino.

"If there is anything good in me, you have put it there," he answered. "Do not take it away ; do not give me the physic of good advice."

"I think you need it more than usual to-night," said his cousin. "You are more than usually foolish, you know."

"You are more than usually wise. But if you tell me to do anything to-night, I will do it."

"Then go away and dance with some one else," laughed Hermione. To her surprise, Alexander rose quietly, and with one gentle glance turned away. Then she repented.

"Alexander!" she exclaimed, almost involuntarily.

"Yes," he answered, coming back, and seating himself again by her side.

"I did not tell you to come back," she said, amused at his docility.

"No — but I came," he replied. "You called me. I thought you had forgotten something. Shall I go away again ?"

"No. You may stay, if you will be good," said she, leaning back and looking away from him.

"I promise. Besides, you admitted a moment ago that I was very good. Perhaps I am too good, and that is the reason why you sent me away."

"I did not say you were good. I said there was some good in you. You always take everything for granted."

"I will take all you grant," said he.

"I grant nothing. It is you who fancy that I do. You have altogether too much imagination."

"I never need it with you, even if I have it," answered Alexander. "You are infinitely beyond anything I ever imagined in my wildest dreams."

"So are you," laughed Hermione. "Only — it is in a different way."

"Why do you think I like you so much?" asked her cousin, suddenly changing his tone.

"Because you ought not to," she answered without hesitation.

"Then you think that as soon as any one tells me that I should not like a thing, I make up my mind to like it and to have it? No, that is not the reason I love you."

"It was 'liking,' not 'loving,' a moment ago," observed Hermione. "Please always say 'liking.' It is a much better word."

"Perhaps. It leaves more to the imagination, of which you say I have so much. The reason I like you so much, Hermione, is because you are so honest. You always say just what you mean."

"Yes. The difficulty lies in making you understand what I mean."

"As the Frenchman said when a man misunderstood him. You furnish me with an argument; you are not bound to furnish me with an understanding. No, I am afraid that would be asking the impossible. It is easier for a woman to talk than for a man to know what she thinks."

"I thought you said I was honest. Please explain," returned Hermione.

"Honesty does not always carry conviction. I mean that you are evidently most wonderfully honest, from your own point of view. If I could make my opinion yours. everything would be settled very soon."

" In what way ? "

" Why should I tell you ? I have told you so often, and you will not believe me. If I say it, you will send me away again. I do not say it, — another proof of my goodness to-night."

" I am deeply sensible," answered Hermione, with a laugh. " Come, I will give you one dance, and then you must go."

So they left their seat, and went into the ball-room just as the musicians began to play Nur für Natur ; and the enchanting strains of the waltz carried them away in the swaying movement, and did them no manner of good. Just such conversations had taken place before, and would take place again so long as Hermione maintained the possibility of converting Alexander to the platonic view of cousinly affection. But each time some chance expression, some softer tone of voice, some warmer gleam of light in the Russian's brown eyes, betrayed that he was gaining ground rather than losing anything of the advantage he had already obtained.

Half an hour later Hermione laid her hand on Paul's arm, and looked up rather timidly into his eyes through the holes in her domino. His expression was very cold and hard, but it changed as he recognized her.

" At last," he said happily, as he led her away.

" At last," she echoed, with a little sigh. " Do you want to dance ? " she asked. " It is so hot ; let us go and sit down somewhere."

Almost by accident they came to the place where Hermione had sat with Alexander. There was no one there, and they installed themselves upon the same sofa.

" I thought you were never coming," said Paul. " After all, what does it matter whether people see us together or not ? I never can understand what amusement there is, after the first five minutes, in rushing about in a domino and trying to mystify people."

" No," answered Hermione, " it is not very amusing. I

would much rather sit quietly and talk with some one I know and who knows me."

"I want to tell you something to-night, dear," said Paul, after a short silence. " Do you mind if I tell you now ? "

"No bad news ? " asked Hermione, rather nervously.

"No. It is simply this : I have made up my mind that I must speak to your father to-morrow. Do not be startled, darling. This position cannot last. I am not acting an honorable part, and he expects me to ask him the question. I know you have objected to my going to him for a long time, but I feel that the thing must be done. There can be no good objection to our marriage, — Mr. Carvel made Griggs understand that. Tell me, is there any real reason why I should not speak ? "

Hermione turned her head away. Under the long sleeves of her domino her small hands were tightly clasped together.

" Is there any reason, dear ? " repeated Paul, very gently. But as her silence continued his lips set themselves firmly, and his face grew slowly pale.

" Will you please speak, darling ? " he said, in changed tones. " I am very nervous," he added, with a short, harsh laugh.

"Oh — Paul ! Don't ! " cried Hermione. Her voice seemed to choke her as she spoke. Then she took courage, and continued more calmly : " Please, please wait a little longer, — it is such a risk ! "

Paul laughed again, almost roughly.

"A risk ! What risk ? Your father has done all but give his formal consent. What possible danger can there be ? "

" No. Not from him, — it is not that ! "

" Well, what is it ? Hermione, what in the name of Heaven is the matter ? Speak, darling ! Tell me what it is. I cannot bear this much longer." Indeed, the man's suppressed passion was on the very point of breaking out, and the blue light quivered in his eyes, while his face grew unnaturally pale.

"Oh, Paul — I cannot tell you — you frighten me so," murmured Hermione in broken tones. "Oh, Paul! Forgive me — forgive me!"

At that moment Gregorios Balsamides passed before their corner, a lady in a red hood and a red mask leaning on his arm.

"Hush!" exclaimed Paul, under his breath, as the couple came near them. But Gregorios only nodded familiarly to Paul, stared a moment at his pale face, glanced at the black domino, and went on with his partner. "I do not want to frighten you, dearest," continued Paul, when no one could hear them. "And what have I to forgive? Do not be afraid, and tell me what all this means."

"I must," answered Hermione, her strength returning suddenly. "I must, or I should despise myself. You must not go to my father, Paul — because I — I am not sure of myself."

She trembled visibly under her domino, as she spoke the last words almost in a whisper, hesitating and yet forcing herself to tell the truth. Paul glanced uneasily at the black drapery which veiled all her head and figure, and with one hand he grasped the carved end of the sofa, so that it cracked under the pressure. For some seconds there was an awful silence, broken only by low sounds which told that Hermione was crying.

"You mean — that you do not love me," said Paul at last, very slowly, steadying his voice on every syllable.

The young girl shook her head, and tried to speak. But the words would not come. Meanwhile the strong man's anger was slowly rising, very slowly but very surely, so that Hermione felt it coming, as a belated traveler on the sands sees the tide creeping nearer to the black cliff.

"Hermione," he said, very sternly, "if you mean that you are no longer willing to marry me, say so plainly. I will forgive you if I can, because I love you. But please do not trifle with me. I can bear the worst, but I cannot bear waiting."

"Do not talk like that, Paul!" cried his cousin in an agonized voice, but recovering her power of speech before the pent-up anger he seemed to be controlling. "Let us wait, Paul; let us wait and be sure. I cannot marry you unless I am sure that I love you as I ought to love you. I do love you, but I feel that I could love you so much more — as — as I should like to love my — the man I marry. Have patience, — please have patience for a little while."

Paul's white lips opened and shut mechanically as he answered her.

"I am very patient. I have been patient for long. But it cannot last forever. I believed you loved me and had promised to marry me. If you have made a mistake, it is much to be regretted. But I must really beg you to make up your mind as soon as possible."

"Oh, pray do not talk like that. You are so cold. I am so very unhappy!"

"What would you have me say?" asked Paul, his voice growing clearer and harder with every word. "Will you answer me one question? Will you tell me whether you have learned to care so much for another man that your liking for him makes you doubt?"

"I am afraid" — She stopped, then suddenly exclaimed, "How can you ask me such a question?"

"What are you afraid of?" inquired Paul, in the same hard tone. "You always tell the truth. You will tell it now. Has any other man come between you and me?"

It was of no use for her to hesitate. She could command Alexander and give him any answer she chose, but Paul's strong nature completely dominated her. She bent her head in assent, and the Yes she spoke was almost inaudible.

"And you ask time to choose between us?" asked Paul, icily. "Yes, I understand. You shall have the time, — as long as you please to remain in Constantinople. I am much obliged to you for being so frank. May I give you my arm to go into the next room ? "

" How unkind you are ! " said Hermione, making an effort to rise. But her strength failed her, and she fell back into her seat. " Excuse me," she faltered. " Please wait one moment, — I am not well."

Paul looked at her, and hesitated. But her weakness touched him, and he spoke more gently as he turned to her.

" May I get you a glass of water, or anything ? "

" Thanks, nothing. It will be over in a moment, — only a little dizziness."

For a few seconds they remained seated in silence. Then Hermione turned her head, and looked at her cousin's white face. Her small gloved hand stole out from under her domino and rested on his arm. He took no notice of the action ; he did not even look at her.

" Paul," she said, very gently, " you will thank me some day for having waited."

A contemptuous answer rose to his lips, but he was ashamed of it before it was spoken, and merely raised his eyebrows as he answered in perfectly monotonous tones :

" I believe you have done what you think best."

" Indeed I have," replied Hermione, rising to her feet.

He offered her his arm, and they went out together. But when supper-time came, and with it the hour for unmasking, Hermione was not to be seen ; and Alexander, who had counted upon her half-given assent to dance the cotillon with him, leaned disconsolately against a door, wondering whether it could be worth while to sacrifice himself by engaging any one in her place.

But Paul did not go home. He was too angry to be alone, and above all too deeply wounded. Besides, his position required that he should stay at least until supper was over, and it was almost a relief to move about among the

gorgeous costumes of all kinds which now issued from the
black, white, and red dominos, as a moth from the chrysalis.
He spoke to many people, saying the same thing to each,
with the same mechanical smile, as men do when they are
obliged day after day to accomplish a certain social task.
But the effort was agreeable, and took off the first keen
edge of his wrath.

He had no need to ask the name of the man who had
come between him and the woman he loved. For weeks he
had watched his brother and Hermione, asking himself if
their intimacy meant anything, and then driving away the
tormenting question, as though it contained something of
disloyalty to her. Now he remembered that for weeks this
thing she had spoken must have been in her mind, since she
had always entreated him to wait a little longer before
speaking with her father. It had appeared such an easy
matter to her to wait ; it was such a hard matter for him, —
harder than death it seemed now. For it was all over.
He believed that she had spoken her last word that night,
and that in speaking of waiting still longer she had only intended to make it less troublesome to break it off. She had
admitted that another man had come between them. Was
anything further needed? It followed, of course, that she
loved this other man — Alexander — better than himself.
For the present he could see only one side of the question,
and he repeated to himself that all was over, saying it again
and again in his heart, as he went the rounds of the room,
asking each acquaintance he met concerning his or her plans
for the summer, commenting on the weather, and praising
the successful arrangement of the masked ball.

But Paul was ignorant of two things, in his present frame
of mind. He did not know that Hermione had been perfectly sincere in what she had said, and he did not calculate
upon his own nature. It was a simple matter, in the impulse of the first moment, to say that all was at an end, that
he gave her up, even as she had rejected him, with a sort of

savage pleasure in the coldness of the words he spoke. He could not imagine, after this interview, that he could ever think of her again as his possible wife, and if the idea had presented itself he would have cast it behind him as a piece of unpardonable weakness. All his former cynical determination to trust only in what he could do himself, for the satisfaction of his ambition, returned with renewed strength; and as he shook hands with the people he met, he felt that he would never again ask man or woman for anything which he could not take by force. He did not know that in at least one respect his nature had changed, and that the love he had lavished on Hermione was a deep-rooted passion, which had grown and strengthened and spread in his hard character, as the sculptor adapts the heavy iron framework in the body and limbs of a great clay statue. In the first sudden revulsion of his feeling, he thought he could pluck away his love and leave it behind him like an old garment, and the general contempt with which he regarded his surroundings after he left Hermione reminded him almost reassuringly of his old self. If his old self still lived, he could live his old life as before, without Hermione, and above all, without love. There was a bitter comfort in the thought that once more he was to look at all things, at success in everything, at his career, his aims both great and small, surrounded by obstacles which could be overcome only by main force, as prizes to be wrested from his fellows by his own unaided exertions.

He had forgotten that Hermione had been the chiefest aim of his existence for several months, and at the same time he did not realize that he loved her in such a way as to make it almost impossible for him to live without her. It was not in accordance with his character to relinquish without a struggle, and a very desperate struggle, that for which he had labored so long, and an outsider would have prophesied that whosoever would take from Paul Patoff the woman he loved would find that he had attempted a dangerous thing. Mere senseless anger does not often last long, and before an hour had passed Paul began to feel those suspicious little thrusts of pain in the breast and midriff which warn us that we miss some one we love. For a long time he tried to persuade himself that he was deceived, because he did not believe himself capable of such weakness. But the feeling was unmistakable.

The dancing was at its height, for all those who did not mean to stay until the end of the cotillon had gone home, so that the more distant rooms were already deserted. Almost unconsciously Paul strayed to the spot where he had sat with Hermione. He looked towards the sofa where they had been seated, and he saw a strange sight.

Alexander Patoff was there, half sitting, half lying, on the small sofa, unaware of his brother's presence. His face was turned away, and he was passionately kissing the cushions, — the very spot against which Hermione's head had rested. Paul stared stupidly at him for a moment, as though not comprehending the action, which indeed was wild and incomprehensible enough; then he seemed to understand, and strode forward in bitter anger. His brother, he thought, had seen them there together, had been told what had passed, and had chosen this passionate way of expressing his joy and his gratitude to Hermione. Alexander heard his brother's footsteps, and, starting, looked wildly round; then recognizing Paul, he sprang to his feet, and a faint color mounted to his pale cheeks.

"Fool!" cried Paul, bitterly, as he came forward. But Alexander had already recovered himself, and faced him coolly enough.

"What is the matter? What do you mean?" he asked, contemptuously.

"You know very well what I mean," retorted his brother, fiercely. "You know very well why you are making a fool of yourself, — kissing a heap of cushions, like a silly schoolboy in love."

"My dear fellow, you are certainly quite mad. I waltzed too long just now, and was dizzy. I was trying to get over it, that was all. My nerves are not so sound in dancing as they were before I was caught in that trap. Really, you have the most extraordinary ideas."

Paul was confused by the smooth lie. He did not believe his brother, but he could not find a ready answer.

"You do not know who sat there a little while ago?" he asked, sternly.

"Not the remotest idea," replied Alexander. "Was it that adorable red mask, who would not leave Balsamides even for a moment? Bah! You must think me very foolish. Come along and have some supper before we go home. I have no partner, and have had nothing to eat and very little to drink."

Paul was obliged to be content with the answer; but he understood his brother well enough to know that if there had been nothing to conceal, Alexander would have been furious at the way in which he was addressed. His conviction remained unchanged that his brother had known what passed, and was so overcome with joy that he had kissed the sofa whereon Hermione had sat. The two men left the room together, but Paul presently slipped away, and went home.

Strange to say, what he had seen did not have the effect of renewing his resentment against Hermione so much as of exciting his anger against his brother. He now felt for the first time that though he might give her up to another, he could not give her up to Alexander. The feeling was perhaps only an excuse suggested by the real love for her which filled him, but it was strongly mixed with pride, and with the old hostility which during so many years had divided the two brothers..

To give her up, and to his own brother, — the thing was impossible, not to be thought of for a moment. As he walked quickly home over the rough stones of the Grande

Rue, he realized all that it meant, and stopped short, staring at the dusky houses. He was not a man of dramatic instincts. He did not strike his forehead, nor stamp his foot, nor formulate in words the resolution he made out there in the dark street. He merely thrust his hands deeper into the pockets of his overcoat, and walked on; but he knew from that moment that he would fight for Hermione, and that his mood of an hour ago had been but the passing effect of a sudden anger. He regretted his hard speech and bitter looks, and he wished that he had merely assented to her proposal to wait, and had said no more about it until the next day. Hermione might talk of not marrying him, but he would marry her in spite of all objections, and especially in spite of Alexander.

Had she spoken thoughtlessly? In the light of his stronger emotion it seemed so to him, and it was long before he realized that she had suffered almost as much in making this sacrifice to her honesty as he had suffered himself. But she had indeed been in earnest, and had done courageously a very hard thing. She was conscious that she had made a great mistake, and she wanted to avert the consequences of it, if there were to be any consequences, before it was too late. She had allowed Alexander to become too fond of her, as their interview that evening had shown; and though she knew that she did not love him, she knew also that she felt a growing sympathy for him, which was in some measure a wrong to Paul. This sympathy had increased until it began to frighten her, and she asked herself where it would end, while she yet felt that she had no right to inflict pain on Alexander by suddenly forcing him to change his tone. Her mind was very much confused, and as she could not imagine that a real and undivided love admitted of any confusion, she had simply asked Paul to wait, in perfect good faith, meaning that she needed time to decide and to settle the matter in her own conscience. He had pressed her with questions, and had finally extorted the confession that another man had come between them. She had not meant to say that, but she was too honest to deny the charge. Paul had instantly taken it for granted that she already loved this other man better than himself, and had treated her as though everything were over between them.

The poor girl was in great trouble when she went home that night. Although nothing had been openly discussed, she knew that her engagement to Paul was tacitly acknowledged. She asked herself how he would treat her when they met; whether they should meet at all, indeed, for she feared that he would refuse to come to the house altogether. She wondered what questions her father would put to her, and how Madame Patoff would take the matter. More than all, she hesitated in deciding whether she had done well in speaking as she had spoken, seeing what the first results had been.

She shut herself in her room, and just as she was, in the beautiful Eastern dress which she was to have shown at the ball when the masking was over, she sat down upon a chair in the corner, and leaned her tired head against the wall. But for the disastrous ending of the evening, she would doubtless have sat before her glass, and looked with innocent satisfaction at her own beautiful face. But the dark corner suited her better, in her present mood. Her cheek rested against the wall, and very soon the silent tears welled over and trickled down, staining the green wall paper of the hotel bedroom, as they slowly reached the floor and soaked into the dusty carpet. She was very miserable and very tired, poor child, and perhaps she would have fallen asleep at last, just as she sat, had she not been roused by sounds which reached her from the next room, and which finally attracted her attention. Madame Patoff slept there, or should have been sleeping at that hour, for she was evidently awake. She seemed to be walking up and down, up and down eternally, between the window and the

door. As she walked, she spoke aloud from time to time.
At first she always spoke just as she was moving away from
the door, and consequently, when her back was turned towards the place where Hermione sat on the other side of
the wall, her words were lost, and only incoherent sounds
reached the young girl's ears. Presently, however, she
stopped just behind the door, and her voice came clear and
distinct through the thin wooden panel : —

"I wish he were dead. I wish he were dead. Oh, I
wish I could kill him myself!" Then the voice ceased,
and the sound of the footsteps began again, pacing up and
down.

Hermione started, and sat upright in her chair, while the
tears dried slowly on her cheeks. The habit of considering
her aunt to be insane was not wholly lost, and it was natural that she should listen to such unwonted sounds. For
some time she could hear the voice at intervals, but the
words were indistinct and confused. Her aunt was probably very ill, or under the influence of some hallucination
which kept her awake. Hermione crept stealthily near the
door, and listened intently. Madame Patoff continued to
walk regularly up and down. At last she heard clear
words again : —

"I wish I could kill him ; then Alexis could marry her.
Alexis ought to marry her, but he never will. Cannot Paul
die !"

Hermione shrank from the door in horror. She was
frightened and shaken, and after the events of the ·evening
her aunt's soliloquies produced a much greater effect upon
her than would have been possible six hours earlier. Her
first impulse was not to listen more, and she hastily began
to undress, making a noise with the chairs, and walking as
heavily as she could. Then she listened a moment, and all
was still in the next room. Her aunt had probably heard
her, and had feared lest she herself should be overheard.
Hermione crept into bed, and closed her eyes. At the end

of a few minutes the steps began again, and after some time the indistinct sounds of Madame Patoff's voice reached the young girl's ears. She seemed to speak in lower tones than before, however, for the words she spoke could not be distinguished. But Hermione strained her attention to the utmost, while telling herself that it was better she should not hear. The nervous anxiety to know whether Madame Patoff were still repeating the same phrases made her heart beat fast, and she lay there in the dark, her eyes wide open, her little hands tightening on the sheet, praying that the sounds might cease altogether, or that she might understand their import. Her pulse beat audibly for a few seconds, then seemed to stop altogether in sudden fear, while her forehead grew damp with terror. She thought that any supernatural visitation would have been less fearful than this reality, and she strove to collect her senses and to compose herself to rest.

At last she could bear it no longer. She got up and groped her way to the door of her aunt's room, not meaning to enter, but unable to withstand the desire to hear the words of which the incoherent murmur alone came to her in her bed. She reached the door, but in feeling for it her outstretched hand tapped sharply upon the panel. Instantly the footsteps ceased. She knew that Madame Patoff had heard her, and that the best thing she could do was to ask admittance.

"May I come in, aunt Annie?" she inquired, in trembling tones.

"Come in," was the answer; but the voice was almost as uncertain as her own.

She opened the door. By the light of the single candle — an English reading-light with a reflecting hood — she saw her aunt's figure standing out in strong relief against the dark background of shadow. Madame Patoff's thick gray hair was streaming down her back and over her shoulders, and she held a hairbrush in her hand, as though the fit of walking had come upon her while she was at her toilet. Her white dressing-gown hung in straight folds to the floor, and her dark eyes stared curiously at the young girl. Hermione was more startled than before, for there was something unearthly about the apparition.

"Are you ill, aunt Annie?" she asked timidly, but she was awed by the glare in the old lady's eyes. She glanced round the room. The bed was in the shadow, and the bed-clothes were rolled together, so that they took the shape of a human figure. Hermione shuddered, and for a moment thought her aunt must be dead, and that she was looking at her ghost. The girl's nerves were already so overstrained that the horrible idea terrified her; the more, as several seconds elapsed before Madame Patoff answered the question.

"No, I am not ill," she said slowly. "What made you ask?"

"I heard you walking up and down," explained Hermione. "It is very late; you generally go to sleep so early " —

"I? I never sleep," answered the old lady, in a tone of profound conviction, keeping her eyes fixed upon her niece's face.

"I cannot sleep, either, to-night," said Hermione, uneasily. She sat down upon a chair, and shivered slightly. Madame Patoff remained standing, the hairbrush still in her hand.

"Why should you not sleep? Why should you? What difference does it make? One is just as well without it, and one can think all night, — one can think of things one would like to do."

"Yes," answered the young girl, growing more and more nervous. "You must have been thinking aloud, aunt Annie. I thought I heard your voice."

Madame Patoff moved suddenly and bent forward, bringing her face close to her niece's, so that the latter was startled and drew back in her chair.

"Did you hear what I said?" asked the old lady, almost fiercely, in low tones.

Sometimes a very slight thing is enough to turn the balance of our beliefs, especially when all our feelings are wrought to the highest pitch of excitement. In a moment the conviction seized Hermione that her aunt was mad, — not mad as she had once pretended to be, but really and dangerously insane.

"I did not understand what you said," answered the young girl, too frightened to own the truth, as she saw the angry eyes glaring into her face. It seemed impossible that this should be the quiet, sweet-tempered woman whom she was accustomed to talk with every day. She certainly did the wisest thing, for her aunt's face instantly relaxed, and she drew herself up again and turned away.

"Go to bed, child," she said, presently. "I dare say I frightened you. I sometimes frighten myself. Go to bed and sleep. I will not make any more noise to-night."

There was something in the quick change, from apparent anger to apparent gentleness, which confirmed the idea that Madame Patoff's brain was seriously disturbed. Hermione rose and quietly left the room. She locked her door, and went to bed, hoping that she might sleep and find some rest; for she was worn out with excitement, and shaken by a sort of nervous fear.

Sleep came at last, troubled by dreams and restless, but it was sleep, nevertheless. Several times she started up awake, thinking that she again heard her aunt's low voice and the regular fall of her footsteps in the next room. But all was still, and her weary head sank back on the pillow in the dark, her eyelids closed again in sheer weariness, and once more her dreams wove fantastic scenes of happiness, ending always in despair, with the suddenness of revulsion which makes the visions of the night ten times more agonizing while they last than the worst of our real troubles.

But the morning brought a calmer reflection; and when

Hermione was awake she began to think of what had passed. The horror inspired by her aunt's words and looks faded before the greater anxiety of the girl's position with regard to Paul. She tried to go over the interview in her mind. Her conscience told her that she had done right, but her heart said that she had done wrong, and its beating hurt her. Then came the difficult task of reconciling those two opposing voices, which are never so contradictory as when the heart and the conscience fall out, and argue their cause before the bewildered court of justice we call our intelligence. First she remembered all the many reasons she had found for speaking plainly to Paul on the previous night. She had said to herself that she did not feel sure of her love, allowing tacitly that she expected to feel sure of it before long. But until the matter was settled she could not let him hurry the marriage nor take any decisive step. If he had only been willing to wait another month, he might have been spared all the suffering she had seen in his face ; she herself could have escaped it, too. But he had insisted, and she had tried to do right in telling him that she was not ready. Then he had been angry and hurt, and had coldly told her that she might wait forever, or something very like it, and she had felt that the deed was done. It was dreadful ; yet how could she tell him that she was ready ? Half an hour earlier, on that very spot, she had suffered Alexander to speak as he had spoken, only laughing kindly at his expressions of love ; not rebuking him and leaving him, as she should have done, and would have done, had she loved Paul with her whole heart.

And yet this morning, as she lay awake and thought it all over, something within her spoke very differently, like an incoherent cry, telling her that she loved him in spite of all. She tried to listen to what it said, and then the answer came quickly enough, and told her that she had been unkind, that she had given needless pain, that she had broken a man's life for an over-conscientious scruple which had no real foundation. But then her conscience returned to the charge, refuting the slighting accusation, so that the confusion was renewed, and became worse than before. For the sake of discovering something in support of her action, she began to think about Alexander ; and finding that she remembered very accurately what they had said to each other, her thoughts dwelt upon him. It was pleasant to think of his beautiful face, his soft voice, and his marvelous dancing. It was a fascination from which she could not easily escape, even when he was absent ; and there was a charm in the memory of him, in thinking of how she would turn him from being a lover to being a friend, which drew her mind away from the main question that occupied it, and gave her a momentary sensation of peace.

Suddenly the two men came vividly before her in profile, side by side. The bold, manly features and cold glance of the strong man contrasted very strangely with the exquisitely chiseled lines of his brother's face, with the soft brown eyes veiled under long lashes, and the indescribable delicacy of the feminine mouth. Paul wore the stern expression of a man superior to events and very careless of them. Alexander smiled, as though he loved his life, and would let no moment of it pass without enjoying it to the full.

It was but the vision of an instant, as she closed her eyes, and opened them again to the faint light which came in through the blinds. But Hermione felt that she must choose between the two men, and it was perhaps the first time she had quite realized the fact. Hitherto Alexander had appeared to her only as a man who disturbed her previous determinations. If she had hesitated to marry Paul while the disturbance lasted, it was not because she had ever thought of taking his brother instead. Now it seemed clear that she must accept either the one or the other, for the comparison of the two had asserted itself in her mind. In that moment she felt that she was worse than she had ever been before ; for the fact that she compared the two men as possible husbands showed her that she set no value on the promises she had made to Paul.

To choose, — but how to choose? Had she a right to choose at all? If she refused to marry Paul, was she not bound to refuse any one else, — morally bound in honor? The questions came fast, and would not be answered. Just then her aunt moved in the next room, and the thought of her possible insanity returned instantly to Hermione's mind. She determined that it was best to speak to her father about it. He was the person who ought to know immediately, and he should decide whether anything should be done. She made up her mind to go to him at once, and she rang for her maid.

But before she was dressed she had half decided to act differently, to wait at least a day or two, and see whether Madame Patoff would talk to herself again during the night. To tell her father would certainly be to give an alarm, and would perhaps involve the necessity of putting her aunt once more under the care of a nurse. John Carvel could not know, as Hermione knew, that the old lady's resentment against Paul was caused by her niece's preference for him, and it would not be easy for the young girl to explain this. But Hermione wished that she might speak to Paul himself, and warn him of what his mother had said. She sighed as she thought how impossible that would be. Nevertheless, in the morning light and in the presence of her maid, while her gold-brown hair was being smoothed and twisted, and the noises from the street told her that all the world was awake, the horror of the night disappeared, and Hermione almost doubted whether her aunt had really spoken those words at all. If she had, it had been but the angry outbreak of a moment, and should not be taken too seriously.

XXI.

It was probably curiosity that induced Professor Cutter to pay a visit to Constantinople in the spring. He is a scientist, and curiosity is the basis of all science, past, present, and future. His mind was not at rest in regard to Madame Patoff, and he found it very hard to persuade himself that she should suddenly have become perfectly sane, after having made him believe during eighteen months that she was quite mad. After her recovery he had had long interviews with Mrs. North, and had done his best to extract all the information she was able to give about the case. He had studied the matter very carefully, and had almost arrived at a satisfactory conclusion; but he felt that in order to remove all doubt he must see her again. He was deeply interested, and such a trifle as a journey to Constantinople could not stand in the way of his observations. Accordingly he wrote a post-card to John Carvel to say that he was coming, and on the following day he left England. But he likes to travel comfortably, and especially he is very fond of finding out old acquaintances when he is abroad, and of having an hour's chat with scientific men like himself. He therefore did not arrive until a week after John had news of his intended journey.

For some reason unknown to me, Carvel did not speak beforehand of the professor's coming. It may be that, in the hurry of preparation for moving up the Bosphorus, he forgot the matter; or perhaps he thought it would be an agreeable surprise to most of us. I myself was certainly very much astonished when he came, but the person who showed the greatest delight at his arrival was Hermione. It is not hard to imagine why she was pleased, and when I knew all that I have already told I understood her satisfaction well enough. The professor appeared on the day before the Carvels were to transfer themselves to Buyukdere. His gold-rimmed spectacles were on his nose, his thick and short gray hair stood up perpendicularly on his head as of old, his beard was as bushy and his great hands were as huge and as spotless as ever. But after not having seen him for some months, I was more struck than ever by his massive build and the imposing strength of his manner.

Several days had elapsed since the events recorded in the last chapter. To Hermione's surprise, Paul had come to the hotel as usual, on the day after the ball, and behaved as though nothing had happened, except that he had at first avoided finding himself alone with his cousin. She on her part was very silent, and even Alexander could not rouse her to talk as she used to do. When questioned, she said that the heat gave her a headache; and as Chrysophrasia spent much time in languidly complaining of the weather, the excuse had a show of probability. But after a day or two she was reassured by Paul's manner, and no longer tried to keep out of his way. Then it was that they found themselves together for the first time since the ball. It was only for a moment, but it was long enough.

Hermione took his passive hand in hers, very timidly, and looked into his face.

"You are not angry with me any more?" she said.

"No, not in the least," he answered. "I believe you did what you believed to be best, the other night. No one can do more than that."

"Yes, but you thought I was not in earnest."

"I thought you were more in earnest than you admitted. I thought you meant to break it off altogether. I have changed my mind."

"Have you? I am so glad. I meant just what I said, Paul. You should not have doubted that I meant it."

"I was angry. Forgive me if I was rude. I will not give you up. I will marry you in spite of everybody."

Hermione looked at him, curiously at first, then with a sort of admiration which she could not explain, — the admiration we all feel for a strong man who is very much in earnest.

"In spite of myself?" she asked, after a pause.

"Yes, almost," he began hotly, but his tone softened as he finished the sentence, — "almost in spite of yourself, Hermione."

"Indeed, I begin to think that you will," she answered, turning away her head to hide a smile that had in it more of happiness than of unbelief. Some one entered the room where they were standing, and nothing more was said ; nor did Paul repeat his words at the next opportunity, for he was not much given to repetition. When he had said a thing, he meant it, and he was in no hurry to say it again.

Meanwhile, also, the young girl had more than once listened, during the night, for any sounds which might proceed from Madame Patoff's bedroom; but she had heard nothing more, and the impression gradually faded from her mind, or was stored away there as a fact to be remembered at some future time. When Professor Cutter arrived, she determined to tell him in strictest confidence what had occurred. This, however, was not what gave her so much satisfaction in meeting him. She had long looked forward to the day when she could enjoy the triumph of seeing him meet Alexander Patoff, alive and well; for she knew how strongly his suspicions had fastened upon Paul, and it was he who had first told her what the common story was.

The professor arrived in the early morning by the Brindisi boat, and Hermione proposed that Chrysophrasia, Paul, Cutter, and herself should make a party to go over to Stamboul on the same afternoon. It was warm indeed, but she represented that as the whole family were to move up the Bosphorus on the following day, it would be long before they would have a chance of going to Stamboul again. Chrysophrasia moaned a little, but at last accepted the proposition, and Paul and the professor expressed themselves delighted with the idea.

The four set off together, descended by the Galata tunnel, and crossed the bridge on foot. Then they took a carriage and drove to Santa Sophia. There was little chance for conversation, as they rattled over the stones towards the mosque. Chrysophrasia leaned wearily back in her corner. Paul and Hermione tried to talk, and failed, and Professor Cutter promenaded his regards, to borrow an appropriate French expression, upon the buildings, the people, and the view. Perhaps he was wondering whether more cases of insanity presented themselves amongst the vegetable sellers as a class than amongst the public scribes, whose booths swarm before the Turkish post-office. He had seen the city before, but only during a very short visit, as a mere tourist, and he was glad to see it again.

They reached the mosque, and after skating about in the felt overshoes provided for the use of unbelievers, Cutter suggested going up to the galleries.

"It is so very, very far!" murmured Chrysophrasia, who was watching a solitary young Sufí, who sat reciting his lesson aloud to himself in a corner, swaying his body backwards and forwards with the measure of his chant.

"I will go," said Hermione, with alacrity. "Paul can stay with my aunt."

"I would rather stay," answered Paul, whose reminiscences of the gallery were not of the most pleasant sort.

So Professor Cutter and the young girl left the mosque, and with the guide ascended the dim staircase.

"Papa wrote you the story, did he not?" asked Hermione. "Yes. This is the way they went up."

The professor looked about him curiously, as they followed the guide. Emerging amidst the broad arches of the gallery, they walked forward, and Hermione explained, as

Paul had explained to her, what had taken place on that memorable night two years ago. It was a simple matter, and the position of the columns made the story very clear.

"Professor Cutter, I want to speak to you about my aunt," said Hermione, at last. The professor stopped and looked sharply at her, but said nothing. "Do you remember that morning in the conservatory?" she continued. "You told me that she was very mad indeed, — those were your own words. I did not believe it, and I was triumphant when she came out — in — well, quite in her senses, you know. I thought she had recovered, — I hope she has. But she has very queer ways."

"What do you mean by queer ways, Miss Carvel? I have come to Constantinople on purpose to see her. I hope there is nothing wrong?"

"I do not know. But I have told nobody what I am going to tell you. I think you ought to be told. My room is next to hers, at the hotel, and I hear through the door what goes on, without meaning to. The other night I came home late from a ball, and she was walking up and down, talking to herself so loud that I heard several sentences."

"What did she say?" asked Cutter, whose interest was already aroused. The symptom was only too familiar to him.

"She said" — Hermione hesitated before she continued, and the color rose faintly in her cheeks — "she said she wished she could kill Paul — and then" —

"And then what?" inquired the professor, looking at her steadily. "Please tell me all."

"It was very foolish, — she said that then Alexander could marry me. It was so silly of her. Just think!"

After all, Professor Cutter was her father's old friend. She need not have been so long about telling the thing.

"She thinks that you are going to marry Paul?" observed the professor, with an interrogative intonation.

"Well, if I did?" replied the young girl, after a short

pause. "If she were in her right mind, would that be any reason for her wishing to murder him ? "

"No. But I never believed she was out of danger," said Cutter. "Did she say anything more ? "

Hermione told how Madame Patoff had behaved when she had entered the room. Her companion looked very grave, and said little during the few moments they remained in the gallery. He only promised that he would tell no one about it, unless it appeared absolutely necessary for the safety of every one concerned. Then they descended the steps again and joined Chrysophrasia and Paul, who were waiting below.

"Aunt Chrysophrasia says she must go to the bazaar," said the latter.

"Yes," remarked Miss Dabstreak, "I really must. That Jew! Oh, that Jew! He haunts my dreams. I see him at night, dressed like Moses, with a linen ephod, you know, holding up that Persian embroidery. It is more than my soul can bear ! "

" But we were going to take Professor Cutter to the other mosques," objected Hermione.

"I am sure he will not mind if we go to the bazaar in-stead, will you ? " she asked, with an engaging squint of her green eyes, as she turned to the professor.

"Not at all, — not at all, Miss Dabstreak. Anything you propose — I am sure " — ejaculated Cutter, apparently waking from an absorbing meditation upon his thumb-nail, and perhaps upon thumb-nails in general.

"You see how kind he is! " murmured Chrysophrasia, as she got into the carriage. " To the bazaar, Paul. Could you tell the driver ? "

Paul could and did. Ten minutes later the carriage stopped at the gate of the bazaar. A dozen Mohammedans, Greeks, and Jews sprang out to conduct the visitors whither they would, — or, more probably, whither they would not. But Paul, who knew his way about very well, fought them off. One only would not be repulsed, and Chrysophrasia took his part.

"Let him come, — pray let him come, Paul. He has such beautiful eyes, such soft, languishing eyes, — so sweetly like those of a gazelle."

"His name is Abraham," said Paul. "I know him very well. The gazelle is of Jewish extraction, and sells shawls. He is a liar."

"Haïr, Effendim — sir," cried Abraham, who knew a little English. "Him Israeleet — hones' Jew — Abraham's name, Effendim."

"I know it is," said Paul. "Git!" — an expression which is good Californian, and equally good Turkish.

They threaded the narrow vaulted passages, which were cool in the warm spring afternoon, taking the direction of the Jews' quarter, but pausing from time to time to survey the thousand articles, of every description, exposed for sale by the squatting shopkeepers. Cutter looked at the weapons especially, and remarked that they were not so good as those which used to be found ten years earlier. Everything, indeed, seemed to have changed since that time, and for the worse. There is less wealth in the bazaar, and yet the desire to purchase has increased tenfold, so that a bit of Rhodes tapestry, which at that earlier time would not have fetched forty piastres, is now sold for a pound Turkish, and is hard to get at that. It may be supposed that the Jews have made large fortunes in the interval, but the fact is not apparent in any way; the uncertainty of property in Turkey forcing them to conceal their riches, if they have any. Their shops are very fairly clean, but otherwise they are humble, and the best and most valuable objects are generally packed carefully away in dark corners, and are produced only when asked for. You see nothing but a small divan, a table, a matted floor, and shelves reaching to the ceiling, piled with packages wrapped in shabby gray linen. It is chiefly in the Mohammedan and Greek "tscharshis" of the bazaar that jewelry, weapons, and pipes are openly exhibited, and laid out upon benches for the selection of the buyer. But the Jews have almost a monopoly of everything which comes under the head of antiquities, and it is with them that foreigners generally deal. They are as intelligent as elsewhere, and perhaps more so, for the traveler of to-day is a great cheapener of valuables. Moreover, the Stamboul Jews are most of them linguists. They speak a bastard Spanish among themselves; they are obliged to know Turkish, Greek, and a little Armenian, and many of them speak French and Italian intelligibly.

Chrysophrasia delighted in the bazaar. The flavor of antiquity which hangs about it, and makes it the only thoroughly Oriental place in Constantinople, ascended gratefully to the old maid's nostrils, while her nerves were continually thrilled by strange contrasts of color. It was very pleasant, she thought, to be really in the East, and to have such a palpable proof of the fact as was afforded by the jargon of loud but incomprehensible tongues which filled her ears. She had often been in the place, and the Jews were beginning to know her, scenting a bargain whenever her yellow face and yellow hair became visible on the horizon. She generally patronized Marchetto, however, and on the present occasion she had come expressly to see him. He was standing in the door of his little shop as usual, and his red face and red-brown eyes lighted up when he caught sight of Miss Dabstreak. With many expressions of joy he backed into the interior, and immediately went in search of the famous piece of Persian embroidery which Chrysophrasia had admired during her last visit to the bazaar.

"Upon my honor" — began Marchetto, launching into praises of the stuff. Patoff and Hermione stood at the door, but Cutter immediately became interested in the bargain, and handled the embroideries with curiosity, asking all manner of questions of the Jew and of Miss Dabstreak. Somehow or other, the two younger members of the party soon found themselves outside the shop, walking slowly up and down and talking, until the bargain should be concluded.

" I could not go up to the gallery in Santa Sophia," said Paul. " I am not a nervous person, but it brings the story back too vividly."

" What does it matter, since he is found ? " asked Hermione.

Patoff was struck by the question, for it was too much at variance with his own feelings to seem reasonable. It was not because he preferred to avoid all reminiscence of the adventure that he had stayed below, but rather because he hated to think what the consequences of Alexander's return had been.

" What does it matter ? " he repeated slowly. " It matters a great deal. What happened on that night, two years ago, was the beginning of a whole series of misfortunes. I have had bad luck ever since."

" Why do you say that ? " asked Hermione, somewhat reproachfully.

" It is true, — that is one reason why I say it. But for that night, my mother would never have been mad. I should never have been sent to Persia, and should not have gone to England during my leave. I should not have met you " —

" You consider that a terrible misfortune," observed Hermione.

" It is always a man's misfortune when he determines to have what is denied him," answered Paul quietly. " Somebody must suffer in the encounter, or somebody must yield."

" Somebody, — yes. Why do you talk about it, Paul ? "

" Because I think of nothing else. I cannot help it. It is easy to say, ' Let this or that alone ; ' it is another matter to talk to you about the bazaar, and the Turks, and the weather, when we are together."

Hermione was silent, for there was nothing to be said.

She knew how well he loved her, and when she was with him she submitted in a measure to his influence ; so that often she was on the point of yielding, and telling him that she no longer hesitated. It was when she was away from him that she doubted herself, and refused to be persuaded. Paul needed only a very little to complete his conquest, but that little he could not command. He had reached the point at which a man talks of the woman he loves or of himself, and of nothing else, and the depth of his passion seemed to dull his speech. A little more eloquence, a little more gentleness, a little more of that charm which Alexander possessed in such abundance, might have been enough to turn the scale. But they were lacking. The very intensity of what he felt made him for the time a man of one idea only, and even the freedom with which he could speak to Hermione about his love for her was a disadvantage to him. It had grown to be too plain a fact, and there was too little left to the imagination. He felt that he wearied her, or he fancied that he did, which amounted to the same ; and he either remained tongue-tied, or repeated in one form or another his half-savage ' I will.' He began to long for a change in their relations, or for some opportunity of practically showing her how much he would sacrifice for her sake. But in these days there are no lists for the silent knights ; there are no jousts where a man may express his declaration of love by tying a lady's colors to his arm, and breaking the bones of half a dozen gentlemen before her eyes. And yet the instinct to do something of the kind is sometimes felt even now, — the longing to win by physical prowess what it is at present the fashion to get by persuasion.

Paul felt it strongly enough, and was disgusted with his own stupidity. Of what use was it that during so many years he had cultivated the art of conversation as a necessary accomplishment, if at his utmost need his wits were to abandon him, and leave him uncouth and taciturn as he had been in his childhood ? He looked at Hermione's down-

cast face; at the perfect figure displayed by her tightly fit-
ting costume of gray; at her small hands, as she stood still
and tried to thrust the point of her dainty parasol into the
crevice between two stones of the pavement. He gazed at
her, and was seized with a very foolish desire to take her
up in his arms and walk away with her, whether she liked
it or not. But just at that moment Hermione glanced at
him with a smile, not at all as he had expected that she
would look.

"I think we had better go back to the shop," said she.
So they turned, and walked slowly towards the narrow door.

"These Orientals are so full of wonderful imagery!"
Chrysophrasia was saying to Professor Cutter as the pair
came in. "It is delightful to hear them talk, — so different
from an English shopkeeper."

"Very," assented the learned man. "Their imagery is
certainly remarkable. Their scale of prices seems to be
founded upon it, as logarithms depend for their existence
on the square root of minus one, an impossible quantity."

"Dear me! Could you explain that to Marchetto? It
might make a difference, you know."

"I am afraid not," answered the professor gravely.
"Marchetto is not a mathematician; are you, Marchetto?"

"No surr, Effendim. Marchetto very honest man.
Twenty-five pounds, lady — ah! but it is birindjí — there
is not a Pacha in Stamboul" —

"You have said that before," observed the scientist.
"Try and say something new."

"New!" cried Marchetto. "It is not new. Any one
say it new, he lie! Old — eski, eski! Very old! Twenty-
five-six pounds, lady! Hein! Pacha give more."

"I fear that the traditions of his race are very strong,"
remarked Chrysophrasia, languidly examining the embroidery, a magnificent piece of work, about a yard and a half
square, wrought in gold and silver threads upon a dark-red
velvet ground; evidently of considerable antiquity, but in

excellent preservation. "Paul, dear," continued Miss Dab-streak, seeing Patoff enter with Hermione, "what would you give for this lovely thing? How hard it is to bargain! How low! How infinitely fatiguing! Do help me!"

"Begin by offering him a quarter of what he asks, — that is a safe rule," answered Paul.

"How much is a quarter of twenty-five — let me see — three times eight are — do tell me, somebody! Figures drive me quite mad."

"I have known of such cases," assented the professor. "Eight and a quarter, Miss Dabstreak. Say eight, — I dare say it will do as well."

"Marchetto," said Chrysophrasia sadly, "I am afraid your embroidery is only worth eight pounds."

The Jew was kneeling on the floor, squatting upon his heels. He put on an injured expression, and looked up at Miss Dabstreak's face.

"Eight pounds!" he exclaimed, in holy horror. "You know where this come from, lady? Ha! Laleli Khanum house — dead — no more like it." Marchetto of course knew the story of Alexander's confinement, and by a ready lie turned it to his advantage. Every one looked surprised, and began to examine the embroidery more closely.

"Really!" ejaculated Chrysophrasia. "How strange this little world is! To think of all this bit of broidered velvet has seen, — what joyous sights! It may have been in the very room where she died. But she was a wicked old woman, Marchetto. I could not give more than eight pounds for anything which belonged to so depraved a crea-ture."

"Hein?" ejaculated the Jew, with a soft smile. "I know what you want. Here!" he exclaimed, springing up, and rummaging among his shelves. Presently he brought out a shabby old green cloth caftán, trimmed with a little tar-nished silver lace, and held it up triumphantly to Chryso-phrasia's sight.

"Twenty-five-six pounds!" he cried, exultingly. "Cheap. Him coat of very big saint-man — diè going to Mecca last year. Cheap, lady — twenty-five-six pounds!"

"I think you are fairly caught, aunt Chrysophrasia," observed Paul, with a laugh.

"Who would have guessed that there was so much humor in an Israelite?" asked Chrysophrasia, with a sad intonation. "I cannot wear the saint's tea-gown, Marchetto," she continued; "otherwise I would gladly give you twenty-five pounds for it. Eight pounds for the embroidery, — no more. It is not worth so much. I even think I see a nauseous tint of magenta in the velvet."

"Twenty-four-five pounds, lady. I lose pound — your backsheesh."

How long the process of bargaining might have been protracted is uncertain. At that moment Balsamides Bey entered the shop. It appeared that he had called at the Carvels', and, being told that the party were in Stamboul, had gone straight to the Jew's shop, in the hope of finding them there. He was introduced to the professor by Paul, with a word of explanation. Marchetto's face fell as he saw the adjutant, who had a terribly acute knowledge of the value of things. Balsamides was asked to give his opinion. He examined the piece carefully.

"Where did you get it?" he asked, in Turkish.

"From the Valide Khan," answered the Jew, in the same language. "It is a genuine piece, — a hundred years old at least."

"You probably ask a pound for every year, and a backsheesh for the odd months," said the other.

"Twenty pounds," answered Marchetto, imperturbably.

"It is worth ten pounds," remarked Balsamides, in English, to Miss Dabstreak. "If you care to give that, you may buy it with a clear conscience. But he will take three weeks to think about it."

"To bargain for three weeks!" exclaimed Chrysophrasia. "Oh, no! It takes my whole energy to bargain for half an hour. The lovely thing, — those faint, mysterious shades intertwined with the dull gold and silver, — it breaks my heart!"

Marchetto was obdurate, on that day at least, and with an unusually grave face he began to fold the embroidery, wrapping it at last in the inevitable piece of shabby gray linen. The party left the shop, and threaded the labyrinth of vaulted passages towards the gate. Cutter was interested in Gregorios, and asked him a great many questions, so that Chrysophrasia felt she was being neglected, and wore her most mournful expression. Paul and Hermione came behind, talking a little as they walked. They reached the bridge on foot, and, paying the toll to the big men in white who guard the entrance, began to cross the long stretch of planks which unites Stamboul with Pera. The sun was already low. Indeed, Marchetto had kept his shop open beyond the ordinary hour of closing, which is ten o'clock by Turkish time, two hours before sunset, and the bazaar was nearly deserted when they left it.

Paul and Hermione stopped when they were halfway across the bridge, and looked up the Golden Horn. Great clouds were piled up in the west, behind which the sun was hidden, and the air was very sultry. A dull light, that seemed to cast no shadows, was on all the mosques and minarets, and down upon the water the air was thick, and the boats looked indistinct as they glided by. The great useless men-of-war lay as though water-logged in the heavy, smooth stream, and the flags hung motionless from the mastheads.

The two stood side by side for a few moments and said nothing. At last Paul spoke.

"It is going to rain," he said, in an odd voice.

"Yes, it is going to rain," answered his companion.

"On parà! Ten paras, for the love of God!" screamed a filthy beggar close behind them. Paul threw the wretched creature the tiny coin he asked, and they turned away. But his face was very white, and Hermione's eyes were filled with tears.

XXII.

A FEW days later the Carvels were installed for the summer in one of the many large houses on the Buyukdere quay, which are usually let to any one who will hire them. These dwellings are mostly the property of Armenians and Greeks who lost heavily during the war, and whose diminished fortunes no longer allow them to live in their former state. They are vast wooden buildings for the most part, having a huge hall on each floor, from which smaller rooms open on two sides; large windows in front afford a view of the Bosphorus, and at the back the balconies are connected with the gardens by flights of wooden steps. In one of these, not far from the Russian embassy, the Carvels took up their abode, and John expressed himself extremely well satisfied with his choice and with his bargain. In the course of their stay in Pera, the family had contrived to collect a considerable quantity of Oriental carpets and other objects, some good, some utterly worthless in themselves, but useful in filling up the immense rooms of the house. Chrysophrasia seemed to find the East sympathetic to her nerves, and was certainly more in her element in Constantinople than in Brompton or Carvel Place. Strange to say, she was the one of the family who best understood the Turks and their ways. In contact with a semi-barbarous people, she developed an amount of common sense and keen intelligence which I had never suspected her of possessing.

As for me, I had gone up to Buyukdere one day, and had then and there changed my mind in regard to my departure. The roses were in full bloom, and everything looked so unusually attractive, that I could not resist the temptation of spending the summer in the place. A few years ago, when I thought of traveling, I set out without hesitation, and went to the ends of the earth. I suppose I am growing old, for I begin to dislike perpetual motion. The little kiosk on the hill, at the top of a beautiful garden, was very tempting, too, and after a few hours' consideration I hired it for the season, with that fine disregard for consequences which one learns in the East. The only furniture in the place was an iron bedstead and an old divan. There was not a chair, not a bit of matting; not so much as an earthen pot in the kitchen, nor a deal table in the sitting-room. But in Turkey such conveniences are a secondary consideration. The rooms were freshly whitewashed, the board floors were scrubbed, and the view from the windows was one of the most beautiful in the world. A day spent in the bazaar did the rest. I picked up a queer, wizened old Dalmatian cook, and with the help of my servant was installed in the little place eight-and-forty hours after I had made up my mind.

The life on the Bosphorus is totally different from that in Pera. Everybody either keeps a horse or keeps a sailboat, and many people do both; for the Belgrade forest stretches five-and-twenty miles inland from Buyukdere and Therapia, and the broad Bosphorus lies before, widening into a deep bay between the two. The fresh northerly breeze blows down from the Black Sea all day, and often all night; and there is something invigorating in the air, which revives one after the long, gay season in Pera, and makes one feel that anything and everything is possible in such a place.

The forest was different in May from what it had been on that bitter March night when Gregorios and I drove down to Laleli's house. The maidám — the broad stretch of grass at the opening of the valley before you reach the woods — was green and fresh and smooth. The trees were full of leaves, and gypsies were already camping out for the season. The woodland roads were not as full of

riders as they are in July and August, and the summer
dancing had not yet begun, nor the garden parties, nor any
kind of gayety. There was peace everywhere, — the peace
of quiet spring weather before one learns to fear the sun
and to long for rain, when the crocus pushes its tender head
timidly through the grass, and the bold daisies gayly dance
by millions in the light breeze as though knowing that their
numbers save them from being plucked up and tied into nose-
gays, and otherwise barbarously dealt with, according to the
luck of rarer flowers.

So we rode in the forest, and sailed on the Bosphorus,
and enjoyed the freedom of the life and the freshness of the
cool air, and things went on very pleasantly for every one,
as far as outward appearances were concerned. But it was
soon clear to me that the matter which more or less interested the whole party was no nearer to its termination than
it had been before. Paul came and went, and his face betrayed no emotion when he met Hermione or parted from
her. They were sometimes alone together, but not often,
and it did not seem to me that they showed any very great
anxiety to procure themselves such interviews. A keen ob-
server might have noticed, indeed, that Hermione was a
shade less cordial in her relations with Alexander, but he
himself did not relax his attentions, and was as devoted to
her as ever. He followed her about, always tried to ride
by her side in the forest, and to sit by her in the boat; but
under no circumstances did I see Paul's face change either
in color or expression. He did not look scornful and cynical, as he formerly did, nor was there anything hostile in
his manner towards his brother. He merely seemed very
calm and very sure of himself, — too sure, I thought. But
he had made up his mind to win, and meant to do it in his own
fashion, and he appeared to be indifferent to the fact that
while his duties often kept him at the embassy the whole
day, Alexander had nothing to do but to talk to Hermione
from morning till night. I fancied that he was playing a

waiting game, but I feared that he would wait too long, and lose in the end. I knew, indeed, that under his calm exterior his whole nature was wrought up to its highest point of excitement; but if he persisted in exercising such perfect self-control he ran the risk of being thought too cold, as he appeared to be. I was called upon to give an opinion on the matter before we had been many days in Buyukdere, and I was embarrassed to explain what I meant.

John Carvel and Hermione, Alexander and I, rode together in the woods, one afternoon. Paul was busy that day, and could not come. It fell out naturally enough that the young girl and her cousin should pair off together, leaving us two elderly men to our conversation. Hermione was mounted on a beautiful Arab, nearly black, which her father had bought for her in Pera, and Alexander rode a strong white horse that he had hired for the short time which remained to him before he should be obliged to return to St. Petersburg. They looked well together, as they rode before us, and John watched them with interest, if not altogether with satisfaction.

"Griggs," he observed at last, "it is very odd. I don't know what to make of it at all. You remember the conversation we had in Pera, the first night after our arrival? I certainly believed that Hermy wanted to marry Paul. She seems to get on amazingly well with his brother; don't you think so?"

"It is natural," I answered. "They are cousins. Why should they not like each other? Alexander is a most agreeable fellow, and makes the time pass very pleasantly when Paul is not there."

"What surprises me most," said John Carvel, "is that Paul does not seem to mind in the least. And he has never spoken to me about it, either. I am beginning to think he never will. Well, well, there is no reason why Hermy should marry just yet, and Paul is no great match, though he is a very good fellow."

"A very good fellow," I assented.   "A much better fellow than his brother, I fancy, — though Alexander has what
women call charm.   But Paul will not change his mind;
you need not be afraid of that."

"I should be sorry if Hermy did," said Carvel, gravely.
"I should not like my daughter to begin life by jilting an
honest man for the sake of a pretty toy soldier like Alexander."

It was very clear that John Carvel had a fixed opinion
in the case, and that his judgment did not incline to favor
Alexander.   On the other hand, he could not but be astonished at Paul's silence.   Of course I defended the latter as
well as I could, but as we rode slowly on, talking the matter
over, I could see that John was not altogether pleased.

Alexander and Hermione had passed a bend in the road
before us, and had been hidden from our view for some
time, for they were nearly half a mile in front when we had
last seen them.   They rode side by side, and Alexander
seemed to have plenty to say, for he talked incessantly in
his pleasant, easy voice, and Hermione listened to him.
They came to a place where the road forked to the right
and left.   Neither of them were very familiar with the forest, and, without stopping to think, they followed the lane
which looked the straighter and broader of the two, but
which in reality led by winding ways to a distant part of
the woods.   When John Carvel and I came to the place, I
naturally turned to the left, to cross the little bridge and
ascend the hill towards the Khedive's farm.   In this way
the two young people were separated from us, and we were
soon very far apart, for we were in reality riding in opposite
directions.

The lane taken by Hermione and her cousin led at first
through a hollowed way, above which the branches of the
trees met and twined closely together, as beautiful a place
as can be found in the whole forest.   Alexander grew less
talkative, and presently relapsed altogether into silence.

They walked their horses, and he looked at his cousin's face, half shaded by a thin gray veil, which set off admirably the beauty of her mouth and chin.

"Hermione," he said after a time, in his softest voice.

The girl blushed a little, without knowing why, but did not answer. He hesitated, as though he could get no further than her name. As the blush faded from her cheek, his cousin glanced timidly at him, not at all as she generally looked. Perhaps she felt the magic of the place. She was not used to be timid with him, and she experienced a new sensation. There was generally something light and gay in his way of speaking to her which admitted of a laughing answer ; but just now he had spoken her name so seriously, so gently, that she felt for the first time that he was in earnest. Instinctively she put her horse to a brisker pace, before he had said anything more. He kept close at her side.

"Hermione," he said again, and his voice sounded in her ear like the voice of an unknown spell, weaving charms about her under the shade of the enchanted forest. "Hermione, my beloved, — do not laugh at me any more. It is earnest, dear, — it is my whole life."

Still she said nothing, but the blush rose again to her face and died away, leaving her very pale. She shortened the reins in her hands, keeping the Arab at a regular, even trot.

"It is earnest, darling," continued her cousin, in low, clear tones. "I never knew how much I loved you until to-day. No, do not laugh again. Tell me you know it is so, as I know it."

The lane grew narrower and the branches lower, but she would not slacken speed, though now and then she had to bend her head to avoid the leafy twigs as she passed. But this time she answered, not laughing, but very gravely.

"You must not talk like that any more," she said. "I do not like to hear it."

"Is it so bitter to be told that you are loved — as I love?

Is it so hard to hear ? But you have heard once — twice,
twenty times ; you will not always think it bad to hear ;
your ears will grow used to it.   Ah, Hermione, if you could
guess how sweet it is to love as I love, you would understand ! ''

"I do not know — I cannot guess — I would not if I
could," answered the young girl desperately. "Hush, Alexander ! Do not talk in that way. You must not. It is
not right."

"Not right ? " echoed the young man, with a soft laugh.
"I will make it right ; you shall guess what it is to love,
dear, — to love me as I love you."

He bent in his saddle as he rode beside her, and laid his
left hand on hers, but she shook his fingers off impatiently.

"Why are you angry, love ? " he asked.   "You have let
me say it lightly so often ; will you not let me say it earnestly for once ? "

"No," she answered firmly.   "I do not want to hear it.
I have been very wrong, Alexander.   I like you very much
— because you are my cousin — but I do not love you — I
will not — I mean, I cannot. No, I am in earnest, too —
far more than you are. I can never love you — no, no, no
— never ! "

But she had let fall the words "I will not," and Alexander knew that there was a struggle in her mind.

"You will not ? " he said tenderly.   "No — but you
will, darling. I know you will. You must ; I will make
you ! "

Again he leaned far out of his saddle, and in an instant
his left arm went round her slender waist, as they rode
quickly along, and his lips touched her soft cheek just below
the little gray veil. But he had gone too far. Hermione's
spurred heel just touched the Arab's flank, and he sprang
forward in a gallop up the narrow lane. Alexander kept
close at her side. His blood was up, and burning in his
delicate cheek. He still tried to keep his hand upon her

waist, and bent towards her, moving in his saddle with the ease of a born horseman as he galloped along. But Hermione spurred her horse, and angrily tried to elude her cousin's embrace, till in a moment they were tearing through the woods at a racing pace.

Suddenly there came a crash, followed by a dull, heavy sound, and Hermione saw that she was alone. She tried to look behind her, but several seconds elapsed before her Arab could be quieted; at last she succeeded in making him turn, and rode quickly back along the path. Alexander's horse was standing across the way, and Hermione was obliged to dismount and turn him before she could see beyond. Her cousin lay in the lane, motionless as he had fallen, his face pale and turned upwards, one arm twisted under his body, the other stretched out upon the soft mould of the woodland path. Hermione stood holding the two horses, one with each hand, and looking intently at the insensible man. She did not lose her presence of mind, though she was frightened by his pallor; but she could not let the horses run loose in such a place, when they might be lost in a moment. She paused a moment, and listened for the sound of hoofs, thinking that her father and I could not be far behind. But the woods were very still, and she remembered that she and her cousin had ridden fast over the last two miles. Drawing the bridles over the horses' heads, she proceeded to fasten them to a couple of trees, not without some trouble, for her own horse was excited and nervous from the sharp gallop; but at last she succeeded, and, gathering her habit in one hand, she ran quickly to Alexander's side.

There he lay, quite unconscious, and so pale that she thought he might be dead. His head was bare, and his hat, crumpled and broken, lay in the path, some distance behind him. There was a dark mark on the right side of his forehead, high up and half covered by his silky brown hair. Hermione knelt down and tried to lift his head upon her knee. But his body was heavy, and she was not very strong.

She dragged him with difficulty to the side of the path, and raised his shoulders a little against the bank. She felt for his pulse, but there was no motion in the lifeless veins, nor could she decide whether he breathed or not. .Utterly without means of reviving him, for she had not so much as a bottle of salts in the pocket of her saddle, she kneeled over him, and wiped his pale forehead with her handkerchief, and blew gently on his face. She was pale herself, and was beginning to be frightened, though she had good nerves. Nevertheless she took courage, feeling sure that we should appear in five minutes at the latest.

It was clear that in galloping by her side at full speed Alexander's head had struck violently against a heavy branch, which grew lower than the rest. His eyes had been turned on her, and he had not seen the danger. The branch was so placed that Hermione, lowering her head to avoid the leaves, as she looked straight before, had passed under it in safety ; whereas her cousin must have struck full upon the thickest part, three or four feet nearer to the tree. At the pace they were riding, the blow might well have been fatal ; and as the moments passed and the injured man showed no signs of life, Hermione's heart beat faster and her face grew whiter. Her first thought was of his mother, and a keen, sharp fear shot through her as she thought of the dreadful moment when Madame Patoff must be told ; but the next instant brought her a feeling of far deeper horror. He had been hurt almost while speaking words of love to her ; he had struck his head because he was looking at her instead of before him, and it was in some measure her fault, for she had urged the speed of that foolish race. She bent down over him, and the tears started to her eyes. She tried to listen for the beating of his heart, and, opening his coat, she laid her ear to his breast. Something cold touched her cheek, and she quickly raised her head again and looked down. It was a small flat silver flask which he carried in the pocket of his waistcoat, and which in the fall had slipped up from its place. Hermione withdrew it eagerly and unscrewed the cap. It contained some kind of spirits, and she poured a little between his parted lips.

The deathly features contracted a little, and the eyelids quivered. She poured the brandy into the palm of her hand, and chafed his temples and forehead. Alexander drew a long breath and slowly opened his eyes; then shut them again; then, after a few moments, opened them wide, stared, and uttered an exclamation of surprise in Russian.

"Are you better?" asked Hermione, breathlessly. "I thought you were dead."

"No, I am all right," he said, faintly, trying to raise himself. But his head swam, and he fell back, once more insensible. This time, however, the fainting fit did not last long, and he soon opened his eyes again and looked at Hermione without speaking. She continued to rub the spirits upon his forehead. Then he put out his hand and grasped the flask she held, and drank a long draught from it.

"It is nothing," he said. "I can get up now, thank you." He struggled to his feet, leaning on the young girl's arm. "How did it happen?" he asked. "I cannot remember anything."

"You must have struck your head against that branch," answered Hermione, pointing to the thick bough which projected over the lane. "Do you feel better?"

"Yes. I can mount in a minute," he replied, steadying himself. "I have had a bad shaking, and my head hurts me. It is nothing serious."

"Better sit down for a few minutes, until the others come up," suggested the young girl, who was surprised to see him recover himself so quickly. He seemed glad enough to follow her advice, and they sat down together on the mossy bank.

"It was my fault," said Hermione, penitently. "It was so foolish of me to ride fast in such a place."

"Women care for nothing but galloping when they are

on horseback," said Alexander. It was not a very civil speech, and though Hermione forgave him because he was half stunned with pain, the words rang unpleasantly in her ear. He might have been satisfied, she thought, when she owned that it was her fault. It was not generous to agree with her so unhesitatingly. She wondered whether Paul would have spoken like that.

"Do you really think you can ride back?" she asked, in a colder tone.

"Certainly," he said; "provided we ride slowly. What can have become of uncle John and Griggs?"

Uncle John and Griggs were at that moment wondering what had become of the two young people. We had ridden on to the top of the hill, and had stopped on reaching the open space near the Khedive's farm, where there is a beautiful view, and where we expected to find our companions waiting for us. But we were surprised to see no one there. After a great deal of hesitation we agreed that John Carvel, who did not know the forest, should follow the main road down the hill on the other side, while I rode back over the way we had come. I suspected that Alexander and Hermione had taken the wrong turn, and I was more anxious about them than I would show. The forest is indeed said to be safe, but hardly a year passes without some solitary rider being molested by gypsies or wandering thieves, if he has ventured too far from the beaten tracks. I rode as fast as I could, but it was nearly twenty minutes before I struck into the hollow lane. I found the pair seated on the bank, a mile further on, and Hermione hailed me with delight. Everything was explained in a few words. Alexander seemed sufficiently recovered from his accident to get into the saddle, and we were soon walking our horses back towards the maidám of Buyukdere. Neither Alexander nor Hermione talked much by the way, and we were all glad when we reached the tiny bazaar, and were picking our way over the uneven street, amongst the coppersmiths, the lounging soldiers, the solemn narghylè smokers, the kaffejis, the beggars, and the half-naked children.

On that evening, two things occurred which precipitated the course of events. John Carvel had an interview with Hermione, and I had a most unlucky idea. John Carvel's mind was disturbed concerning the future of his only daughter, and though he was not a man who hastily took fright, his character was such that when once persuaded that things were not as they should be, he never hesitated as to the course he should pursue. Accordingly, that night he called Hermione into his study, and determined to ask her for an explanation. The poor girl was nervous, for she suspected trouble, and did not see very clearly how it could be avoided.

"Sit down, Hermy," said John, establishing himself in a deep chair with a cigar. "I want to talk with you, my dear."

"Yes, papa," answered Hermione, meekly.

"Hermy, do you mean to marry Paul, or not? Don't be nervous, my child, but think the matter over before you answer. If you mean to have him, I have no objection to the match; but if you do not mean to, I would like to know. That is all. You know you spoke to me about it in England before we left home. Things have been going on a long time now, and yet Paul has said nothing to me about it."

It was impossible to put the matter more clearly than this, and Hermione knew it. She said nothing for some minutes, but sat staring out of the window at the dark water, where the boats moved slowly about, each bearing a little light at the bow. Far down the quay a band was playing the eternal *Stella Confidente*, which has become a sort of national air in Turkey. The strains floated in through the window, and the young girl struggled hard to concentrate her thoughts, which somehow wound themselves in and out of the music in a very irrelevant manner.

"Must I answer now, papa?" she asked at last, almost desperately.

"My dear," replied the inexorable John, in kind tones, "I cannot see why you should not. You are probably in very much the same state of mind to-night as you were in yesterday, or as you will be in to-morrow. It is better to settle the matter and be done with it. I do not believe that a fortnight, a month, or even a longer time will make any perceptible difference in your ideas about this matter." He puffed at his cigar, and again looked at his daughter.

"Hermy," he continued, after another interval of silence, "if you do not mean to marry Paul, you are treating him very badly. You are letting that idiot of a brother of his make love to you from morning till night."

"Oh, papa! How can you!" exclaimed Hermione, who was not accustomed to hearing any kind of strong language from her father.

"Idiot, — yes, my dear, that expresses it very well. He is my nephew, and I have a right to call him an idiot if I please. I believe the fellow wears stays, and curls his hair with tongs. He has a face like a girl, and he talks unmitigated rubbish."

"I thought you liked him, papa," objected Hermione. "I do not think he is at all as silly as you say he is. He is very agreeable."

"I have no objection to him," retorted John Carvel. "I tolerate him. Toleration is not liking. He fascinated us all for a day or two, but it did not last long; that sort of fascination never does."

There was another long pause. The band had finished the *Stella Confidente*, and ran on without stopping to the performance of the drinking chorus in the *Traviata*. Hermione twisted her fingers together, and bit her lips. Her father's opinion of Alexander was a revelation to her, but it carried weight with it, and it aroused a whole train of recollections in her mind, culminating in the accident of the afternoon. She remembered vividly what she had felt during those long minutes before Alexander had recovered consciousness, and she knew that her feelings bore not the slightest relation to love. She had been terrified, and had blamed herself, and had thought of his mother; but the idea that he might be dead had not hurt her as it would have done had she loved him. She had felt no wild grief, no awful sense of blankness; the tears which had risen to her eyes had been tears of pity, of genuine sorrow, but not of despair. She tried to think what she would have felt had she seen Paul lying dead before her, and the mere idea sent a sharp thrust through her heart that almost frightened her.

"Well, my dear," said John, at last, "can you give me an answer? Do you mean to marry Paul or Alexander, or neither?"

"Not Alexander, — oh, never!" exclaimed Hermione. "I never thought of such a thing."

"Paul, then?"

"Papa, dear," said the young girl, after a moment's hesitation, "I will tell you all about it. When Paul came, I firmly intended to marry him. Then I began to know Alexander — and — well, I was very wrong, but he began to make pretty phrases, and to talk of loving me. Of course I told him he was very foolish, and I laughed at him. But he only went on, and said a great deal more, in spite of me. Then I thought that because I could not stop him I was interested in him. Paul wanted to speak to you, but I would not let him. I did not feel that my conscience was quite clear. I was not sure that I should always love him. Do you see? I think I love him, really, but Alexander interests me."

"But you never for a moment thought of marrying Alexander? You said so just now."

"Oh, never! I laughed at him, and he amused me, — nothing more than that."

"Then I don't quite see" — began John Carvel, who was rather puzzled by the explanation.

"Of course not. You are a man, — how can you understand ? I will promise you this, papa : if I cannot make up my mind in a week, I will tell Paul so."

"How will a week help you, my dear ? Ever so many weeks have passed, and you are still uncertain."

"I am sure that a week will make all the difference. I think I shall have decided then. I am in earnest, dear papa," she added, gravely. "Do you think I would willingly do anything to hurt Paul ? "

"No, my dear, I don't," answered John Carvel. "Only — you might do it unwillingly, you know, and as far as he is concerned it would come to very much the same thing." And with this word of warning the interview ended.

When I went home to dinner, I found Gregorios Balsamides seated on the wooden bench under the honeysuckle outside my door. He had escaped from the dust and heat of Pera, and had come to spend the night, sure of finding a hearty welcome at my kiosk on the hill. I sat down beside him, and he began asking me questions about the people who had arrived, giving me in return the news and gossip of Pera.

"You have a very pretty place here," he said. "A man I knew took it last summer, and used to give tea-parties and little fêtes in the evening. It is easy to string lanterns from one tree to another, and it makes a very pretty effect. It is a mild form of idiocy, it is true, — much milder than the prevailing practice of dancing in-doors, with the thermometer at the boiling point."

"It is not a bad idea," I answered. "We will experiment upon our friends the Carvels in a small way. I will ask them and the Patoffs to come here next Saturday. Can you come, too ? "

The thing was settled, and Gregorios promised to be of the party. We dined, and sat late together, talking long before we went to bed. Gregorios is a soldier, and does not mind roughing it a little ; so he slept on the divan, and declared the next day that he had slept very well.

XXIII.

MADAME PATOFF had not received the news of Alexander's accident with indifference, and it had been necessary that he should assure her himself that he was not seriously hurt before she could be quieted. He had been badly stunned, however, and his head gave him much pain during several days, as was natural enough. He spent most of his time on the sofa in his mother's sitting-room, and she would sit for hours talking to him and trying to soothe his pain. The sympathy between the two seemed strengthened, and it was strange to see how, when together, their manner changed. The relation between the mother and the spoiled child is a very peculiar one, and occupies an entirely separate division in the scale of human affections; for while the mother's love in such a case is sincere, though generally founded on a mere capricious preference, the over-indulged affection of the child breeds nothing but caprice and a ruthless desire to see that caprice satisfied. Madame Patoff loved Alexander so much that the belief in his death had driven her mad; he on his side loved his mother because he knew that in all cases, just and unjust, she would defend him, take his part, and help him to get what he wanted. But he never missed her when they were separated, and he never took any pains to see her unless in so doing he could satisfy some other wish at the same time. He was selfish, willful, and obstinate at two-and-thirty as he had been at ten years of age. His mother was willful, obstinate, and capricious, but as far as he was concerned she was incapable of selfishness.

What was most remarkable in her manner was her ease

in talking with Professor Cutter, and her indifference in referring to her past insanity. She did not appear to realize it; she hardly seemed to care whether any one knew it or not, and regarded it as an unfortunate accident, but one which there was little object in concealing. As the scientist talked with her and observed her, he opened his eyes wider and wider behind his gold-rimmed spectacles, and grew more and more silent when any one spoke to him of her. I knew later that he detected in her conduct certain symptoms which alarmed him, but felt obliged to hold his peace on account of the extreme difficulty of his position. He felt that to watch her again, or to put her under any kind of restraint, might now lead to far more serious results than before, and he determined to bide his time. An incident occurred very soon, however, which helped him to make up his mind.

One afternoon we arranged an excursion to the ruined castle of Anadoli Kavák, on the Asian shore, near the mouth of the Black Sea. Mrs. Carvel, who was not a good sailor, stayed at home, but Miss Dabstreak, Madame Patoff, and Hermione were of the party, with Paul, Macaulay Carvel, Professor Cutter, and myself. Macaulay had borrowed a good-sized cutter from one of his many colleagues who kept yachts on the Bosphorus, and at three o'clock in the afternoon we started from the Buyukdere quay. There was a smart northerly breeze as we hoisted the jib, and it was evident that we should have to make several tacks before we could beat up to our destination. The boat was of about ten tons burden, with a full deck, broken only by a well leading to the cabin; a low rail ran round the bulwarks, for the yacht was intended for pleasure excursions and the accommodation of ladies. The members of the party sat in a group on the edge of the well, and I took the helm. Chrysophrasia was in a particularly Oriental frame of mind. The deep blue sky, the emerald green of the hills, and the cool clear water rippling under the breeze, no doubt acted soothingly upon her nerves.

"I feel quite like Sindbad the Sailor," she said. "Mr. Griggs, you ought really to tell us a tale from the Arabian Nights. I am sure it would seem so very real, you know."

"If I were to spin yarns while steering, Miss Dabstreak," I said, "your fate would probably resemble Sindbad's. You would be wrecked six or seven times between here and Kavák."

"So delightfully exciting," murmured Chrysophrasia. "Annie," she continued, addressing her sister, "shall we not ask Mr. Griggs to wreck us? I have always longed to be on a wreck."

"No," said Madame Patoff, glancing at her foolish sister with her great dark eyes. "I should not like to be drowned."

"Of course not; how very dreadful!" exclaimed Miss Dabstreak. "But Sindbad was never drowned, you remember. It was always somebody else."

"Oh — somebody else," repeated Madame Patoff, looking down at the deep water. "Yes, to drown somebody else, — that would be very different."

I think we were all a little startled, and Hermione looked at Paul and turned pale. As for Cutter, he very slowly and solemnly drew a cigar from his case, lit it carefully, crossed one knee over the other, and gazed fixedly at Madame Patoff during several minutes, before he spoke.

"Would you really like to see anybody drowned?" he asked at last.

"Why do you ask?" inquired Madame Patoff, rather sharply.

"Because I thought you said so, and I wanted to know if you were in earnest."

"I suppose we should all like to see our enemies die," said the old lady. "Not painfully, of course, but so that we should be quite sure of it." She laid a strong emphasis on the last words, and as she looked up I thought she glanced at Paul.

"If you had seen many people die, you would not care for the sight," said the professor quietly. "Besides, you have no enemies."

"What is death?" asked Madame Patoff, looking at him with a curiously calm smile as she asked the question.

"The only thing we know about it, is that it appears to be in every way the opposite of life," was the scientist's answer. "Life separates us for a time from the state of what we call inanimate matter. When life ceases, we return to that state."

"Why do you say 'what we call inanimate matter'?" inquired Paul.

"Because it has been very well said that names are labels, not definitions. As a definition, inanimate matter means generally the earth, the water, the air; but the name would be a very poor definition, — as poor as the word 'man' used to define the human animal."

"You do not think that inanimate matter is really lifeless?" I asked.

"Unless it is so hot that it melts," laughed the professor. "Even then it may not be true, — indeed, it may be quite false. We call the moon dead, because we have reason to believe that she has cooled to the centre. We call Jupiter and Saturn live planets, though we believe them still too hot to support life."

"All that does not explain death," objected Madame Patoff.

"If I could explain death, I could explain life," answered Cutter. "And if I could explain life, I should have made a great step towards producing it artificially."

"If one could only produce artificial death!" exclaimed Madame Patoff.

"It would be very amusing," answered Cutter, with a smile, folding his huge white hands upon his knee. "We could try it on ourselves, and then we should know what to expect. I have often thought about it, I assure you. I once had the curiosity to put myself into a trance by the Munich method of shining disks, — they use it in the hospitals instead of ether, you know, — and I remained in the state half an hour."

" And then, what happened when you woke up ? "

" I had a bad headache and my eyes hurt me," replied the professor dryly. " I dare say that if a dead man came to life he would feel much the same thing."

" I dare say," assented Madame Patoff ; but there was a vague look in her eyes, which showed that her thoughts were somewhere else. We were close upon the Asian shore, and I put the helm down to go about. The ladies changed their places, and there was a little confusion, in which Cutter found himself close to me.

" Keep an eye on her," he said quickly, in a low voice. " She is very queer."

I thought so, too, and I watched Madame Patoff to see whether she would return to the subject which seemed to attract her. Cutter kept up the conversation, however, and did not again show any apprehension about his former patient's state of mind, though I could see that he watched her as closely as I did. The fresh breeze filled the sails, and the next tack took us clear up to Yeni Mahallè on the European side ; for the little yacht was quick in stays, and, moreover, had a good hold on the water, enabling her to beat quickly up against wind and current. Once again I went about, and, running briskly across, made the little pier below Anadoli Kavák, little more than three quarters of an hour after we had started. We landed, and went up the green slope to the place where the little coffee-shop stands under the trees. We intended to climb the hill to the ruined castle. To my surprise, Professor Cutter suggested to Madame Patoff that they should stay below, while the rest made the ascent. He said he feared she would tire herself too much. But she would not listen to him.

" I insist upon going," she said. " I am as strong as any of you. It is quite absurd."

Cutter temporized by suggesting that we should have coffee before the walk, and Chrysophrasia sank languidly down upon a straw chair.

"If the man has any loukoum, I could bear a cup of coffee," she murmured. The man had loukoum, it appeared, and Chrysophrasia was satisfied. We all sat down in a circle under the huge oak-tree, and enjoyed the freshness and greenness of the place. The kaffeji, in loose white garments and a fez, presently brought out a polished brass tray, bearing the requisite number of tiny cups and two little white saucers filled with pieces of loukoum-rahat, the Turkish national sweetmeat, commonly called by schoolboys fig-paste.

"Why was I not born a Turk!" exclaimed Chrysophrasia. "This joyous life in the open air is so intensely real, so profoundly true!"

"Life is real anywhere," remarked Cutter, with a smile. "The important question is whether it is agreeable to the liver."

"Death is real, too," said Madame Patoff, in such a curious tone that we all started slightly, as we had done in the boat. My nerves are good, but I felt a weird horror of the woman stealing over me. The imperturbable scientist only glanced at me, as though to remind me of what he had said before. Then he took up the question.

"No, madam," he said, coldly. "Death is a negation, almost a universal negation. It is not real; it only devours reality, and then denies it. You can see that life is to breathe, to think, to eat, to drink, to love, to fear, — any of these. Death is only the negation of all these things, because we can only say that in death we do none of them. Reality is motion, in the broad sense, as far as man is concerned; death is only the cessation of the ability to move. You cannot predicate anything else of it."

"Oh, your dry, dry science!" exclaimed Chrysophrasia, casting up her green eyes. "You would turn our fair fields and limpid — ahem — skies — into the joyless waste of a London pavement, or one of your horrid dissecting-rooms!"

" I don't see the point of your simile, Miss Dabstreak,"
answered Cutter, with pardonable bluntness. " Besides,
that is philosophy, and not science."

" What is the difference, Mr. Griggs ? " asked Hermione,
turning to me.

" My dear young lady," said I, " science, I think, means
the state of being wise, and hence, the thing known, which
gives a man the title of wise. Philosophy means the love of
wisdom."

" Rather involved definition," observed the professor, with
a laugh. " There is not much difference between the state
of being wise and the state of loving wisdom."

" The one asserts the possession of that which the other
aspires to possess, but considers to be very difficult of attainment," I tried to explain. " The scientist says to the world,
' I have found the origin of life : it is protoplasm, it is your
God, and all your religious beliefs are merely the result of
your ignorance of protoplasm.' The philosopher answers,
' I allow that this protoplasm is the origin of life, but how
did this origin itself originate ? And if you can show how
it originated from inanimate matter, how did the inanimate
matter begin to exist ? And how was space found in which
it could exist ? And why does anything exist, animate or
inanimate ? And is the existence of matter a proof of a
supreme design, or is it not ? ' Thereupon science gets very
red in the face, and says that these questions are absurd,
after previously stating that everything ought to be questioned."

" Science," answered the professor, " says that man has
enough to do in questioning his immediate surroundings,
without going into the matter of transcendental inquiry."

" Then she ought to keep to her own proper sphere," said
I, waxing hot. " The fact is that science, armed with miserably imperfect tools, but unbounded assumption, has discovered a jelly-fish in a basin of water, and has deduced
from that premise the tremendous conclusion that there is no
God."

"That is strong language, Mr. Griggs, — very strong language," repeated the professor. "You exaggerate the position too much, I think. But it is useless to argue with transcendentalists. You always fall back upon the question of faith, and you refuse to listen to reason."

"When you can disprove our position, we will listen to your proof. But since the whole human race, as far as we can ascertain, without any exception whatsoever, has believed always in the survival of the soul after death, allow me to say that when you deny the existence of the soul the *onus probandi* lies with you, and not with us."

Therewith I drank my coffee in silence, and looked at the half-naked Turkish children playing upon the little pier over the bright water. It struck me that if the learned scientist had told them that they had no souls, they would have laughed at him very heartily. I think that in the opinion of the company I had the best of the argument, and Cutter knew it, for he did not answer.

"I have always believed that I have a soul," said Macaulay Carvel, in his smooth, monotonous tone. But there was as much conviction in his tone as though he had expressed his belief in the fact that he had a nose.

"Of course you have," said Hermione. "Let us go up to the castle and see the view before it is too late. Aunt Annie, do wait for us here; it is very tiring, really."

"You seem to think I am a decrepit old woman," answered Madame Patoff, impatiently, as she rose from her chair.

Paul felt that it was his duty to offer his mother his arm for the ascent, though the professor came forward at the same moment.

"Dear Paul, you are so good," said she, accepting his assistance as we began to climb the hill.

I saw her face in that moment. It was as calm and beautiful as ever, but I thought she glanced sideways to see whether every one had heard her speech and appreciated it.

Little was said as we breasted the steep ascent, for the path was rough, and there was barely room for two people to walk side by side. At last we emerged upon a broad slope of grass outside the walls of the old fortress. A goatherd lives inside it, and has turned the old half-open vaults into a stable for his flocks. We paused under the high walls, which on one side are built above the precipitous cliff, with a sheer fall of a hundred feet or more. Towards the land they are not more than forty feet high, where the grass grows up to their base. There is a curious gate on that side, with the carved arms of the Genoese republic imbedded in the brick masonry.

Some one suggested that we should go inside, and after a short interview with the goatherd he consented to chain up his enormous dog, and let us pass the small wooden gate which leads to the interior. Inside the fortress the falling in of the roof and walls has filled the old court so that it is nearly on a level with the walls. It is easy to scramble up to the top, and the thickness is so great that it is safe to walk along for a little distance, provided one does not go too near the edge. We wandered about below, and some of us climbed up to see the beautiful view, which extends far down the Bosphorus on the one side, and looks over the broad Black Sea on the other. Madame Patoff still leaned on Paul's arm, while the professor gallantly helped the languid Chrysophrasia to reach the most accessible places. Macaulay was engaged in an attempt to measure the circumference of the castle, and rambled about in quest of facts, as usual, noting down the figures in his pocket-book very conscientiously. I was left alone with Hermione for a few minutes. We sat down on a heap of broken masonry to rest, talking of the place and its history. Hermione was so placed that she could not see the top of the wall which overhung the precipice on the outer side, but from where I sat I could watch Paul slowly helping his mother to reach the top.

" It belonged to the Genoese, and was built by them," **I**

said. "The arms over the gate are theirs. Perhaps you noticed them." Paul and his mother had reached the summit of the wall, and were standing there, looking out at the view.

"How did the Genoese come to be here?" asked Hermione, digging her parasol into the loose earth.

"They were once very powerful in Constantinople," I answered. "They held Pera for many years, and " —

I broke off with an exclamation of horror, starting to my feet at the same instant. I had idly watched the mother and son as they stood together, and I could hear their voices as they spoke. Suddenly, and without a moment's warning, Madame Patoff put out her hand, and seemed to push Paul with all her might. He stumbled, and fell upon the edge, but from my position I could not tell whether he had saved himself or had fallen into the abyss.

I suppose Hermione followed my look, and saw that Madame Patoff was standing alone upon the top, but I did not stop to speak or explain. I sprang upon the wall, and in a second more I saw that Paul had fallen his full length along the brink, but had saved himself, and was scrambling to his feet. Madame Patoff stood quite still, her face rigid and drawn, and an expression of horror in her eyes that was bad to see. But I was not alone in coming to Paul's assistance. As I put out my arm to help him to his feet, I saw Hermione's small hands lay hold of him with desperate strength, dragging him from the fatal brink. But Paul was unhurt, and was on his legs in another moment. He was ghastly white, and his lips worked curiously as his eyes settled on his mother's face.

"How did it happen?" asked Hermione, as soon as she could speak, but still clinging to his arm, while she glanced inquiringly at her aunt.

"I do not know," said Paul, in a thick voice, between his teeth.

"I was dizzy," gasped Madame Patoff. "I put out my hand to save myself " —

"Do me the favor to come down from this place at once," I said, grasping her firmly by the arm, and leading her away.

"Paul, Paul, how did it happen?" I heard Hermione saying, as we descended.

But Paul's lips were resolutely shut, and he would say nothing more about it. Indeed, he was badly startled, but I knew his paleness was not caused by fear. In my own mind the conviction was strong that his mother had deliberately attempted to murder him by pushing him over the edge. I remembered Cutter's warning, and I wondered that he should have allowed her to go out of his sight since he recognized the condition of her brain, but a moment's reflection made me recollect that I had understood him differently. He had meant that she might try to kill herself, not her son; and that had been my own impression, for it was not till later that I learned how she had spoken of Paul to herself, that night in Pera, after the ball. At that time the professor knew more about the matter than I did, for Hermione had confided in him when they were alone in Santa Sophia.

I think Madame Patoff tried to explain the accident to me as I got her down into the ruined court, but I do not remember what she said. My only wish was to get the party back to Buyukdere, and to be alone with Cutter for five minutes.

"Patoff has met with an accident," I said, as the others came up. "He stumbled near the edge of the wall, and is badly shaken. We had better go home."

There was very little explanation needed, and Paul protested that he had incurred no danger, though he acquiesced readily enough to the suggestion. I did not let Madame Patoff leave my arm until we were once more on board the little yacht, for I was convinced that the woman was dangerously mad. The drawn expression of her pale face did not change, and she soon ceased speaking altogether. I noted the fact that in all the excitement of the moment she expressed no satisfaction at Paul's escape. It was not until we reached the water that she said something about "dear Paul," in a tone that made me shudder. We were a silent party as we ran down the wind to Buyukdere. Cutter sat beside Madame Patoff, and watched her curiously ; for the expression of her face had not escaped him, though he had no idea of what had happened. Sitting on the deck, at the edge of the wall, she looked down at the water as we rushed along.

"What do you see in the water?" asked the professor, quietly. The answer came in a very low voice, but I heard it as I stood by the helm : —

"I see a man's face under the water, looking up at me."

"And whose face is it?" inquired Cutter, in the same matter-of-fact tone.

"I will not tell you, nor any one," she answered. Cutter looked up at me to see whether I had heard, and I nodded to him. In a few minutes we were alongside of the pier. I refused Chrysophrasia's not very pressing invitation to tea, and, bidding good-by to the rest, I put my arm through the professor's. He seemed ready enough to go with me, so we walked along the smooth quay in the sunset, arm in arm.

"I wanted to speak to you," I said. "You ought to know what happened up there this afternoon. Madame Patoff tried to push Paul over the edge. It was a deliberate attempt to murder him." Cutter stopped in his walk and looked earnestly into my face.

"Did you see it yourself? Did you positively see it, or is that only your impression?"

"I saw it," I answered, shortly.

"She is quite mad still, then. No one but a mad woman would attempt such a thing. What is worse, it is a fixed idea that she has." He told me what Hermione had confided to him.

"Then Paul's life is not safe for a moment," I said, after a moment's pause.

" Unless his brother marries Miss Carvel, I would advise him to be on his guard when he is alone with his mother. He is safe enough when other people are present. I know those cases. They are sly, cautious, timid. She will try and push him over the edge of a precipice when nobody is looking. Before you she will call him ' dear Paul,' and all the rest of it."

" That looks to me more like the cunning of a murderess than the slyness of a maniac," I said.

" Most murderers are only maniacs, mad people," answered the professor. " Men and women are born with a certain tendency of mind which makes them easily brood over an idea. Their life and circumstances foster one particular notion, till it gets a predominant weight in their weak reasoning. The occasion presents itself, and they carry out the plan they have been forming for years in secret, or even unconsciously. If in carrying out their ideas they kill anybody, it is called murder. It makes very little difference what you call it. The law distinguishes between crimes premeditated and crimes unpremeditated. Murder, willful and premeditated, involves in my opinion a process of mind so similar to that found in lunatics that it is impossible to distinguish the one from the other, and I am quite ready to believe that all premeditated murders are brought about by mental aberration in the murderer. On the other hand, manslaughter, quick, sudden, and unplanned, is the result of more or less inhuman instincts, and those who commit the crime are people who approach more or less nearly to wild beasts. For the advancement of science, murderers should not be hanged, but should be kept as interesting cases of insanity. Much might be learned by carefully observing the action of their minds upon ordinary occasions. As for homicides, or manslaughterers, — I wish we could use the English word, — they are less attractive as a study, and I do not care what becomes of them. The brain of a freshly killed tiger would be far more interesting."

"What do you propose to do with Madame Patoff?" I asked. "You do not suppose that Miss Carvel will marry Alexander Patoff in order to prevent his mother from murdering Paul?"

"She ought to," answered Cutter, quietly. "It would be most curious to see whether there would be any change in her fixed dislike of the younger son."

"And do you mean that that young girl should sacrifice her life to your experiments?" I asked, rather hotly. I hated the coldness of the man, and his ruthless determination to make scientific capital out of other people's troubles.

"I can neither propose nor dispose," he answered. "I only wish that it might be so. After all, she could be quite as happy with Alexander as with Paul. I doubt whether she has a strong preference for either."

"You are mistaken," said I. "She loves Paul much more than she herself imagines. I saw her face to-day when Paul was lying on the edge of the precipice. You did not. I have watched them ever since they have been together in Constantinople, and I am convinced that she loves Paul, and not Alexander. What do you intend to do with Madame Patoff? You know I have a little party at my cottage on Saturday, — you promised to come. Is it safe to let her come, too?"

"Perfectly," answered my companion. "The only thing to be done at present is to prevent her remaining alone with Paul."

"Suppose that Paul tells what happened this afternoon. What then?"

"He will not tell it. I have a great admiration for the fellow, he is so manly. If she had done worse than that, he would not tell any one, because she is his mother. But he will be on his guard, never fear. She will not get such a chance again. Good-night."

The professor left me at the door of the garden through which I had to pass to reach the little kiosk. I walked slowly up through the roses and the flowers, meditating as I went. Paul had a new enemy in the professor, who would certainly try and help Alexander, in order to continue his experiments upon Madame Patoff's mind. Poor Paul! He seemed to be persecuted by an evil fate, and I pitied him sincerely.

XXIV.

It was Saturday afternoon, and my preparations for my little tea-party were complete. Gregorios Balsamides had arrived from Pera, and we were waiting for the Carvels, seated on the long bench before the house, where the view overlooks the Bosphorus. The sun had almost set, and the hills of Asia were already tinged with golden light, which caught the walls of the white mosque on the Giant's Mountain, — the Yusha-Dagh, where the Mussulmans believe that Joshua's body lies buried; Anadoli Kavák was bathed in a soft radiance, in which every line of the old fortress stood out clear and distinct, so that I could see the very spot where Paul had fallen a few days before; the far mouth of the Black Sea looked cold and gray in the shadows below the hills, but down below, the big steamers, the little yachts, the outlandish Turkish schooners, and the tiny caïques moved quickly about in the evening sunshine. My garden was become a wilderness of roses in the soft spring weather, too, and each flower took a warmer hue as the sun sank in the west, and slowly neared the point where it would drop behind the European foreland.

The kiosk was a wooden building, narrow and tall, so that the rooms within were high, and the second story was twenty feet above the ground. I had caused hundreds of lamps to be hung within and without, to be lighted so soon as the darkness set in, and my man, who has an especial talent for all sorts of illuminations, and in general for everything which in Southern Italy comes under the head of 'festa,' had borrowed long strings of little signal-flags and streamers, which he had hung fantastically from the house to the surrounding trees. When once the lamps should be lighted the effect would be very pretty, and to the eyes of English people utterly new.

Gregorios sat beside me on the garden seat, and we talked of Madame Patoff and her latest doings. My mind was not at rest about her, and I inwardly wished that some accident might prevent her from coming that day. I had more than once almost determined to speak to my old friend John Carvel, and to tell him what had occurred at Anadoli Kavák. Nothing but my respect for Professor Cutter's opinion as a specialist had prevented me from doing so; but now, at the last moment, I wished I had not been overruled, for I had an unpleasant conviction that his prudence had been forgotten in his desire to study the case. For men of his profession there seems to be an absorbing interest in deciding the question of where crime ends and madness begins, and to put Madame Patoff under restraint would have been to cut short one of the most valuable experiences of Cutter's life. He probably knew that in the present stage of her malady such a proceeding would very likely have driven her into hopeless and evident insanity. I could have forgiven him if I had thought that he regarded the question from a moralist's point of view, and balanced the danger of leaving the unfortunate woman at large against the possible advantage she herself might gain from enjoying unrestricted liberty. But I was sure that the scientist was not thinking of that. He had expressed interest rather than horror at her attempt to push Paul over the edge of the wall. He had answered my anxious questions concerning the treatment of Madame Patoff by a short dissertation on insanity in general, and had left me to continue his studies, regardless of any danger to his patient's relations. The moral point of view shrank into insignificance as he became more and more absorbed in the result of the case, and I believe that he would have let us all perish, if necessary, rather than consent to relinquish his study. He might have regretted his indifference afterwards, especially if he had arrived at no satisfactory conclusion in regard to the unhappy woman; but in the fervor of scientific speculation, minor considerations of safety were forgotten. Cutter is not a bad man, though he is ruthless. He would be incapable of doing any one an injury from a personal motive, but in comparison with the importance of one of his theories the life of a man is no more to him than the life of a dog. I said something of that kind to Balsamides.

"My dear fellow," he answered, "do you expect common sense from people who waste their lives in such a senseless fashion? Can anything be more absurd than to attempt to explain the vagaries of a diseased mind? They call that science in the professor's country. They may as well give it up. They will never ultimately discover any better treatment for dangerous lunatics than solid bolts and barred windows."

"I believe you are right," I said. "If we could put medicine into the head as we can into the stomach, something might be accomplished. It is very unpleasant to think that I am to entertain a lady at my tea-party who only the other day tried to murder her son in my sight."

"Very," assented Gregorios. "Here they come."

We heard the sound of voices in the garden, and rose to meet the party as they came up towards the house. None of them had been to see me before, except Paul, and they at once launched into extravagant praises of the view and of the kiosk. Chrysophrasia raved about the sunset effects, and Hermione was delighted with the way the flags were arranged. Macaulay consulted his pocket barometer to see how many feet above the sea the house was built, and declared that the air must be far more healthy in such a place than on the quay. Madame Patoff looked silently out at the view, leaning on Alexander's arm, while John Carvel and his wife stood close together, smiling and appreciative, the ideal of a well-assorted and perfectly happy middle-aged couple. Cutter talked to Balsamides, and Paul followed Hermione as she slowly moved from point to point. I stood alone for a few moments, and looked at them, going over in my mind all that had happened during the last seven months, and wondering how it would all end.

These ten people had lived much together, and had found themselves lately united in some very strange occurrences. With the exception of Balsamides and the professor, they were all nearly related, and yet they were as unlike each other as people of one family could be. The gentle, saintly Mary Carvel had little in common with her æsthetic sister Chrysophrasia Dabstreak, and neither of them was very like Madame Patoff. Sturdy John Carvel was not like his sleek son Macaulay, except in honesty and good-nature. Alexander Patoff was indeed like his mother, but Paul's stern, cold nature was that of his father, long dead and forgotten. As for Hermione, she presented a combination of character derived from the best points in her father and mother, marred only, I thought, by a little of that vacillation which was the chief characteristic of her aunt Chrysophrasia. Cutter and Balsamides were men of widely different nationalities and temperaments : the one a ruthless scientist, the other an equally ruthless fatalist ; the one ready to sacrifice the lives of others to a fanatic worship of his profession, the other willing to sacrifice himself to the inevitable with heroic courage, but holding other men's lives as of no more value than his own. A strange company, I thought, and yet in many respects a most interesting company, too.

"Shall we go in-doors and have tea?" I said after a few moments, collecting my guests together. "The view is even better from the windows above."

I led them into the stone-paved vestibule of the wooden house, and up the wooden stairs to the upper story. Presently they were all installed in the large room where the preparations for the small festivity had been made, and I began to do the honors of my bachelor establishment. In a Turkish family, the room where we sat, and the three others upon the same floor, would have been set apart for the harem, for one door separated them from the staircase and from all the rest of the house, — a large strong door, painted white, and provided with an excellent lock and key. I had selected one room for my bedroom, and the rest were furnished with Oriental simplicity, not to say economy. But Balsamides had sent down a bale of beautiful carpets, which he lent me for the occasion, and which I had hung upon the walls and spread upon the floors and divans. Tea, coffee, sherbet, a beautiful view, and a little illumination of the gardens, constituted the whole entertainment, but the enthusiasm of my guests knew no bounds, probably because they had never seen anything of the kind before.

"Griggs is growing to be a true Oriental," said Balsamides, approvingly ; "he understands how the Turks live."

"Yes," I answered, "I present you the thing in all its bareness. You may take this as a specimen of an Eastern house. People are apt to fancy that those long, latticed houses on the Bosphorus conceal unheard-of luxuries, and that the people live like Sybarites. It is quite untrue. They either try to imitate the French style, and do it horribly, or else they live in great bare rooms like these."

"What do the women do all day long?" asked Chrysophrasia. "I am sure they do not pass their time upon a straw matting, staring at each other, — so very dreary!"

"Nevertheless they do," said Gregorios. "They smoke and eat sweetmeats from morning till night, and occasionally an old woman comes and tells them stories. Some of them can read French. They learn it in order to read novels, but cannot speak a word of the language."

"Dreary, dreary!" sighed Chrysophrasia. "And then, the division of the affections, you know, — so sad."

"Many of them die of consumption," said Gregorios.

"It would be curious to watch the phases of their intelligence," said the professor, slowly sipping his coffee, and staring out of the window through his great gold-rimmed spectacles.

The sun had gone down, and the darkness gathered quickly over the beautiful scene. At one of the windows Hermione sat silently enjoying the evening breeze; Alexander was seated beside her, while Paul stood looking out over her head. Neither of the two men spoke, but from time to time they exchanged glances which were anything but friendly. Outside, my man and the gardener were lighting the little lamps, and gradually, as each glass cup received its tiny light, the festoons of white and red grew, and seemed to creep stealthily from tree to tree. The conversation languished, and the deepening twilight brought with it that pleasant silence which is the very embodiment of rest descending at evening on the tired earth.

"It is like an evening hymn," said Mrs. Carvel, whose gentle features were barely visible in the gloom.

No one spoke, but I fancied I saw John Carvel lay his hand affectionately on his wife's arm, as they sat together. There was a light above the eastern hills, brightening quickly as we looked, and presently the full moon rose and shed her rays through the low open windows, making our faces look white and deathly in the dark room. It shone on Madame Patoff's marble features, and cast strange shadows around her mouth.

"Shall we have lights?" I asked. There was a general refusal; everybody preferred the moonlight, which now flooded the apartment.

"It seems to me," said Chrysophrasia, half sadly, — "it seems to me — ah, no! I must be mistaken, — and yet — it seems to me that I smell something burning."

"I think it is the lamps outside," I answered. No one else took any notice of the speech, which jarred upon the pleasant stillness. I myself thought she was mistaken.

"What a wonderful contrast!" said Hermione. "I mean the lamps and the moonlight." Then she added, sud-

denly, " Do you know, Mr. Griggs, there is really something
burning. I can smell it quite well."

A fire in a Turkish house is a serious matter. The old
beams and boarded walls are like so much tinder, and burn
up immediately, as though soaked with some inflammable
liquid. I rose, and went out to see if there were anything
wrong. As I opened the door which shut off the whole
apartment from the stairs, I heard a strange crackling sound,
and outside the window of the staircase, which was in the
back of the house, I saw a red glare, which brightened in
the moment while I watched it. I did not go further, for I
knew the danger was imminent.

" Will you be good enough to come down-stairs ? " I said,
quietly, as I re-entered the room where my guests were assembled. " I am afraid something is wrong, but there is
plenty of time."

A considerable confusion ensued, and everybody rushed
to the door. Protestations were vain, for all the women
were frightened, and all the men were anxious to help them.
The sight of the flames outside the window redoubled their
fears, and they rushed out, stumbling on the dusky landing.
In the confusion of the moment I did not realize how it all
happened. Chrysophrasia, who was mad with fright, caught
her foot against something, and fell close beside me. The
other ladies were already down-stairs, I thought. I picked
her up and carried her down as fast as I could, and out into
the garden.

" Come away from the house ! " I cried. " Away from
the trees ! " Chrysophrasia was senseless with fear, and I
bore her hastily on till I reached the fountain, some twenty
yards down the hill. There I put her down upon a bench.
There were two buckets and a couple of watering-pots there,
and I shouted to the other men to come to me, as I filled
two of the vessels and ran round to the back of the house.
I passed Madame Patoff, standing alone under a festoon of
ittle lamps, by a tree, and I remember the strange expres-

sion of gladness which was on her face. But I had no time
to speak to her, and rushed on with my water-cans.

Meanwhile the flames rose higher and higher, crackling
and licking the brown face of the old timber. There was
small chance of saving the building now. My men had been
busy lighting the lamps in the garden, but I found them already on the spot, dipping water out of a small cistern with
buckets, and dashing it into the fire with all their might,
their dark faces grim and set in the light of the flames. I
worked as hard as I could, supposing that all the party were
safe. I had no idea of what was going on upon the opposite
side of the house. In truth, it was horrible enough.

Paul and Cutter were very self-possessed, and their first
care was to see that all the four ladies were safe. They had
Hermione and her mother with them, and, taking the direction of the fountain, they found Chrysophrasia upon the
bench where I had left her, in a violent fit of hysterics.
Madame Patoff was not there.

"I was going back for aunt Annie," said Macaulay Carvel, "for I counted them as they came out, and missed her.
She ran right into my arms as I stood in the door. She is
somewhere in the garden; I am quite sure of it."

Cutter hurried off, and began to search among the trees.
Already the bright flames could be seen in the lower story,
and in a moment more the glass of one of the windows
cracked loudly, and the fire leapt through. Then from the
high windows above a voice was heard calling, loud and
clear, to those below.

"The door is locked! Can any one help me?" The
voice belonged to Gregorios, and the party looked into each
other's faces in sudden horror, and then glanced at the burning house.

"Save him! Save him!" cried Hermione. But Paul
had already left her side, and had reached the open door of
the porch. Alexander stood still, staring at the flames.

"He saved you," said Hermione, grasping his arm fiercely.
"Will you do nothing to help him?"

"Paul is gone already," answered Alexander, impatiently. "There is nothing the matter. Paul will let him out."

But the other men were less apathetic, and had followed the brave man to the door. He had disappeared already, and as they came up a tremendous puff of smoke and ashes was blown into their faces, stifling and burning them, so that they drew back.

"Jump for your life!" shouted John Carvel, looking up at the window from which the voice had proceeded.

"Yes, jump!" cried Alexander, who had reluctantly followed. "We will catch you in our arms!"

But no one answered them. Nothing was heard but the crackling of the burning timber and the roaring of the flames, during the awful moments which followed. Stupefied with horror, the three men stood staring stupidly at the hideous sight. Then suddenly another huge puff of smoke and fiery sparks burst from the door, and with it a dark mass flew forward, as though shot from a cannon's mouth, and fell in a heap upon the ground outside. All three ran forward, but some one else was there before them, dragging away a thick carpet, of which the wool was all singed and burning.

There lay Gregorios Balsamides as he had fallen, stumbling on the doorstep, with the heavy body of Paul Patoff in his arms. Hermione fell on her knees and shrieked aloud. It was plain enough. Paul, without the least protection from the flames, had struggled up the burning staircase, and had unlocked the door, losing consciousness as he opened it. Gregorios, who was not to be outdone in bravery, and whom no danger could frighten from his senses, had wrapped a carpet round the injured man, and, throwing another over his own head, had borne him back through the fire, the steps of the wooden staircase, already in flames, almost breaking under his tread. But he had done the deed, and had lived through it.

He looked up faintly at Hermione as she bent over them both.

"I think he is alive," he gasped, and fainted upon the ground.

They bore the two senseless bodies to the fountain, and laid them down, and sprinkled water on their faces. Behind them they could hear the crash of the first timbers falling in, as the fire reached the upper story of the kiosk; at their feet they saw only the still, pale faces of the men who had been ready to give their lives for each other.

But Cutter had gone in search of Madame Patoff, during the five minutes which had sufficed for the enacting of this scene. He had found her where I had passed her, looking up with a strange smile at the doomed house.

"Paul is looking for you," said the professor, taking her arm under his. She started, and trembled violently.

"Paul!" she cried in surprise. Then, with a wild laugh, she stared into Cutter's eyes. He had heard that laugh many a time in his experience, and he silently tightened his grip upon her arm.

"Paul!" she repeated wildly. "There is no more Paul," she added, suddenly lowering her voice, and speaking confidentially. "Hermione can marry my dear Alexander now. There is no more Paul. You do not know? It was so quickly done. He stayed behind in the room, and I locked the door, so tight, so fast. He can never get out. Ah!" she screamed all at once, "I am so glad! Let me go — let me go" —

At that moment I came upon them. Relinquishing all hopes of saving the house, and wondering vaguely, in my confusion of mind, why nobody had come to help me, I called my two men off, and was going to see what had become of the party. I found Madame Patoff a raving maniac, struggling in the gigantic hands of the sturdy scientist. I will not dwell upon the hideous scene which followed. It was the last time I ever saw her, and I pray that I may never again see man or woman in such a condition.

Meanwhile, the two men who lay by the fountain in the

moonlight showed signs of life. Gregorios first came to himself, for he had only fainted. He was in great pain, but was as eager as the rest to restore Paul to consciousness. Patoff was almost asphyxiated by the smoke, his hair and eyebrows and mustache were almost burnt off, and his right hand was injured. But he was alive, and at last he opened his eyes. In a quarter of an hour he could be helped upon his feet. Balsamides was already standing, and Paul caught at his hand.

"Not that arm," said Gregorios calmly, holding out the other. In his fall he had broken his wrist.

In answer to my cries, the two Carvels left the injured men and came to our assistance, while we struggled with the mad woman, who seemed possessed of the strength of a dozen athletes. Hermione was left by the fountain.

"I was quite sure it would be all right," said Alexander to her, presently. It was more than the young girl could bear. She turned upon him fiercely, and her beautiful face was very white.

"I despise you !" she exclaimed. That was all she said, but in the next moment she turned and threw her arms about Paul's neck, and kissed his burnt and wounded face before them all.

.   .   .   .

There is little more to be said, for my story is told to the end. When I found them all together, Gregorios took me aside and drew a crumpled mass of papers from his pocket with his uninjured hand.

"I stayed behind to save your papers and your money," he said quietly. "I have seen houses burn before, and there is generally no time to be lost."

I wonder what there is at the bottom of that man's strange nature. Cold, indifferent, and fatalistic, apparently one of the most selfish of men, he nevertheless seems to possess somewhere a kind of devoted heroism, an untainted quality of friendship only too rare in our day.

Hermione Carvel is to be married to Paul in the autumn, but there is reason to believe that Alexander, who has rejoined his regiment in St. Petersburg, will not find it convenient to be at the wedding. When Balsamides was crying for help from the upper window, and when Alexander stood quietly by Hermione's side while his brother faced the danger, the die was cast, and she saw what a wide gulf separated the two men, and she knew that she loved the one and hated the other with a fierce hatred.

Poor Madame Patoff is dead, but before he left Constantinople Professor Cutter spent half an hour in trying to demonstrate to me that she might have been cured if Hermione had married Alexander. I am glad he is gone, for I always detested his theories.

So the story is ended, my dear friend; and if it is told badly, it is my fault, for I assure you that I never in my life spent so exciting a year. It has been a long tale, too, but you have told me that from time to time you were interested in it; and, after all, a tale is but a tale, and is a very different affair from an artistically constructed drama, in which facts have to be softened, so as not to look too startling in print. I have given you facts, and if you ever meet Gregorios Balsamides he will tell you that I have exaggerated nothing. Moreover, if you will take the trouble to visit Santa Sophia during the last nights of Ramazán, you will understand how Alexander Patoff disappeared; and if you will go over the house of Laleli Khanum Effendi, which is now to be sold, you will see how impossible it was for him to escape from such a place. In the garden above Mesar Burnu you will see the heap of ashes, which is all that remains of the kiosk where I gave my unlucky tea-party; and if you will turn up the bridle-path at the left of the Belgrade road, a hundred yards before you reach the aqueduct, you will come upon the spot where Gregorios threatened to kill Selim, the wicked Lala, on that bitter March night. I dare say, also, that if you visit any of these places by chance you will remember the strange scenes they have witnessed, and I hope that you will also remember Paul Griggs, your friend, who spun you this yarn because you asked him for a story, when he was riding with you on that rainy afternoon last month. I only wish you knew the Carvels, for I am sure you would like them, and you would find Chrysophrasia very amusing.

www.ingramcontent.com/pod-product-compliance
Lightning Source LLC
Chambersburg PA
CBHW030238030726
47493CB00023B/134